ONE CRAZY SUMMER . . .

*Goals for the Week of June 9–15*

*1) Read one book at age-appropriate reading level.*

*2) Do 10 pages in the Sixth-Grade Math Review Workbook.*

*3) Limit TV to two hours a day—educational programs only.*

*4) Survive the first week of Intensive Summer Language Learning.*

*5) Survive the first week of babysitting for Edison Blue.*

*6) Try not to think about what the other guys are doing at the pool.*

*7) Try not to think about what the other guys are doing at the park.*

*8) Remember that summer is only 10 weeks long. Motto: This too shall pass.*

Also by Claudia Mills

*Dinah Forever*

*Losers, Inc.*

*Standing Up to Mr. O.*

# CLAUDIA MILLS

# You're a Brave Man, Julius Zimmerman

## SCHOLASTIC INC.

New York   Toronto   London   Auckland   Sydney
Mexico City   New Delhi   Hong Kong   Buenos Aires

ISBN 0-439-30936-0

12 11 10 9 8 7 6 5 4 3 2 1                    1 2 3 4 5 6/0

Printed in the U.S.A.                    40

First Scholastic printing, September 2001

*To Beverly Reingold,*
*again and always,*
*and this time to Abby Sider, too*

# You're a Brave Man,
# Julius Zimmerman

# 1

At nine o'clock in the morning on the first day of summer vacation, when he should have been sleeping late or heading off to the pool, Julius Zimmerman was speaking French. Not really *speaking* French, but he was opening his mouth, and French words, words in the French language, were coming out.

"*Bonjour, Madame Cowper,*" Julius repeated with all the others. "*Comment allez-vous?*" He knew he was saying it all wrong. When it came to school, even to summer school, Julius usually did everything all wrong.

"*Non! Non! Non!*" Madame Cowper, whose real

name was Mrs. Cowper, corrected them emphatically. Julius had already learned that the word for "No" in French is *"Non,"* pronounced with a long "o" to rhyme with *bone*, but said in a funny, nasal way, as if the speaker had a terrible, stuffy head cold and didn't know enough to blow his nose.

*"Non! Non! Non! Comme ça!* Like this!" Madame Cowper paused and then repeated the phrase, drawing out each syllable with exaggerated enunciation. When she said "Cowper," it sounded like "Cow-pear," but with about five "r"s at the end: "Cow-pearrrrr." If a word had one "r" in it, why give it five? When she said *"vous,"* her lips pursed as if she were about to kiss somebody. Julius couldn't believe how much work it was in French to say, "Good morning, how are you?" He wished they would learn the French for "Goodbye, I'm outta here." And then all go home.

He caught the eye of his best friend, Ethan Winfield, and they shared a quick grimace. It was Julius's fault, not Ethan's, that they were going to be spending three hours a day, five days a week, for five whole weeks in Intensive Summer Language Learning. Or, rather, it was Julius's mother's fault. She had found out about the program first, and signed up Julius, and then she had told Ethan's mother about it, and Mrs. Winfield had signed up Ethan, too.

Other kids' mothers must have found out about it, as well, because there were twenty-three students in

4

the class, even some other boys, like Alex Ryan, who looked as sheepish as Julius felt. Only Lizzie Archer, AKA the Lizard, seemed to be in her element. Lizzie had a long-standing crush on Ethan and was probably looking forward to being able to write bilingual love poems to him, half in English, half in French.

When the class finally satisfied Madame Cowper on "How are you?" she turned to the chalkboard. From the front, she was a remarkably large woman; from the rear, she looked even larger.

Alex leaned forward. "Madame *Cow*per. Get it?"

Marcia Faitak giggled.

Julius hoped Madame Cowper hadn't heard. If she had, she didn't show it. She wrote on the board, in large, neat handwriting: *Je m'appelle* _____ .

Then she turned back to the class and adjusted her glasses. They were definitely strange-looking glasses, the tortoiseshell frames rising to a pointy little peak on the outside of each eye. Had she actually picked out those frames on purpose at the glasses store? Maybe they had been the only pair on sale.

*"Je m'appelle Madame Cowper,"* Madame Cowper said then. *"Comment vous appelez-vous?"* She stood still, obviously waiting for someone to answer.

Julius didn't get it. How could you give an answer when you didn't understand the question? He looked at Ethan. Ethan plainly didn't get it, either.

*"Je m'appelle Madame Cowper. Comment vous*

5

*appelez-vous?"* Madame Cowper repeated, her voice registering a hint of impatience.

Lizzie Archer raised her hand. *"Je m'appelle Lizzie Archer,"* she ventured.

*"Bien! Bien!* Good! Good! *Elle s'appelle Lizzie Archer. Comment vous appelez-vous?"* Madame Cowper pointed at Ethan.

Ethan managed to give his answer: *"Je m'appelle Ethan Winfield."*

Julius had begun to figure out that they were supposed to say their names. Okay, he could do that. He could say his name. He had had plenty of practice over the past twelve years saying his name.

One by one, almost all of them got through their names, though Marcia started to giggle again during hers, and when Alex said his, it sounded a lot like *"Je MOO-pelle Alex Ryan. Comment MOO appelez-MOO?"* Madame Cowper pretended not to notice. So she must have heard Alex's remark before.

Julius felt himself getting more and more nervous as his turn approached. All he had to do was say one sentence in French. That couldn't be so hard—even if he was going to have to speak French all by himself this time, just him, saying those strange, unintelligible words.

Finally Madame Cowper pointed at Julius. *"Comment vous appelez-vous?"*

Julius swallowed hard. Maybe he didn't have to say

6

the whole sentence. She had asked for his name; well, he'd tell her his name. "Julius Zimmerman," he said.

"*Non! Non! Non!* You must say, '*Je m'appelle Julius Zimmerman.*'" Madame Cowper adjusted her glasses again as she waited for Julius to repeat the full sentence.

He had heard the sentence twenty times already. Why couldn't he remember it now?

"*Je m'appelle . . .*" Madame Cowper prompted him.

"*Je m'appelle,*" Julius repeated miserably.

"Your name, Monsieur Zimmerman. You must say your name."

"Julius. I mean, Julius Zimmerman."

"*Non, non.* You must say, '*Je m'appelle Julius Zimmerman.*'"

Somehow Julius stammered it out. He thought he heard Alex say, "*Je m'appelle Julius Ding-Dong.*"

Forty-five minutes into Intensive Summer Language Learning, it was already clear who was the worst student in the class. It felt strangely familiar. It felt strangely like the rest of Julius's life.

Julius could still hear his mother explaining her plans for his summer. "Listen, honey, last summer we had a lazy summer, and I admit it was a lot of fun, but then—well, lazy habits developed over the summer can be hard to break, and you have to be disappointed, too, about your report cards this past year. So this summer we're going to concentrate on setting a good foundation for seventh grade."

A good foundation, Julius was finding out, meant Intensive Summer Language Learning in the morning, and a *job* in the afternoon, which he would be starting in another few hours. His mother had read that jobs helped adolescents learn about responsibility, so she had signed him up to babysit for one of the children from Ethan's mother's preschool. She had pointed out that this way he'd have spending money of his own, plus he could start his own savings account for college. *College!* And a good foundation meant keeping a weekly goal-setting journal. Julius's mother loved goals and resolutions. She was the only person Julius knew who, in addition to New Year's resolutions, made new month's and new week's resolutions, too.

"Now, I'm not going to be reading your journal," she had told Julius when she handed him the green-covered, seventy-page, college-ruled, spiral-bound notebook. "But I want you to promise that you'll write in it faithfully."

Julius had promised. It wasn't as if he had a choice. So that morning he had written on the first page:

> *Goals for the Week of June 9–15*
> *1. Read one book at age-appropriate reading
> level.*

2. *Do 10 pages in the Sixth-Grade Math Review Workbook.*
3. *Limit TV to two hours a day—educational programs only.*
4. *Survive the first week of Intensive Summer Language Learning.*
5. *Survive the first week of babysitting for Edison Blue.*
6. *Try not to think about what the other guys are doing at the pool.*
7. *Try not to think about what the other guys are doing at the park.*
8. *Remember that summer is only 10 weeks long. Motto: This too shall pass.*

It was a pretty grim list. His mother had suggested the first three items on it; she had signed him up for the next two. Only the last three were his own, plus the motto. So far he hadn't even survived the first hour of the first day of Intensive Summer Language Learning. He still had a lot of goals to go.

At last Madame Cowper announced that it was time for a fifteen-minute break. When they returned, they would watch a video on France and learn some French songs. Julius bet the songs would be *"Frère Jacques"* and *"Sur le Pont d'Avignon."* He hoped they wouldn't have to all hold hands and dance. The image of

Madame Cowper skipping back and forth on the bridge of Avignon made Julius grin to himself, but he stifled the thought. Tall and gangly, he had been the butt of enough klutz jokes to cure him permanently of wanting to laugh at how anybody else looked.

It felt good to be outside, however briefly. Julius and Ethan slumped down on the blacktop, their backs against the brick wall of West Creek Middle School, where all the summer language programs were being held. Alex ambled over to join them.

"So what do you think of the Cow?" Alex asked.

"She's okay," Julius said uncomfortably.

"Okay? You've got to be kidding. Like, is this for real? We're going to be doing this all summer?"

"Just five weeks," Ethan said. Right then it sounded to Julius like a very long time.

"Five *weeks*? Five weeks out of our *lives*?" Alex's voice rose to an indignant squawk.

"Do you have to take it?" Julius asked. "Like, would your parents let you drop it? My mom's making me take it." *And* making him work a job. *And* making him read age-appropriate books.

"Mine, too," Ethan said, though Julius knew that Ethan's mother would let him drop it if he wanted to. Julius also knew that Ethan was the kind of friend who would never desert him. They had been friends since second grade, through thick and thin.

"My dad's going to France on a business trip this

fall, and he's taking my mom and me," Alex said. "They want me to learn a little French before we go."

Well, Julius wasn't going to France. He wasn't going anywhere. Nowhere fast, that was where he was headed.

"What do you say we shoot some hoops?" Ethan asked. "I brought my ball."

They had just enough time for Julius to miss two baskets before Madame Cowper appeared at the door, saying something to them in French that apparently meant it was time for the video. Julius barely watched it, and he tuned out during *"Frère Jacques"* and *"Sur le Pont."* Then they spent the rest of the morning discussing the weather. Julius learned that *"Il fait beau"* meant "The weather is beautiful." It was, too: clear, sunny, hot, but not too hot, perfect weather for biking, swimming, basketball, hiking—anything but Intensive Summer Language Learning.

When Julius biked home for lunch, his mother was there to greet him. She worked at home most days. She was a writer, but she didn't write novels or short stories or poetry, although Julius knew she wanted to. She wrote computer manuals. Boring computer manuals. Every once in a while she tried to slip in a little humor, she had told Julius, but the editors always took it out.

"Hi, honey. How *was* it?"

It was an ordinary question, but the tone was too eager. Julius knew she wanted him to say that he had fallen in love with the French language and that at long last he had discovered the subject that would turn him into a straight-A student.

"It was okay."

Her face showed a flicker of disappointment. Disappointing his mother was the one thing that Julius *was* good at.

"What's your teacher like?"

Should he tell her? No. She had enough problems of her own, writing dry, dull manuals all day when she wanted to write Pulitzer Prize–winning novels.

"She was okay, too."

"What's her name?"

"Mrs. Cowper. Only we have to call her Madame Cow-pear."

"I take it she's not another Ms. Gunderson?"

Julius flushed. Ms. Gunderson was the beautiful student science teacher who had come to West Creek Middle School last winter. Half the boys had had crushes on her, including Julius and Ethan. She had liked Ethan best, probably because Ethan had knocked himself out to impress her with a super-duper science fair experiment. For a while there, Julius had been pretty annoyed with Ethan. But now Ms. Gunderson was a fond memory, Julius was best friends with Ethan again, and Julius was through with love forever.

"No," he said. "She's not another Ms. Gunderson."
It was the understatement of the millennium.

"Oh, you're going to be so glad you took this course.
Think how far ahead you'll be when you start a foreign
language in eighth grade," his mother said.

Did she really believe that? She wouldn't if she had
been in French class that morning, when Julius had
been the only student in the room who couldn't even
say his name. The question for Julius was never how
far ahead he would be but how far behind. It was only
the first day of Intensive Summer Language Learning,
and already he felt so far behind that there was no way
he could ever catch up.

## 2

As they ate their lunch of macaroni and tuna salad, Julius's mother kept using her hopeful-sounding, overly enthusiastic tone of voice. "And this afternoon you start your first *job*! Mrs. Blue told me on the phone that she knows you're going to be wonderful with little Edison. She thinks he'll do better with a male babysitter."

The comment suggested that Edison hadn't done particularly well with his last, female babysitter.

"And you'll be able to do all those fun *boy* things with him."

As if Julius weren't a total klutz at most "boy things."

14

"I'll try," he said lamely.

Apparently it was the right response. His mother's face brightened. "I know you will, honey. That's what it's all about in life: trying. Doing your best, whatever else happens."

Julius had met Edison and his parents briefly at his job interview two weeks ago. Edison had been pretty quiet and mopey from his nap, dragging a dingy blanket along behind him. Edison was three. In the mornings, he went to the Little Wonders preschool, where Ethan's mother was his teacher; in the afternoons, his mom stayed home with him. But this summer Mrs. Blue needed to work some extra hours and had decided to hire a babysitter to fill the gap. Mrs. Blue had called Mrs. Winfield, and Mrs. Winfield had called Mrs. Zimmerman. And the rest was history, as Custer had no doubt remarked when he looked up and saw the Indians.

At one o'clock on the dot, Julius rang the bell at the Blues' small brick split-level, about a mile's bike ride from home.

Mrs. Blue opened the door right away. She was short, considerably shorter than Julius. Her hair was pulled back in an untidy ponytail. "Oh, Julius, I'm so glad to see you. Come on in! Edison has been very . . ." She lowered her voice. "He thinks he doesn't want a babysitter. I'm afraid he's quite *adamant* about it. But

15

I'm sure you'll be able to win him over." Julius had never heard anybody sound less sure of anything.

"Edison!" Mrs. Blue called in the same falsely cheerful tone Julius had heard his own mother use an hour ago. Did all moms go to some special intensive summer course on gushing? Didn't they know kids figured out right away that the more cheerful their mothers sounded, the worse the fate that lay in store for them?

A small boy appeared in the doorway. He was wearing shorts and a T-shirt that said: "I ♡ Virginia Beach." But from the scowl that darkened his grubby little face, it looked as if Edison didn't ♡ anything.

"I don't think there's anything else I need to tell you before I go," Mrs. Blue said uncertainly. "Eat anything you want in the fridge. Be sure to put sunblock on Edison if you go out in the yard. I'm a little low on wipes, so use them sparingly. I'll be back at four. I've left his dad's and my work numbers on the bulletin board, in case there're any emergencies."

The mention of "emergencies" made Mrs. Blue look more uncertain than ever. She lowered her voice. "I've read that it's better for the mother not to prolong the goodbyes. The book said that even if the child cries, it's usually only for a minute or so, and it's worse if the mother lingers. But you'll tell me if he cries longer than that, won't you?"

Julius nodded numbly. He hoped Edison wouldn't cry. He hated it when people cried.

16

"Bye, angel!" His mother blew an obviously guilty kiss to Edison, who promptly burst into stormy sobs. Then she was gone. Julius's first afternoon of babysitting had begun.

Edison hurled himself at the front door, through which his mother had disappeared, beating his small fists against it.

"Hey, buddy," Julius said awkwardly. "She's coming back."

In three more hours.

Edison stood on his tiptoes and tried to turn the doorknob. To Julius's horror, the door began to open.

"Whoa!" Julius leaped forward to push it shut.

For the next few minutes, Edison strained to pull the door open, while Julius leaned against it to keep it closed. At least Julius had size and strength on his side. But Edison had willpower on his.

Something Mrs. Blue had said in parting was beginning to occupy the part of Julius's mind not taken up by his struggle with Edison. *Put sunblock on him.* That sounded bad enough: was Julius supposed to hold the door with one hand while he applied sunblock with the other? *Use wipes sparingly.* What kind of wipes? Did Edison howl so much that his parents bought special wipes for his chapped little nose? Or did she mean . . .

Julius looked down at Edison, still pulling at the door with all his might. Maybe his shorts did seem a little bulgy.

But the kid was three! He was a toddler, not a baby! Toddlers didn't wear diapers anymore—did they?

No. Julius's mother wouldn't have done this to him. She wouldn't have signed him up for a job where he would have to change diapers. He had never changed a diaper. He was never going to change a diaper. He didn't know how to change a diaper. Diapers had . . . *stuff* in them. Stuff Julius didn't even want to *think* about, let alone *look* at, let alone *wipe*.

"Come on, buddy," Julius said. "This is getting boring. Let's go do—" What? What did three-year-olds like to do? Besides have tantrums.

"I have an idea!" Julius said in an excited voice, as if he had reached into his pocket and found two free tickets to Disney World. "Why don't you show me your room? I bet you have a *cool* room!" Ten minutes into the job, Julius was already starting to sound like somebody's mother.

"No!" Edison said. But at least he let go of the doorknob. Julius grabbed the spare house key from the hook next to the door and quickly locked the deadbolt.

"Why don't you show me your toys?"

"No!"

"Why don't you show me your backyard?"

"No!"

Julius had an inspiration. "Why don't you show me nothing?"

"No!"

"You don't want to show me nothing? Okay, don't show me nothing. Show me something. What do you want to show me?"

Edison had to think that one over. "Nothing," he finally said, but Julius could tell Edison knew he had lost the first round.

"Ooh, I like your nothing!" Julius said. "Wow, Edison, that nothing is so cool!"

Edison giggled. Julius felt a small stir of satisfaction. So far, on the first day of summer, he had accomplished one thing. He hadn't been able to say his name in French, but he had made Edison Blue laugh.

Edison was still in a good mood when he finally led Julius upstairs to his room. "Edison's bed!" he shouted, leaping into the middle of a smaller-than-regular-size bed covered with a Winnie-the-Pooh bedspread.

He ran to the bureau. "Edison's clothes!"

He ran to what was unmistakably a changing table. A *diaper*-changing table.

"Edison's *diapers*!" The word caused him to burst into gales of laughter. Sure enough, there was a stack of disposable diapers in one of the bins beneath the changing table.

Julius's blood ran cold.

There was no way that he, Julius Zimmerman, was

going to change anybody's diaper. That was final. Edison was going to have to wait until four o'clock on weekday afternoons to put anything in his diapers. If he did pee or poop before then, Julius was going to pretend that it had happened as Mrs. Blue was walking in the door. Three hours wasn't that long. A kid could wait three little hours to have his diaper changed. Pioneer kids crossing the prairie in covered wagons had probably waited a lot longer than that.

Still, Julius wanted to get as far away from the changing table as possible. "Hey, buddy, show me Edison's yard."

He managed to get sunblock smeared on Edison's chubby arms and legs. His face was harder. Or rather, his face was impossible. On little kids' faces, everything was so close together that their cheeks and noses were right next to their eyes. Sunblock in your eyes could really sting. And the harder someone pulled away from you, the harder it was even to dab on sunblock, let alone rub it in. Julius got one little dot of sunblock on Edison's left cheek before he gave up, hoping that you couldn't get skin cancer in an afternoon.

Finally, they were ready to go outside. But as soon as they reached the large, square sandbox that stood next to the redwood play set, Edison turned difficult again. Instead of digging sand, he began throwing it. Julius could tell that he wasn't throwing sand because he wanted to throw sand; he was throwing sand to see if Julius would stop him.

Julius said his line: "Hey, buddy, no throwing sand."

Edison threw another handful of sand, a bigger handful this time.

Julius had tried being his mother; now he'd try being his father. He put on a sterner voice: "I said, *no throwing sand.*"

Edison threw his sand toward Julius.

Maybe with Edison you had to explain the reason for a rule. "Look, buddy, if you throw sand, it can get in somebody's eye. In Edison's eye. Edison no like sand in eye. Edison have to go to doctor. Doctor dig sand out of Edison's eye. Ooh, that hurts Edison's eye."

Edison held his next handful of sand. Was he considering this line of argument, or wondering if his babysitter had suddenly lost the power to speak coherent English? Then he threw it.

Julius was getting angry now. He knew he wasn't allowed to spank Edison, but he could give him a time-out. Mrs. Blue had discussed "guidelines for discipline" with him at the interview. She had told him he could place Edison in a time-out chair for a couple of minutes. She had also told him that the only problem with this was that Edison wouldn't stay in a time-out chair for even a couple of seconds.

"That does it, buddy! You're in time-out!"

Julius swooped down and gathered up a kicking, screaming Edison and set him down on the picnic bench.

"No!" Edison ran back to the sandbox.

Again, Julius carried him to the picnic bench.

Edison ran back to the sandbox.

Was Julius supposed to hold him in the time-out chair? He could, if he had to.

He carried Edison to the picnic bench once more. This time he held Edison, squirming and struggling, in place. Julius might be a spindly version of a twelve-year-old, but compared to a three-year-old's, his physique was magnificent. He had Edison this time.

Until Edison bit him. On the hand. Hard.

"Owwww! You little—"

Edison burst free and ran back to the sandbox, to the exact same spot where he had been standing before Julius first carried him away.

Julius heard merry laughter. He looked up. Watching them from over the neighbors' fence was a girl. Apparently she had been watching the whole time.

# 3

If babysitting for Edison Blue was bad, worse was babysitting for Edison Blue in front of an audience.

"I suppose you could do better," Julius said defensively.

"I wouldn't even try," the girl said.

Julius remembered Mrs. Blue's remark to his mother about how Edison might do better with a male babysitter. He had a sneaking suspicion that this girl with the mocking eyes had been the female babysitter who hadn't worked out. It was only reasonable that the Blues would have started with their next-door neighbor before turning to him.

"I bet you did," he said. "I bet the only reason I'm here making a fool of myself is that you already tried and failed."

"You lose. I don't sign up to do things I'm going to fail at."

With the fence between them, Julius could see only her head and shoulders. She was around his height, and even though she looked sixteen, somehow Julius could tell that she only *looked* sixteen; he would guess that she was actually close to his own age. She was undeniably pretty, with straight dark hair that fell past her shoulders and large dark eyes. She certainly didn't look like someone who'd ever failed at anything.

Julius turned to check on Edison, who was still standing in the sandbox, silently watching them and *not* throwing sand. Julius realized that he had discovered something important: three-year-olds can be distracted.

He turned back to the girl again, wondering if he could steer the discussion in a friendlier direction. He wasn't used to chatting casually with someone who was so pretty.

"So do you babysit for any other kids?" Most of the girls Julius knew loved little kids and had counted the months until they were old enough to babysit.

The girl gave him a scornful look. "Life is too short."

She had a point there. Forget life: *summer* was too

short to spend babysitting, much less learning French, and yet somehow Julius was doing both.

Julius tried to think of something else to ask her. He wanted to prolong the conversation that was distracting Edison so effectively. "What do you do instead?"

"I dance. I sing. I act."

It was easy to imagine her on the stage. She was definitely a dramatic figure, with her dark coloring and her expressive face.

"Do you want to be an actress?" Julius asked.

"I *am* an actress. I played Juliet last year in the Waverly School's production of *Romeo and Juliet*." The Waverly School was a fancy private school. It figured. "And I'm auditioning for the Summertime Players production of *Oklahoma!* in a couple of weeks."

She studied Julius with what seemed to be genuine interest. "What about you? What do you do when you're not babysitting *l'enfant terrible*?"

Julius didn't understand the last part of the question, though something about it sounded vaguely familiar. *Lon-fon terrr-eebl*?

"It's French for 'the terrible child.' "

"Actually, I've been studying French." Maybe that would impress her.

"How long?" she demanded skeptically, as if anyone who had studied French for more than one day would know the French words for "terrible child."

"One day," Julius admitted. So much for impressing her.

*"Comment vous appelez-vous?"* she asked.

Wait a minute. He knew what *that* meant. Julius couldn't believe that less than two hours out of his first French class he was being asked a question in French that he could not only understand but maybe even answer. He gave it a try: *"Je m'appelle Julius Zimmerman."*

He must have said it right, because the girl smiled. She had an incredible smile that seemed to say the person she was smiling at was her favorite person in the whole entire world. *"Je m'appelle Octavia Aldridge."*

Julius glanced back to check on Edison again. A stinging handful of sand struck him on his bare arm.

"I think this is my cue for an exit," Octavia said. *"Au revoir, Julius.* I wish you luck. Lots of luck."

Julius didn't know if he was relieved or sorry to see her go. He glanced at his watch. Two more hours. Two more hours to be the target of Edison's sand-throwing.

Distraction, he remembered. Distraction was the key.

Julius suggested a nap. Edison didn't want to take a nap.

Julius suggested a story. Edison didn't want to hear a story.

Julius suggested a nap again. Kids small enough to be wearing diapers should still be taking afternoon naps. But Edison hadn't changed his anti-nap stance since the previous suggestion.

Then Julius suggested a snack. He himself was ravenous, as if he'd been working all day at hard labor on a chain gang. This time, Edison followed Julius into the kitchen.

The snack worked out pretty well, although Edison spilled his juice all over his I ♡ Virginia Beach shirt and had a tantrum when Julius wouldn't let him eat a crumbled cookie that had fallen onto the Blues' none-too-clean kitchen floor. In the end, Julius let him eat it. Kids had probably eaten worse things than that and survived.

It was only two-fifteen. Suddenly Julius remembered: TV. Edison's mother had told him at the job interview that she didn't want him and Edison to spend their time together staring at the TV, but Julius decided she couldn't possibly have meant it. Besides, they weren't spending their *whole* time together watching TV. Edison had spent almost half of it having tantrums.

Anyway, he'd turn it off at three fifty-five and hope that Edison had the sense not to tell.

Julius clicked around the channels until he found the Flintstones. He had written in his goals journal that he would watch two hours a day of TV, maximum, educational programs only, but surely cartoons with Edison didn't count toward his own limit.

Peace descended on the Blue household. There were

two couches in the family room. Julius sprawled on one. Edison sprawled on the other. The Flintstones were followed by Bugs Bunny. Bugs Bunny was followed by Porky Pig. The afternoon wasn't turning out so badly, after all.

At three-fifty, to be on the safe side, Julius announced in his now-perfected fake-cheerful voice, "All right, buddy! We have to let the TV rest now!"

No sooner had he clicked the power button than a loud wail arose from Edison.

"More TV!"

"No, no, buddy. The TV's tired. Poor TV! It needs to go for a nice little nap."

"TVs don't take naps!"

All right, so the kid wasn't dumb. "Well, it doesn't need to take a nap, exactly, but it can break if we don't turn it off for a while and let the circuits cool down."

Edison considered this explanation. He seemed to know that it was better than the first one Julius had given, but it still wasn't good enough.

"More TV!"

Julius was getting desperate. Desperate enough to try the truth. "Look, your mom said we weren't supposed to watch TV. She's going to be here any minute, and if she finds us watching TV, we're going to be in big trouble. Both of us. You and me."

The mention of Edison's mother turned out to be a mistake.

"I want my mommy!" The cry was so loud that Octavia could probably hear it a house away.

"She's coming! Any minute now!" At least Julius hoped she was. If she was late, he didn't know what he'd do.

But she wasn't late. Mrs. Blue appeared promptly at four, just as Edison had stopped shrieking, "I want my mommy!" and had gone back to shrieking, "More TV!"

Mrs. Blue flew to Edison and caught him up in a big hug. It wasn't a fake hug, either, as far as Julius could tell. Hard as it might be to believe, Edison's mother actually loved him.

Then, when Edison was finally quiet, Mrs. Blue turned to Julius. "How did it go?"

"Pretty well," Julius said, relieved that she hadn't asked what Edison had meant by crying "More TV!" And it *had* gone pretty well, all things considered. Edison hadn't pooped in his diaper, though Julius could smell that he had deposited a generous quantity of pee-pee in it. There had been no visit to the emergency room, no frantic calls to 911. The house was still standing.

"Julius, what was Edison saying about more TV?"

Julius kept his tone professional and polite. "I had some trouble getting him calmed down after his snack, so we watched a little bit toward the end."

"Just a little bit, though." Luckily she didn't pause for confirmation. "I guess that's all right. I know the afternoons can get a bit . . . long sometimes. Speaking of which: angel, it's time for us to say goodbye to Julius."

"Bye, Edison!" Julius said. If there was ever a contest for the two most beautiful words in the English language, he had his entry ready.

"No! Julius stay!"

To Julius's great surprise, Edison sprang across the room and attached himself to Julius's leg.

"Hey, buddy, I'll be back! I promise!"

For the next few minutes, Julius's leg was the scene of a tug of war. Edison tugged on Julius's leg; Mrs. Blue tugged on Edison. Finally, fortunately for Julius, Mrs. Blue won.

Julius didn't linger for another round of farewells. He bolted out the door to freedom. Though he had to admit that he had found Edison's last tantrum oddly gratifying. Maybe you weren't a total failure as a babysitter if the kid cried when it was time for you to leave.

As he unlocked his bike, he heard from the family room the unmistakable theme music of Looney Tunes. Afternoons with Edison could get long, all right.

Julius made a beeline for Ethan's house. He and Ethan hung out and shot a few baskets until six o'clock. They were both lousy players, but liked playing, anyway. Then Julius headed home. His mom had a deadline looming on a writing project, and his dad was working late at his accounting office, so dinner was leftover Chinese carryout that Julius heated up for his mom and himself in the microwave.

"Okay, *now* tell me," his mom said as she picked up her chopsticks. "How was your first day at your very first *job*?" She emphasized the word as if Julius were a little kid, Edison's age, and she was trying to make him feel important. "Did you get off to a good start with Edison?"

*Had* he gotten off to a good start with Edison? His hand still hurt from where Edison had bit him, but he also still felt secretly pleased that Edison had cried when it was time for him to go. "I guess so," he said.

"What kinds of things did you do with him?"

Julius thought over his possible answers: *Let him bite me, let him throw sand at me, watched a bunch of dumb cartoons on TV.*

"Just things," he said.

His mother didn't look satisfied, but she changed the subject.

"I took a little break this afternoon and went to the library," she said. "I came home with more books than I can possibly read in two months, let alone two weeks, but I couldn't resist. How about you? Have you picked out which book you want to read this week?"

She had to be joking. It was only *Monday*. He wasn't going to start on his week's reading goal on a *Monday*. Besides, how could he come home from a morning

31

spent with Madame Cowper and an afternoon spent with Edison Blue and then spend his evening reading age-appropriate books and filling in pages in his Sixth-Grade Math Review Workbook? His mother couldn't expect him to attempt the impossible. Fortunately, he had made this discovery in time to revise his week's goals.

After dinner, Julius opened his green-covered journal and wrote:

*Goals for the Week of June 9–15, Revised*
1. *Try not to make a fool of yourself in French class.*
2. *Get Edison Blue to stop throwing sand.*
3. *Limit Edison's TV to one hour per afternoon—no sex or violence.*
4. *Try to keep Edison from pooping in his diaper.*

It was a good thing his mother had said she wouldn't be reading his goals journal. Maybe he could reinstate the reading goal and the math goal when he had the summer more under control. *If* he ever had the summer more under control.

He studied the list again. Then he added:

5. *Find out more about Octavia Aldridge.*

# 4

After three more days of Intensive Summer Language Learning, Julius was an old pro at "My name is Julius Zimmerman" and "Good morning, how are you?" He was getting pretty good at "What is the weather like?" "It is fine." "It is raining." "It is snowing."

But he still felt it was a mistake on Madame Cowper's part to insist on talking to the class so much of the time in French. Hadn't she noticed that none of them could understand French? Unless the others all understood. Was Julius the only one who sat there in a fog of stupefaction?

And in less than five weeks they were going to have

to put on a play for their families and friends—performed entirely in French! That was what Madame Cowper had said—unless Julius had misunderstood her. Which was all too possible. She couldn't really have meant that he, Julius Zimmerman, was going to speak in French in front of an audience. Maybe it would be a play in which the characters mainly exchanged their names and talked about the weather.

At least they were also going to cook French foods. And eat French foods. Friday was to be their cooking day, and so on that Friday they met for class in the middle-school Family Living room.

Right away Madame Cowper said something in French that ended with the words *quiche Lorraine*. Julius decided she must be saying, "Today we will make quiche Lorraine." He had never heard of quiche Lorraine, but he figured it had to be a kind of food, and any kind of food sounded good to Julius.

He made sure to stick close to Ethan as they divided into groups of four for the cooking, each group claiming its own individual kitchenette, complete with stove, sink, and refrigerator. Unlike most of the kids Julius knew, and unlike Julius himself, Ethan could cook. Ethan and his older brother, Peter, cooked dinner at their house most Saturday nights. At Julius's house, nobody cooked on most nights. Julius's mother liked the joke, "What does a working mother make for dinner?" "Reservations!" In her case, it was phone calls for carryout pizza, carryout Chinese, carryout Vietnamese, and carryout Italian. There was no carryout French restaurant in the vicinity of West Creek, which was why the Zimmermans never ate quiche.

Alex and Marcia were in Julius's group, too. Lizzie was probably disappointed at not getting to be with Ethan, and Ethan was probably relieved at not having to be with Lizzie.

Madame Cowper held up a package of store-bought piecrusts. "Today we will cheat just a little bit," she said, speaking for once in plain ordinary English. "We will use packaged piecrusts for our quiche. But I must tell you that this the French would never do. *Non, jamais!* In France all the food is prepared fresh, from the freshest possible ingredients."

She demonstrated how to fit the piecrust into the piepan.

"I'll do ours," Marcia said importantly, snatching up their piecrust and awkwardly smooshing it in place. Julius was sure that Ethan was a better cook than Marcia.

"Look," Alex said in a loud whisper. "There's going to be one quiche for each group, and one for La Cow. A whole pie just for her." This time he oinked instead of mooing.

"*Maintenant, la préparation.* Now, the filling," Madame Cowper went on when all the piecrusts were in their pans and had been placed in the oven to bake for five minutes. "I must say this is going to be a very naughty day for dieters!"

"I bet it's not her first naughty day," Alex said.

Julius felt embarrassed for Madame Cowper. He wished she would explain the recipe without calling attention to how fattening it was. Didn't she know she was giving kids like Alex more opportunity for mean remarks?

"One of you can have my piece," Marcia said to the boys. "I'm trying to cut back on calories."

She looked at the others as if expecting one of them to say, "*You* don't need to worry about calories." And she didn't. Marcia was the skinniest girl in the class, except for Lizzie, who was the skinniest and the shortest.

"Yeah, you're really a tub," Alex said.

"I am not!" Marcia said, pretending to pout, but plainly pleased at how obviously false his statement was.

"Can you pinch an inch?" Alex leaned over to pinch whatever fat was available from Marcia's slim waist.

Julius was pretty sure that Alex liked Marcia. Marcia squealed and shoved him away. Maybe she liked him, too.

Madame Cowper gave them both a cold look. "Monsieur Ryan, Mademoiselle Faitak, I hope I will not have to ask anyone to leave during our first cooking demonstration."

Alex and Marcia stopped their horsing around, but they didn't look happy about it.

"As I was saying," Madame Cowper went on, "the filling for our quiche Lorraine is very rich. It is made of bacon, cheese, cream, and eggs. *Du bacon, du fromage, de la crème, des oeufs*. We will begin with the bacon."

Madame Cowper gave each group a slab of uncooked bacon to chop into one-inch pieces. Ethan efficiently chopped theirs and placed it in the frying pan, then set about capably separating the sizzling bacon pieces with a fork. Julius felt a quick surge of admiration for his friend, mingled with jealousy. Ethan liked to act as if he and Julius were lousy at all the same things—basketball, math—but Ethan was good at a lot of things, too. Having an older brother probably helped. When you were an only child, you had nobody to show you things. You fumbled and bumbled around on your own.

After Madame Cowper approved the doneness of their bacon, Ethan transferred the bacon bits onto a paper towel and then poured the fat from the pan into a waiting jar.

"Ick," Marcia said.

"That's what Madame Cow would look like if she melted. 'Help, I'm melting!' " Alex screeched in what was clearly intended to be an imitation of the Wicked Witch of the West.

"Monsieur Ryan," Madame Cowper called above the general din. "This is your second warning."

While Alex and Marcia prepared the egg and cream filling, Ethan set Julius to work dicing a block of Swiss cheese. Julius managed to do it without dicing any part of his fingers. Then, as directed by Madame Cowper, he scattered the cheese in the bottom of the piecrust, and Ethan sprinkled in the bacon bits.

"*Bien! Bien!* Now we will pour in our filling. *Comme ça!* Like this!" Madame Cowper demonstrated on her own quiche. It was true that she had made one just for herself.

Ethan poured in the filling, almost spilling it when Alex jostled him while trying to pinch another nonexistent inch of fat from Marcia's skinny frame.

"Monsieur Ryan! You have had two warnings. I do not give three warnings." Madame Cowper's voice was unpleasantly shrill. "I must ask you to leave us. You may sit in the hall outside our room and read in your textbook while the rest of us finish preparing our quiche. Needless to say, you will not be joining us when we eat our quiche, either."

At first Alex hesitated, as if he was thinking about defying Madame Cowper. But then he mustered a sneer and sauntered out to the hall.

"Now carefully, *very* carefully, carry your quiche to the oven. Place it on the center rack. It will need to bake for thirty-five to forty minutes."

Madame Cowper came over to their group. "Monsieur Zimmerman, will you do the honors?"

Julius swallowed hard. He had expected Ethan, the chef, or Marcia, the know-it-all girl, to do the honors. Madame Cowper apparently didn't know that his nickname in fifth grade had been Klutzius.

Ethan opened the oven door for him. The oven had been preheated, and Julius felt a blast of scorching-hot air.

Madame Cowper was still waiting. Julius picked up the quiche, his hands slightly shaking. The filling sloshed from one side of the pan to the other. It seemed alive.

"Be careful, Monsieur Zimmerman! *Faites attention!*"

If only she would stop watching him. Julius could never perform when people watched him. Having Madame Cowper watch him try to put a quiche in the oven was like having Octavia Aldridge watch him try to keep Edison Blue in time-out, or like having the whole class watch him try to stammer out his name. Some people performed better under pressure; Julius didn't.

Julius sensed the disaster before it happened. He

39

had a fleeting vision of losing control of the pan and spilling the quiche all over the floor. Then, just as he was about to slide it onto the rack, he lost control of the pan.

Julius watched, helpless, as the quiche spilled all over the oven door and dripped onto the floor.

Marcia giggled. Ethan groaned. Julius felt his cheeks flame hotter than the preheated oven.

Madame Cowper let his group eat her quiche. It made Julius feel better about Madame Cowper, but it didn't make him feel any better about himself.

That afternoon Julius took Edison in his stroller to the park, half a mile or so from the Blues' house. The stroller was one of the few things in his life that Edison definitely liked. All Julius had to do was strap him in, and off they went. When Julius was out pushing Edison in his stroller, he felt capable and purposeful, as if he knew what he was doing and where he was going. He felt the way Octavia Aldridge looked.

Compared to the quiche disaster, the past few days of babysitting for Edison Blue hadn't been too bad. Julius had avoided the backyard, in order to avoid the sandbox. This also meant that he had avoided Octavia, whom he hadn't particularly wanted to avoid. He felt the need to redeem himself somehow in her eyes. Of course, with Edison in tow, he could easily end up only embarrassing himself further.

At the park, Julius made the mistake of letting Edison out of his stroller to play, for within minutes Edison had figured out that the pleasures of throwing gravel were very like the pleasures of throwing sand.

"You're going to have to keep your little brother from throwing the gravel," one of the mothers there told him.

Did she really think Julius wanted his "little brother" to throw gravel? Did she really think Julius could stop his "little brother" from throwing gravel?

"Hey," Julius said to Edison. "Did you hear what the lady said? No throwing gravel."

Unimpressed, Edison continued to throw gravel.

"He could get that in somebody's eye," the woman said.

Julius tried again. "The lady doesn't like it when you do that."

More gravel flew by.

Julius had to do something. "Edison, if you don't stop, I'm putting you in your stroller right now and taking you home."

This time the flying gravel struck Julius's leg.

He had made the threat; now he had to carry it out. Wishing the lady weren't still watching him, he straightened his shoulders to signal that he meant business. But he had a hunch that forcing Edison into the stroller was not going to be particularly easy.

Sure enough, it wasn't.

Edison kicked and hit and bit. Somehow Julius succeeded at stuffing him in his seat and securing the seat belt. As the mothers watched, Julius wheeled the screaming Edison away from the park playground.

All the way home, Edison howled. Julius was surprised that nobody stopped them to accuse him of kidnapping. Not that anybody in his right mind would want to kidnap Edison Blue.

Octavia was in her front yard, sitting in a swing that hung from the big tree by the house. She was wearing a long white dress—her *Romeo and Juliet* costume, maybe. Her timing was impeccable.

"*Bonjour, Julius,*" she said. "I see Edison is his usual good-natured self today."

Julius felt better. Octavia had made it seem as if the problem lay with Edison's being Edison rather than with Julius's being Julius.

"He and I had a little disagreement over throwing gravel at the park," Julius said.

"And you won."

"If you call this winning." Julius wasn't sure he did. Edison's tears streaked the dirt that had mingled with the sunblock Julius had applied to his cheeks. At least Julius had learned how to get enough sunblock on his tiny face.

Octavia leaned back in the swing. "Do you mind if I ask you one question?"

"No," Julius said cautiously.

"*Why?*"

"Why what?"

"Why are you doing this?" She sounded as if she really wanted to know.

The question embarrassed him. "Why do you think? To earn money, that's why." Not that he had gotten any yet. Mrs. Blue was going to pay him every Friday, so he wouldn't get his first pay for another hour. He could hardly wait.

"No," Octavia said. "There're easier ways to earn money. I can think of at least five hundred."

Apparently, Julius hadn't fooled her. "My mom signed me up. She wants me to have a job this summer. I'm supposed to be learning about responsibility."

"And are you?"

Julius shrugged. He felt the color rising in his face. "I'm learning something, I guess."

Octavia laughed, not a mean laugh. "I bet you are."

Julius glanced down at Edison. He had fallen asleep. He seemed so innocent when he was sleeping. Octavia pushed off gracefully with her sandaled feet and resumed her swinging. Julius wheeled Edison around to the back of the house, then managed somehow to maneuver the stroller up the steps and inside the door. Whatever he was learning this summer, it was something he didn't particularly want to know.

# 5

Julius knew he was going to have to make some new goals for the coming week. He definitely didn't want the second week of summer vacation to be anything like the first. Reviewing the week's goals: he had made the biggest possible fool of himself in French class; he hadn't gotten Edison to stop throwing sand *or* gravel; he and Edison had watched more than an hour of TV on several days. He had had a conversation with Octavia, but instead of finding out more about her, he had let her find out more about him, which wasn't on his list at all. The only accomplishment he had to show for the week, when you got right down to it, was that Edison hadn't pooped in his diaper. That was it. Period.

Well, that wasn't quite all. He had earned the first non-allowance money of his life, and that felt pretty good. But what could he possibly buy with it that was worth what he had gone through to earn it?

His mother seemed worried about him, too, but for different reasons. "Honey, you didn't read *any* books this week?" she asked him on Sunday night, when he came home from playing water basketball with Ethan and some of the other guys at the pool. "I know you've been busy with your class and your job and your friends, but everyone needs to make time for *reading*."

Of course, she had been reading herself when he came in. She was always reading. Too bad he hadn't caught her at the end of the book. When his mother was within the last hundred pages of a book, the house could burn to the ground and she wouldn't notice. She usually cried at the end, too. Julius was invariably relieved when he saw that it was a book she was crying over, rather than the memory of his last report card.

Julius hesitated. "I started one, but I haven't finished it yet," he lied.

"What is it?" she asked eagerly.

"I—um—I don't remember the title."

She looked so disappointed that Julius tried to think of a title, any title. Ethan had read *A Tale of Two Cities* last year when he was trying to impress Ms. Gunderson.

"It was something about cities. Two cities. *A Tale of Two Cities*. That's it."

Her face brightened. "You're reading *A Tale of Two Cities*? Julius, that's a wonderful book! No wonder you didn't get it finished in a week. That's hardly a book you whip right through. And it fits in so perfectly with your French class, too."

Why did it fit in well with his French class? Were the two cities somewhere in France? Julius felt his face betraying him.

"You're not reading it." His mother turned away.

"But I'm *going* to," Julius said. He hated it when the light went out of her eyes that way, all because of him. "Ethan read it last year, and he said it was really good."

"I don't want you to read a book for me, I want you to read it for yourself."

"That's what I'm going to do. I'm going to read it for myself."

His father came in. Julius's dad was a tall, heavyset man, not a Mr. Cow, but someone who could stand to lose twenty pounds around his middle. Julius had seen pictures of his dad as a tall, skinny boy like himself. He sometimes wondered if he would have a middle like that someday, and wear a suit and carry a briefcase to his accounting office. The thought made his heart sink, although there wasn't anything else he was planning to become.

"You're going to read what for yourself?" his father asked.

"*A Tale of Two Cities.*"

"Good luck," his father said.

"Dan! Don't discourage him! *A Tale of Two Cities* is a perfectly thrilling book. I loved it when I was his age."

His father gave Julius a look that said: I doubt you'll like it, but you might as well humor your mother. Come to think of it, his father didn't read books. He read two newspapers every morning, but Julius couldn't remember the last time he had seen his father reading a book.

Julius made a quick call to Ethan. "How long is *A Tale of Two Cities*?"

"Four hundred twenty-two pages." It didn't surprise Julius that Ethan could still give the exact answer. "Why?"

"My mom wants me to read it."

"It's good," Ethan said. "It starts out kind of slow, but then it gets good."

So Julius put it on his list.

*Goals for the Week of June 16–22*

*1. Make Ethan do all the cooking on cooking day.*

*2. Limit Edison to three tantrums a day, none in front of Octavia Aldridge.*

*3. Keep Edison from pooping in his diaper— VERY IMPORTANT!!!!*

4. *Start reading* A Tale of Two Cities, *by*
   *Charles Dickens (422 pages). Find out if the*
   *cities are in France.*

This week's list seemed even more gruesome than last week's. Week two of summer vacation looked as if it was going to be, if anything, worse than week one.

On Monday, Julius and Ethan passed Lizzie as they biked together to West Creek Middle School. She was walking. Julius had never seen Lizzie on a bike. Maybe she was the only kid in Colorado who couldn't ride one, just as last year she had been the only kid in Colorado who couldn't light a match to start the bunsen burner in science class.

Lizzie caught up with them while they waited at the next traffic light. "Hi," Julius said, to break the awkward silence.

"Hi," Ethan echoed.

Lizzie flushed with pleasure. Julius thought she'd probably sit all morning writing "Hi" over and over again in the notebook she always carried with her.

The light was taking a long time to change. Ethan was beginning to get the desperate, trapped look he often got around Lizzie. Julius tried to help out. "How's it going?" he asked her.

"Wonderful! Don't you love French? I dreamed I was

in Paris last night, living in a garret on the Left Bank, in the Latin Quarter, selling flowers on the streets all day and then writing poetry all night. By the light of one flickering candle."

"They have electricity in France," Julius couldn't resist pointing out.

"In my dream they didn't. Maybe it was long-ago Paris, like in *La Bohème*, or maybe I couldn't afford electricity because I was so poor and nobody would buy the flowers I was selling."

She paused. "Except you, Ethan. You were in my dream, too, and you were the only person who bought any flowers from me."

"The light's green now," Ethan said in a strangled voice.

"See you later," Julius said for both of them as they pushed off, Ethan in the lead, pedaling as furiously as a rider in the final time trial in the Tour de France.

Julius didn't usually tease Ethan about Lizzie— Ethan got teased enough by the other kids—but this time he couldn't help himself.

"What kind of flowers did you buy from her?" he asked when they were locking their bikes.

Ethan punched him in the arm. "Cut it out."

Lizzie arrived a few minutes later. "You bought a bouquet of purple violets," she said to Ethan, as if the conversation at the traffic light had never been interrupted. "One small bunch of half-wilted purple violets."

Julius noticed then that Lizzie was wearing a wilted-looking artificial violet in her bright red, curly hair.

That day they were learning the French words for the parts of the body. *La tête*. The head. *La main*. The hand. *Le pied*. The foot.

"Now we will play *un petit jeu*, a little game," Madame Cowper announced. "I believe you all know how to play it. *Allons, debout!* Get up, everybody! You will form a circle, *un cercle*. And we will play *la version française* of *le* Hokey Pokey."

The first question that occurred to Julius was: Is this really happening? Were they really going to put their right *pied* in, take their right *pied* out, put their right *pied* in, and shake it all about?

Apparently they were. Madame Cowper produced a portable tape player, and pushed the play button, and the familiar music for the Hokey Pokey began to fill the room, only whoever was singing it was singing it in French. Julius tried to listen for words he knew, the parts-of-the-body words, but they were all jumbled together with the words for *put, in*, and *shake it all about*. It was easier to watch Madame Cowper and do what she did.

But Julius almost couldn't bear to watch her shaking

different body parts all about. Instead he watched his classmates. Ethan wasn't as good at the Hokey Pokey as he was at frying bacon. He kept getting his body parts in and out a second after everybody else.

Lizzie had managed to find a place next to Ethan in the circle. Julius could tell she was really listening to the tape and trying to hear the announcement of each body part as it came. Her face wore the look of rapt concentration that it did when she was writing her poems.

Alex and Marcia were laughing so hard they could barely turn themselves around for the last line of each verse. The more Madame Cowper shook, the more they laughed. Julius hoped she thought they were laughing at the silliness of the game itself.

The French voice kept on singing. The other kids kept on shaking their body parts. Julius tried to shake the same body parts, but he was one of the world's less talented Hokey Pokey players. If only he could be at the pool doing the backstroke instead.

The tape came to an end. "Monsieur Zimmerman," Madame Cowper said, turning to him.

Uh-oh.

"I think you are having some trouble with *le* Hokey Pokey, *non*?"

Was he supposed to answer? "Um—I guess I got a little mixed up in a couple of places."

"Monsieur Zimmerman, you must listen to the

words—*écoutez bien*—rather than watching your classmates. *Encore.*"

The music began to play again. Put your something in, put your something out. Julius tried to listen, he really did, but the words ran together so fast he couldn't do it. He stole one glance at Lizzie. She was shaking her foot. He looked again. Her left foot. But now the music was on to the next body part.

Madame Cowper clicked off the tape. She was red and panting from the exertion of Hokey-Pokeying. *"Alors!"* she said. "We have had our exercise for today, *non*? Go outside, *mes enfants*, and have a little recess. If we have time at the end of class, maybe we will do *le* Hokey Pokey again. Monsieur Zimmerman, would you please stay here?"

Alex casually hummed a few bars of Chopin's Funeral March as he headed toward the door with all the others.

When Julius was left alone with Madame Cowper, she said in what was obviously meant to be a kindly tone, *"Maintenant*, Monsieur Zimmerman, we will try it again. *Allons-y!* Come! I will give you *une leçon particulière*, a private lesson, in *le* Hokey Pokey."

Julius knew then that he had reached rock bottom in his life. Lower than a private lesson in *le* Hokey Pokey you could not sink.

The tape began to play. Put your something in.

Julius strained to listen. *Pied? Main? Tête?* Tentatively, he twitched his right foot.

"*Non, non, le pied gauche,* the left foot." Awkwardly, Julius wiggled the other foot. This was like kindergarten, when he couldn't remember which hand he was supposed to put over his heart during the Pledge of Allegiance.

As the tape wore on, Julius shook his way through each body part under the sharp eyes of Madame Cowper, who seemed to be correcting practically every one. By the second time through, he still couldn't hear what that French voice on the tape was saying, but he had managed to get the order of the body parts fairly well memorized. The song ended with shaking your whole self. He knew that much for sure.

As if to celebrate the progress they had made, Madame Cowper joined in on the final verse, shaking her whole self, too. Julius made the mistake of glancing toward the classroom window. Half the class had their faces pressed up against the glass, watching Julius and Madame Cowper shaking themselves frantically in their private little Hokey Pokey duet.

Why couldn't he have learned something useful in French class, such as what the French Foreign Legion was, and how soon he could join it?

# 6

Edison still howled when his mother left every afternoon and then, three hours later, he howled when
Julius left. This might have shown how attached he
was to his mother and Julius, or it might have shown
how attached he was to howling.

That Monday afternoon, Edison howled as usual
while he watched his mother's station wagon back out
of the driveway. Julius had learned that it was best to
ignore Edison's tantrums. He picked up a few toys
from the family room floor, but Edison, still shrieking,
snatched them out of the toy box and repositioned each
one exactly where it had been before.

Finally, Edison's tantrum subsided. His thumb went into his mouth like a little round plug.

"Hey, buddy," Julius said, "want to go in your stroller to the library?" He needed to get *A Tale of Two Cities* if he was ever going to read it.

"Edison's stroller!" Edison shouted happily. He scrambled up off the floor and ran over cheerfully to stand in front of Julius.

But then his face changed. He pressed his lips together. He shut his eyes. He gave a little grunt. His cheeks turned red.

"No, Edison, no!"

It was too late. An unmistakable odor filled the room. Edison's face looked normal again, or, rather, normal for when he wasn't howling. But Julius could feel all the color draining out of his own. He couldn't believe that little kids could just ... *go* ... like that, standing up, in front of other people, their faces giving away the terrible secret of what was going on in their pants.

Julius checked his watch. It was only one-fifteen. Could he really leave Edison like that for two hours and forty-five minutes and then pretend it had just happened? Wouldn't the contents of Edison's diaper be squished in a telltale way by then? Besides, Julius wasn't looking forward to two hours and forty-five minutes spent in the company of someone who smelled the way Edison smelled.

"Edison's stroller!" Edison sang out again, as if nothing had happened. He headed toward the back door, where his stroller stood waiting.

"Wait a minute, buddy! You can't go like that."

Storm clouds gathered over Edison's face. Was it time for tantrum number two already?

"You have . . . you know . . . you can't *sit* in that stuff. I have to—we're going to have to change your diaper."

At least Edison didn't launch into another round of howling. Apparently he didn't mind having his diaper changed. Little kids were strange: they minded stupid, unimportant things, such as having their shirts changed, but they didn't mind catastrophic, cataclysmic disasters, such as having their diapers changed.

Julius followed Edison up to his room. He was going to have to change a diaper. He was just going to have to do it. Every day millions of people in America changed diapers. They survived. Julius would survive, too.

No. He couldn't do it. He wasn't like millions of other people. That millions of people in France spoke French didn't mean Julius could speak French. People were different. Some spoke French, and some didn't. Some changed diapers, and some didn't.

He'd have to call someone to come over and change it for him.

His mother? She had gotten him into this mess in

the first place. And she had to know how to change a diaper, because once upon a time she had changed Julius's own diapers—a sickening thought. So he could call his mother. But, according to his mom, the job was supposed to be teaching him about responsibility. Would she think he was learning about responsibility if he called her for every single catastrophe?

Octavia lived right next door. But she had already said that life was too short for babysitting. And life was definitely too short to deal with the contents of diapers. Maybe Octavia could pretend she was a character in a play and that changing a diaper was part of the script? Julius suspected that there wasn't a single diaper-changing scene anywhere in the complete works of Shakespeare.

His only hope was Ethan. Julius could almost imagine his friend briskly and efficiently changing a diaper, the way he had briskly and efficiently fried the bacon.

Almost, but not quite. But there wasn't anyone else he could call.

"Edison, stay right here. I have to make a phone call. Stay right here and *don't sit down*."

Luckily, Ethan was home and not at the pool.

"What's up?" Ethan asked.

"I'm at Edison Blue's house. There's a problem. A big problem. Can you come over?"

"Sure. What kind of problem?"

Julius had to tell him. Ethan would never forgive him if he didn't. But it was all he could do to say it out loud. "He . . . *went* in his diaper," Julius whispered into the phone. "I have to change it."

There was a long pause on Ethan's end of the line. Then Ethan said, "Number one?"

"Number two." There was another, longer pause. "Listen, if you can't, forget it."

"What's the address?"

Julius told him. Then, weak with gratitude, he hung up.

Upstairs, Julius found Edison sitting on the floor playing with his wooden train tracks. How could he sit in it? And the smell—couldn't he smell himself? Maybe Julius needed to start a list of lifetime goals in the back of his journal.

*Goals for the Rest of My Life*
*1. Don't have kids.*

Though maybe he could adopt one who had already been toilet-trained.

A few minutes later, he heard the doorbell. Ethan hadn't wasted any time biking to the rescue. Julius let him in, and the two of them hurried upstairs.

"Edison, this is my friend Ethan. He's going to help me change your diaper."

"No!"

Edison hadn't objected to the prospect of the diaper change before. What was his problem now? Not that Edison was famous for consistency.

"Hi, Edison," Ethan said. "My mom is Mrs. Winfield, your teacher at school."

"My teacher is Patty!" Edison contradicted him.

"That's her! That's my mom!" Ethan said.

"*Not* Mrs. Winfield."

"Patty Winfield. Patty is her first name, Winfield is her last name."

"*Not* Mrs. Winfield!"

Julius decided to cut the conversation short, fascinating as it was. "Okay, buddy, let's get that diaper changed."

"No! *You* don't change Edison's diaper. *Edison* change Edison's diaper!"

Julius thought for a minute. Could Edison really change his own diaper? If he could, Julius's problems were over. Still, he really ought to stick around and supervise, in case anything . . . fell out.

"Okay, Edison, *you* change your diaper. Ethan and I, we're only here to help."

Edison looked suspiciously at Ethan.

"That's right," Ethan confirmed. "We're just your helpers, your diaper-changing helpers."

"Don't look," Edison commanded them.

Julius pretended to shut his eyes, keeping them open just enough to squint through his eyelashes.

Edison pulled down his shorts. Then he tugged at the little sticky tabs on the sides of the diaper.

"Hey," Julius interrupted, "maybe we should do this in the bathroom." Someplace where there wasn't light-colored wall-to-wall carpet.

A brilliant idea he should have had fifteen seconds ago. Off came the diaper, and down onto the middle of the wall-to-wall carpet covering Edison's bedroom floor. Fortunately, it looked as if it fell clean side down.

"Edison need wipes!"

Ethan was able to unroot himself first. He grabbed the box of wipes from the diaper table and placed it on a chair next to Julius.

"Come on, buddy." Julius recovered his voice. "Let's go do this in the bathroom."

"Mommy changes me *here*!"

"Yeah, but Mommy's not changing you now. Julius and Ethan are changing you now—well, helping to change you—and we think we should be doing this in the bathroom."

"No! Here!"

For answer, Julius took Edison by the arm and began to lead him down the hall to the bathroom.

"No!" Edison yanked himself away and tried to run back to his bedroom, his shorts still bunched around his ankles. "Edison do it here! Like Mommy!"

Just as he got back to the bedroom, he tripped and fell, unwiped-bottom side down, and began to howl. But not as loud as Julius and Ethan were howling.

By the end of the afternoon, Julius was pretty certain that there was one thing worse than changing a diaper: scraping and scrubbing the contents of that diaper off a light-colored carpet. He would owe Ethan for this one for the rest of his life.

Luckily, once they managed to open the childproofed cupboard of cleaning products, they found one bottle for removing "pet stains." Apparently, pets stained carpets in much the same way that three-year-olds did. By the time they were done, only a suspicious antiseptic-smelling wet spot on the carpet remained.

When Mrs. Blue came home, Ethan was gone and Edison was getting ready for his closing tantrum. Everything was back to normal. But, not surprisingly, Julius hadn't gotten to the library to check out *A Tale of Two Cities*. He wouldn't have had the strength to start reading it that night, anyway.

# 7

Julius didn't take Edison to the library until Friday. He would have gone sooner, but the weather turned hot, and he couldn't face the long trudge to the library in the blazing sun when he could lie on the couch in Edison's air-conditioned family room, watching TV. Besides, the diaper episode had definitely unnerved him—not that he had all that much nerve in the first place. What if Edison pooped *again* in his diaper? In public. For example, right in the middle of the children's room at the public library. Julius could imagine the lady from the park appearing out of nowhere to sniff and say, "I think you need to change your little brother."

One thing Julius had to say for that lady, though, was that Edison hadn't thrown any more sand since the incident at the park. They had gone outside to the sandbox twice that week, when Julius had started to feel guilty about all the TV they were watching. Both times Edison had picked up a handful of sand, looked at Julius, then dropped it and looked away. So maybe there was something to the discipline idea, after all. It was worth thinking about.

The heat affected everybody in Intensive Summer Language Learning, too. West Creek Middle School wasn't air-conditioned, so that when it got hot, it got *hot*. Julius felt even sorrier for Madame Cowper when the temperature hit ninety degrees by midmorning. On those days, she didn't just perspire under her arms and on her high, glistening forehead; she sweat all over, so that big, blotchy dark stains appeared on the front and back of the tops of her too-tight polyester pantsuits.

On Friday morning, in French cooking class, the menu was something horrible called a *croque-monsieur*. It was a kind of ham and cheese sandwich on french toast. Julius liked ham and cheese sandwiches and he liked french toast, but he couldn't get used to the idea of the two together. He had to break the eggs for the french toast, and one splattered all over the counter. Still, better one egg on the counter than a whole quiche Lorraine all over the floor.

That day, despite the heat, Julius decided he had better go to the library so he would have something to tell his mother if she asked. He loaded a remarkably cheerful Edison in his stroller, and off they went.

The library was air-conditioned. Every pore of Julius's skin sang with relief as the cool air flowed over him. After the intense midday sun, his eyes took a moment to adjust to the dimmer light inside the library. When they did, he saw Lizzie Archer, curled up on a couch by the window, lost to the world in a book. On the couch facing her, watching him with her dark, amused eyes, sat Octavia Aldridge.

Should he go over and say hi? Julius practiced the line in his head: "Hi." He decided against it. Instead he gave a quick, casual wave and briskly wheeled Edison over to the computer catalog. Luckily, Edison had fallen asleep on the way to the library. With any luck he'd sleep, poop-free, through the whole visit.

Julius typed in DICKENS, CHARLES. The guy had sure written a lot of books. He scrolled down until he found *A Tale of Two Cities*. Status: IN. Julius wasn't surprised. Few people would consider *A Tale of Two Cities* summer reading. He turned from the monitor to find Octavia at his side.

"Hi," he said, glad to have the line ready and rehearsed.

"Hi," she said. *"Comment ça va?"*

Julius didn't miss a beat. *"Très bien, merci, et toi?"*

There was a word for how he must look, chatting away in French to Octavia Aldridge, and the word was *debonair*.

Or the word was *idiotic*.

But he did feel a twinge of pride at being able to respond to Octavia so promptly and smoothly in a foreign language. Taking French wouldn't be so bad if he could actually *learn* some.

Octavia peered over his shoulder at the computer monitor. Then she looked at Julius, as if waiting for an explanation.

"My mom thinks I don't read enough."

"Your mom."

Julius remembered that the last time he had talked to Octavia, he had told her that his mom had signed him up to babysit for Edison. He added, defensively, "My friend Ethan said it was pretty good."

"Oh, it's good," Octavia said. "It's great. Almost as great as ice cream. Speaking of which, do you want to go get some? Ice cream. As soon as you get your book."

"Sure," Julius said. Had she just invited him to go out for ice cream? She *had* just invited him to go out for ice cream. "I mean, sure."

Five minutes later, *A Tale of Two Cities* wedged in the stroller next to a still-sleeping Edison, Julius and Octavia entered the ice cream parlor across the street from the library. At that moment an unpleasant thought occurred to Julius. He didn't have any money. His earnings were stashed in a jar in his bureau drawer. All he had with him was fifteen cents.

"What're you going to have?" Octavia asked. "I'm going to have a double scoop of black raspberry."

"Actually . . ." Julius groped again, desperately, in his pocket. All he felt was the same dime and nickel. "I'm not that hungry."

Octavia glared at him. "Then why did you say you'd go for ice cream?"

"Well, I thought I was hungry, but now . . . I'm not."

He searched the menu board for anything that might cost fifteen cents. Then he saw it: water. This was one of the cheapskate places that charged people money for a lousy paper cup of water. "Maybe I'll have some water."

"Water? You're going to watch me eat? And make me feel like a total and complete pig? While you drink water?"

It was time to start over again. "Actually," Julius said, "I *am* hungry."

"A minute ago you actually weren't hungry, and now you actually are hungry?"

"I actually am hungry. But I don't actually have any money. So can I borrow some?"

Octavia laughed. "No. This is my treat."

Even though it charged for water, the ice cream parlor was a pleasant place, with frilly curtains and little old-fashioned wrought-iron tables and chairs. Julius and Octavia claimed a table by the window and pushed the third chair away to make room for Edison's stroller.

Julius took a first lick of black raspberry ice cream. He didn't usually go in for fruity flavors, but he had thought it was safer to order the same thing as Octavia. Of course, once he had ordered it, she had told him, "You don't have to copy me." It was good, though.

"My *Oklahoma!* audition is next week," Octavia said after she had licked her cone down to a manageable point.

Julius thought about mentioning that he was going to be in a play, too, in French, no less. But he could tell it wouldn't impress her.

"What part are you trying out for?" It seemed a good, low-key question to start off with.

"Laurey. That's the lead. Ado Annie is a better part in some ways—you know, she's the one who sings, 'I Cain't Say No'—but there's a long ballet sequence for Laurey, and I can do ballet as well as regular stage dancing."

"Do you think you'll get it?"

Octavia gave him a withering look. "So far in my life, I've been to nine auditions, and I've gotten the part I've tried out for every single time."

"Wow," Julius said, since Octavia obviously expected some response along those lines. But as much as he envied her confidence, it made him a little uneasy, too. What if someday she didn't get a part? He hesitated for a moment, then plunged in. "But nobody gets the part they want *all* the time." Was that true? It sounded true. It sounded almost as true as the law of gravity.

"Maybe nobody *does*. But somebody *could*. Because it all depends on talent, and preparation, and being right for the part. I couldn't get *any* part I tried out for, but if I pick parts that I'm suited for—like Laurey— and prepare like crazy for the audition, which I've been doing, then I'd say my chances are pretty good."

"But what if two people are both suited for a part, and they're both really talented, and they both prepare like crazy?"

"Well, obviously only one of them can get it." Octavia sounded impatient at having to explain such an elementary point to Julius. "All I'm saying is that so far that's never happened to me. I want things more than other people want them, and I'm willing to do what I have to do to get them. Your cone is dripping."

Julius caught the drip with his tongue and for the next minute concentrated on licking his cone. There was no point in trying to challenge Octavia's confidence in herself, and he wasn't even sure why he wanted to. Except it couldn't hurt to consider the idea that sometime in your life something might not work out the way you wanted it to. Julius's own operating principle was that things would never work out the way he wanted them to.

"So why do you like acting so much?" he asked, hoping he was retreating to safer territory. He expected Octavia to toss back some scornful reply, but instead she seemed to be genuinely considering the question.

"Well, partly it's that I like plays so much. I still remember the first one I ever went to. *South Pacific*. I was only four, but one of the teachers in my preschool was in the chorus, so my parents took me, and when the curtain went up . . . it was magic. It was like having a magic ring that could take you to another time and place. And the *music*. Those *songs*. My parents bought me the CD of the first Broadway production, and I learned all the songs by heart, with the same motions I'd seen on the stage. My parents thought it was funny, and they'd put the CD on when their friends came over and have me do my version of 'Some Enchanted Evening' and 'There Is Nothin' Like a Dame.' And their friends would all clap for me, and I'd curtsy, and I knew that this was *it*. This was what I wanted to do with my life."

Octavia stopped. For the first time since Julius had met her, she looked self-conscious. "I bet you didn't expect a speech. Believe it or not, I don't always talk

69

about myself this much. So what about you? Do you have a first memory of something like that?"

Julius tried to think of a memory to match Octavia's. But he knew he had nothing. "Nah," he said.

"What's your very first memory? Any memory. Do you know what it is?"

Julius thought back. His family had moved into their current house when he was three and a half, so any memory of their first house had to be an early one.

"I remember the garage. Our house now has an automatic garage-door opener, but our first house, when I was really little, didn't have one, and I remember my mom getting out of the car and bending down to lift the door and how it came rolling right up."

Octavia stopped licking her cone. "Your first memory is of your garage door?"

Okay, it wasn't much compared with Octavia's memory of *South Pacific*. But she had asked for his first memory, and that was what he had come up with.

Another memory, dimmer than the garage door, began to form.

"Wait a minute. There was a little kid on our street, and there was something wrong with her, or something." It was strange recalling a memory, like watching a picture develop on a Polaroid snapshot. "It was her eyes. They didn't look in the same direction. One of them always turned in. And this other kid—

Jimmy—Jimmy Jardullo—he was laughing at her, and she was crying, so I punched him in the stomach, and I got put in time-out for hitting him, but he didn't get put in time-out for making her cry. I guess my mom thought I felt like punching people in the stomach that day."

Julius stopped. The memory, when it had finally come, had been so vivid, so real. He looked sheepishly at Octavia. "I bet you didn't expect a speech, either."

"I like your memory," she said softly.

"I like yours, too."

Julius heard a howl. Edison was awake, pointing at the remains of Julius's soggy, dripping cone. "Edison wants ice cream!"

"Okay, buddy, calm down, I'll get you some ice cream." He felt in his pockets for his money, then remembered. "Or how about some water? A nice cool cup of yummy water?"

"Edison wants ice cream!"

"Julius." Octavia touched his hand. "I said, this is my treat. What kind of ice cream do you want, Edison? Julius and I had black raspberry."

"*Not* raspberry."

"How about vanilla?" Julius asked.

"*Not* vanilla."

"Listen, buddy," Julius said, "I'll read you the whole list and you pick. Ready? Vanilla."

"*Not* vanilla."

"Chocolate."

"*Not* chocolate."

"Strawberry."

"*Not* strawberry."

Edison had vanilla. It dripped all over him, and all over the stroller, and all over the plastic cover of *A Tale of Two Cities*, but Julius didn't care. He felt too good to care about anything.

"**H**ow are you coming along with *A Tale of Two Cities*?" Julius's mother asked him Sunday afternoon, as she was fixing potato salad for a family barbecue that evening.

"Well, I got the book," he said. "From the library," he added, watching the hopeful look fade from her eyes. "I didn't get a chance to go over there until Friday."

"Honey, we *have* the book. It's right there on the bookshelf in the living room."

She put down the mayonnaise spoon and led Julius to the living room, where one whole wall was lined with bookshelves from floor to ceiling.

"Here, with all the other Dickens novels." Sure enough, there was *A Tale of Two Cities*, flanked by *David Copperfield* and *Great Expectations*. "I still remember how long I worked when we moved in to get our books arranged. I had always wanted to live in a house with a library, a real library, the kind with a little moving ladder that rolled from shelf to shelf. I think that's what sold this house to me, all the built-in bookcases."

But there was no moving ladder. Maybe Julius would save his Edison Blue money and buy her one for Christmas. He'd like a moving ladder himself. He would have had a wild time riding on one when he was a little kid.

"Don't you ever browse here?" Julius's mother's tone had shifted from nostalgia to worry. "When I was a child, I read every book my parents owned; I think I read half the books in our tiny public library. And now we have a house full of books, and I sometimes wonder whether you even look at them."

Julius tried to think of something to say to make her feel better. It was true that his mother's books had never had any appeal to him. There were so many of them, all lined up in those long, straight rows, like the army of statues from a dead emperor's tomb he had seen once in the museum. He knew his mother wished he were a reader like—the thought came to him— Lizzie Archer. He could imagine the little squeal of

74

delight Lizzie would give if she ever saw the Zimmermans' books. His mother should have had Lizzie for a daughter. Instead she had Julius for a son.

"I look at them," he said. He looked at the books every day; he just never looked inside them.

As Julius headed upstairs to try to read at least the first chapter of *A Tale of Two Cities* before dinner, he heard his dad say to his mom, "Times have changed, Cindy. A lot of kids today aren't readers."

Julius knew he shouldn't linger at the top of the stairs, but he couldn't help himself. It felt good to hear his dad taking his side.

"There's still nothing like a book," his mom said sorrowfully. "You can't curl up on the couch with a computer. And plenty of kids still read. Ethan read *A Tale of Two Cities* last winter."

Julius should never have told her that.

"It just breaks my heart that Julius doesn't read." Julius could hear the despair in her voice. "When you love something, you can't help but hope your children will love it, too. And children who read do better in school. It's a proven fact. They do."

"But these days, even in schools, kids are watching TV and using the Internet," Julius's dad said gently. "They get their information in other ways."

"Tell me," his mother said, "how much information does someone get from *The Flintstones*?"

"Well, maybe he learns something about the Stone Age."

His dad laughed and, to Julius's relief, his mom laughed, too. Upstairs in his room, he opened his library copy of *A Tale of Two Cities*. "It was the best of times, it was the worst of times." That sounded like a dumb first line to Julius. *Best* and *worst* were opposites. If it was the *best* of times, it couldn't be the *worst* of times. What kind of book began with an outright contradiction?

Julius closed the book. He'd pick it up again later, when his mother's look and tone of disappointment weren't so sharp in his memory.

After dinner, instead of starting in right away on *A Tale of Two Cities*, he made his goals list:

*Goals for the Week of June 23–29*
1. *Don't go out without money.*
2. *Don't disgrace yourself in French class.*
3. *Don't put off reading* A Tale of Two Cities.
4. *Don't let Edison poop in his diaper again—VERY IMPORTANT!!!!*

Even Julius had to admit that the list was pathetic. Octavia's list—he was sure she had one—would say "Astonish them at the audition for *Oklahoma!*" or

"Memorize all the lines of all the heroines in Shakespeare." Julius's goals were all negative: don't do this, don't do that. It was as bad as the list of rules posted by the side of the pool.

He decided to rewrite the list, making it more positive.

*Goals for the Week of June 23–29*
1. *Carry money with you—at least $2.00.*
2. *Do your best in French class.*
3. *Read one chapter a day of* A Tale of Two Cities.
4. *Toilet-train Edison Blue????!!!!*

The new list looked more impressive. It also looked impossible. Toilet-train Edison Blue? Who was he kidding?

Julius took a five-dollar bill from his Edison Blue jar and stuffed it in the pocket of the jeans he had tossed on the bottom of his bed, the jeans he would wear tomorrow. There. He had already taken care of goal number 1. But goal number 4 was the killer. Goal number 4 was a killer and a half.

When Julius and Ethan arrived at Intensive Summer Language Learning on Monday morning, their classroom had been transformed into an art museum. Every wall was covered with reproductions of what

Julius supposed were great works of French art. He couldn't help but notice that some of the great works of French art featured female persons wearing few, if any, clothes.

"*Ce vendredi*, this Friday, we will go to *le musée d'art*, the museum of art, in Denver, to see an exhibit on *l'impressionnisme français*, French Impressionism," Madame Cowper announced. In her funny mixture of half French, half English, she went on to say that, after touring the exhibit, they would have lunch at a French restaurant; the class would run until three that day. Then Madame Cowper handed out permission slips for the trip, luckily in English.

Julius's first thought was: Edison Blue. Would Mrs. Blue be able to find someone else for that afternoon? Would Edison miss him? Or would he cling as hard to the new babysitter's leg when it was time for him or her to go? Julius was surprised that he almost minded the thought of skipping work. Anyone in his right mind would be overjoyed at the thought of an afternoon without Edison Blue.

Madame Cowper spent the first part of the class talking about French art. One by one, she told the class about each of the pictures displayed in the classroom, even the pictures of the ladies with no clothes on.

"And this is *Odalisque*, by Jean Auguste Dominique Ingres," she said, pointing to a portrait that showed a whole entire naked lady, mostly her back, but one little bit of her front. "Note the exquisite sense of color," Madame Cowper said. Julius chiefly noted the use of a *lot* of skin tones.

"What happened to her clothes?" Alex called out.

To her credit, Madame Cowper didn't blush. *"De l'antiquité*, the human body has always been a favorite subject for *les artistes."*

As Madame Cowper turned to the next picture, Alex shot a rubber band across the room at *Odalisque*. It hit her square on the backside with a loud *ping*.

"Monsieur Ryan! Today I am giving only one warning. If you cannot treat these works of art with the proper respect, you will not accompany us to the museum on Friday." Apparently Madame Cowper could speak in English when she wanted to make a point clear enough. *"Comprenez-vous?* Do you understand?"

Alex glared at her, but she held his gaze. He didn't make any more smart-alecky remarks as she showed the class little naked baby angels on a ceiling painting by Fragonard and naked girls in Tahiti painted by Gauguin. But as the class was getting ready to file outside for the morning break, Alex collected his rubber band from the floor beneath *Odalisque*, and snapped it at one of the naked baby angels.

Instantly Madame Cowper bore down upon him. Julius caught in his breath.

*"Monsieur Ryan, donnez-le-moi."*

Alex gave her the rubber band.

"*Donnez-moi votre* permission slip."

His face completely sullen and resentful now, Alex returned to his desk, picked up his permission slip, and handed it to Madame Cowper. As the rest of the class stared, she ripped it in half, then in half again, and deposited the pieces in the wastepaper basket.

Alex lost his temper. "You can't stop me from going. This isn't school. My dad *paid* for this class."

"We shall see, Monsieur Ryan, we shall see."

Julius couldn't help but be thankful that for once the person in trouble was not Monsieur Zimmerman. He might not be able to pour quiche or do *le* Hokey Pokey, but at least he was able to stay out of trouble in French class, and to look at French paintings of naked ladies without cracking up.

Julius arrived a few minutes early at Edison's house that afternoon. He wanted a little extra time to talk to Mrs. Blue.

He took a deep breath and made himself start in: "Um—Mrs. Blue—I was wondering—well—do you think it's time for Edison to start using—the—um—the potty?" He kept his voice low so that Edison, busily playing with his trucks at the other end of the room, wouldn't hear.

Mrs. Blue sighed. "I don't know. We bought him a little potty some time ago—you may have seen it in the bathroom—but so far he's shown no interest in using it. And the books I've read all say that parents should wait until the child shows interest. But one of my friends said that her children never showed any interest, so she just had to train them anyway. She used stickers."

"Stickers?"

"As a reward. She made a chart and put it on the refrigerator. But I don't know. Edison is such a sensitive little boy . . . And he gets upset so easily."

Julius wasn't about to disagree.

"Edison's daddy doesn't seem worried about it, but he doesn't really worry about anything. What do *you* think, Julius? You've gotten to know Edison pretty well during the past two weeks. Do *you* think he's ready?"

It took Julius a moment to realize that Edison's mom was actually asking *him*—a twelve-year-old boy—for advice. Somehow he had always assumed that moms just knew these things, like what foods their kids should eat, and what time their kids should go to bed, and when their kids should start using the potty. But Mrs. Blue plainly didn't have a clue.

Julius thought about her question. He was ready for Edison to be potty-trained, but was Edison ready?

"I think so," he finally said. "The other day, when I was changing his diaper, he told me that he wanted to change it himself." Never before had so many gruesome details been left out of a story.

"Maybe you're right. On my way home today, I'll stop and buy some stickers. You might try mentioning it to him—casually at first, so as not to put him off. You know how negative he is."

Julius made no comment.

"Maybe you could play some sitting-on-the-potty games."

"Sure," Julius said, as if he had been playing sitting-on-the-potty games all his life.

Sitting-on-the-potty games sounded pretty terrible, but not as terrible as changing-poopy-diaper games. Julius had taken his first step—a small step, but nonetheless a real step—toward his biggest summer goal. It might not be his mother's top-ranked goal for him, but for Julius it would be a real accomplishment.

# 9

Ever since the conversation in the ice cream parlor, Julius had started actually to like Octavia Aldridge. He had been intrigued by her right from the start: for one, she was beautiful; for another, *she* obviously thought she was terrific. But now he genuinely liked her, too. It seemed impossible that she could ever genuinely like him, and yet she *had* asked him out for ice cream. That, however bizarre and unbelievable, was a fact.

So Julius made a point of suggesting to Edison that they play outside. The heat had broken; the breeze was brisk and refreshing.

"Let's go play outside, buddy."

"No!"

"You can ride your bike." It was just a little plastic trike, and Edison didn't even pedal it; he scooted it along with his feet, like something out of *The Flintstones*. Still, Julius knew that Edison was proud of it.

"No!"

"You can make chalk pictures on the driveway."

"No!"

Desperate, Julius cast about for another idea. "You can . . . sit on your potty."

This suggestion didn't trigger the standard response. "My potty isn't outside."

"We can *take* it outside. Maybe the potty would like to see Edison's yard. Poor potty, stuck all day in a yucky bathroom. Let's take the potty on a little outing."

Edison giggled. Julius took that for a yes.

He got a reasonable amount of sunblock on Edison and then went into the upstairs bathroom to get the potty. It occurred to Julius that emptying that potty would not be appreciably more pleasant than changing a diaper. But he would cross that bridge if he ever came to it.

At the back door, he suddenly had a pang of doubt about carrying the potty into the yard. Forget *A Tale of Two Cities*. He should be reading a book on potty training to see what it said about taking a potty out of the bathroom. You didn't want to make the kid think the whole world was one big bathroom. But you also had to make going to the potty seem like fun.

It was too late, anyway, now that he had said all that stuff about how the potty needed fresh air and sunshine.

"All right, Edison! Out we go!"

In the yard, Edison tried putting the potty in different places: on the patio, next to the grill, in the sandbox, laughing hysterically at each one.

"My potty likes the sandbox," Edison said, still laughing so hard that he almost tumbled over.

"Okay. Leave it in the sandbox. But no throwing sand, potty!"

"Hi, Julius, hi, Edison." Octavia was leaning over the fence. She *would* have to appear in time to overhear Julius engaged in conversation with a potty. Julius was willing to bet things like that had never happened to Romeo. Should he make a joke about it? No. It was better to pretend that the potty wasn't there.

"How's it going?" he asked, getting up and taking a couple of steps away from the potty. That way it wouldn't be in her direct line of vision when she looked at him.

"Fine. Why is there a potty in the middle of the sandbox?"

Edison looked up, evidently pleased at the question. "My potty *likes* the sandbox."

Julius shrugged apologetically, as if he couldn't be expected to understand the strange workings of the three-year-old mind. In a low voice, he said, "We're playing potty games today. You know, to get him used to the idea of using it."

"Potty games." Octavia had a way of repeating Julius's words that made them seem totally inane. Then she laughed, the merry, affectionate laugh he had heard before. "You're a brave man, Julius Zimmerman."

Sheepishly, Julius laughed with her. Her laugh would be a good stage laugh; it made her audience want to join in.

"When is your audition?" Julius asked.

"Wednesday. Down in Denver, at my drama school. My mom works there, so I ride in with her."

"Do they tell you right away if you get it?" He tried to make the question sound casual, but he could tell it annoyed her.

"No, they don't tell you right away if you get it." Her sarcastic mimicry of his words stung. "They'll post the cast list on Friday. Want to hear one of my songs?"

Julius was relieved that her voice had turned friendly again. "Sure."

Lightly, Octavia swung herself over the fence. Julius hoped it was all right. Mrs. Blue had told him he couldn't have friends over during his babysitting hours. Of course, Ethan had come, but that had been a rescue mission, not a social call. And this was a performance, not a social call. And Octavia wasn't exactly a friend. Anyway, it couldn't matter that much which side of the fence she was standing on.

Julius seated himself on Edison's little wooden swing. To his amusement, Edison sat down comfortably on the potty. Julius wondered if Octavia had ever performed to an audience seated on a potty before.

" 'Many a New Day.' " Octavia announced her selection as formally as if they had been in Boettcher Concert Hall in Denver. Then she opened her mouth and sang.

If Julius hadn't decided at the beginning of the summer that he was through with love forever, he would have fallen in love with Octavia the moment the first notes poured out. She had an amazing voice, clear and true and lilting. And her face as she sang was alive with expression, the kind of face a movie camera would love, the kind of face you could watch forever without being bored.

When she finished, Julius applauded, clapping so hard his palms stung. For once agreeable, Edison joined in from his potty-seat perch.

"You'll get the part," Julius said, all doubt banished now. There couldn't be two girls who sang like that and who looked like that when they sang.

"That's the plan," Octavia said. Although she sounded as calm and conceited as ever, it was clear that she was pleased by Julius's response.

"How long does the play run?" he asked.

"Eight performances."

If he weren't through with love, Julius would attend all eight and use his Edison Blue earnings to buy her a bigger bouquet of roses each evening. And on the final night he'd send her so many flowers that her entire dressing room would be filled with them and she'd have to hire a limousine to take them home with her.

It was a good thing that he was through with love.

On Tuesday, apparently daunted by Madame Cowper's swift and terrible punishment of Alex, no one else shot any rubber bands or spitballs at the art pictures.

During the break, Alex announced to the others loudly, "I told my dad that the Cow ripped up my permission slip for Friday, and he's going to call her tonight and make her let me go."

Julius marveled at how differently his own parents would have responded. They would never take his side against a teacher. His mother, especially, always seemed willing to assume that Julius was in the wrong. Julius knew other kids whose parents came complaining to the teacher when they got bad grades. But when Julius got bad grades, his mom came complaining to him.

He was glad they weren't getting a grade in Intensive Summer Language Learning. Though maybe Julius wouldn't have done too badly. He was starting to understand more and more of what Madame Cowper said to the class, and that morning he had had the right answer twice when she called on him.

"Do you think he can?" Ethan asked. "Make her? I mean, it's her class, isn't it?" Julius knew that Ethan's parents were more like his than they were like Alex's.

"My dad's a lawyer," Alex said, "and when he says, 'Jump,' other people say, 'How high?' You'll see. Madame Cowper's going to be the Cow that jumped over the moon."

On Wednesday, Julius realized that he had forgotten to ask Octavia what time her audition was. Morning? Afternoon? He wanted to be able to beam good-luck thoughts to her. Not that she needed luck. As far as Julius was concerned, she was ready for Broadway.

That afternoon, Edison hurried out cheerfully to his potty, still stationed in the sandbox. His new favorite game was to hide things in it. The day before, he had spent the whole afternoon filling the potty with matchbox cars and then taking them out again. He loved best the moment when he raised the lid to reveal his hidden treasures. Today the treasures were pinecones, gathered from under the three tall trees that bordered the Blues' backyard.

Toward three o'clock Octavia appeared in her yard.

"Hey, Octavia!" Julius called over to her, trying not to sound too eager for her news. "How's it going?"

"Okay," she said, coming over to the fence. "Good," she corrected herself. Had Julius imagined a hint of self-doubt in her first reply?

He hoped she would volunteer information about the audition, but when she didn't, he made himself ask, "How was the audition?"

This time she had the correct answer ready: "Fine."

"Fine?"

"It was an audition, all right? I read, I sang, I danced. What else do you want to know?"

"Do you think you did okay?"

"What is this, the Inquisition?"

"It's called friendly interest," Julius said stiffly. Was it too much to assume that he and Octavia were friends?

"Look!" Edison interrupted. As Julius and Octavia watched, he pointed to the potty, filled almost to overflowing with pinecones.

"Wow!" Julius said, as he had the last six times Edison had shown him the pinecones.

"I'm sorry," Octavia said. "All right, since you asked: there was another girl there, who auditioned after me. She was good, that's all."

Julius stopped himself from asking: As good as you

90

are? And he didn't tell her she was sure to get the part, because he could tell how lame it would sound.

"How're the potty games coming?" Octavia asked then, obviously glad to change the subject.

"Great," Julius said truthfully. Even if Edison never learned to use the potty for its proper purpose, he had been so happily absorbed in playing with it that he hadn't had a single tantrum this week. You couldn't ask much more of a potty than that.

On Thursday Julius was beginning to wonder if the potty that had served as a garage for model cars, a seat in a concert hall, and a storage container for pinecones would ever serve as a potty.

Edison was busy filling the potty with sand, excavated from the sandbox with his toy backhoe. It was hard work for a hot afternoon, and his cheeks were pink with exertion. His hair clung damply to his small head.

"Hey, buddy," Julius began tentatively. "Most people don't put sand in a potty." As if Edison had ever shown any sign of caring about what "most people" did. "You know what most people put in a potty?"

Edison obviously wasn't listening. Julius lowered his voice to a whisper, as if he were about to communicate some fascinating secret. "They put in pee-pee."

At that Edison looked up. "What?"

How much of the speech had Edison missed? Probably the whole thing. But Julius just repeated the last word: "Pee-pee."

Edison burst out laughing, as if *pee-pee* was the funniest word in the English language. Which maybe it was. Then he asked, "What's pee-pee?"

He had to be kidding. Pee-pee was . . . pee-pee. Julius didn't know how to define it for Edison better than that. It was probably one of those words they didn't even put in the dictionary.

"It's a kind of water that you make in your diaper," he finally said.

Suddenly Edison's face cleared. "Wee-wee?" he asked.

"Yes!" Julius should have asked Mrs. Blue what term she used with Edison. "Pee-pee is wee-wee!"

If the word alone had been funny, the sentence defining it was funnier. Edison tried to say it himself, but his tongue tripped over the two rhyming pairs of repeated syllables. "Say it again!" he begged between gasping giggles.

Feeling exceedingly foolish, and hoping that for once Octavia wasn't around to overhear, Julius repeated, "Pee-pee is wee-wee."

"Again! Say it again!"

Okay. Anything in the service of the cause. "Pee-pee is wee-wee."

"Say it again!"

Julius had an inspiration. "Look, I'll say it again *if* you make some pee-pee in your potty." Who needed stickers?

"My potty has sand in it."

"We can take it out. I'll help you."

Eagerly, Julius dumped out the sand. Then, for good measure, he took the potty out of the sandbox and gave it a good dousing with the hose. All clean and empty now, it sparkled invitingly in the afternoon sun.

Not invitingly enough, apparently.

"No!" Edison practically screamed. "Edison doesn't *want* to make pee-pee wee-wee in his potty."

"Okay." Julius tried to keep his voice cheerful. Book or no book, he knew enough about potty-training, or at least potty-training Edison Blue, to realize he shouldn't make an issue of it, lest Edison feel honor-bound to turn against the potty for life. "Whatever you say, buddy. Whenever *you* want to. And when you do, I'll say the funny rhyme again. Deal?"

Edison still glared at him suspiciously, but he didn't howl.

From next door, Julius heard Octavia warbling her warm-up voice exercises, sliding up and down a series of ever-higher scales. If she was still worried about yesterday's audition, it didn't show: her voice rang out loud and clear.

# 10

Julius's spirits lifted when he saw the school bus parked in front of West Creek Middle School on Friday morning. Yes! They soared still higher when he saw that Alex was not there. Even if the bus was old and bumpy and their destination was just the Denver Art Museum, still, a class trip without Alex Ryan was a clear improvement on ordinary life, at least on ordinary life in Intensive Summer Language Learning.

Mrs. Blue had understood when Julius asked for the afternoon off. She would stay with Edison that day, so Julius didn't have to worry whether Edison would like his new babysitter better, or whether the new babysitter would wonder why there was a sparkling-clean potty in the middle of the sandbox.

Julius and Ethan grabbed two seats together on the bus, as far back as Julius could sit without getting carsick.

"Can you sleep over tomorrow night?" Ethan asked, once Madame Cowper had counted *nez* in French and the bus was on its way.

"Probably," Julius said. "I have to ask my mom. But I think she'll let me. I mean, I have to have *some* fun this summer."

"How's Edison doing?"

"Okay. He's a pretty good kid, really."

Ethan looked skeptical. "Have you had any more . . . problems?"

"Not since the Big One. Right now I'm trying to get him to use the potty."

"Man!"

Julius felt embarrassed by Ethan's admiration, especially since he seemed as far away from that goal as ever. "So Alex isn't here," he said. "I guess his dad didn't call her, after all."

"I bet he did, and she didn't let him push her around. Have you ever met Alex's dad? He's a lot like Alex. The time I saw him, it was at the pool, and he was making fun of Alex in front of all the other guys.

He called him a chicken when he wouldn't jump in the deep end. I'd hate to have a dad like that."

"Me too," Julius said. He thought gratefully of his own gentle, good-natured dad. And even his mother—she was always after him for one thing or another, but she never picked on him in front of anybody else. He had to give her credit for that. He just wished that he could be the son she had always wanted, or else that she could learn to want the son she already had.

"Do your parents bug you about stuff?" Julius asked Ethan.

"Sure," Ethan said. "Not during summer much, but when we're in school, yeah, they bug me about homework, getting it done, checking my work. But not like Alex's dad."

"Sometimes . . ." It was hard for Julius to get the sentence out. "Sometimes I don't think my mom likes me very much."

He thought Ethan might look shocked, but he didn't. All he said was "Oh, moms always love their kids. Just because they yell at us sometimes doesn't mean they don't love us."

Julius knew his mom *loved* him—she still wanted to hug him and kiss him, even though he thought he was too big for that now. But he didn't know if she really *liked* him. His mom liked people who did well in school, people who read books, and not any old books, but long, hard, boring, age-appropriate books.

Julius let the subject drop.

When they got off the bus at the museum, Madame Cowper counted *nez* again. *Vingt-deux.* Twenty-two. Didn't she know that the number would be the same as it had been when they got on the bus, since they had made no stops along the way?

Once inside, Madame Cowper led them grandly to the French Impressionist exhibit, where a museum lady was going to give their group a special tour. The museum lady and Madame Cowper must have been friends, because they acted thrilled when they saw each other.

"Lila!" the museum lady said to Madame Cowper.

"Angie!" Madame Cowper said to the museum lady.

Then they hugged each other. It was embarrassing to watch, but it made Julius feel better to know that Madame Cowper had at least one friend, someone who obviously thought of her as a person, not as a French teacher. Or as a cow. For the first time, he wished Alex were on the trip.

Madame Cowper's friend certainly knew a lot about French Impressionist painting, and Madame Cowper did, too. The pictures themselves were terrific, much better than *Odalisque* or those naked baby angels.

Even when Monet painted the same haystack over and over again, it was always different. The guy could paint. His pictures almost made Julius want to try painting. He could paint a picture of Octavia dancing, like the Degas paintings that hung near the Monets. But painting people had to be harder than painting haystacks. Probably he should start out with haystacks.

The exhibit was a large one, with paintings on loan from museums all over the world. When the tour was over, Madame Cowper counted *nez* again.

*"Dix-huit. Dix-neuf. Vingt. Vingt et un."*

Twenty-one.

She counted again. *"Vingt et un."* Twenty-one. Who wasn't there?

Ethan was the first to figure out who was missing. "Lizzie," he said.

Madame Cowper gave a cluck of worried irritation. "Monsieur Winfield, Monsieur Zimmerman, would you go back through the galleries to see if perhaps she is lost? The rest of us will wait here."

Together, Ethan and Julius retraced their steps. The galleries had become crowded, and there was no sign of Lizzie anywhere. Then, in the very first gallery, Julius caught a glimpse of her familiar red curls. She was standing, motionless, in front of one of Monet's water lily paintings.

"Hey, Lizzie," Ethan said.

She didn't move.

"Lizzie," he said again, and touched her on the arm.

She gave a little scream. "Ethan?" She looked puzzled to see him.

"Madame Cowper sent us to find you," Ethan said. "The tour is over. We need to get on the bus to go to lunch."

Julius wondered if Lizzie would be upset that she had missed almost the whole tour, and 90 percent of the Impressionist paintings. If she loved paintings so much that she could spend almost two hours in just one room, it was a shame she had missed looking at so many. But she didn't seem to mind. Maybe if you looked at a couple of paintings that long and hard, you didn't need to look at any others.

"I'm never writing poetry again," Lizzie whispered as she followed Ethan and Julius through the museum. Julius glanced at Ethan to see if he looked relieved. Last year, much of Lizzie's poetry had been about Ethan. Ethan mainly looked intent on getting back to the others without losing Lizzie to any more rhapsodies.

"Unless . . ." Lizzie stopped walking, so the boys had to stop, too. "Do you think someone could do *that* with words? Write a poem about water lilies that would make people see them—really *see* them—understand them—the way Monet did?"

Ethan didn't answer, plainly at a loss for what to say.

"Maybe," Julius ventured. It seemed a safer answer than yes or no.

Lizzie turned to him. "Do you really think so?"

What Julius really thought was that he hoped the bus hadn't left without them. His stomach yearned for the restaurant.

"Sure," he said.

"Sure," Ethan echoed.

Lizzie sighed blissfully and allowed herself to follow the boys again. If *Ethan* said it, apparently that made it true.

When they rejoined the group, Madame Cowper's face lit up with relief. "Mademoiselle Archer, we were beginning to worry."

"I was looking at the water lilies," Lizzie explained softly.

"*Monsieur Zimmerman, Monsieur Winfield, merci beaucoup!*" Madame Cowper didn't scold Lizzie for not staying with the group, perhaps because she loved the paintings, too, in her own way, as much as Lizzie did. "*Allons-y!*" she said. "*C'est l'heure du déjeuner.* It is time for our lunch."

Julius couldn't have agreed more.

Julius's family seldom came to Denver, so Julius didn't know the city very well. When the bus stopped to drop them off, he didn't know which part of the city they were in, except that it was some part without sky-scrapers or the gold dome of the State Capitol.

After the nose count, the class filed off the bus and waited on the sidewalk for Madame Cowper to lead them to the restaurant. They had walked half a block, past several restaurants and shop windows, when, across the street, Julius saw a girl who from the back looked exactly like Octavia. Could it be Octavia? Her acting school was somewhere in Denver. But what if he called her name and some strange girl turned to look at him scornfully?

What if he called her name and Octavia herself turned to look at him scornfully?

He took the plunge. "Octavia?"

She turned around. It *was* Octavia. And, unbeliev-ably, incomprehensibly, Octavia was crying.

Julius didn't hesitate. He ran up to Ethan. "If Madame Cowper misses me, tell her I'll be there in a few minutes."

"What's happening?"

"I can't talk now. I saw a girl I know, and she's in some kind of trouble."

As Ethan hurried to catch up with the rest of the class, Julius darted across the street to where Octavia was still standing.

Suddenly he knew what was wrong. "You didn't get the part."

Octavia turned away from him so he couldn't see her face, but she didn't run away. She just stood there, facing the dingy brick wall of some drab Denver apartment building, sobbing soundlessly.

"Hey," he said gently. What could you say to someone who had had a big disappointment, someone who had never been disappointed before? Every possible line he could think of was inane or insulting. Still, he had to say something. "It'll be okay," he said. Inane *and* insulting.

Octavia whirled around to face him. "No, it won't!" At least she was angry now, rather than defeated.

"All right, it's *not* going to be okay." At that moment, talking to Octavia felt oddly like talking to Edison.

"Oh, shut up." She turned away again, and Julius could tell from her shaking shoulders that she had resumed her silent sobbing.

He tried shutting up, but after a moment of uncomfortable silence, he couldn't help asking, "Did you get *any* part?"

Without turning around, Octavia spat out, "If you can call it a part. Not Laurey, not Annie. I'm in the chorus, but I have a few speaking lines. Do you call that a part? I don't call that a part. I call that a joke."

"Were there some people who didn't get anything?"

The question provoked Octavia to turn around and face Julius again, the better to discharge her fury. "Of *course* there were people who didn't get anything. And

102

I'm supposed to be *happy—grateful—thrilled*—not to be one of them? Lucky me, there are some people in the world who are worse off than I am? Lucky me, at least I'm not starving on the streets of Calcutta?"

The reference to starving made Julius think of the rest of his class, seated in the French restaurant, waiting to order. How angry would Madame Cowper be when this time his turned out to be the missing nose?

But he couldn't leave Octavia in the state she was in. He tried again: "I didn't mean it like that. I meant that I'm your friend"—was that too presumptuous?—"that I *want* to be your friend, and if you feel bad, I feel bad, too. And if I could think of something to say that would make you feel better, I'd say it."

"Oh, Julius." To his shock, Octavia hugged him and then stayed there, within the circle of his arms, leaning against him and crying fresh tears.

"Come on, don't cry." He kept his arms awkwardly in place and struggled to think of something else to say. "Every actress has setbacks, right?" That had to be true.

"I'm not an actress anymore."

"Of course you are."

"No, I'm not." Octavia broke free from Julius. "If I'm going to be a second-rate actress, I'm not going to be an actress at all. Second-rate doesn't happen to be my style."

Were you second-rate because you didn't get one

part? But Julius knew better than to argue with her. He looked down the street, searching for inspiration.

There it was: an ice cream parlor, two doors down. He had already missed the beginning of lunch; he might as well miss the middle of it, too.

"Look," he said, "actress or not, what you need right now is ice cream."

Madame Cowper would be furious with him, even more furious than she had been with Alex. But that couldn't be helped. He'd get Octavia some ice cream, make sure she was okay, and then find the French restaurant—how many French restaurants could there be in that part of Denver?—and try to explain.

# 11

The restaurant turned out to be easy to find. Luckily, it had a French-restaurant-type name: Chez Jacques. Julius didn't want to go in. Facing Madame Cowper after he had run off on his class trip felt like facing his mother on report card day.

He made himself push open the restaurant door and peer into its dim interior. He could see small tables with red-checked tablecloths; on each one stood a wine bottle holding a candle. Toward the back, a large group was seated at two long tables. His class.

"*Alors!* Monsieur Zimmerman, what have you to say for yourself?" Madame Cowper left the table and came forward magnificently to confront him.

"Nothing," Julius muttered. The less he said, the sooner the conversation would be over with.

"*Rien?* Come, come, Monsieur Zimmerman. We have been waiting for you for *une demi-heure.* Half an hour. You must have some explanation to give us."

When Julius didn't answer, she went on, as if to prompt his memory, "Monsieur Winfield told us that you saw *une amie.* A friend. Is that true, Monsieur Zimmerman?"

Glad that the others were out of hearing, Julius replied, half under his breath, "She was crying, okay?"

"And you leave your class in the middle of a class trip whenever you see *une amie qui pleure*—a friend who cries?"

Well, how often was that? Finding a crying friend on the street in Denver was hardly an everyday occurrence. And finding a crying Octavia was like being struck by lightning and winning the lottery on the same day: the odds were definitely against it.

"Yes," Julius said, a note of defiance in his voice. "I do."

Madame Cowper's expression softened. "*Asseyez-vous, Monsieur Zimmerman.* Sit down. It is too late for you to order a meal—you must tell your friend not to cry so long next time. But perhaps you would care to join us for dessert."

Julius took the seat Ethan had saved for him and

tried, without success, to slip into it inconspicuously as Marcia Faitak giggled and the rest of the class stared. For dessert, everyone ordered crepes filled with various kinds of jam. Julius chose strawberry. It was delicious.

Julius's mother was out at some kind of boring computer meeting all day Friday and Friday evening, too. So Julius didn't see her until Saturday morning, when she settled down on the couch next to him while he was watching some cartoons. He hoped she wouldn't get on his case about watching them. He hadn't seen *Rugrats* in ages.

"So how was the class trip?" she asked him.

"It was okay." He kept one eye on *Rugrats* as he answered. Tommy and Chuckie in their dopey, drooping diapers reminded him now of Edison.

"What was the exhibit like?"

Julius shrugged. "It was a bunch of pictures. Some of them were pretty cool."

"Which was your favorite artist?"

Julius tried to remember the name of the guy who had painted all the haystacks. It started with "M." On the TV, Tommy and Chuckie were stealthily climbing out of their cribs.

"Um . . ." Julius said. "I forget his name."

"Julius!" His mother clicked off the TV with emphatic abruptness. Julius knew she was mad at him now. "What happened to all your goals and resolutions? I thought you were going to give up cartoons this summer. Remember? Less TV, and educational programs only?"

"There's nothing on but cartoons on Saturday mornings," Julius said.

"Then why watch anything?" she said. "Tell me, Julius, tell me honestly, have you read *any* of *A Tale of Two Cities* this summer? Have you read even the first chapter?"

There was no point in stalling. "Well, not yet."

"Three weeks of summer vacation have gone by, and you haven't read anything!"

"I've read a bunch of books to Edison." That much was true. He had started with *Once Upon a Potty*, for obvious reasons, but then he had found a little bookshelf in Edison's room with a whole bunch of books he had loved when he was a little boy: *Mike Mulligan and His Steam Shovel*, *Curious George*, *The Happy Lion*. One afternoon last week he and Edison had been so busy reading the books they had forgotten to watch their cartoons. Did that count?

"Julius, I'm glad you're taking your job seriously, I really am, but when we talked about your reading goals for the summer, we were talking about something more ambitious than picture books."

So it didn't count.

"Julius, I know you have a lot on your plate this summer, and you need some time to relax on the weekends, but it's just as easy to relax with a good book as with TV. Reading is so important! It's the foundation of everything else you do in school, and your schoolwork is the foundation of everything else in your life. Honey, you're going to grow up and have a *job* someday. Have you given any thought to that, any thought at all?"

Julius shook his head. So far all he knew was that he didn't want to write computer manuals like his mom, or be an accountant like his dad.

He hoped his mother wasn't going to cry. That was the worst, when his mother cried. She had cried over his final sixth-grade report card, and the memory of it had made Julius feel sick inside for days. She wasn't crying this time—yet—but she was looking pretty close to it.

As he fiddled with the remote control for the TV, he accidentally turned it on.

"Julius!" His mother snatched the remote away from him and clicked the TV off again. "I think we're going to have to make some *rules* limiting television in this house if your resolutions aren't working. I don't want you watching any more TV until you've made some real progress on your reading goals."

As if to make the banishment of TV more concrete, she laid the remote on the highest shelf of the built-in bookcase in the family room. There might have been something funny about the gesture, for Julius was taller than his mom now and could reach higher than she could. But nothing was funny when his mother was so upset with him.

She stalked out of the room, leaving Julius alone with the blank TV screen.

Should he call Octavia over the weekend to ask her if she was okay? Julius could imagine Octavia giving one of two answers to the question. A scornful no, as in: *Of course I'm not okay. My whole life as an actress has been ruined forever. How could I possibly be okay?* Or a scornful yes, as in: *Oh, that. I've already forgotten about that. But thanks for reminding me about one of the most humiliating afternoons of my life.*

He decided against calling.

Midmorning he made himself ask his mother if he could go to Ethan's house. "He asked me yesterday if I could sleep over."

She hesitated.

"I won't watch any TV while I'm there, if you don't want me to."

His mother sighed. "Oh, honey, that's not the issue. Of course you can go, and if Ethan's family is watching TV, you can watch it with them. I really don't want to be an evil ogre here. It's just that cartoons are such a waste of time. They're a complete and utter waste of time. I want you to use your time better than that this summer. And I think turning off the TV here at home is going to help."

She brushed back his hair from his eyes. At least she didn't seem mad anymore.

"You're not mad at me?"

"I'm not mad at you," she said, with an attempt at a smile.

But he knew that even if she wasn't angry at him, she wasn't happy with him, either. By now Julius thought he understood how his mother's mind worked. When she was upset about one thing, it acted as a magnet in her mind for all the other things she had ever been upset about. So he was sure she was walking around thinking: My son likes TV better than reading. My son got three C's on his last report card. My son got nothing at the sixth-grade awards assembly.

Sunday evening, back at home, he remembered to make up his goals list for the coming week. Needless to say, he hadn't made much progress on *A Tale of Two Cities* at Ethan's house, though he had taken the book along with him. Still, carrying it around wasn't the same thing as actually reading it.

Reviewing his other goals: Julius *had* made some progress on toilet-training Edison, though so far nothing had been deposited in the potty besides cars and pinecones and sand. He hadn't humiliated himself a single time in French class, if you didn't count missing half of the class-trip lunch as humiliating. And he had had money with him when he invited Octavia to have ice cream in Denver. The week wasn't a total loss.

> *Goals for the Week of June 30–July 6*
> 1. *Get Edison to make pee-pee in the potty. Or at least to try.*
> 2. *Cheer up Octavia. If she still needs cheering up. And if she'll let you be the one to cheer her.*
> 3. *Keep up the good work in French class (ha ha).*
> 4. *Read Chapter 1 of* A Tale of Two Cities. *Read it or die!*

On Monday morning Alex was quieter than usual. He must have minded missing the class trip more than he'd let on. He spent the first half of the morning staring down at his desk instead of spouting his usual wisecracks.

At the break, he became more himself again, coming up to Julius to say, "I hear the Cow had a cow on the dumb class trip. Give me five, man." Alex held up his hand; reluctantly, Julius high-fived him. You couldn't leave somebody's hand up there in the air, waiting for nothing.

"It wasn't like that," Julius said then. "I didn't mean to upset anybody. I just saw this friend I had to talk to."

"Yeah, yeah, but first the Lizard gives the Cow the slip, then you."

But Madame Cowper hadn't seemed all that flustered after either incident on the trip. The class trip from hell, Julius knew, would have been one with Alex Ryan on it.

And this morning Madame Cowper seemed positively exuberant. "*Il est temps, mes amis*, it is time, my friends, for us to plan *la présentation spéciale*, the special presentation, which we will give to your families and friends on the last day of class, a week from this Friday."

Was the last day of class coming so soon? Julius had the surprising thought that he would almost miss French class, miss the sight of Madame Cowper adjusting her funny-looking glasses. Since the class trip, when she had been so understanding, Julius had begun to forgive her for the private tutorial in *le* Hokey Pokey.

"So," Madame Cowper went on, "we will sing for your families, yes? And show them our collection of

French paintings? And dance *le* Hokey Pokey. And we will give a performance together of *Cendrillon*."

Julius didn't recognize the name.

"You know it, I believe, as *Cinderella*."

*Cinderella*! Seventh graders acting out *Cinderella*! The last time they had acted out a fairy tale, Julius remembered, was when they did *Thumbelina* back in second grade. Lizzie was Thumbelina because she was then, as now, the shortest girl in the class.

Apparently oblivious to the horrified silence that had fallen over the room, Madame Cowper began handing out copies of the French script for *Cendrillon*.

"Now, as Cendrillon has *beaucoup de* lines *à dire*, to speak, we must choose a Cendrillon who has shown herself an outstanding pupil of French, *n'est-ce pas*? Is it not so? Mademoiselle Archer, you will be our Cendrillon."

Lizzie flushed with pleasure. At the compliment? Or at the thought of starring in the play?

"Now we must choose our prince," Madame Cowper went on.

Julius shrank back in his seat to make himself as inconspicuous as possible. He knew that every other boy in the class was doing the same.

As Madame Cowper's beady eyes surveyed the room for possible princes, Alex called out nastily, "How about Ethan? He'd make a great prince. He and Lizzie are both short, and besides . . ." He let his voice trail off meaningfully. It was clear that he meant to say they liked each other. Alex had been merciless in teasing Ethan about Lizzie's crush on him last winter.

"Monsieur Winfield," Madame Cowper said approvingly, "will you serve as our prince?"

She didn't wait for an answer. Julius would have defined true misery as the look on Ethan's face when he heard his fate.

Marcia was chosen as the wicked stepmother. Two other girls volunteered to be wicked stepsisters. A pretty girl named Alison was the natural choice as fairy godmother. Julius felt lucky that there were so many more major speaking parts for girls than for boys in *Cinderella*.

"Now we need a rat who will turn into a coachman."

Julius shrank back again, but not far enough, for Madame Cowper said, "Monsieur Zimmerman, will you be our rat?"

At least the rat would have few, if any, lines to speak, unlike the royal trumpeter, who had more lines to speak than any boy except the prince. That part went to a tall kid named Joey. Alex was picked to be one of the mice who became horses. Other boys became pages at the royal court.

As they began laboriously reading through the play,

Julius suddenly thought of Octavia. He and Ethan hated being in plays, but Octavia loved it. Or had loved it. Was she really through with acting? She couldn't be. If only he could find some way to make her see that. The question was: How?

# 12

By Wednesday, Julius was getting worried. He hadn't caught even a glimpse of Octavia since last Friday's encounter in Denver. He sat on Edison's wooden swing, gazing gloomily at the potty, which that afternoon was filled with erasers. Edison loved erasers, though he didn't use them to erase anything. He just liked clutching them, and lining them up in rows, and, now, putting them in a white plastic potty and then taking them out again.

Julius and Edison were at a stalemate regarding pee-pee in the potty. So far that week they'd had the same conversation about it every day.

"Say 'Pee-pee is wee-wee,' " Edison would demand.

"I'll say it when you make some pee-pee in the potty," Julius would reply.

"No!" Edison would shout.

And Julius would turn away, trying to act as if he didn't care what Edison decided, either way.

Maybe he *should* call Octavia. Or knock at her door. It would be so easy to walk next door with Edison and ring her doorbell. Edison could even push the button for him. Little kids loved pushing buttons.

No, there was nothing at all hard about it. Except taking the first step. And the next step. And the step after that.

"I have to make wee-wee," Edison announced suddenly. Julius leaped up as if stung by a bee. Edison had never made an announcement about his pee-pee/wee-wee before. He had just *made* it, with no preliminary discussion.

In one swift motion, Julius scooped the erasers out of the potty. "Here?" he asked, his voice practically squeaking from excitement. "Do you want to make it in the potty?"

Maybe he shouldn't ask it as a question. "Here," he said, forcing his voice lower. "You can make it in your potty."

Edison looked at the potty uncertainly.

"Let's take off your diaper," Julius suggested. Edison

118

could hardly make pee-pee in his potty while he still had his diaper on.

Julius was kneeling down beside Edison to help him undo the sticky flaps on his diaper when Edison said, "I don't have to go anymore."

"Sure you do."

"No I don't."

"You will in another minute."

"No I won't. My wee-wee already came out." Julius groaned. "In my diaper."

More disappointed than he had thought he would be, Julius resumed his seat on the swing. He made a mental note to tell Mrs. Blue to buy Edison those diapers that pulled up and down like underpants. How did any kid in the history of the world ever get toilet-trained when toilet training was so hard?

How did anybody ever do anything when *life* was so hard? Julius's mother was still upset with him. She hadn't made any more critical or nagging comments since Saturday; she hadn't even asked him about *A Tale of Two Cities*, which he still hadn't managed to start reading. But the way she wasn't saying anything gave Julius the distinct impression that his mother had given up on him.

His mother had given up on him, Octavia had given up on acting, Julius was close to giving up on potty-training Edison. The only person who hadn't given up on her projects was Lizzie. During rehearsals, when Cendrillon gazed adoringly at her prince at the ball, it wasn't acting on Lizzie's part, that was for sure.

Lizzie actually made a pretty good Cinderella. She didn't have Octavia's talent for acting, but she was great at memorizing lines. And being picked on by stepmother Marcia and being in love with prince Ethan both came naturally to Lizzie.

The biggest problem with the play right now was Ethan. The problem, to put it bluntly, was that Ethan couldn't act. At all. To save his life. Especially not when he had to act as if he were in love with Lizzie Archer. During rehearsals Ethan forced out his lines as if they were being extracted by torture.

At that moment Julius had the best idea he had had in a long time. What Ethan needed was acting lessons. And the person he needed them from was Octavia.

Was she home? Julius whisked up Edison, whose diaper had the aroma of pee-pee/wee-wee about it, and hurried inside to the phone. From his weekend debates over whether or not to call her, he already knew Octavia's number by heart.

She answered on the second ring. Cowardice overcame Julius. He hung up. But at least he knew she was home.

He called Ethan.

"What's up?" Ethan asked, sounding nervous.

"Nothing," Julius said reassuringly.

"Nothing?" Ethan's voice cracked with relief. "Aren't you at Edison's?"

"Yeah, I'm here. I thought you might want to come over." He'd better not mention the play. "Just to hang out for a while."

"Are you sure it's okay?"

No, he was sure it wasn't okay. Mrs. Blue had told him distinctly that he wasn't supposed to have friends over while he was babysitting. But she hadn't told him he wasn't supposed to go to a friend's house while he was babysitting.

"Actually, we'll come over there."

"Over here? With Edison? You're coming here?"

"Yeah. And . . . I'm bringing another friend, too. See you in ten." And Julius hung up.

Now he had a reason to ring Octavia's doorbell. Or, rather, to let Edison ring it. Five times.

"Oh, it's you," Octavia said ungraciously when she answered it. But Julius almost thought she looked happy to see him. He was certainly happy to see her. She didn't look heartbroken or distraught, or in any way like someone who had shut herself off from the world forever.

"Would you do me a favor?" Julius asked, hoping he would have the nerve to finish the request.

"It depends on what it is."

"You know that French class I'm taking? Well, we're putting on a play, and . . ."

He saw Octavia's face harden. "And?"

Julius made himself continue. "It's *Cinderella*. Only they're calling it *Cendrillon*."

"You're Prince Charming."

He knew he blushed then. "No, I'm the rat who turns into a footman, but my friend Ethan is Prince Charming, only he's not very charming. Partly because in real life Cinderella is in love with him, and in real life he's not in love with Cinderella. Oh, and in real life she's not Cinderella, she's Lizzie. Edison, you can stop ringing the doorbell now."

"And the favor is?"

"I think he needs acting lessons. Edison, that's enough."

"From me."

Julius tried to offer a dazzling smile. "Who better?"

" 'Those who can, do. Those who can't, teach.' Is that the idea? I can't act, so I can teach?"

Leave it to Octavia to twist everything around. "No! That's not the idea. Edison, *stop* it! The idea is—" He broke off. He could hear the incessant ding-dong of the doorbell echoing through Octavia's house. He was certainly glad her parents weren't home.

"The idea is to butter me up and make me believe in myself as an actress again." Octavia's voice was weary now, instead of angry. "Nice try, Julius."

"No! Or, rather, yes, but—anyway, Ethan really does need help. If the prince stinks, the whole play stinks. Couldn't you give him a couple of pointers?"

"When?"

"Now."

Octavia suddenly smiled. "Ice cream afterward?"

Julius felt in his pocket; yes, he had enough money. "Ice cream afterward," he agreed.

Julius pried Edison away from Octavia's doorbell and ignored the howls as he strapped him into the stroller. They were off. Now all Julius had to do was explain to Ethan why he had shown up at his door accompanied by an acting coach who happened to be a gorgeous middle-school girl. But the hardest part was behind him.

They found Ethan shooting baskets in his driveway. Edison's eyes widened when he saw Ethan. "Your mommy is Patty," he said.

Ethan's eyes widened when he saw Octavia. He didn't say anything.

Julius figured he might as well jump in. "This is Octavia. Octavia, Ethan. Octavia is an actress. A really terrific actress. And I thought maybe she could . . ." It was getting hard to finish the sentence. Julius deliberately avoided Ethan's eyes. "Maybe she could give us some help getting ready for the play."

The *us* was a nice touch. Julius didn't need any help

being a rat who turned into a coachman. A rat was just a rat. A coachman was just a coachman. He had only two lines to speak, total.

"Um . . . sure," Ethan said slowly. Julius kept his eyes elsewhere while Ethan led them around to the backyard.

Octavia broke the awkward silence. "Okay. Julius. Let's start with you."

Julius felt alarmed. He had *said* "us," but he hadn't *meant* "us."

"Actually," Julius said, "I only have two lines to speak. The rest of the time I don't say anything."

"That's the hardest kind of acting," Octavia told him. "Mime. All your thoughts and emotions portrayed without words."

"I don't think my characters have any thoughts and emotions."

"Julius. I thought you brought me over to help you. Do you want my help or not?"

He had brought Octavia over to help Ethan—and to help *her*. But if Octavia was bent on helping *him*, he didn't see any way out of it.

"Yes," he said meekly. "I want your help."

He unstrapped Edison from the stroller. Edison immediately began picking the gone-to-seed dandelions next to Ethan's patio and blowing the wispy seeds, with all the breath he could muster, all over the next-door neighbor's immaculate, manicured lawn.

"I'm ready," Julius said.

"You are a rat," Octavia said, fixing her eyes on him. "You have whiskers, and a long tail, and sleek gray fur, and a bad disposition."

Julius stood there, waiting for Octavia to say more.

"Show me," Octavia said. "I see Julius Zimmerman. I want to see a rat. Whiskers, tail, fur, general disagreeableness."

Ethan chuckled. Julius would get him for that later.

"Um—am I . . . should I be on all fours?"

"How many rats do you know who walk on two legs?"

Cursing his long, awkward legs, Julius got down on all fours. He would take the Hokey Pokey over this any day.

"Your tail, Julius. Where's your tail?"

Feebly, Julius twitched his rear end.

"Whiskers."

Feeling the crimson surge into his face, Julius made an attempt at twitching his nose.

"That's better. Good! Now look furtive."

Julius wasn't sure what the word meant.

"Sly. Sneaky. Used to darting behind the woodwork. Knowing that Cinderella's stepmother will throw a shoe at you if she sees you. Looking for treasures to steal. Willing to bite if cornered."

Julius tried to put an expression on his red, twitching face that would convey all those things. He didn't need Octavia to tell him that he failed miserably. He didn't need Ethan to tell him that he looked ridiculous.

"I'll show you." Octavia flung herself down on all fours. Before Julius's eyes, she became a rat. How she did it, Julius didn't know, but he saw her long, thin tail and quivering whiskers and beady eyes. As Julius and Ethan stared, Octavia constructed an elaborate pantomime, sniffing about for food, darting behind one of Ethan's bushes at an imagined sound, greedily snatching up a stray morsel of cheese and devouring it with her sharp rodent's teeth.

Then, as suddenly as she had become a rat, she was a girl again.

"Like that," Octavia told Julius.

*Oh. Like that.*

Julius tried once more, but it was Edison who really seemed to have taken Octavia's demonstration to heart. Down on his hands and knees, with his diapered bottom twitching in the air, he looked more like a little rat than Julius ever could.

But Octavia was full of encouragement. "That's it, Julius! Yes, Edison! Twitch those tails!"

Then Octavia turned to Ethan. By the time she was done with him, he sounded considerably more like a lovesick prince than he had before. However, the real test would come when he had to say his lines not to Octavia but to Lizzie Archer. It was easy, Julius thought, to act as if you were in love with Octavia. He felt almost jealous watching Octavia and Ethan rehearsing their scenes together.

Ethan didn't join them for ice cream, though he flashed Julius a quick thumb's-up sign of approval when Octavia's back was turned. For once, Julius was eager to leave his friend behind.

Octavia showed her merry side at the ice cream parlor. She kept Edison amused the whole time by speaking in different accents, from a Southern drawl to upper-class English to the talk of a tough New Yorker.

But then Julius made his big mistake. "You're a great actress, Octavia. You know you are. Just because you didn't get one part in one play—"

Octavia cut him off. "Give up, Julius. I'm not a great actress, not that *you* would know a great actress if you saw one."

Julius knew Octavia was so cutting because his clumsy words had opened her wound. He'd thought maybe she had healed by now. Apparently she hadn't.

# 13

When Julius made his goals for the week of July 7–13, he had an easy time doing it. The only thing he wrote in his journal was:

*Goals for the Week of July 7–13*
*See Goals for the Week of June 30–July 6.*

Edison still hadn't made pee-pee in the potty. Octavia still wasn't cheered up. Maybe getting Octavia to help Ethan with the play counted as keeping up the good work in French class; in any case, Julius needed to keep it up some more. And he still hadn't started *A*

*Tale of Two Cities*. He just couldn't make himself do it. Every time he opened the book, he felt overcome by the weight of his mother's disappointment in him. The book lay on his bedside table, like a silent reproach, saying to him all the things his mother wasn't letting herself say.

He picked up his pen and added a fifth goal:

*5. Help my mom feel better about*

About what? About having a son who was a mediocre student at best and who didn't like to read and who got a two-line part in the *Cendrillon* play because his French accent was so bad? But he couldn't write all of that in his goals list. So he wrote:

*5. Help my mom feel better about things.*

On Monday, after another afternoon in which Edison's pee-pee came out in his diaper, but not in his potty, Julius was almost ready to give up on goal number 1.

Mrs. Blue seemed ready to give up, as well. As soon as she returned home and gave Edison his hug and kiss, she turned to Julius. "Any luck?"

He knew what the question meant. "No," he told her.

Mrs. Blue put Edison down. He ran back to his potty, which now stood in the middle of the family room, still filled with erasers.

"Oh, Julius, I had such a feeling that it would happen today, while you were here. You know, another boy, an older boy, someone he looks up to."

"It'll happen," Julius said, sounding more confident than he felt. "He won't be going off to college wearing diapers." He had heard this kind of remark made to other mothers about other things. He even remembered neighbor ladies telling his own mother, when she had worried about his thumb-sucking, "Well, he won't be going off to college sucking his thumb."

"It's not college I'm worried about, it's kindergarten," Mrs. Blue said miserably.

"That's still two years away. A lot can happen in two years."

"Oh, Julius." Mrs. Blue seemed close to tears. What was it about Julius that attracted crying females? "It's so hard being a mother sometimes. I lie awake at night, wondering if Edison will ever use the potty, if he'll ever stop being so negative, if he'll ever outgrow biting."

"He doesn't bite me anymore," Julius offered. "He hasn't done it since the first week." If it was hard to be a mother generally, how much harder it must be to be the mother of Edison Blue.

Or of Julius Zimmerman?

"Sometimes I think that if he would just make wee-

wee in the potty, I'd never worry about anything else ever again." She laughed. "Famous last words."

"It'll happen." Julius hoped it would happen before Edison went off to kindergarten. What he really hoped was that it would happen that summer. While he was babysitting. So that there would be one shining moment of achievement in his sixth-grade summer.

"Listen," Julius said awkwardly. "This French class I'm taking? We're putting on this play on Friday, you know, to show our families and friends what we've learned about French language and culture. We're doing *Cinderella*, in French, and I only speak two lines, but I'm the rat who turns into a coachman, and, anyway, if you think Edison might like it . . ."

"He'd love it!" Mrs. Blue said. "I can take off work that morning. Edison, honey, Julius is going to be in a play! He's going to be the rat in *Cinderella*! Do you want to go see him? Mommy will take you on Friday."

"No," Edison said.

"You don't want to see Julius being a rat?"

"Yes," Edison said then.

"Yes, you don't want to see the play, or yes, you do want to see the play?" Julius asked him.

"I want to see it," Edison said.

On Tuesday, Julius debated with himself for the better part of the afternoon whether or not to leave an invitation to the play in Octavia's mailbox. While Edison loaded up his potty with small plastic action figures, Julius took one of the flyers Madame Cowper had given the class and tentatively wrote Octavia's name on the back of it. Then, at the bottom, hoping it didn't sound too mushy, he wrote:

> *Thanks for all your help. Ethan is a great prince now. I am getting better with my tail, too.*

He hesitated, then added:

> *You are a wonderful actress, whatever you say.*
> > *Sincerely,*
> > *Julius Zimmerman*

Not that saying it would make her believe it. He could hear her mocking voice in reply: "Thank you, Julius. If *you* believe in me, then of course I should believe in myself."

Before he could change his mind, he scooped up Edison, went next door, and slipped the flyer in Octavia's mail slot, careful not to let Edison ring her doorbell even a single time.

Instantly he was sorry he had done it. But the worst thing that could happen was that she would tear up the invitation and not come to the play. She probably couldn't come, anyway.

.  .  .

Ethan was a good prince now, if not a great one. Julius was an adequate rat now, if not a good one. Lizzie's French lines tripped off her tongue as fluidly as if she had been born in Paris, helped no doubt by all the time she had spent selling flowers there in her dreams.

One thing still bothered Julius. At every class concert or play that he had ever seen, somebody came up to the microphone and made a speech thanking the teacher and giving her a present from the class. Somebody's mother always made sure it happened. This time nobody seemed to be making sure it happened. Julius hoped it wasn't up to him to do it. Or was that what his mother meant by learning about responsibility?

During the break on Tuesday, Julius tried broaching the subject with some of the others.

"Do you think . . ." Julius began, wishing that he had the kind of voice that would make people take seriously any idea that came from his lips. He didn't. "Do you think we should get a present for Madame Cowper, you know, to give her at the play?"

Ethan said right away, "Yeah. Like all chip in a dollar for it."

Quickly Julius called the rest of the class over to join them. "Hey, guys? Do you want to chip in a dollar to buy Madame Cowper a thank-you present?"

"You're kidding, aren't you?" Alex asked. "Tell me you're kidding."

"No," Julius said. "I'm not kidding. Look, you don't have to contribute if you don't want to."

Lizzie was the first to produce her dollar. Some kids told Julius they needed to get their money from home, but promised to bring it tomorrow. Alex ended up being the only kid to refuse. Fine! Julius figured they could get a pretty terrific present for twenty-two dollars, a dollar for every *nez* in the class except one.

That evening, after supper, Julius went up to his room and took *A Tale of Two Cities* off his bedside table. *Read it or die!*

He was pleasantly surprised to discover, when he actually made himself open the book, that the whole first chapter had only three pages. If he had known that, he would have forced himself through it weeks ago. He forced himself through it now, and found that not only was it much shorter than he had feared, it was also much more boring—something about a Woodman and a Farmer, and the year of Our Lord one thousand seven hundred and seventy-five. Why not just say "1775"? What was the point of writing in such a long-winded way?

Julius pushed on to Chapter 2. It was a little bit better, because at least there was some dialogue in it, between some people named Tom and Joe and Jerry. But he didn't get the sense that they were main characters, and he still didn't have the faintest idea what was supposed to be happening. Had Ethan really read this book and *liked* it? It was hard to believe.

At the end of Chapter 3, Julius gave up. What was the point? There were forty-five chapters in all, which meant that, with three down, there were still forty-two to go. Forty-two! Grimly, he opened his goals journal and crossed off goal number 4. But he felt no surge of satisfaction. A great classic of world literature, one of his mother's all-time favorite books, and it was all he could do to get through three chapters of it.

On Wednesday Edison announced three different times that he needed to use the potty. Three different times Julius rushed to help Edison whip off his pull-on diaper and ready himself for the Big Moment. Three different times the Big Moment didn't come.

Edison looked as downcast as Julius felt. "My wee-wee doesn't like potties," he said sorrowfully. "My wee-wee just likes diapers."

"It has to learn to like potties," Julius said. "That's all. It takes time for it to learn. Give it time."

But not too much time. Julius couldn't take any more of watching Mrs. Blue's face fall when she came home to discover, once again, that Edison's diaper was wet and Edison's potty was dry.

"Oh, Julius," she said to him later that afternoon as he was getting ready to go home, "Jackie across the street told me that her little girl trained herself—trained herself completely—when she had just turned two."

"Well, girls are different." It was another line he remembered people telling his mother, when he'd had trouble learning to write in cursive back in third grade. They would tell her boys had more trouble learning cursive than girls did—conveniently ignoring that all the other boys in Julius's class could write in cursive.

"I guess so," Mrs. Blue said. "I asked Patty Winfield at Little Wonders, and she said this was normal, that some children don't learn till they're four. Four!"

Julius tried to put on a sympathetic face, but four didn't sound so old to him. Four was nothing. Four was a million years ago, when life was simple and no one expected you to teach little kids to use the potty or to talk in French or to read four-hundred-page-long novels by Charles Dickens.

"Dad and I are both planning on coming to your program this Friday," Julius's mother told him that night at dinner.

"You don't have to do that," Julius said. "I only have two lines to speak in the play. 'Cinderella, your coach is here.' And 'Off to the ball!' You don't have to miss work to hear me speak two lines."

"But there's more to the program than the play, isn't there?" his mother asked.

"We sing some songs, and we . . ." He could hardly bring himself to say it. "We do the Hokey Pokey in French."

A smothered guffaw came from his dad.

"So it's really okay if you don't come," Julius concluded.

"I don't often get the chance to see the Hokey Pokey done in French," his dad said. "I'll be there."

"Do you realize," his mother asked, "that when your class ends on Friday, summer vacation will be half over?" She hesitated. "Are you making any progress on your summer goals? Now that we've turned off the TV, you haven't had as many distractions."

Julius thought about the dry potty, about Octavia's depression, about *A Tale of Two Cities*, which he knew now he would never finish.

"Not really," he admitted. "I mean, I've been making lists every week in my journal, but . . ." He trailed off.

"This is your big chance, Julius," his mother said, a note of desperation creeping into her voice. "A whole summer to work on those academic skills you're going to need for seventh grade, to get ready to make a new start in school next year." As if afraid she would say more, she got up to start clearing the table.

"Look, honey, he's taking a class, working a job . . . And he's only twelve," his dad said gently.

"Twelve!" his mother said. She sounded like Mrs. Blue saying, "Four!" "When I was twelve . . ." This time she was the one who trailed off.

"When you were twelve, you were perfect." Julius finished the sentence for her, surprised at the intensity of his own response. "When you were twelve, you read books all day long, and you won prizes, and your mother bragged to all her friends about how wonderful you were."

He tried to stop himself, but the words, held in too long, came tumbling out: "Well, you want to know something? I'm not you."

"Julius." His mother reached out her hand to him, but he didn't take it. Instead he left the table and went upstairs to his room, trying not to indulge in the childish satisfaction of slamming the door.

There, he opened his goals journal and ripped out the five pages he had written so far that summer. He crumpled them into five little balls and hurled them, one by one, at his wastepaper basket.

For the first time in his life, his aim was perfect.

Ten minutes later, he heard his mother's soft knock at his door. He wanted to tell her to go away. Instead he mumbled, "Come in."

"May I sit down?" she asked him. Her eyes were red and glistening, as if she had been crying. For answer, Julius sat up on his bed and moved over to make room for her.

"Julius."

He stared down at his bare feet.

"Julius, I'm sorry if I've put too much pressure on you this summer. God knows, I've made mistakes over the years. But I'm your mother. It's my job to try to help you grow and develop into all you can be."

"I know," Julius said. He hoped she wouldn't start in on the speech about reading.

Sure enough, she did. "It's just that reading—well, reading is so important, Julius, for whatever else you decide to do in your life. And reading is—if you love to read, then the whole world is open to you. It's all there, everything is there, in books. I know you haven't had a lot of time to read this summer. Maybe I shouldn't have signed you up for a class *and* a job. Anyway, whatever I did, I did because I thought it was best for you."

"I know," Julius said again. She didn't understand that it wasn't the class or the job that he minded; it was thinking that whatever he did, it wasn't enough to please her, could never be enough, because he wasn't the person she wanted him to be.

"I won't ask you about your reading again," his

mother said. She gave a wry, wan smile. "Or at least I'll try hard not to. Okay?"

"Okay," Julius said. He made himself return her smile, over the lump in his throat.

After she left, he stared down again at his feet. He knew she was trying to be a good mother to him, the way Mrs. Blue was trying to be a good mother to Edison. He just wished she could see that, in his own way, he was trying, too.

# 14

On Friday morning Julius was more nervous than he had thought he'd be.

What if Octavia came? What if Octavia didn't come?

Would Madame Cowper like her present? Julius had thought it was perfect when he found it at the mall yesterday afternoon, but what did he know about anything? And would he make a fool of himself giving it to her?

Would Madame Cowper tell his parents that he had run off with Octavia on the class trip? That would hardly be a story to gladden his mother's heart. Would his mother be disappointed in him yet again when she heard him stammer his two pathetic lines in the play, with the worst French accent in the class?

When Ethan came to get Julius so they could ride to school together, Ethan looked as miserable as Julius felt. His face bore the set look of a soldier about to have his leg amputated without anesthesia.

"It'll be over in three hours," Julius told him, trying to sound encouraging.

"One hundred and eighty minutes," Ethan said. "Ten thousand eight hundred seconds."

Put that way, it didn't sound encouraging at all.

In the classroom, all was chaos, as kids muttered their lines to themselves and scrambled into their makeshift costumes. Julius wore black sweatpants and a black sweatshirt to be the rat, with a rat mask he had made out of a paper bag. Once he became the coachman, he would quickly slip off his mask and slip on a fancy jacket that Madame Cowper said belonged to her husband. So there was a Monsieur Cowper. That was a strange thought.

Ethan wore a prince costume loaned by the middle-school drama teacher, with the pants pinned up because Ethan was shorter than the typical middle-school prince. Lizzie had brought in her own rags —maybe the ones she had worn in her garret in Paris?—but her ball gown was also a drama department loan. She actually looked pretty when she had it on, with her blue eyes blazingly bright and her red curls bouncing. Julius wondered if Ethan had noticed.

The program would be performed in the school all-purpose room. The first guests began arriving at ten. Julius waved to his parents, glad that Madame Cowper was too busy with last-minute costume adjustments to chat with anybody. So far, so good. He saw Ethan's mom and older brother, Peter; Ethan's dad had to work. He recognized Lizzie's mother, short, like Lizzie, with hair almost as red.

"Julius! Julius! Julius!"

Edison ran up to him, and, touched by the exuberance of the greeting, Julius swung him up for a hug. Behind Edison came Mrs. Blue, looking sheepish, pulling Edison's little red wagon.

In the little red wagon sat Edison's potty.

"One of my parenting magazines came yesterday," Mrs. Blue began apologetically, "and it had an article on toilet training, and it said that for the crucial first weeks of training, it's important not to go away from home, and if you do go, to take the potty with you."

Julius stared at her.

"I hope you don't mind," Mrs. Blue said, her face suddenly anxious.

"Mind? No! Of course not!" If Alex found out that one of Julius's guests for the play was a potty, and teased him about it for the rest of his life, that was the way it would be.

"My potty likes plays!" Edison said. Julius had never

realized how piercing Edison's high little voice was until he uttered this particular sentence in hearing range of all Julius's classmates.

"Well, I hope it will like this one," Julius told him.

Back with his class again, he scanned the room for Octavia. Remarks about potties were usually her cue for a grand entrance. He didn't see her anywhere.

Not that he had thought she would come.

Only he *had* thought she would come.

In any case, she wasn't there.

It was time for the program to begin. Madame Cowper, magnificent in a flowing Moroccan caftan, which suited her better than her usual pantsuits, stepped up to the microphone. She beckoned to the cast, in their costumes, to crowd around her.

"*Bonjour, mesdames et messieurs, amis et familles*, friends and families. Today we present for you *une petite pièce*, a little play." She went on with a speech about all they had learned in the past five weeks and about how much she had enjoyed having them as students. Julius knew she couldn't have enjoyed having him as a student—someone who couldn't put a quiche in the oven without spilling it all over the floor, someone who couldn't even put his right foot in and take his right foot out.

As Madame Cowper's speech wound to a close, Julius's palms turned clammy. It was time for him to make his speech. Since it was his idea to give Madame Cowper the present, he felt it was his responsibility to do it.

"*Excusez-moi,*" Julius said, stepping forward from the rest. "*Nous avons un cadeau pour vous.* We have a present for you. *Merci beaucoup.* Thank you very much." He felt foolish saying it in French, especially in *his* French, but he had decided to do the thing all the way if he was going to do it at all.

"*Un cadeau? Pour moi?*"

Madame Cowper sounded so genuinely pleased and surprised that Julius wondered fleetingly what Alex was thinking right then. Was he a little bit sorry he hadn't contributed anything?

She tore off the wrapping paper and lifted the top of the box. Then she pulled out a scarf with Monet's water lilies printed on it. Julius hadn't been able to believe his eyes when he had found it on sale in the regular department store in the mall.

"Ohhh!" Madame Cowper gave a long sigh of ecstatic appreciation, sounding almost like Lizzie Archer, as she held up the scarf for everyone to see. The applause was loud and long. Ethan and Lizzie were clapping hardest, of course, but the others were clapping as well, including Marcia. Even Alex was clapping, as hard as if he had picked out the present himself and helped to pay for it.

The play began. Lizzie-as-Cinderella sat alone in her ashes. Marcia-as-wicked-stepmother was mean to her. So far it seemed like ordinary school. During his few moments onstage, Julius acted as much as he could like a rat, even though Octavia wasn't there to critique his tail. Cinderella's fairy godmother appeared. Yes, Cinderella *was* going to the ball!

Just as Julius whipped off his rat mask and got ready to whip on his coachman jacket, a piercing little voice from the side of the stage summoned him.

"Julius, my wee-wee is ready to come out!"

Mrs. Blue had hurried after Edison and was trying to shush him. "Edison, Julius has to be in the play now, honey!"

Edison, hopping from one foot to another, clutching his shorts, looked exceedingly like a toddler who had to go.

"I want my wee-wee to come out in my potty!" Edison wailed.

Julius shot a frantic look at the fairy godmother. She was still working on transforming Cinderella's rags into a ball gown. He had a minute, maybe two.

He dropped his jacket and mask, slipped off the stage, and raced with Edison, Mrs. Blue, and the little red wagon out to the hall.

"Oh, Julius—do you think . . . ?" Mrs. Blue breathed.

Julius expertly tugged at Edison's pull-on diaper and positioned the potty for him to sit on.

There came a small tinkling sound that could mean only one thing.

"It came out!" Edison danced around his potty as best he could with his shorts and diaper still bunched around his ankles. "Look, Julius, look! My wee-wee came out!"

Julius looked, hoping this was the last time in his life he would be called upon to admire anyone's wee-wee. Then, from inside the all-purpose room, he heard the fairy godmother's voice, tinged with exasperation, announcing in emphatic French that *now* this rat would become a coachman.

Oops!

Julius sprinted back to the stage. Panting, he shrugged into his jacket and presented himself to the irate fairy godmother.

A long silence followed. Wasn't somebody supposed to say something?

*He* was supposed to say something. Lizzie, radiant in her ball gown, whispered the line to him: *"Cendrillon, votre carrosse est ici!"* Julius gasped it out.

He was supposed to say another line, too. Now, or later on?

There was another long silence.

Okay, he was supposed to say it now.

*"Allons au bal!"* Julius said.

At last the play was over, and all that was left was *le* Hokey Pokey. Julius shook his body parts as best he could, knowing that half the time he was putting the right foot in when he was supposed to be taking the left foot out. The reality of what had happened outside in the hall finally hit him. Edison had made pee-pee in the potty! And the glory of that moment belonged to him, Julius!

When they returned for refreshments back in their classroom, Julius grabbed a croissant. He took one big buttery bite and turned around to find his mother standing right in front of him.

"Oh, Julius," she said. Her "Oh, Julius" carried such a different meaning from Mrs. Blue's "Oh, Julius."

"Where did you go? I felt so sorry for that girl playing the fairy godmother. She stood there without the faintest idea what to do."

His mother looked as if she was trying to keep herself from saying more, but she couldn't do it. "Julius, the whole point of the babysitting job was to help you learn to be more responsible. Oh, Julius, what am I going to do with you?"

"Nothing, I guess," Julius muttered. "There's nothing you can do with me." His post–pee-pee exhilaration had evaporated.

He felt someone tugging at his leg. Edison. The little boy's tight hug brought to Julius's eyes the tears that hadn't come with his mother's scolding.

Mrs. Blue put her hand on Julius's mother's arm. "You must be very proud of Julius."

Julius's mother hesitated before responding, as if wondering what feature of Julius's performance in the play or the Hokey Pokey could have inspired such a comment. "Oh, we are," she said slowly.

"He is just working wonders with Edison this summer. Edison is blossoming because of Julius. That's the only word for it. Blossoming. And do you know what happened just now?" Mrs. Blue lowered her voice as if the miracle about to be revealed were too sacred to be spoken out loud.

"Edison used the potty! For the first time! Right now! During the play! And Julius was kind enough to rush away from the play to help him do it. I don't know any other boy his age who could give so much to a young child. Julius, I can't thank you enough for this morning, and for everything."

Julius let himself look at his mother. Now *she* looked ready to cry.

"I think Julius has a gift, a real gift, for working with children," Mrs. Blue went on. "I was telling Patty Winfield about him, and she said Edison talks about Julius all the time at school, too. Patty said when Julius is old enough to get a real summer job, she'd be glad to help him get one at Little Wonders."

A job working with lots of little kids like Edison Blue, all day long? Julius never would have believed that the thought of it could make a slow smile spread across his face.

His dad came up to them then. "Son, I sure enjoyed that Hokey Pokey," he said with a big grin.

As Julius's dad led Mrs. Blue and Edison to the refreshment table, Madame Cowper appeared and pumped Julius's mother's hand. For a moment, Julius thought she was going to kiss his mother on both cheeks, but she didn't. "Madame Zimmerman, I have so enjoyed knowing Julius."

Was she kidding?

Madame Cowper put her arm around Julius's shoulder. *"Julius a un grand coeur."* She said the words with unusual distinctness, to help Julius's mother understand what she was saying. She couldn't, of course. Julius couldn't, either.

"Julius has a big heart," she translated, with the same exaggerated emphasis on each word. "On our class trip, he leaves us. For half an hour, he leaves us. I worry, I fret, my hair turns gray. Why does he leave us? Because he sees a friend, and she is crying. That is Julius."

Madame Cowper fingered the Monet scarf, which she had tied around her neck. "And this scarf. It is not an easy task to find the right present for *une femme d'un certain âge.* An old woman. A woman whom some call the Cow. Eh? *Non*, Julius Zimmerman, he has a big heart."

With that, she left to talk to other parents.

"Oh, Julius."

He turned to face his mother.

"I had no idea . . . Somehow I thought . . . I thought things this summer *weren't* working out for you. Did you really toilet-train Edison? And all those things your teacher said . . . Oh, Julius, you and I are so different, it's hard for me sometimes to see that—well, your goals may not be the goals I picked for you, but they're *your* goals, and I'm proud of you for accomplishing them. I hope you know that. I'm proud of *you*."

She reached out her arms to him, and Julius gave her a quick, stiff hug, then pulled away, to bring himself back under control.

It wasn't turning out to be such a bad summer. Intensive Summer Language Learning and Edison Blue had both been his mother's ideas, but Julius had to admit they had worked out all right in the end, even if they hadn't worked out exactly the way his mother had planned. Unbelievable as it seemed, he had accomplished almost everything on his goals list. He had redeemed himself in French class and even learned some French. Edison had used the potty. His mother understood him a little better.

The only things he hadn't done were cheer up Octavia and read *A Tale of Two Cities*. He'd return the book tomorrow; maybe he'd check out some books on child development instead.

Mrs. Blue returned and touched his elbow. "I almost forgot to give you this."

It was a folded piece of paper. Julius opened it and read:

> *Dear Julius,*
>
> *I'm so sorry I can't be at your play today. Twitch that tail for me!*
>
> *The reason I can't be there is because I have an audition in Denver. Wish me luck!*
>
> *Octavia*
>
> *P.S. If I get the part, I'll buy you ice cream.*
> *P.P.S. If I don't get the part, I'll buy you ice cream.*

Edison tugged at Julius's leg again, and Julius picked him up for another hug.

# secret sex

# secret sex

## an anthology

edited by

## RUSSELL SMITH

Publisher: Kwame Scott Fraser | Acquiring editor: Russell Smith
Cover designer: Laura Boyle
Cover image: Laura Boyle

Library and Archives Canada Cataloguing in Publication

Title: Secret sex : an anthology / edited by Russell Smith.
Names: Smith, Russell, 1963- editor.
Identifiers: Canadiana (print) 2023049899X | Canadiana (ebook) 20230499163 | ISBN 9781459752429 (softcover) | ISBN 9781459752443 (EPUB) | ISBN 9781459752436 (PDF)
Subjects: LCSH: Erotic stories, Canadian—21st century. | LCSH: Short stories, Canadian— 21st century. | CSH: Erotic stories, Canadian (English) | CSH: Short stories, Canadian (English) | CSH: Canadian fiction (English)—21st century
Classification: LCC PS8323.E75 S32 2024 | DDC C813/.6083538—dc23

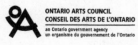

We acknowledge the support of the Canada Council for the Arts and the Ontario Arts Council for our publishing program. We also acknowledge the financial support of the Government of Ontario, through the Ontario Book Publishing Tax Credit and Ontario Creates, and the Government of Canada.

Care has been taken to trace the ownership of copyright material used in this book. The author and the publisher welcome any information enabling them to rectify any references or credits in subsequent editions.

The publisher is not responsible for websites or their content unless they are owned by the publisher.

Printed and bound in Canada.

Rare Machines, an imprint of Dundurn Press
1382 Queen Street East
Toronto, Ontario, Canada M4L 1C9
dundurn.com, @dundurnpress

Angie Abdou

Jean Marc Ah-Sen

Tamara Faith Berger

Jowita Bydlowska

Xaiver Michael Campbell

K.S. Covert

francesca ekwuyasi

Anna Fitzpatrick

Drew Hayden Taylor

Victoria Hetherington

Marni Jackson

Andrew Kaufman

Michael LaPointe

Pasha Malla

Sophie McCreesh

Lisa Moore

Heather O'Neill

Lee Suksi

Susan Swan

Heidi von Palleske

Aley Waterman

Zoe Whittall

David Whitton

Michael Winter

# Contents

# Introduction

I WAS RECENTLY EDITING A NOVEL WITH STRONG AUTO-
biographical elements that had quite a bit of sex in it. When
the sex was between men and women, it was described in some
physical detail, but when there was sex between two women,
I noticed the language became vague. I asked the author why
that was. She said, "Because I know my family will read it."

I guessed she didn't want to come out to them in that in-
direct way.

A few days later, I was on another manuscript. There was
a sex scene with a person of uncertain gender whose body was
not described in any physical way. I queried the author and she
replied, "I can't go into details — my ex will read it." Here the
fear was of damaging someone else's privacy.

These are tricky waters.

I'm not sure if readers realize how much authors — even
much published, seasoned authors, like many of those gathered
here — agonize over the question of how people are going to

respond to any description of sex, and how nervous authors are about accidentally revealing details of their own sexual predilections by fictionalizing them.

Writing sex scenes is notoriously difficult: one walks a tightrope between the crude and the laughable (especially in English, a Germanic language that lends itself to the silly or the ugly). When describing body parts, one must choose between the correct word — which can sound clinical, as if one is reading a medical textbook — and a slang word, which almost always sounds more crass than the rest of the language one's character is using.

Add to that the anxiety over coming out to one's family and mortifying one's mom. And add to that an anxiety over being mocked for imagining sex at all. A particular strain of conservative critic tends to imagine the authors themselves in all the positions described, because that's almost always amusing.

And childish. Even the Canadian media report excitedly on the annual Bad Sex in Fiction Award, a British tradition that is simply a mean-spirited exercise in playground mockery and repression. It could only come from the Brits, such a powerful dismissal; indeed, the Bad Sex Award was co-founded by Auberon Waugh, a political and social conservative, whose stated rationale was "to draw attention to the crude, tasteless, often perfunctory use of redundant passages of sexual description in the modern novel, and to discourage it." In other words, it wasn't bad sex writing he was opposed to, it was any sex writing; sex scenes themselves were tasteless and redundant.

Are they?

At any given moment, there are millions of people having sex, just as millions are eating. If you live in a city, there are probably a hundred people having sex within a five-minute walk of where you are. There is likely someone having sex on your block right now. Someone you know is having sex right this second. And sex — or the lack of it, or its discomforts and threats — is important to relationships. But dinner scenes are far more common in literary fiction than sex scenes. The general nervousness that comes from living in an intellectual environment that is so ready to pounce with great glee on anything possibly embarrassing ... well, it pushes one into reticence. That's why novelists end up panning to the window, like a camera in an old film, when their characters fall into bed.

It's a shame, I think, because I can't imagine understanding characters without understanding what they do in bed. (In fact, I might say this about real people too.)

The fact that readers also like sexual detail is proved by the massive popularity of clumsily written S/M erotica. But these blunt instruments of fantasy usually involve multimillionaire or otherwise powerful male antagonists, so they are in effect a subgenre of romance fiction. There is little in common between them and the world of Booker-and-Pulitzer-prize–winning novelists.

So what would happen, I wondered, if I gave a selection of published literary writers the opportunity to write sex scenes, or reflections on sex, and share them, without any fear of identification? Would they write more explicitly, more openly about desire if they knew that their parents and their exes and Twitter would not be able to tell which of the scenes they were responsible for?

The answer is a dramatic yes. In the stories I have collected here, you will find stories that are graphic and stories that are shocking, as well as stories that are yearning and beautiful. Some are explicit. They veer from heartfelt to satirical to purely fantastical. A couple are slapstick. There is at least one murder and one vampire. One is constituted entirely of Pornhub video titles. One is narrated not by a person at all, but by an archaic word (you'll understand when you read it).

The authors range in age from their twenties to their seventies, and they are from across the country. Some have had their books translated into many languages and have won nominations for the Giller Prize; others are in the first years of their career. All have been astonishingly honest. They have written, for this book, the scenes they cut out of their published novels, or the scenes they simply wouldn't dare publish.

I will tell you who they all are, but I won't tell you who has written which story. You will have to guess. Some of these guesses won't be easy, as several of these writers have used invisibility to abandon their usual tone or subject.

Note that I have not used the word *erotica* to describe this collection. Erotica suggests that the pieces are written primarily in an attempt to arouse. I would be surprised if you felt no arousal on reading some of these, but that is not their point. These are pieces about sex good and bad, about its disappointments as well as its ecstasies.

Are they particularly Canadian? Well, one scene does in fact take place in a canoe. More importantly, in their heterogeneity they are deeply Canadian. They are snapshots not just of the variety of sexual experience but also of the wide range of literary approaches the country is currently producing. Usually in secret.

— Russell Smith

Sext

hey
u up?

*Nope. Sleeping. Zzzzz.*

hope you're having sexy dreams at least

*I'm on a pirate ship surrounded by swarthy
buccaneers and I was just about to do it with all
of them but then my phone started buzzing.*

not gonna lie, that sounds disgusting
pirate ships are breeding grounds for bacteria
if you think about it, im p much saving you from a painful uti

*So is this why you're texting?
To slut-shame my subconscious and put me in
the mood by talking about infections?*

hey, you'll never catch me shaming a slut

huge slut fan over here
and if i wanted to put you in the mood, first thing i'd do is
get you far away from any pirate ship

*Where would you take me?*

dinner, dancing, maybe take in a broadway show

*Sounds expensive.*

you're telling me. you haven't even seen the five-star hotel
room i booked for us yet

*Oh yeah?*

yea. mirrored ceilings, incredible views, king-sized bed, those
little mint things on the pillows

*Hope the walls are thick.*

thick walls, and even thicker ... well, you know

*I do know.*
*It's why I texted you back.*

so what d'ya say. is my fantasy hotel enough to get you off
your fantasy pirate ship

*Hmm, well I do get seasick easily.*
*And I did get a new nightie that would*
*just be all wrong for the ocean.*
*Aesthetically speaking, I mean.*

Oh yea?

*You know. Black. Silk. Little bit of lace on top. Not quite long*
*enough to cover my full ass, but it does put in an honest effort.*

you do have a magnificent ass
belongs in a museum, i always say

> *So maybe I'm sprawled on your hotel bed, and*
> *maybe I'm wearing my nightie, and maybe there's*
> *nothing on underneath. What next?*

well obviously i'd come over and start kissing you deeply

> *A good start.*

I wasn't done
I'd run my hands over your body, feeling the warmth of you
under the silk. cup your left breast with one hand and run the
other down your thigh, giving it a good squeeze.

> *The left breast is my favourite.*

I know.
I'd give the other lots of attention, too. Take my time. Touch
every exposed inch of you.

> *When did you start using punctuation?*

Don't interrupt me.
When I feel you squirm the right amount, that's when it's
time to raise your nightie. I'd kiss up and down your thighs,
getting closer to your pussy.
Is it shaved?

> *Never.*

Perfect.
I'd start covering you in kisses, gently at first, before spread-
ing open your lips and using my tongue. Tracing every fold,
finding the parts that make you moan.

> *Mmmmmm.*
> *That's good.*
> *Stay down there.*

Nope.

> *???????*
> *What do you mean, nope?*

I mean, I got you all warmed up.
Now it's my turn.

> *Fair enough.*
> *Can I stay on my back at least?*
> *This hotel bed is so comfortable.*

Say please.

> *You're not the boss of me.*

Is that so?
You're getting a spanking for that one.

> *I'd like to see you try.*

I'm flipping you over.
You get your wish. You get to stay on the bed, but you're on
your stomach now.

> *A real monkey's paw situation over here.*

She just can't shut up!
I've got the cure for that.
SPANK
That's one.
SPANK.
Two.

*(Wait, pause. Can we skip the part where*
*you actually type out the spanks?)*
*(I get what you're going for, it just takes*
*me out of the rhythm a little bit.)*

(ah i gotcha)
(k how about:)
I give your naughty ass the spanking that it so clearly needs.

*(Ok yeah, that works)*
*Ahhh no, it hurts so much! I promise I'll behave for you.*

That's right.
On your knees. On the ground. Bed privileges revoked.

*Yes, sir.*

I slowly undo my belt and fly. I take my time, and I know it's
killing you.

*My mouth is open, waiting.*

Finally, I pull out my cock. Hard, erect, throbbing.

*I love how big your uncut cock is.*

?????
I'm circumcised

*Wait.*
*Are you sure?*
*Coulda sworn you were uncut.*

uhhhhh yea this is the kinda thing im definitely sure about

*Wow my bad.*
*I haven't seen you in forever!*

*I guess I've been seeing too many fore-*
*skinned dicks lately and got mixed up?*

Alright, no more talking from you.
I grab your hair and slam my very big, very much cut cock
into your mouth, facefucking you.

*nnnnnnnnnggggggfthjaksdfh (that's me being facefucked)*

You're drooling. Tears down your face. Messy little slut.

*Definitely not going to forget this cock again.*
*I mean*
*nnnnnnnnnggggggfthjaksdfh*
*Also*
*\*choking noises\**

Ok enough of that.
I pull you to your feet.

*Don't forget to take the cock out of my mouth first.*

You get a few more hard spanks for that sass.
I'm bending you over the bed so your ass is raised high in the
air, you're face down on the comforter.

*Yaaaaaay.*
*I missed you, bed.*

More spanks. Pay attention.

*I'm on my tiptoes, locked and loaded.*

Not yet, you're not.
I tease your dripping wet pussy with the tip of my cock, making sure you're nice and ready.

*Hold on.*
*Get a condom first.*

(wait are you doing a bit or do you want me to put on a fantasy condom in this fantasy scenario)

*(im totally kidding, bud)*

(lolllll)

*(like, in real life, you absolutely better)*
*(but for now you're fine.)*
*(all my fantasy condoms are expired anyway)*
*Please fuck me, sir, I need you inside me.*

Attagirl.
I thrust into you, fucking you hard.

*Hell yes.*

You feel incredible.

*I reach down and touch my clit.*
*You fill me up perfectly. Every time you slam into*
*me I feel it against the sting of my spanked ass.*

That's right, baby.
You're my slut.

*All yours.*
*Will you pull my hair?*

Of course.
I love it when you squirm under me.
I'm so close.

*Cum inside me.*

secret sex

I'm going to.

> *Do it soon.*
> *I'm almost there too.*

It's coming.

> *Me too.*

Fuuuuuuuuuuuuuuuuuuuuuck

> *nnnnnnnnggggggfthjaksdfh*

Wow.
did u really cum?

> *In the fantasy?*
> *Definitely.*

no i mean actually
i came so hard

> *That's rad!*

you too right?

> *That was fun.*
> *I had fun.*

did you need to finish? we can keep going …

> *I really need to sleep.*
> *Sometime again though?*

no for real, I can go again if you give me like 15
let me get some water, get my heart rate down first
hold on …
alright im back

Don't think I'm done punishing you for that attitude you
gave me earlier ...
hey are you still there
hey
u up?

# Tulip

I TRIED TO CALL A MAN TO TELL HIM HOW I FELT. THIS was before cellphones, before internet. I walked into a phone booth in Amsterdam, giddy from the pink-lit coffee shop. The booth was infiltrated with stickers of women bent over multicoloured 1-800s. Their legs bore the imprints of garters, thick ledges of flesh. Their eyes were redacted, but still they all smiled. I thought, *This was the power of tantalization.* Of craftiness, facelessness, spiders spinning fat-thighed. Back then, I thought sex was better than love. Love was glued on to sex, just a salty veneer. Sex was the zenith, the rainbow, the ring. In Amsterdam, I slept on the floor of my friend's gallery. By night, I dressed up like a nurse and performed "surgery." Everything, especially communication, has changed a lot between now and then. But performance art and whoredom have remained exactly the same.

When I returned home, toxin-ridden, I immediately started working out. I decided to ignore the man that I'd telephoned from abroad. I thought about 1-800s, being tied and bent in half. My cunt was a geyser. I thought I should be paid for prowess.

*Fuck my pussy once*, I wrote in the classified ad. *Fuck my pussy once and you'll never forget.* I advertised myself as girl-in-basement alone. Girl looking for new experiences. All natural. Bookworm.

I secured one client quickly. A lawyer, he said. Back then, I really did live in a basement. The family who owned the house was my friend's brother and his wife. They were also lawyers, out of the house by eight. My lawyer said he wanted Monday to Friday, before nine. He told me he had a white BMW, but I never went outside to check. I made sure the door was unlocked. My basement smelled like freezer burn. The place was one long, mouldy passageway, the bedroom a box to the left. The lawyer liked it best when I pretended to be asleep. He wore a black suit with straight lines down the legs. When I heard him enter, I started the dream. I arranged myself one leg out of the covers, headless, zigzagged.

"I need pussy first thing in the morning," he'd said on the phone.

He breathed way too loud, like he was running, winded.

The aura of the lawyer was essentially a cleaner's bag. Rippling sheath, hung up, chemically clean. There was something about his bravado that spoke directly to me.

"Once I get it," the lawyer had told me, "I can go about my day."

In my cell, he took off his suit and laid it on the one chair. He got into bed hard. He said he wanted to snuggle for a bit. But he didn't want to snuggle. He just wanted my heat. He really liked it when I kept pretending not to be conscious yet. I had already showered and shaved. I radiated willingly.

A woman I admired, the queen of performance art, once told me never to touch a flower, its petals, inside or out. She said touching a flower was violence. She called flowers "decapitated cunts." She said you can even scar them with your gentle fingerprints.

In my classified ad, I'd named myself Tulip. I thought, *Tulips grow in the basement. Tulips wobble in the wind.*

"Fuck, yeah, Tulip, your pussy's so wet."

With his cock at my back, I pushed into it. I dreamt in that basement of waves crashing through city streets. His dick like the arm of a clock. His Monday knuckles like rocks. I thought, *Tulip's tight and she's wet and she hugs on each notch.* She just wants to be fucked from behind, where she doesn't care about love. She doesn't want to be with that man she'd called from abroad. A lawyer's fingering her pussy. Tulip is squealing from it. He has a near-to-full cock and he's paying her rent. He pays three hundred dollars to feel her pussy like this. Tulip's five mornings are perfectly defiled. After his fingers, he puts his cock in. One claw lifts her thigh and Tulip moans for real. He has an appendage, robotic and flecked. The lawyer's cock is so desperate to disappear and reappear. He lifts her leg higher, fucks her into mush. Tulip wants to think about what she's doing later, but his fuck hypnotizes.

*T, I love your tight pussy. I can still smell you on me.*

The lawyer started sending Tulip emails at lunch.

*See you tomorrow, bright and early. One day, we'll go out for a drink.*

The lawyer arrived at quarter past eight and was gone by a quarter to nine.

One day, a Wednesday, Tulip decided that she wanted to add another man. This one wasn't from the classified. She met this one at yoga and told him exactly what she did.

"*Wild*," he said, eyebrows wiggling. "Sex work's a lost art."
He was grizzly, a line cook. He was almost exactly her type.
After they'd had sex a few times at his place, he wanted to pay
her in the basement. He said he wanted to be a part of that part
of her life.

This man wanted breath work, for his kundalini to rise.
The first time he came to her crumbling basement, Tulip didn't
shower or shave. Tulip knew kundalini loved pussy. Kundalini
loved blood and light.

"Sorry I can't do lotus," the cook said, cross-legged, naked
on her bed.

His clothes had been thrown on the oatmeal carpet in a
pile. His cock was not yet exactly sticking straight up. Tulip
didn't look him in the eyes. She held his little dick head in
her hands. She cradled it as she eased the cook down on her
headboard-less bed. Then she swivelled and crawled on him,
slathering his dick. In that moment, she felt like she really loved
men. She kept on the cook's cock, like she was the one fingering him. She let him look at her pussy, up close, from behind.
It felt like a butterfly bulb: globular, infrared. She'd charged the
cook one hundred dollars. She gave him a deal. The cook split
Tulip in half from behind and he chomped, licking in.

The artist who told Tulip never to touch a flower's skin also
once told her that Satan had a tail. *Kundabuffer*, she said. That's
Latin for animal cock. Kundabuffer, she said, is why women
were burned at the stake.

Kush, Kundabuffer. This was kundalini. The grizzly line
cook breathed his fire inside of me. My landlord lawyers upstairs had specified no smoke. But I floated on the cook's belly,
incredibly stoned as he flicked his tongue in and out of my
infrared cunt. Basements are coated with bugs. They are lush.

I turned burnt as I sucked him. I rubbed back and forth. Then, the cook sprayed in my mouth and I came in his face like a slug.

There were six months in my basement when the lawyer and cook crossed. Wednesdays, mid-week, the day I had them both. On Wednesdays, for six months, I felt really good. I mean, mentally in shape. I was making us all better human beings. The lawyer started to emote. The cook said he slipped love into food. I was making more money than I ever had in my life. I became the most powerful artist, dirty and clean.

Then I read a book called *Cherry* and it disturbed me a lot. It was written by a guy in prison, an ex-military heroin addict. I guess the part that messed me up most was when the guy shot cum up a girl's nose. It was his girlfriend, apparently, and afterward, he said he felt lonely and sick. He said he felt sick that *this* was what life was about for him. You feel sad because that's all there is in this world: your cum and her face with its holes to corrupt. The author of *Cherry* thought this was existential. But it occurred to me that maybe *I* was like his girlfriend. Not with the lawyer or the cook, but with the man that I'd called from abroad. I thought, *A girlfriend absorbs semen, the frequency of it.* A girlfriend looks for love from low-energy sex. Cherry didn't want the Kundabuffer. He didn't want to fuck five times a week. He didn't want love slipped into his food. He didn't need a girlfriend, that was all.

My end with the lawyer was really, really bad. I wouldn't go out with him to dinner and he threatened to sue me for procurement. Then the kundalini cook started fucking other girls. He said he kept wanting to split yoga pants. I thought about that. I liked yoga pants, too. I thought, from behind or the front, there's this yawning seed shape. That seed is split stitches, a house of mirrors of slits. In the phone booth in Amsterdam, my thoughts felt like cursive, blown glass. The man didn't ask about my nurse performance. All he wanted to know: When was I coming back? I was his dumbbell receiver, inside and out. There was nothing redacted on my face or up my nose. Tulips open and beckon. I thought, *Love is being roughed up.*

# Comets

A HOME MOVIE OF US MAKING LOVE. THE BEDROOM BACK on Mercer Avenue. The bedroom was painted pale green back then and the headlights of passing traffic from the bay window, a strip of glass above the curtain rod, bored into the mirror on the opposite wall like comets, shedding a swarm of glitter, until the car turned the corner and the light fizzed out and shot back through with the next car.

But it's not that dark yet. Not at the beginning of the movie. Nobody has their headlights on. It's early afternoon. It looks like spring from the light. Maybe early spring, when it's still cold.

It happens, though. It gets darker during the lovemaking, that's how long it goes on. It gets darker in the room; the corner of the bureau becomes soft in the shadows. The mound of laundry. There's a blink or glitch and the camera adjusts to how dark it's getting.

There's no sound.

I say, Turn it up. You hit the button, but there's no sound.

We look so young. Our bodies are beautiful. I mean, both of us. So beautiful it's a shock. I feel acute sadness. But also, I'm horny for us as we were then. Or horny because we're watching them as we are now, or who knows why.

It's easy to slip and think that we are still them. They look so familiar. I remember what they smelled like, what they felt. How turbulent. How everything mattered, the smallest slight, the tiniest kind of a gift. How slick and wet it all is. What we want. Always wanting.

It's easy to think they are us.

They *are* us.

I can't believe how beautiful we are.

We forget about the camera. First, we know about the camera. We are aware, hyperaware of the camera, but we don't look at it. We're acting. A very stiff, pretend-there's-no-camera kind of acting.

Very serious, Bergman serious. As if quite often, in everyday life, we find ourselves walking toward the bed, one at a time, naked, la la la, and lying down on the bed and waiting to be joined by the other, and not looking at the camera. As if we were up to that kind of thing all the time.

That bedroom was always cold. Sometimes you could see your breath. Like, in the fall we had a space heater that put out a roiling heat you could see as little collapsing waves that made a patch of the room look Vaseline smeared. But only in a narrow space of about two feet in front of the heater. You'd have to be standing right in front of the metal grill, and then only your shins would be hot. If you were wearing pants it felt like they'd catch fire. The space heater was old and loud.

The bedsheets were the cheapest Walmart had, some polyester blend; it caused shivers it was so unnatural. Yellow roses and they were faded and there's even a hole, you can see it in the home movie, with a ladder of threads, and you can see the mattress through it. The mattress was new. We had a new mattress and we'd saved for it. It was the most expensive thing we ever bought. It was more expensive than the car we bought, which didn't go for very long, and cost everything we had. We were always spending everything we had, and we never noticed it was gone. We'd go to the bank machine and there'd be zero, or minus a thousand. Or we had lots.

We had to get the bus out there to Walmart — I did, it was somebody else's day to have the car — to get those sheets and then standing at the bus stop in the weather, waiting for the bus, trying to get back before the kids were finished daycare. Arriving late when your kids were the only ones left. The teachers already in their coats and softly clapping their mitted hands, once, twice, like, Okay then, let's go.

Once you got six extension cords and joined them all together because you'd bought an electric muscle massager at a garage sale, and I was out there in the lawn chair at the edge of the field and you crept up behind me and told me *shhh* and turned that thing on and put it on the Lycra crotch of my bathing suit, made me come almost instantly. So fast and hard. All the leaves flickering their silver undersides.

Once, in the canoe, the lake was still but the ripples went out when I came, I mean they shattered the reflection of the side of the red canoe and the rocks at the edge of the lake and the trees, shattered into pieces all quivering and they floated back together, and I came again. Then you put a knee on either side of me and the thing rocked and we nearly tipped over. We stayed still for a minute and then, as you fucked me, the canoe jut-jutted forward, ploughing the water apart and smashing the reflections of all the trees again.

On the honeymoon, that guy we met who kept following us around because he was afraid he'd be mugged in the market, him banging on our hotel room door, banging, and saying, Are we going to the restaurant now? Me, hopping around, trying to get my sock on and make my voice normal, like I wasn't just fucking my brains out, and you telling me not to answer him, not to answer, Don't fucking, don't answer, and me saying, Yes, just a minute. Because, I hissed at you, it'd be rude not to answer him and you jacking off before I could get the door open.

The red-tiled shower, the young woman who brought us back to her house for breakfast when we were going back and forth to different cities a night's sleep apart on the Eurail pass, because we couldn't afford the hostels and slept on the trains, cities a night's sleep apart, back to her house and she wondered, Are you together? If we were together, did we want to get in the shower together? The big clouds of steam and the kissing sound when I unpeeled my back from the red tiles, legs wrapped around you, and the squeak of your palm on the tiles near my head, shampoo running all over us into our eyes. The hot water and the table set with silver platters of meats and cheeses and breads and fruit, and her looking into my eyes, the woman, my face flushed, every part of me blushing, a drip of water running from a strand of my hair down my neck, and she touched me. She caught the drip of water with the back of her hand, this woman we met on the train, and she lifted her hand, put her mouth over the drip, all the while looking into my eyes, then rubbed her lips together as if tasting me, something I whispered to you later, grinding against each other in the dark on the floor of the train, roaring toward Vienna.

People on the bus from Walmart, sinking deep into their puffy winter coats, half asleep, eyelids drooping, the snow flying, erasing all the buildings, and the other cars zooming past, their headlights splintering up in the dark, snakey red tail lights, bright as fresh blood on the black, wet asphalt ahead, reflections of faces in the windows floating over the box stores Canadian Tire, Home Depot, Staples, Dominion, Old Navy, Mark's Work Wearhouse, the kids all getting their coats on in the daycare porch, waiting for me, the bus driver getting out and disappearing around the corner for a smoke, the bedsheets in the plastic bag that I held on my lap.

I had a book, Raymond Carver, or *Midnight's Children*, or *Crime and Punishment*, or *First Love*, Turgenev with that whip, wasn't there a woman on horseback with a whip, doesn't she strike someone across the cheek? D.H. Lawrence and *The Fox* and the man shooting at it as it disappeared in the long grass with its white tail up exposing its asshole. This would be the only time I'd have to sink into a book, to let it take hold, the engine of the bus thrumming through me; sometimes on the bus, Lawrence could make me horny, make me come even, any fiction could. Knowing the house would be noisy, homework, bath time, combing the tangles, tears, math, and I came on the bus, the plastic bag with the sheets scrunched in my fists, laundry, and the phone, somebody's tears over having to eat carrots and hating carrots, hating them, hating them, the glass of water tumbling, shattering, There, now, that's broken. Are you happy now?

Somebody crying about somebody else deciding what DVD and the bloody fire truck, kicking the toy fire truck down the hall with the lights and sirens. This all made me horny, and it was nothing to lock the door to the laundry room and climb up on the dryer and slide down on top of your cock with my jeans hanging off one leg and one boot still on and somebody yelling and yelling I'm wanted on the phone, and your hand over my mouth and coming like that with the vibrations of the dryer and spilled fabric softener on one cheek of my ass, blue and viscous.

There's mostly just the bed in the frame but there are also clothes on the floor. Not just the clothes we were wearing. A pile of laundry and toys, one of those chunky Fisher-Price plastic kitchens for little kids with thick plastic frying pans hanging from hooks. And a xylophone that looked like a snake slithering on wheels as you pulled the string, the tongue darting out. The pony on a metal stand and rusted springs that had been in the garden, but our youngest wanted it inside since we wouldn't have real pets, and sometimes if I came, the head and neck with its wild, pale mane nodded at me, lascivious, the white of the eye, and the springs creaked and the rust from the springs dropped off in a fine curtain of dust; the painted eye would catch the light and give me the creeps with its faux gaiety and depth.

From behind.

Gripping the bar of the metal headboard. Your hand on the small of my back, the other gripping my hip, sticking my bum up to you, come on, come on. Do it.

Outdoors at sunset in the snowstorm, the pinging of the snow on your nylon snowsuit, the quilted fluorescent orange padding inside, I can taste the colour orange, the shiny rub of it, enough to make me come or the smell of gas or engine oil or blue exhaust from the broken-down snowmobile, and put it in my mouth, come on, come on. Hit the back of my hot orange throat.

There were hundreds of hours of home videos. I don't know how you found this one of us making love. Mixed in with the one of parties and people smoking who don't smoke anymore, gave up smoking years ago, Look, Marie smoking, just look, look at her. There's that guy who came from Australia with his big broad chest and he stayed, and someone broke his heart, then he left for good and nobody ever heard tell of him again; then we don't say anything because the camera is lingering on someone who is dead now, has died, but is singing a ballad, belting it out. Though there's no sound.

It must have been near Halloween, no it wasn't spring; it's midafternoon, it's the fall, because there were those chocolate gold coins, one of the kids had dropped them all over the floor from trick-or-treating. The car headlights hitting the coins and you unwrapped the gold foil and pressed the chocolate coins between the cheeks of my ass and licked them. Didn't you get the job around then? We went right out and bought the new mattress. Suck my nipple, suck my nipple, can you? Hard. Put your tongue. Finger me. Finger me now. Touch my ass. Can you just. Oh. Oh.

You must have already got the job. We were okay. We were going to be okay. We put the old mattress out on the sidewalk.

But mostly it's just the bed with the bedsheet in this video. No blankets. You must have pulled all the blankets off for the home movie. Set design.

Once in a new house and there were the boxes, still packed up, everything, and you had come back from the supermarket with a package of chicken breasts and I was making myself come in the only armchair, with the streetlight coming in through the crack in the curtains, still in that astrakhan coat with the high collar, and the bone buttons, and all that flaming satin on the inside, you dropped the package of chicken on the floor and your mouth on me, your tongue, and me all slippery and stick it in me, okay? Can you? Fuck, yeah.

At the beginning the bed takes up most of the movie's frame.

Once, coming back from the bar, and I had that taffeta dress the colour of bubble gum I'd bought second-hand and you tore it open from the neck to the hem, and the sound of tearing fabric made me come, or it was your tongue, or I couldn't get you in me fast enough, and I just came and kept coming and the dress was also — you'd spilled a glass of red wine all over me.

I come around the corner and I'm naked and get on the bed. That was when I was running. Look at me. And you were running. God we really had nice bodies. Must have been the nineties. Big hair, jackets with rhinestone buttons, and skirts with six flounces. Heart of glass, girls wanting to have fun. The time I climbed up on the tabletop in the fake leopard skin miniskirt, and in the alley you came on it. All over my good fake, two-dollar, sale-bin, raggedy-hemmed leopard skin miniskirt.

We had to be so fast back then. We had to go to the laundry room. Or in the bathroom. Or out on the back deck when we had the tarp up so nobody could see down on us from the balconies next door and the rain hitting the tarp. The side of it came loose and the water sloshed down with a big noise, very close; we nearly jumped out of our skin. Or in the tub and the water walloping out every time you thrust me up, waves slapping the linoleum. The water weeping through the plaster ceiling of the porch, making a chunk fall off.

This was elaborate, setting up a camera on a tripod. This must have taken precious time. Where did we get the time to screw the camera down onto the threaded bolt that sticks up out of the metal base on the top of the tripod, the camera jerking around three-sixty, and the whole room whir-jerk, whir-jerk, the pixels discombobulating with each twist and following in a tail of pixelated diamond dust, like a snow globe of our lives back then. How did we have the time for that? To adjust the focus. Get it sharp. The image, the bed, your chest, your cock in the black curly glistening hair, it's all so sharp.

I let my hand drop over the side of the canoe and stirred up the water and the trees and the stones, broke them apart flicking my fingers, and I honestly can't come again, I really can't, okay, okay, yes, okay. Yes, on my face. Come on my face.

Sometimes the kids would be gone for an hour. Maybe half an hour and we dropped everything. The ladle splatting back into the pot of spaghetti sauce, droplets all over the counter, the wall. That's how urgent to get up over the stairs and strip down and get in the bed and fuck.

We both had shift work. Different shifts. We had to co-ordinate our schedules, whoever got home first made dinner. If the other one was late getting home, it was a fight. If the other one went out for a beer with people from work. There was a raging fight and tears, doors slamming. Voices raised. Or it was we'd give each other a break.

You go out, go out with your friends.

No, you go on.

Go on, you go.

Or brought people home. We had sex fast. Really fast. As fast as two people could have sex and still both come and sometimes come more than once. Or only one of us came. Before someone called out they were hungry, or there's someone at the door, or I hurt my knee, or she pushed me.

Lots of times I came lots of times, even though it was really fast, or didn't come, and we were only half undressed and my bra not undone but wrenched up around my chin, and someone knocking on the bathroom door, and saying, What are you doing in there? I need to go.

Because we could get started and someone would be through the front door calling up the stairs, Anybody home?

Then we forget about the camera. Because when you are fucking there comes a time when that's all you are or can do or feel or think or be.

We watch the home movie together because you say: I found this, and I want to know if you want me to erase it?

Have you looked at it?

Some of it.

How much of it?

Some, you know. The first bit.

I can't remember doing it — I don't know what will happen next in the film. I have no recollection because I was in it. Am in it. I am the co-star. Starring in. The fitted bedsheet with the faded yellow roses that slips off the corner of the bed nearest the camera and inches up over the mattress. His toes, the ball of his foot finding purchase on the icy blue, bare, cold corner of the mattress but we're not cold now. Not cold. His foot, the ball of his foot pressing so hard into the mattress, driving all of this into me, and it doesn't look — it looks slow is what it looks.

It looks like there's no movement at all. It's almost still.

It's duration. It's an extended, unending fucking that can't ever stop because everything else stopped around it.

We're arching into it, we're both arching into it. A clench that builds, fusing, sends shivers. Fingers pressing so hard on my ass, his fingers go white. Holding the cheeks on my ass. Gripping me.

First there's just the bed and a jerk to the side while the camera was screwed onto the tripod. Then he must have adjusted the aperture a few times because the empty mattress goes dark and darker; then it lightens up. Is blasted with light so it disappears in a white blaze and back to the print of the bedsheet, to ordinary daylight. All these adjustments, but it's surprisingly artless. Unfabricated, once we get into it.

I walk into the frame completely naked and he does the same. We are self-conscious about it, but we pretend we aren't. And then we aren't self-conscious. We aren't pretending. You can see the pretending slide away from our skin like taking off his shirt, like my skirt falling off. Except we aren't wearing clothes when we walk into the frame; we're already naked, we don't disrobe, there's nothing cheesy like that. But we walk into the frame and our awareness falls off like some flimsy fabric thing. We are unaware. We were pretending but then we are just fucking *there*. Because however elaborate the pretending is, it cannot be maintained. It falls away.

Like we were always *there* back then. We are still here. We are always in a clench so hard and fast and muscle riven, coated with slipperiness, bone, claws, need, never awkward or anything other than just what it is. What is it? Give it to me.

This is: Do you want me to erase it? Because who is it for?

Once I was reading on the couch in front of the woodstove and the ice cream machine going in the kitchen, the heat from the stove stultifying. It was dark except for the fire in the woodstove and the headlamp for reading. You come out in the dark, hold out a spoon, and put it in my mouth, feed me it, a spoonful of ice cream, to see if it needed anything, extra sugar? Creamy, so creamy.

Did it need anything? I pulled down my jeans and you went back into the kitchen and got another spoonful, and this was with my headlamp focused downward, ice cream edged off the spoon with your thumb onto my clit, Lick it off, lick it off, please, please, it's so cold. Please. Please? How hot your tongue was, little sticky darts of your tongue, all the cream dripping.

Once after a terrible storm we went off on the Ski-Doo and the throb of that between my thighs, the bogs frozen over so we went places we'd never been before between valleys and the sun setting, and we fucked there right out in the open in the freezing cold. I saw the eyes of something flash green in the forest behind black branches.

So, we watch it, and I think it was actually winter when this thing was shot. The light I realize now, yes, it's winter. We can't keep our hands off each other while we watch the home movie because it is so fucking sexy and then we are kissing, but turning slightly from the kiss to keep watching, both of us, pawing each other, watching ourselves.

And without being aware of it, we are doing what they are doing — you are on top of me and I must have said, Wait, wait, because I reach out and touch the screen, and the tips of my fingers go through the glass, and I am stroking your hard cock on the new mattress shiny and icy blue and silver, silver like the underside of leaves, the mattress, on the other side of the screen and I am just running the back of my index finger over your cock, tracing a vein, and now my whole hand is in, up to my wrist and then my arm. I am passing through the screen, brittle, thin like ice over a puddle shattering us into the other

side, shattering the us making out while we watch and I tug
you through with me. I grip you by the cock as hard as I can as
I come and tug you through.

Then we are both coming, and we can't watch and come at
the same time, so we miss some; we miss some, we are missing
it, but we keep watching after that, and we both come in the
home movie and then we come with them, in them, are them.

The thing is, they were completely naked. More naked than
I remember. I am only seeing now how naked they were, and
they didn't know it.

I wanted to touch them, I wanted to put my wet fingers
through the plasma screen and touch them. I sucked two of
my fingers, making them good and wet, and drove them into
the puckering tight screen and it clenched around my fingers
over and over, and I stirred the pixels into chaos, a glitchy static
hissing, and before the pixels could swarm back into the solid
shape of our bodies back then, we got deep inside them.

# Niche Parade: Hotel Maid Compilation

[COMPILED ENTIRELY FROM VIDEO TITLES ON PORNHUB]

1.

When I went to an e-sports hotel, I met a maid who played with me.

My dirty maid was so sexy, I offer her money. I offer money to this hotel maid that she is pregnant so that she has sex with me. I give money to the cleaning lady and she fuck me. Businessman buys with his dirty money the clueless morality of this maid.

"You wanna play the game? My penis wants to play with you."

A game of taste. Sexy maid sucks dirty after cleaning.

Dirty maid.

2.

"You find me dressed as a French maid in your cupboard?"

Old hotel. The maid brought towels. My maid very very sexy.

3.

A maid in a hotel room is alarmed when she sees a big dick.

"It excites me to show myself while looking at the big cock of our maid's husband. Can I put some pressure there?"

Sexy maid decided that my dick was dusty and fixed it.

"I'll pee with two dicks."

"It's just a cannon!!!"

"Can't you hear it next to you? Peeing pounding."

"Stop it sir I'm going to cum!"

"Don't make a voice."

"Where are you going?! You can't untuck me now!"

That's what it means to be lucky with a maid!

4.

My stepsister will go walk with me only after I fuck her and make her shake.

How a romantic walk around Prague turns out: after a walk in the park, she abruptly attacked my dick.

In the middle of the city! Public sperm walk! How the people look!

A walk with my stepsister in the bushes. Kmart cum walk, cum walk in the airport, amateur cum walk at the mall, cum walk on beach and through town, spermawalk in der nachbarschaf, public cum walk in a crowded street of Barcelona, cum walks to the park, Christmas cum walk, found her vaginal balls after a walk, hotel walk, diaper walk hotel.

I had to walk to hotel with cum all over me.

My stepsister wanted to take a nap, but my cock is awake. She went to have a nap and asked to wake her up shortly, would you do it differently? I spy on my stepsister but I get caught jerking off, I lick my ass balls.

It was like a dream — the maid spied on us.

The sexy hotel maid wakes me up with a blowjob, fucks me and makes me cum twice and cleans everythin'.

## 5.

The female boss seduced the male subordinate to teach her to swim and went to the hotel to have sex.

"This is what you wanted so much. Your ass is in my power now."

Ashamed to pretend to be a hip and a nasty big ass, sexy man in lawyer uniform and stockings and high heels gets cumshot by man. Naughty waist pretending to be a handsome member of society — a handsome member of society who puts up with it as much as possible, a handsome member of society who is unexpectedly pleasant to be bullied.

The maid walked in on us.

The housemaid wants to eat the boss's cock. My cleaning lady knows only love's language.

"I got a French maid to pick up my bras and play with her boobs, I love to be the horny boss."

Naughty maid clothes? It was too comfortable to keep being blamed by her erotic erotic maid costume. Wear it and get acme with rich masturbation.

Big tits maid takes care of boss cock. Maid takes dick in boss's ass.

The maid forgets to close the bathroom door and her boss comes in. Squirt, pee, hiding from the boss. Secret of the boss and his maid! Cleaning maid making the bed as you like.

## 6.

Caution! I've got cum on my face.

I ate cake with cum.

I hired this naughty maid and look what she did. Naughty maid.

## 7.

Lonely girl plays with her maids. The maids clean my dick. Loyalty test!

Let's enjoy the slippery pussy after shaving a fat lady. Capture the dirty pussy of a potato woman sucking! A perverted woman leaking with a toy.

The arsehole still squirts in pussy. Hair and mouth in sperm.

My sex in a hotel room with the cum in my mouth.

It was a day when I masturbated.

## 8.

I found a succubus on my bed.

Giggly mommy succubus puts you in a trance! Succubus grabbed the man to take semen, succubus sister squeezed the man's semen with her body. She sucked all my life force. Hungry succubus drains you. Still waters run deep.

Succubus transform. Horny turns into a succubus. Mesmerising succubus. Succubus sits on you! She is a maid that does it all.

The maid used me like her personal toy.

Beautiful love making, two lovers in hotel room late night.

## 9.

Unexpected alone time at hotel. The house is alone so, it's time to fuck.

Morning sex with wife. I love her big tits. Big thighs and wife in cation.[1] Beautiful body suit and lots of smile. Fisherman hasn't no clue that one hot naughty mom is having fun.

Husband got very special first row place in shower when wife washes and shaves herself. Cuck hubby dries cheating hot-wife after shower in hotel before she leaves for date in hotel bar. This hotel have amazing service.

Found this nerd to ride in the hotel bar. Husband let stranger guy from the hotel bar to fuck his big boob blond wife in their hotel room. Be this big boob MILF husband or lover and fuck her until you cum! Ritz Carlton with a true swinger hotwife.

Wife fucks her friend while his cuckold husband is working. "I'm a cuckold, please."

I invited my friend to fuck my wife together, she wants to eat two cocks. "I fuck the hot guy and the loser cleans it all."

Double cuckold humiliations: I ate two sausages with anal.

I'm your French maid … but I think I flirted too much.

---

1   A positively charged ion.

## 10.

"Finally, will it feel good with me?"

Do not believe what this man dared to do, when his wife retired.

# At the Wreckers

THE GROUND ITSELF WAS SLICK WITH GREASE — DEEP
sedimentary layers of black grease. Hundreds and thousands
of old or dead or smashed-up cars had left their oil on the earth
here, down by the lake, at the wrecking yard on Commissioners
Road. I was there to claim payment — ninety dollars — for my
old Chevette. They told me to wait for Jerry, the owner. I knew
this might take a while.

The office was the size of a trailer. The men in it were also
covered in theatrical amounts of grime. They looked like pir-
ates, or like bad, bad men who wanted to make that clear right
from the start. One of them was clean-shaven, though, and
dressed in pristine overalls. That was sinister in itself. Another
was entirely bald and smudged all over; the only shine on him
was from his single silver earring. A third was raddled in the
face, with a sailor's blue eyes, a phlegmy cough, and a rakish
smile — a man who did as he pleased in life. Now it pleased
him to be around the crushed, haunted carcasses of cars.

I had come down to the wrecker the day before, ready to abandon my car, but forgot to bring along proof of ownership. For some reason they needed proof of ownership before they could compress, eviscerate, or in other ways demolish my 1981 Chevette Scooter. My bicycle was clasped horizontally in the hatchback, with the lid of the trunk held down by a bungee cord. That was my ride home.

The bike and the Chevette had been partners, like Don Quixote and Sancho Panza. Many, many mornings, I had driven the Chevette back to wherever I had left my bicycle locked up the night before, then taken a cab home when it was too sleety to ride, or I was too drunk. Maybe I'd gone over to Eric's place, against my better judgment. The next morning would come with the guilt of having left my bike locked outside alone, overnight, in the city. I'd drive across town full of dread, like I'd finally pushed everything too far. Then I'd turn a corner and see my bicycle still there, a small miracle. Handlebars tilted sideways like a bird with its head tucked into its wing. I'd flip the back seat of the Chevette down flat, unlock the bike, and heave it into the car, knowing the chain might leave black teeth marks on the beige vinyl of the interior. But it didn't matter; the back seat was too small for all but the most desperate or temporary of passengers (i.e., Eric and me). I would stretch the bungee cord from a crevice in the lid of the trunk down to a secretive ridge under the bumper. Then came the cautious drive home, trying to keep the trunk lid from bouncing as the bike's rear wheel spun free in the air. Like a brittle insect held in the mouth of a lizard.

The bike, the car, and me alone in the Scooter. My universe intact again.

The gold-coloured Chevette was my first car after belatedly getting my driver's licence in my midthirties. Before that, I was auto-phobic, or at least afraid of the merge ramps on highways. The whole concept of *merge* basically eluded me. Anyway, in the city I preferred to bike. Even in the dead of winter it was always warmer riding than standing in a glass shelter, waiting for the bus. When my cousin, a car collector, passed the Scooter on to me, for whatever time it had left, I figured I'd use it for trips out of town.

As it turned out, I drove it for the next nine years. It had been perfectly maintained, slumbering away in his vast Mississauga garage. But my boyfriend and I lived in a Parkdale apartment that only had street parking, so the Chevette was re-introduced to life in the wild. Every night I would drive around the block, looking for an empty space. Life got tougher for the Scooter, as rain and salt and snow fell on it.

About a week after I got my licence, as I was pulling out of a lot on Queen Street, I put a ding in the side of the Chevette. That felt tragic, like a thoughtless, cruel insult you can never take back. First dents are the worst. After that, nothing changed about the Scooter for years. It used almost no oil. It always started. When the arm of the turn indicator fell off, I kept it on the dashboard for months, jiggling it back into place for significant turns. Otherwise, the car was indestructible, a pit pony.

The Scooter years were my Eric years, too. A while back, when my boyfriend was rethinking things and still seeing the hygienist, as I called her (she was, in fact, a psychotherapist, his), Eric called me up. I'd been off and on with him, trying to quit him, like smoking. Anyway, he called me up when he was working late one Friday night and I was alone. I agreed to meet him downtown for a drink. "Just a drink," I said sternly, already revealing my agenda. Eric was a rower and had these muscular, tanned forearms. Always my weakness. He and his big-time biologist wife had just had twins — that made a total of three kids under twelve — and he was going out of his mind, he said. Before the Scooter, when we first started seeing each other again on the side, he was always talking to me, kidding around about us having kids together. Giving them names, and then nicknames. I never trust that in a man, to tell the truth. I think men don't really get it til the baby's there.

After we drank most of a bottle of Pinot at a stockbroker bar that was annoying but full of energy, I offered to drive Eric back to his office tower, where he kept his car in an underground lot.

Well, we both knew what that entailed. I steered the Scooter down and down into the concrete abyss. We were both speechless with lust. "It's the dark green Toyota," he said, with an apologetic shrug. A family van. I was the one who was set on having kids when we met in our third year of college. We worked at the same summer camp, where we spent our nights lying under the stars, truant and unquenchable, and our days in a stupor of exhaustion, covered in insect bites.

"There it is."

I parked with drunken aplomb beside his Windstar and cut the engine.

The lighting in underground lots is not good. These places call out for criminal activity.

"If we're into this, we have to get into the back," I said briskly. We got out, flipped the Scooter's front seat forward, and inserted ourselves into the back seat, snug as a condom.

Ah, the melting of former lovers who should know better. Our faces hinged together searchingly, for a long time. It was always good with Eric. The thing is, the Scooter was so small, it wasn't physically possible to fit our bodies together. But we managed anyway. I loved the way his sweat rained down on me, copiously. Then we disengaged, flooded with the usual remorse and second thoughts. There were clothes to be straightened and reassurances to offer. I buttoned his shirt, a soft blue shirt with long tails. Someone slammed a car door farther down the row and we crept into the front seats. I angled the visor mirror toward him to make sure he was presentable and touched that familiar mottled flush that he got on the side on his neck. I calmed it with my hand.

"Drive home slowly, let it fade," I said, wifelike. This would never ever happen again, we both agreed.

For once, this was a promise we would keep, because the next morning the Scooter wouldn't start. I got a tow from the CAA to Sunjan, our mechanic. He could get it back on the road, he said, but this would just keep happening. On the way home I double-parked outside Eric's office. He came down and got in the front seat with me. I told him that I would be taking the Chevette down to Commissioners Road, that Sunjan had said it wasn't worth fixing. He was surprisingly upset. He kissed the dashboard above the radio, then buried his face in my lap.

THE OWNER, JERRY, WAS TAKING HIS SWEET TIME, SO I left the trailer and walked back into the lot, to see if I could find my car and maybe salvage the turn indicator, as a souvenir.

I made my way up and down the rows of cars and vans and trucks, all frozen in different spasms. T-boned in the side, crushed from a rollover, a hood gaping open like a beak. I finally spotted the Scooter, with the red parking permit still taped to the windshield. The front doors were open. I slipped into the driver's seat.

But something was different — the seat was farther away from the wheel and angled back. On the floor I saw two empty take-out food cartons and a plastic fork. A stranger had eaten and possibly spent the night in my Chevette. One of the pirate men? The back seat had been half torn out as well — the cushion stuffing, a light green color, fresh and unsullied, spilled forth like guts. I looked over at the Honda Civic beside me, still relatively intact; there was a roll of yellowing foam rubber inside, tied with a bandana. The abandoned cars on Commissioners Road clearly functioned as some sort of last-exit motel.

I spied a tube of lipstick on the floor of the Chevette. So women stay here, too. I took the cap off and twirled it up. Not my colour. Still, I hoped this final passenger of mine had been able to sleep and dream in my car, undisturbed. Like my bicycle, abandoned for the night down some city lane but safe.

I left the doors open the way I'd found them and went back inside the trailer, where Jerry was sorting out bills at the cash.

"I can only give you seventy," he said, looking thoughtfully into his till.

"But yesterday another guy told me ninety," I said. "It has a brand new starter motor."

It was summer. I was wearing black bike shorts and a black T-shirt, and big tortoiseshell sunglasses. It's very hard to stand your ground in bike shorts. A sign on the wall said, "Prices vary according to the customer's attitude."

"The car still runs," I added, as my voice crept higher. "And the other guy really did say ninety." The phone rang. Jerry took his time dealing with the call. Then the weirdly clean man I had seen before came over. I smiled and told him I was waiting for my ninety dollars. The new starter alone had cost me $124. I only had it put in, I explained, because I felt sorry for Sunjan, our mechanic. His garage had just burnt down. When I saw Sunjan in his overalls, his face still looking shocked a month after the fire, with a special glove on his badly burned hand, I felt so bad I said, fine, let's put in a new starter. I didn't tell him I was only going to use the car to drive down to the wreckers' yard.

I get into trouble all the time with guys like that.

Jerry was still on the phone. Sunjan is a saint, I thought, compared to the men at the wrecking yard, unregenerate, metal-herding men who rip the guts out of old cars saturated with memories and dreams. They are organ thieves, tire plunderers, vinyl slashers. They have no feelings for my Chevette, with Eric's coins still jammed in the crease of the back seat, and now they're going back on their word to me.

The landscape around the wreckers' place is strangely bucolic — you can smell the lake from there. Fields of Queen Anne's lace and small blue wildflowers lie beyond the ziggurats of broken cars. But inside the trailer, even the beige computer in the office is greasy. Everything must be dirty, that's the only rule they submit to here. The Chevette, the most private thing in my possession, was now sheltering strangers, with a wisp of my spirit still trapped in it, a residue of all the hours I had spent feeling the vivid in-between-ness of time in a car, time suspended in the pregnant, still hopeful nowhere between destinations.

From the trailer office I could see the port where the European freighters dock. Big black rusty ships called *Lusitania* or *Reikksgarten* that nose their way deep into these man-made slips of water and then languish for weeks or months at anchor. You never see crew on their decks; the boats just slumber here. Container ships. Imagine a wreckers' yard for just old container ships — emptiness amplified!

I went outside to make sure my bike was still leaning against the bench. I shouldn't be so trusting, I thought, because a bike is, after all, just another form of metal. Potential scrap. But I had less sentiment for my bicycle than for the Chevette; there aren't many things you can do on a bike apart from riding it. I threaded a cable through the frame and the wooden slats of the bench anyway, then spun the padlock. I didn't want to be careless anymore.

Not having a car would help me to not see Eric, I thought, which would mean less carelessness. Commissioners Road used to be one of our spots, in fact. On summer afternoons we would drive out into the middle of one of these orphaned fields and get into the back seat, where the view of the city was like the screen of a big drive-in movie. I'd lie against his chest and he'd wrap his arms around me, both of us passengers, facing forward.

I went inside and Jerry came over with a pink fifty-dollar bill — and a twenty.

"Fresh out of the machine," he said. I looked at the bill, then couldn't see it clearly, because the tears were running down my face.

"Hey, hey," Jerry said. He looked at a grimy cloth that hung beside the till but thought better about handing it to me.

"It's really worth more," I gulped. "In my view."

He went back to the till and took out another fifty. The other guy on the phone was looking our way now.

"You take this then," Jerry said. "Buy yourself a better lock for your bike. Anybody can snap that little cable."

I thanked him. A ship's horn gave a loud blast and that let us both off the hook.

"There she goes," the clean guy said. We watched the ship slide eastward, on its way to the St. Lawrence and the Atlantic.

"It feels like we're moving instead."

"Some of them carry scrap metal." He smiled at me. "Your car might end up in Rotterdam, in a bridge." He was trying to make me feel better.

"Here is okay, too," I said as I headed for the door.

"You take care."

INSTEAD OF GOING HOME ALONG COMMISSIONERS ROAD, I rode my bike along a sandy path that led through the fields of Queen Anne's lace. On my right arm, I felt the currents of cool air flowing off the lake. Behind me, the late afternoon sun flashed off the metal skin of the cars in the yard. All this wild land by the lake was slated for development soon, so I was glad I had come down here before that happened and that I got to send the Chevette off properly. I was thankful for this chance to see the raw end of something — pure, glittering wreckage, out in the open.

# Restoration

EDNA X WAS THIRTY-FOUR YEARS OLDER THAN ME. WE
had just had sex in the spare bedroom of her house that overlooked the lake that provides a water supply to the city. She
began putting on an earring. Unlike my girlfriend she didn't
immediately go to the bathroom and sit on a toilet. She left my
cum inside her. Maybe after I left she took care of that. I used
the narrow staircase and the back door that, I guess, a generation before was meant solely for servants and deliveries. They
had a big brick house from her husband's family's merchant
days. Or maybe the house was from Edna's political side of
the family. It's been thirty years; it's possible I have the history
mixed up.

I had just come back from travelling for six months. I'd
done a degree and then started working in an art gallery. I
remember getting up in the morning and a friend of mine was
still on his way to the university. He was enrolled in a master's
program. I had forgotten you could do that, keep learning. I

had a job now. I had my own apartment. I didn't study. I met
Edna X at the gallery. She was on the board and she was a pa-
tron to the arts. She had a limp and a cane. The woman who
ran the gallery asked me to lug in a bankers box out of the back
of Edna's German station wagon. When she was seven Edna's
family had moved for two years to New York City. There was a
lot of upheaval and she was the youngest of three. The infection
wasn't noticed until it was too late. Edna's leg was amputated
just below the knee.

When we were in bed I tried not to fetishize the stump.
But the truth is the stump made me hard. Or perhaps it was
her admonition. My cock and her leg communicated directly.
The way the skin folded over the ball cap of the knee joint,
the ancient evidence of heavy staples. The roughness and haste
on such a calm and elegant body. Edna kept in shape — yoga
on the TV — and that contrast made me want to fuck the
knee. The savage scar made up for the fact that she was old and
beautiful. There was an indentation in the stump crenellations
that I rubbed my cock on until she said, "Don't do that." I did
it anyway. I did it until she grabbed my cock and told me to
stop. At work, while xeroxing, I thought, *If she wants me to fuck
her then she's going to have to let me use the knee.*

I waited in my cheap coat under the cold fall leaves of the
maples, waited until her husband's diesel tail lights stopped
at the end of their gated street. Then I went inside and put
my damp gloves on the radiator, ran up the back stairs, and
bent her over and rubbed my cock on her knee. It was on my
way to other things. I saw, in Edna's face, that look of taboo.
This friction was never talked about except to say stop it. This
gathering of my cock, my God, I could have come all over the
inside of her leg! I was only twenty-two and she was fifty-six.

She was married to this man who ran a bottling plant for soft drinks. I heard, during lunch at work one day, that he was a trivia answer on the radio noon hour, as if the man who managed to supply ginger ale to a province should have a statue in the park next to the last Indigenous person. "That's unkind," Edna said. His ancestors ran the business of this entire country, "when we were a country." There are many components to growing a successful business, dozens of complex relationships that demand coddling, the fostering of talent, and keeping that talent. "We used to be the centre, but then we got fucked over, and now we are the hinterland."

I was shocked by her anger, her "fucked over" comment. "It's only a can of soda," I said.

"It's jobs," she replied. "Don't underestimate him." Edna's father and grandfather were politicians. But the truth was, both Edna and her husband were weathering a personal decline in family prestige.

The house, though grand, was poorly insulated, and they didn't like to spend on heat. Several of the rooms had portable electric heaters and this was nice, this localized island of heat. There was a den with a fireplace and it burned coal. I'd never seen coal before. The hard black glass. There were brass lamps that were gimballed for they were from a racing yacht in the 1940s that Edna X's father had skippered and held a record one year in one of the Boston states. They had grown children older than me; they had gone to Oxford and Acadia and one was still at McGill. They were bilingual. I can't think why Edna had decided on me.

I was there for the last vestiges of privilege. I could be impressed by this heritage because I had grown up poor from an unknown family. I relished this appetite for the old structures and it thrilled me to be inside the bare legs of an institution. The bead of pre-cum sitting in the slit of my cock, I rubbed this on Edna's knee. Then I put my mouth on her and her fingers opened the brown weathered fold to her pink clit, and she showed me, tapping with an index finger, where to put the flat of my tongue. It was Edna who taught me how to go down, how to use my tongue. It was Edna who made me understand the joy of just relaxing and having my cock deeply sucked. She had an amazing mouth. She didn't like the white flab of her belly, the sag of it when on top of me, how it puckered around her belly button. I was thrilled by it, the ancient face, the intricate gold earrings below an expensive hairstyle, the feel of her hard wedding band as she jerked me off. My girlfriend had never offered instruction and I admire a woman's direction. After following Edna's orders I suddenly stopped and fucked her with vigour. I pulled her down from the headboard. I prevented her wrists from reaching below and she was surprised that she loved this submission. I held her hands over her head and sank my cock into her. "Harder," she said. "Press my ass." I had only made gentle love to my girlfriend. I had heard as a teenager in the bunk bed above me a girl say to my older brother, "Not so hard." I vowed, at the age of fifteen, when my time came to be with women, to be gentle. To be considerate. I had seen enough cruelty in the world, and I didn't want to add to it. I would provide goodness. But Edna loved it rough. She liked putting her good leg over my shoulder. She loved sucking my cock. She made a choking noise. I said, with judgment, "That's pornographic," and even though she was older, this juvenile tone hurt her. When I was working at the art gallery, or seeing a movie with my girlfriend, or having a beer with my friend who was doing a master's, I thought about my decadence with Edna and was ecstatic about it. There was a directory of correct thinking in front of us at all times, and it was easy to pull a chapter out and follow the rules. But in a file in a drawer three inches below grade, down in the dirt and worms, there was an instruction for badness that produced a tremendous feeling of being alive. I got into the pornography of our fucking.

I'd seen Edna X with her husband at a gala. She was wearing this pale wool outfit that was French (later I checked the label in her wardrobe while she was making us a tomato sandwich — her husband wore Dunhill suits). I was a young painter and the premier and his wife were in attendance. Edna curtsied. A curtsy turns a grandmother into a young woman. I hung onto that curtsy as I fucked open that old carapace. Our fucking was full of unsaid taboo. Edna and her husband sat several rows behind me, and I could see Edna's bent knees, the sheer tights, and the hem of that skirt. I just loved how much of a woman she was, never jeans or sneakers, always wool, cashmere, linen. Edna never looked at me but later, as I came over her belly in bed, she said she saw me with my friends in that little gallery, and it hurt her to the core to think of herself as an old bag and that I had all of this to look forward to. In the gallery I had served hors d'oeuvres to her husband while he was listening to the wife of the premier, and I almost dropped the tray when the entire white shelf of his teeth moved — he had dentures.

Edna had two little grandchildren. Photos on a night table in the bedroom that I was not allowed in, though I went in. The bed was raised off the floor with a box spring and platform with wood legs — it was only a proper bed but at the time I thought it grand. The apartment I inherited already had a futon and I felt lucky to get it for free, but now when I slept there I could feel the polyester blend in the sheets, the nubbly quality to the fabrics, and I ached to have Edna's good, smart things. I pulled a pubic hair from my crotch and left it on her husband's pillow. Above his night table a little landscape. It was by a Dutch painter, possibly a fishing village in eastern Canada, the 1700s — it needed restoration. I ran my hand over the Italian and French designer clothes, the hem of a houndstooth skirt, and the diaphanous collar of a blouse I had opened while my cock was planted in Edna's mouth, making her earring touch the blouse. I noticed her makeup. The cut of her hair — she and her husband went to New York twice a year to see plays and eat at restaurants, and she bought clothes and had her hair done and returned with boxes, replenished, to begin again a winter in this eastern city with her greenhouse and tomatoes and subscription to opera on the radio and the latest gadgets like a remote television and a microwave oven. She shied away from nothing new.

The girlfriend I had, she moved on. She broke up with me. She said I was too isolated. It hurt her to leave me; she worried about the turbulence she was making. She was so considerate (she had studied social work and had a job with disadvantaged youth). She didn't want to cause upset. I looked at it all with great distance and immediately phoned Edna's answering machine and booked an afternoon. We lay in her amazing sheets and stared up at that moulded tin ceiling. There were angels up there and the fronds of things that don't grow here. It was like visiting a ruin in Pompeii, something I'd done in the past six months. The apartment I had didn't have mouldings; the ceiling joined the walls in a manner I found discourteous. Everything in Edna's house was antique or expensive or brand new. In the cutlery drawer there was a compartment for eight silver grapefruit spoons with a serrated edge used once annually: when the family came home at Christmas. "No," Edna said, "it's because you were looking for another and your girlfriend saw it." All this time she had been thinking about my girlfriend breaking up with me. I told Edna I had been happy with the way things were, but she shook her head again. "You're too beautiful to walk away from," she said. "You're like no one else in this small city and for a girl her age."

She looked at me as if she couldn't believe her luck. I was too young to believe her. This city was big enough, I thought, but she had lived in it her entire life while travelling to larger places. I had just come back from the Mediterranean countries, staying in youth hostels, visiting the pyramids and the caryatids, and swimming in the hot white pools of Pamukkale. But this city still felt satisfying because, while I'd passed through London and Athens and Istanbul and Cairo, what I'd visited were ruins. It's taken me thirty years to realize, looking back, that I may have had a distinct face, an attractive bearing, at least a countenance that was different (because my parents were immigrants), and for some, that difference is appealing. I am now the age Edna X was when she took me to bed. I did not know I was handsome until Edna, and this innocence made it only more unbearable for some of the women who have, over the years, fallen in love with me while I could not love them back. I'm not proud of this — who can create a face? It was none of my doing, but it's true I did not exploit it; I had no idea I possessed a quality.

Edna's prosthetic leg. It lay on a chair while we fucked. I saw it out of the corner of my eye. It lay on several magazine subscriptions and a new book — Michael Ondaatje's *In the Skin of a Lion*. I rubbed the barrel of my cock on her knee, produced a bead of pre-cum (such a great colour and surface tension, that viscous blue). Then, as we fucked, I studied that contraption, the harness and buckle and rubber slot made by a precision plastics company in Germany. Her pussy was a good angle for my cock, I felt the ribs of my shaft inside her, but it was that plastic and rubber cup and the badness of that brown belt of leather that sat in repose on a Windsor chair that filled me with a desire to fuck a machine. There was a photocopier at the art gallery, and when the machine was churning out paper, that sound I kept in my head as I glanced at Edna's prosthetic limb, and I made the sounds of the photocopier as I exhaled. I was reproducing. If there was a flange or an opening in that photocopier that would have permitted entry of my cock I would, when alone, have fucked it while thinking of Edna. Instead I was in Edna's spare bedroom fucking and becoming a photocopier — I guess one of her kids used to live in this room and would be back at Christmas for half a pink grapefruit. I was creating duplicate pulses of orgasm. Edna knew something was going on, something kinky and mechanistic deep in my mind that she could not condone, but she was astonished at her luck, to have a lover that pounded her and got even more excited to make the nipples on her flat breasts move with each thrust. Did I think of her daughter at McGill? Maybe I did. There was a picture of her with her parents and she was beautiful. It is okay to close your eyes and think of someone else. Edna had money and privilege and a family name but no love, and she was selfish for this love. Her father had been upset with himself over the leg. The New York doctor's disdain, "It is too late" — meaning, if it had been caught in time, this undiagnosed osteomyelitis. Her parents had a lot of money, and it bothered her father that they had neglected her. "He died grieving the loss of my leg."

This absorption in business indicated an inability to love. No one had loved Edna except, possibly, her children, and now those children were gone and the only way to return to love was to become a child. Or fuck a twenty-two year old. And have that young man think of your own daughter. I didn't love her; I was involved in a youthful exploration of taboo. I was plunging myself into riches I'd never experienced growing up the son of a plumber. I loved the paintings and her husband's antiques, that there was a tall narrow closet at the top of the stairs for linens, and the history Edna's family had with the development of this province. I had no anchor. I was deracinated (my parents were not from here). I attached myself to Edna's heritage much like she donned her prosthetic limb. I fucked her like a plumber unclogs a toilet fed with the water from a lake, a lake out there beyond this window, a lake that supplies a city with drinking water, a lake tagged with a municipal lease to provide water for a bottling plant.

I tasted her ass and the taint of shit. This absolutely shocked her with delight. "I need you inside," she said. "Split me in two." And I happily banged her, her good leg around my neck, pulling my eyes down to her eyes, where her faced changed, and if there was one thing I loved about Edna it was her face changing because of my cock deep inside her, the backs of her thighs against my chest. She grabbed my chest hard and turned me over and sat on my face and told me there, there, right there. And she squeezed my head with her thighs so hard I thought I might pass out. The stump of her leg pressed into my side. I asked her to not squeeze so much and she said, "Sorry, sorry," but the next time it was just as hard.

"Touch yourself," she said once, when she had come and was sore but I had waited and was brimming with pent-up cum. I lay on her bed while she sat above me, her bad leg tucked in, though I could feel the vicious work of surgery and amputation with my free hand. I looked in her eyes and then felt the stump, and I stroked myself hard and arched my back and groaned and I came and my cum spurted over me, it landed on my own face — hot cum on my surprised lips.

"Oh my God," she said, "that is so hot."

She went away to New York for a week with her husband, and the next Thursday (those were the afternoons he was surely away at the bottling plant) I went over and found a present on the chair wrapped in expensive floral paper. I unwrapped it carefully, to save the paper. A dark blue shirt made in England. The fabric was stiff it was so thick; it was like a shirt from the 1930s of wonderful quality.

I was walking to work one afternoon wearing that English shirt, in the rain, when the German diesel pulled up. It was her husband. Edna was in the passenger seat. He rolled down the window. "Get in, son." Edna was on her way to an early morning board meeting and he knew of me. The windows steamed up and I rubbed the window clear with the cuff of my sleeve, and the husband said, quickly, "Don't do that." His *don't* was humiliating, but it also made my cock prickle. He had pressed the defogger and turned the fan up a notch. I realized my circular motion was leaving a mark on the window, a mark he did not want on his expensive car. He had turned when he saw me wiping with the cuff of my shirt. He noticed the shirt's imported quality. He knew everything.

I write this, thirty years later. I went to graduate school and moved to the mainland. I got a job in a museum in the nation's capital. I'm a consultant now in art restoration and conservation — this provides me with a nice salary. I own a condo that overlooks both the river and the market. I'm comfortable and hardly think about my life out east. I have developed an opinion on forgeries, and occasionally I think, back then in my adulthood, I had lived an inauthentic life. I wanted to write my first girlfriend a letter to apologize. These are small impulses that I never acted upon. But recently I received a piece of mail forwarded to me by the woman out east who ran that art gallery — my first job. The mail contained an obituary notice. Edna X had recently passed away surrounded by her family. Left to mourn a loving husband, children, grandchildren. I did a search on the husband — he continues to inhabit a position as national adviser to the soft drink industry.

# Timeless Sophistication

I'M STANDING IN THE BATHROOM WHERE YOU WASH YOUR face and body. The sink's basin is so low that my eyes get pulled down to the vanity mirror just above it, and my eyelash dangles like a hangnail, moving in and out of vision like the autofocus of my phone's camera. I am having a nice time.

I manoeuvre my naked body through your cluttered furniture, a couch stained with red wine, an empty mini-bar, a desk with an open notebook mad with short lines and drawings of skulls. I'm dodging the window you warned me to avoid. You said your neighbours can see in here.

I land in your bedroom triumphant as if avoiding unwanted leers from strangers is a privileged feat. And what if they saw? You are playing with a silver hairbrush spiked with sharp bristles bragging a floral gold plating on the back, resembling a hairbrush one would use if one were in a moral fairy tale about a woman with long hair.

I watch your eyes melt into an expression of null relaxation. The bed you recline on resembles that of a college student, unkempt with patterned sheets that don't match. You have put so much effort into the rest of the room, highlighting framed scientific drawings of rapacious birds and various animal bones in mounted cabinets.

The wooden bed frame that you built creaks when we're on top, and it was a disaster when you realized.

"A gift?" I gesture to the brush. This item of exorbitant luxury looks like it should belong to someone who has never doubted anything.

"For you." You toss the brush in the air and I scramble for it.

"Thank you." I hold it as if it could disintegrate. A gift is nice considering that I will be saying goodbye to you in the coming weeks. The years have left us both bored and alone.

I have been thinking about how to do that. It's hard, you see. You're so beautiful. You have a good grasp of reality. Sometimes after we fuck the paranoia comes right back, and you are one of the only souls I trust to bring me out of it.

Right now, I'm focusing on the floral design etched into the brush and the fact that another woman has probably left it here. I will not bring that up. I am here under the condition that I don't care.

"Your plants are turning yellow."

"I tried to repot them."

"Repot them?

"That's what you do when they get infected."

"Infected with what?"

"Tiny insects."

"That must have taken forever."

"A whole day. I changed every pot." You stretch your arms over your head.

I find our exchanges stilted like the ones included as examples in my French exercise book: surface conversations about ordinary things chosen to improve the comprehension of a language.

"I'm heading home to eat, I guess."

"Nice." You are looking at your phone.

"Want to come?"

"I can't."

"Want to call me a cab?"

"Sure yeah, sorry."

I'm confident that I can flip through at least fifty different apps in the span of ten seconds. In order to test this theory, I'd have to invite someone into my world, someone I trust enough to introduce to my plan. They could possibly watch over my shoulder while using the timer on their own phone, but I don't want anyone to know how much I look at the damn thing.

You're slow on the phone. Are you doing it on purpose to keep me here longer? Then, you say your own name out loud. I assume you've been asked who the cab is for. If you were more thoughtful, you would anticipate the driver asking what my name is when I get in the car.

You'd have given them mine.

"The drivers all call me Noah."

"I bet you love that."

"Who wouldn't?"

A recent dream of mine left me unsettled. A woman I used to know in a place we called boarding school was there. We all called it that because we were forced to be there for a number of hours a day. It was only for driving school. We'd never learned when we were young. The place had such a smothering atmosphere that we'd had to imagine it into something else.

In the dream I was visiting her, but I didn't know why. We snuck past imaginary guards while they were walking with their backs to us, dodging past them like spies. I was holding her candy. I never knew her well.

Then she melted out of the dream and I couldn't find her. I felt disturbed that she was lost. I couldn't call her because it was back in a time without easy correspondence. I woke up and checked my phone for a clue.

When I get home, I walk straight to the bathroom to wet my fingers and wipe them on the bar of soap in the dish. I massage the soap onto my hands hoping to get the smell of cigarette off forever. Then I wash my face methodically with a delicate cleanser made for dry skin. I pat it with a face cloth I stole from a hotel. There are various ointments I apply. I turn and put a metal doorstop shaped like an owl in the door. I feel dizzy as I walk down the hall, aiming to collapse on my bed, which smells like sweat.

I flick through an abundance of low-quality, stimulating content, then open my message history with you. I want to try and figure out what quality has drawn me back for all these years.

Watching the videos after I have just seen you seems stupid. My favourite one is this time where you fuck me from behind. It would look like the video was being sped up if it weren't for the irregular movements of your head when you flip your long hair. My ass is in the air. I love the fact that I'm being filmed, and I imagine you showing it to someone or even posting it somewhere. The camera acts as a witness. When you slap me, I breathe in and anticipate when it will happen next. That is the fun of it. Why I come back.

At one point, your face veers out of the shot, but you can see the edge of your mouth smiling in a cruel way. I consider your smirk to be the best part.

I keep turning up the sound because it's an important element of the video. You're slapping my ass. I want to hear that. A muffled noise rises from my bag on the floor. It's from these Bluetooth headphones I have.

It seems like I look okay most of the time that I'm being fucked. I consider this an accomplishment. The purpose of the videos? I watch them later and get more out of them than when they were happening. I recline on my bed with my vibrator, recreating what happened, and feeling the way you slapped me while imagining someone watching. I don't know who you'll show the video to. I don't really care. The phone recording us was a voyeur, and now I am the same, watching the portable machine that made it all possible.

I wish I had a friend to show the videos as I'm certain I would be complimented one way or another. I disconnect the Bluetooth headphones from my phone and play the video again.

I need rest. A time that excludes me from myself, one filled with realistic dreams of improvements to my life, or simply escapades of joy. Sleep is my best chance for that, to avoid the hovering blow from your indifference. And waiting is like a slow high. I think of ways to change my life. An exit from myself and the people I interact with, measuring their motivations until I'm too tired to do it anymore, until I'm too tired to try and find someone good.

# The Politics of Passion

HE SAT THERE, AT THE CONFERENCE TABLE, WATCHING her. Not in a dangerous, obscene manner, but more like a bored man looking for something of interest in a desolate and potentially hostile land. Consequently, he found her unexpectedly interesting, for she gave off an air of confidence. Groomed, not a single follicle out of place. An obvious sense of intelligence. And for those who still cared (and let's face it, that is most of us), she had a definite pleasing physical aesthetic. However, she was, as the Indigenous community called her and her people, colour challenged. Pigment denied. A person of pallor.

He was tall, with a ponytail carrying just a hint of grey. And it was long and thick. He had noticed that women like that. Smartly dressed, with tight pants and a loose shirt. Cheekbones high enough to give altitude sickness. And a smile that told of strange and desirable secrets. Therefore, he was Anishinaabe.

Between them sat a conference on treaty issues. Rows of tables and chairs, peopled with those having an opinion on the topic. Occasionally there would be flare-ups of anger, interruptions of procedure, and long boring soliloquies detailing past indiscretions and unfulfilled obligation. And wants for the future.

Much like prom night, she thought. A lawyer for the government, she often grumbled about how so many years of hard education and attention to legal detail had ended up with her here, waging a battle against Indigenous people and their causes.

Personally, she had nothing against them. In fact, her time working with them had given her an appreciation. Somewhere deep in her closet, she had moccasins. She was sure of it. She'd once had chili made with moose. And that actor, Adam Beach ... well, the less thought about him in such a public environment the better. In fact, there was a gentleman across the floor that in another time and place might make for an interesting sharing of apple strudel recipes (a favourite euphemism used by her girlfriends).

She'd seen him talk earlier, about the importance of tradition. His voice could be heard across the room easily without the aid of a microphone. It boomed. Rattled. More than anything it was the confidence in that voice that had caught her attention. She always liked people who had something to say and knew how to say it. And this man ... his name escaped her ... definitely had that quality.

Next to a Chief from some community the vast majority of Canadians couldn't pronounce sat the man. Much of this political and bureaucratic masturbation frequently left him unsatisfied. He was a man of the people and of their culture. He knew all the prayers, all the songs, and all the stories. He fairly dripped with indigeneity. Many of his friends joked that the man practically peed in a truly Indigenous way, maybe even to the Four Directions. He was here because, once you got past all the governmental bullshit, the trickle-down theory indicated some of this non-stop chatter might make its way to the people. And that was worth his attention.

And it was nice to occasionally make it off the Reserve. He loved his life there dearly, where he was related to 70 percent of the people, which had both benefits and drawbacks for sure. A change of scenery and perspective frequently reinforced his convictions in life. It was also hard to get good Thai or Korean food on the Rez.

Meeting new people was always good. Like that woman at the third table from the back. There was something about her. Her hair was short, which was not always what he looked for in a woman. But he knew there was always more to a person than the length of their hair. It was the way she studied the crowd and the people who rose to speak that piqued his interest. He could tell she was looking inside their souls. She was a lawyer, after all, assessing their strengths and weaknesses. For the government. That did not bode well. In old movies bad guys usually wore the black hats. In today's world, they usually wore black or, at the very least, dark suits. As was she. That was so many Xs against her in his box. But still, he would surreptitiously glance at her. Looking was free and it was sure a hell of a lot better than all the old white men in overpriced suits that mostly filled that side of the room.

The meeting dragged on. Energy wavered. Imaginations wandered, sometimes not to an altogether favourable place. Eventually a coffee and pee break was called ... what with the two frequently going hand in hand. Bones cracked as aged Chiefs and politicians rose to their feet, as coffee and pee exercised its right to unify disparate cultures.

As with Marriott policy, washrooms were located just down the hall, to the right. Suddenly there was a flood of people herding like caribou to those two rooms, unified in cause and purpose, soon followed by a different kind of flood. Soon afterward, people were milling about, grabbing coffee and cookies, as the fate of several thousand square kilometres of land was put on hold. These were, after all, tasty oatmeal cookies.

There they met, by the coffee urn. Being a gentleman, he flipped the lever for her and watched as her cup filled with industrial coffee. She smiled back at him. After filling his own cup, they moved off to the side and began an awkward conversation. The discussion was light and frequently dealing with the treaty issue at hand. At first, their laughter was strained and forced, but as the precious minutes of the coffee/urine break dribbled away, it grew deeper and more honest. Progressively so.

Almost reluctantly they had to part as the negotiations restarted. Accordingly, they filed back into the room and took their seats, again at opposite ends of the room. There definitely had been a connection made. What kind? Too early to say but the rest of the afternoon was filled with glances, smiles, and a joint lack of focus on the issues they had been sent to participate in. It had been nothing, they both knew, coffee and a brief conversation. Did it mean anything? That was for the Gods of Treaty negotiations to decide. The man and woman were mere pawns in their capricious will.

Later, as the day's events came to an end, briefcases were closed and laptops turned off. Chairs scraped against the surprisingly bright, vivid carpet as dozens of people rose to leave. The woman glimpsed the man being surrounded by a throng of other Indigenous people, all seemingly interested in his perspective. There was no throng to surround her, and she left alone for a post-negotiation meeting with her fellow lawyers, sprinkled with the odd bureaucrat. The world had to continue. The man, glancing toward the door, saw the woman leave. Three different people were talking all at once, none of whom really had much to say. They wanted his opinion on what the Elders of the past would have wanted in this situation. Even with his attention split, he tried to be positive. The man managed to come up with something pithy about the fact the Elders would rather be out hunting or fishing than be here. That got a good laugh, a momentary laugh, then they wanted something deeper. The man sighed. When you're a man of tradition, people thought everything had to be deeper. On occasion he'd have to tell people stepping in bear shit is not a sign from the Creator. Oddly, people recurrently looked disappointed.

Later as the afternoon turned slowly into the evening, a primal instinct soon took over all the varied participants of the conference. It was called hunger. Supper was somewhere in the building, roaming free range. One by one, individuals registered at both the hotel and conference made their way to the hotel's restaurant. There the supper awaited. Few civilians knew this was where the real negotiations at these events happened. Here and in the bar, of course. But first things first.

The man entered the restaurant, curious and hungry. The aroma wafting out of the room into the hall told of marvellous cuisine hidden somewhere in those four walls. Thus, he was on the hunt for such savoury delights. Normally he was a man of simple tastes back home. But he was not back home. He was here, in the belly of the Marriott, eager to sample its sins.

As he walked past the tables, he saw much of what he desired. Two Chiefs from just north of his community were sprinkling cheese on their pasta … penne primavera, he believed. Next to them were a lawyer and a bureaucrat sampling each other's veal and chicken piccata. To his left a woman, possibly a research assistant, was deep into her Waldorf salad. Instinct told him she was a vegetarian.

Then there, looking over a portable tray layered tall with tiramisu, cannoli, and some flan, she sat. Concentration was etched across her face. Stopping in his tracks, he watched her, wondering what her decision would be. You see, dessert choices said a lot about an individual. It could be a Rorschach test. If it was flan, he would be disappointed. To him, flan was a choice of last resorts. Bland and forgettable. Tiramisu was better but still a safe choice. If there was a cannoli in her immediate future, the man knew she had potential. After a second of indecision, she caught the waiter's attention, and pointed solidly and confidently to the cannoli. It looked decadent, with the cream-like ricotta oozing out one end. The man was impressed. Not just impressed, but intrigued.

No sooner had the small pale plate been gently but efficiently placed in front of the woman, then the man approached. With her fork halfway through the crust, she looked up at the looming presence that was now standing beside and above her table. It was him.

He complimented her on her choice

She said there was no choice. It was simple.

They both laughed. It was a socially acceptable, polite kind of laugh that denoted a certain "the journey has begun. Let's see where it takes us."

A brief time later, he was sitting at her table, asking a waiter for a second fork. Before either knew it, the cannoli was history. But the positive thing was it had initiated a conversation.

Discussions of dreams, experiences, past adventures, and government policy were soon on the menu. Laughter came and went repeatedly. A little too frequently one leg would ever so casually brush against another. To be social, he ordered a glass of wine himself. Always concerned about the effect alcohol sometimes had on his community, he was strong in his convictions that one glass of pinot noir would not destroy the world. He nursed it the next half an hour. Neither of them were heavy drinkers but the intoxication of the evening, of their chemistry, required a catalyst.

The bar was the next stop of the evening. Again, his second glass of wine was nursed as the chat became more intimate and revealing. There was a constant loud buzz forcing them to lean in closer to each other's ear. There, they breathed in the sweet essence of one another. Both their heads were swimming, partly due to the wine, and partly due to each other's company. Another hour swept past. Inhibitions soon weakened and it quickly became time to put politics to bed.

Attendees from the conference were sprinkled throughout the bar, glancing occasionally at the pair, some wondering what amendment or particular policy required such intense discussion. No doubt, they thought, two people married to their work that can't let loose for the evening and have some fun.

As things of this nature normally progress, a subtle offer was made. From which of our participants, it's not important. But that offer was accepted and moved upon. Soon the man and the woman were leaving the bar and progressing to the logical conclusion of the evening.

The key card in the door. The fumbling of belts and shoes. The creaking of the bed. And like the grand entry of a pow-wow, the fun commenced, and the drumming began.

The two roamed the bed like a bison herd, occasionally stopping only for water. Motions were made, followed by countermotions. As was the true purpose of the conference, much time was spent, using the vernacular, decolonizing each other, until they were well decolonized. Prejudices, preconceived notions, and patriarchal/matriarchal perspectives were lost in the dark.

And then, when the moon climbed to its zenith late into the night, both the man ... and the woman ... reached a mutual and satisfactory reconciliation.

It was, after all, treaty negotiations. Somebody was bound to get fucked.

# Bite

I WANT TO BITE.

I look on the face of my beloved and smile, exposing the teeth I would sink into his body.

I have no desire to feed on the meat and bone of him. No wish to pierce his skin, cause him to bleed.

I just want to feel him shudder as I trap his flesh between my teeth.

I kneel beside him, surveying the topography of his form as it is laid out naked before me on the starched white sheets of the hotel bed. Blindfolded, he cannot anticipate my movements, follow me with his eyes.

He is long and slender, bronzed skin, body hair covering him like flocking on wallpaper, soft and rough. I swipe my palm from navel to nipple, against the nap, watch the hair settle back in its place. His skin is warm from our bath, soft from the light oil we rubbed into each other's bodies.

I close my eyes and seek with fingertips the spot at the hip where bone juts out, barely covered by skin and muscle.

Then I lean over him, rest my cheek against his body. I bare my teeth, run their smooth enamel across the bone. I open my jaw over his skin then ratchet it gently closed. He and I discover at the same time how much flesh I can gather there.

He whimpers quietly through the silk gag I've tied over his mouth.

I lift my head, picking the fold of skin up away from his body, worrying it with my tongue, tasting salt and sweat and soap. I suck it gently, watching nerves quiver in his biceps and toes.

I leave a mark, the kind of imprint one leaves on the skin of an apple when one starts to bite, then, distracted, stops before tearing away the crisp flesh.

That was a good bite, but it does not satisfy.

Where to next?

There are many places I could choose where the skin is virgin, or hardly used. The small of my lover's back, for instance, has felt the pinch and scratch of my fingernails, the press and scrape of my heels, but not my teeth.

I have left him untied so that I may move him as I choose. I turn him onto his side. Again my fingertips reach out to mark the spot first, for teeth are not so sensitive; they cannot feel how his skin twitches away in nervous anticipation.

It is difficult to bite here, the dips and curves and taut muscle do not allow much purchase. I will have to burrow my face into his back, above his buttocks, there, where the tailbone begins at the end of the spine. My teeth will scrabble for hold until they find just enough to catch between them.

It is not so easily cajoled, the mouth, into believing it has had enough, and it is even more difficult to trick the teeth, which even now have finished toying with their last prey and seek more areas of resistance.

The buttocks tempt. I grab a mouthful there, my tongue enjoys the clenching and unclenching of muscle.

The well-developed quads. Behind the knee. The instep. The toes.

Above the waist now. The furrow at the back of the neck, where hair grows into a dark V. The crease between the neck and shoulder. The cap of the shoulder.

Two bites, when there are a matching pair.

And always my hands seek. My tongue licks, my lips suck, my teeth leave a mark.

My lover on his back again.

I admire his throat, a gleaming column before me. My eyes follow his Adam's apple as he swallows. My teeth bob. Catch.

I wait for him to swallow again, for him to take my mouth along with the movement, like a toy ship on a wave.

The inside of the elbow, that little fold of flesh so sensitive, so often ignored by all but Frenchmen in old movies who kiss their way up ladies' arms. Anyone can bite and suck fingertips, with all their incumbent, unsubtle suggestion, and I do. But I return to the nuances of the inner elbow, to watch the vein raised by my mouth throb with a sudden tensing, a gush of blood.

The nipples, like the fingers, are obvious choices but irresistible. First to take the entire areola between my teeth, then just the tip. Just the exquisite tip, the hard little nub standing tall for my tongue.

I nearly forgot the cheekbone. A bite on the cheekbone so sweet the mouth waters.

The jaw, near the ear.

The navel, beneath the belly button, just above the velvety pubic hair.

"Shh," I caution, as he groans and his hips rise from the bed, his cock reaching into the air. "Not yet."

The tender inside of the thigh, tasting of the private parts which swing between, rub against as my tongue now rubs.

The crease of the leg where thigh meets hip.

Finally my teeth have had their fill. This is not where this night ends, or even where my pleasure ends. It is not the end of my tongue meeting his flesh, my lips caressing it, or my teeth massaging it.

But I have finished, for the moment, pleasuring myself.

The teeth marks I have left, the indentations fading — but not, I hope, the impression — are a map to my pleasure. Made, as all maps are, in the hope that someone will follow.

I remove his gag and blindfold so that he may begin.

# Watching You Watching Me

MY LAWYER LAUGHED WHEN YOU STIPULATED THAT I couldn't write about you after the divorce. She cupped her chin in her hand, staring at your wording on the computer screen. That's the only time I saw her happy. Mostly, she terrified me.

"What do we do?" She reined her laughter into a bemused smile. "I mean, it's weird. Right? An odd demand. Isn't it?"

She'd never represented a writer before.

"I don't care. I'll sign it."

After twenty-three years of marriage, you did not understand my career, my process, or me. I only wrote about subjects that interested me, people I wanted to understand, themes I felt like thinking about.

I did not feel like thinking about you.

I would have told you so myself, explained that you needn't worry, but we'd cut off all direct communication by then. Some dangerous transformation had occurred, the energy between us suddenly lethal. We couldn't talk about even the most non-controversial topics — a pack of gum, a baseball game, a bottle of dish soap — without you slamming your head into the wall (next to our bedroom light switch, I can still see a dent, the exact size of your forehead) or me attempting to claw off my own face ("I ran into a tree while biking, a mean tree with very sharp branches"). I had a suspicious number of bike accidents in our final hot summer together.

In some marriages, energy trickles away, each year a little less spark — as if a relationship is a well-used string of Christmas lights. You can get by for a few years taking care of the odd fried bulb (date nights, dildos, raunchy underwear, home movies, anal beads) until the whole string goes limp, the effort of maintenance no longer worth the weak flickers.

Our marriage wasn't like that. We never lost energy. We experienced more of an energy transfusion, like we had the same voltage, but fireworks exchanged for demolition explosives. One day we were fucking hard on a wooden chair in a cheap hotel room in Banff and the next we were screaming into each other's faces (over whatever — unequal division of chores, addictions, kids' report cards, neglect, empty toothpaste tubes, infidelities, dead love, Visa bills — all the same).

In Banff, we escaped the tourist-filled streets (remember the guy flat on the sidewalk having a heart attack in front of lululemon, the crowd of shoppers simply flowing around him, diverting course but not slowing pace?). You placed a chair in front of a full-length mirror, instructed me to sit on your lap facing the glass, bouncing up and down on your cock, while you dug your nails into my hip bones, ran your rough palms along my torso, grabbed my breasts, my nipple poking between your fingers, rubbing against the cool gold of your wedding ring. *"Look at you"* — holding my chin toward the mirror. *"Open your eyes. Just look at you."*

I didn't want to look at my body. Watching you watching me, that's what turned me on. I came so loud, too loud for this cheap hotel with its thin walls. You braced your forearm across my mouth, but your breath in my ear felt gentle. *"Shhh. Shhh. Shhh."* You liked making me scream like that. "What would you say," you asked me afterward, your smile self-satisfied, your posture boastful, the chair on its side, us tangled together on the double bed, "on a scale of one to ten?" You took your pointer finger and with confident precision placed it exactly on my clit (that's an upside of marriage — you could always push my buttons, bad and good). "A nine?" Your touch on the swollen nub stayed so light, barely a whisper of connection. It was a game with you — how little effort you could put into making me come. Lightly, lightly, back and forth. "Maybe even a ten?" There … then not … (as if you already knew it was your leaving that excited me).

"Eleven," I said, my breath speeding up again, my body arching into your absent touch. "Oh my … please … God … *eleven!*"

For the rest of our married life, especially in front of our boys, whenever you said the word *eleven*, I blushed.

You could make me scream in ways you liked less too, ways we both liked less. I remember the day we'd had enough, the good energy no longer worth the bad. The thought came to me so clear, that I would never again put your cock in my mouth (you loved when I'd take you deep in my throat, rubbing my own pussy while I sucked and licked, pretending to come as I almost swallowed you whole. "How," you'd gasp, "*how* do you do that?").

I thought being suddenly single in my fifties, solo parenting three teenage kids, would involve a spell of celibacy. It didn't go that way. My sister and I numbered my men at first, so we could talk about them without granting them the Major Life Significance of names. When the counting got confusing, we switched to cities: Vancouver Boy. Montreal Moneypants. The Winnipeg Wonder. My France Friend. He who stays in Vegas. The Tiger in Toronto. The Constantinople Cutie.

Some philosophers say attraction is about recognition, perceiving something of yourself in another. A true knowing. Soul seeing soul.

I don't buy it.

Attraction sparks to life in our animal selves, not in our souls, the physical craving a response to hormones, energy, electrical currents. Dopamine. Oxytocin. Serotonergic systems. Goosebumps. Sweat. Spit.

Still deep in grief at our explosive ending, mere days into trying to understand my new life, I sat across a conference breakfast table from a lanky, bearded action photographer from Istanbul and I knew. All the light bulbs were on. He and I had only just said hello when I caught myself wondering if I could really make out with that giant beard. (The comparison between facial hair and toilet seats, their capacity for carrying bacteria, had recently been all over the news. You'd always preferred a clean-shaven face.)

He and I danced around each other the first two days of the conference, fingers glancing in the lunch line, a hand pressing on my lower back, guiding me to my auditorium seat, a taste from his martini glass while I puzzled over the infinite options on the lounge menu. The way our eyes took each other in — hard, direct, available — made our course unambiguous.

I called my sister on the third and final day. "I've been single like five minutes."

"Just do it. The fastest way to get over someone is to get under someone else." Typically, my sister avoided clichés, but she allowed an exception for her dumped sister who needed to get laid. "I'll make you themed T-shirts. *We'll always have Constantinople.* I mean Istanbul." She broke into song on the other end of the line. *Istanbul (Not Constantinople).*

That last evening, he found me drinking a beer in the lobby with a film editor from Japan. Not put off that I already had a male companion, the Constantinople Cutie pulled out the chair beside me and sat, just out of the editor's earshot. My Turkish climbing photographer moved through his argument with impressive efficiency — early flight, complimentary bottle of wine in his suite, an aversion to waste, his hotel room number. When he finished, he leaned across me to smile a wave at the editor, stood, pushed his chair into the table, and left.

Fifteen minutes later, I was knocking.

Even though we both knew where we were headed, we drank nearly the whole bottle of wine to raise the courage to get there. I'm not sure how proficient he was in English (he told me his languages in this order: Turkish, Arabic, French, and then English), but that didn't matter. Our conversation was more about the distance of our chairs, the gradual shuffle together, knees nearly touching, knees touching, my excuse to put a hand on a quad, his excuse to tangle fingers in hair.

On the bed, his body, so unlike yours, felt lean and wiry, ready to spring, all those climber's muscles taut. We ripped at our clothes, clutched bodies, pulled hair, bit shoulders. Where sex with you was all absence and teasing and wanting, this man's movements spoke always of presence: *I'm here, I'm here,*

*I'm here.* I didn't worry about his beard, even when he pulled his face from mine, a thread of spit stringing between us. "Oh God" — he smiled, no hesitation in his communication now — "we both needed this." He rolled off me, his arm falling heavy across my naked torso. "But we don't have any condoms. We should have gotten the condoms."

He was more active in the game and its rules than I. I wouldn't have minded about condoms, so urgently did I need him deep inside me.

Let's admit, then, that attraction and its follow-through are not only animal instinct, but also a subtly coded invitation. The way I watched him and his beard, right from that first hello, announced my availability. Even after all those years of near-monogamy, I still knew how to tell a stranger about the dark emptiness inside me and how badly I needed to be filled, by anyone.

But without condoms, he would not fill me tonight. We dressed and walked downtown to the final conference banquet. I hardly registered the world around me. Too consumed by my hunger for his body on mine, I'd become one giant swollen clit. *Fuck me, fuck me, fuck me.* But he talked of other things now. His child. Its mother. He lit a joint. "My vice," he said, offering me none. "You and I can have an arrangement. People think they can be with someone right after a marriage breaks, but they can't. I met an Italian woman when my marriage ended, but I was so broken. I still see her sometimes. I love her, I guess." (The *I guess* reminded me of you — always one foot in, one foot out.) "I see my son's mother too. She wants me when she can't have me and then when she can have me, she wants rid of me." He held the smoke in his lungs, looking at the dark street ahead of him rather than meeting my eye. "She will be so nice. *You don't need a hotel. You come stay with us.* She and I have been around it and around it. My brother tells me — well, never mind my brother. You and I can have an arrangement."

"How old is your brother?" I don't know why I asked that. I couldn't think of anything else to say. All his talk of broken marriage made me think of you when I least wanted to.

"Around my age. Thirty-one."

*Thirty*-one? The number hit me like a cold shower. I could be this man's mother. His beard hid his face — I now imagined the skin underneath smooth and fresh and full of healthy colour — and I hadn't paused in our steady march to his bed to consider his age. I am not naive enough to think of these types of rendezvous as more than smoke and mirrors, but I did not want anything to do with a mirror reminding me I'd been playing at the game so long I could have birthed this hairy, lustful creature.

The mirror you held up at the end sure didn't appeal to me either. God, the list of names you called me: Martyr. Controlling. Liar. Irresponsible. Delusional. Inadequate. You said I eclipsed you. I stole all the light. I left you no room for yourself. "With you," you said, "I don't even know who I am." Arrogant. Unfaithful. Mean.

*Look at you* — holding my chin toward the glass. *Open your eyes. Just look at you.*

No matter how different my men, this part stayed the same, the way self-knowledge faded in response to competition from someone else's version of me, a man's idea of who I was and what he thought I wanted overshadowing the conscious, breathing me standing right in front of him.

I tried an older guy for the first time, thinking his age might make me feel young and fit and desirable. My sister called him

Montreal Moneypants. That one was smart enough to understand the imaginary aspect of relationships, to manipulate the fantasy, to use the make-believe of it all to his advantage. Holed up in the sleeping cubby of his Mercedes Sprinter Van (remember how badly you always wanted one of those?), he and I kissed until my lips chapped. "You take care of everyone." *Kiss kiss.* "Imagine if someone took care of you. Imagine!" *Kiss kiss kiss.* "Even one day a week, if I said, *You carry everyone. Let me carry you.*" *Kiss kiss kiss.* "I'll take care of you." *Long kiss, fingers stroking my collarbone, the base of my neck.* "What about Tuesdays? I'll take care of you on Tuesdays."

Montreal Moneypants wasn't always so gentle though. Once his full soft lips had lulled me into drowsiness, he liked to clasp both hands around my neck and squeeze. He didn't stop my breath, but the choking scared me. You'd never done that. I didn't know how to respond. Should I have stopped him?

"Can I slap you in the face," he asked me once, his eyes glazed with lust. "Do you like that? Do you like being hit in the face?" He pushed up on his forearms, holding his body above mine, lifting one hand to my cheek. "I'd like to hit this face. You want it?"

No. God. No.

But I did let him spank me.

I posed for him on the floor of his van, my pants around my knees, my ass in the air. The excitement came in the waiting, the vulnerability, the absolute transfer of power, but also later, in the red and swollen skin, the lasting sting.

"I spanked you so hard," he said gently, as we ate by candlelight on a picnic table next to his van, scallop pasta with cherry tomatoes. "There's no point spanking at all, unless it's hard." He looked so pleased with himself, his smile reminding me of yours all those years ago in Banff. *Oh my ... please ... God ... eleven.*

I smiled back, not knowing what else to do, unable to put together an appropriate sentence, all my attention drawn to this new kind of pain, the cheeks of my ass raw and burning.

That imagined day that he offered me? The one where he would take care of me, the day on which he would carry my load? That Tuesday never came, of course. I learned to say yes to all his ideas — yes, let's go mountain biking in Utah, skiing in Austria, surfing in Bali; yes, I'll come to your conference in New York, your friend's wedding in the Baha, your research trip to France; sure, we'll read that book / see that film / go to that band / run that marathon together together together together — knowing none of it would happen. He had a way of making sure I knew not to press him, or even question.

"I'm a busy man."

He was there when he was there. He offered what he offered.

Montreal Moneypants liked to grab my hair at the nape of my neck just before I came. He pulled hard enough to snap my head. "It's primal" — he'd grin into my face — "pulling your hair hard like this. Right at the base of your skull. So raw." He yanked. "So animal. You like it. I know you do, you and your hunger, your needs. You like it." I worried his hand would jerk away with a chunk of my scalp. "You hungry, hungry woman. *You like it.*"

It was exciting, I guess, to let a situation get so very far out of my control.

The family guy from Winnipeg was the gentlest and kindest — no man had ever treated me so well — but one idea haunted me, a belief, just starting to come into focus, that being with him — being with anyone — required the invention of an unreal version of myself.

With his two boys and my three, we had a full hockey line, challenging other families on the cul-de-sac to take us on. The joining of families brought so much joy to me and the kids in those early sad months after you extracted yourself from our lives. Bonfires and chairlifts and hot springs and board games. Chocolate fondues and pizza nights and BeaverTails and burger-building contests. The children made life better, and then Winnipeg Wonder and I added the thrill of keeping our adult-time secret, that delicious contrast between the sunny, playful afternoons and the certain dark things that one man and one woman can get up to while children sleep.

He always wanted more of my body — rubbing it, stroking it, clutching it. He loved to talk about the pleasure he took in me, to describe the struggle of entering me, how tightly my pussy grabbed his cock, how he had to force his way in. The first times we fucked, he apologized for how fast he came, but eventually he believed me when I said I loved how quickly he lost control in my arms, his overwhelming excitement at being inside me, the instant release. Afterward, he stroked my pussy, still wet with his cum, making me convulse and shiver and scream, again and again. One time, he rolled away from me, laughing. "I think you're shitting me, how much you orgasm, you just keep doing it. It's too easy."

He was so different from you, who always took my orgasmic talents as clear evidence of your own skill.

I would have stayed with this arrangement for a long time — the family movies in the evening and the slippery, throbbing fun in the dark — but he became difficult, always wanting more of me, too much, texting all day long.

*I just had a shower, thinking of you,* he'd text. *I'm still steaming.*

I got that message standing in line at the bank, when I didn't want to know what he was doing in his shower.

*I'm in bed with you on my mind. I love remembering the noises you make.*

That one came while I sat in the principal's office at my oldest kid's school, talking about math. It felt intrusive, non-consensual, to have his bed and my noises appear at the school.

Even this one — *Are your kids in a shit mood today? Mine sure are* — bothered me.

"I hate all the iPhone time," I told him. "You text, text, text. I can't even breathe. I despise texting. Stop! Just stop it!"

Truthfully, it wasn't the texting I hated but the way his text messages made clear that he wasn't fixated on me but on a version of me who lived only in his head, a version whose kids were bad on the same days his kids were bad, a version who was always thinking about fucking him at the exact same moment he was thinking about fucking me.

All flings depend on this foundation of fantasy, the relationship with a phantom other who lives only in our head. Constantinople Cutie. Montreal Moneypants. The Winnipeg Wonder. All different, yet the same. But marriage is a fantasy too, the most elaborate one of all. The fantasy of a secure future. The fantasy of knowing an other, of being known, of knowability itself.

Even after decades together, you don't know me.

I certainly do not know you.

I cut the phrase out of our legal agreement, all your "shall not write about … in either fiction or nonfiction …" business, and I taped it above my computer screen.

I highlighted SHALL NOT WRITE.

A promise to not write is like a promise of celibacy.
Impossible to keep.

A year later, I began a story.

# Praying Mantis

## 1.

HOW ARE YOU? YOU SEEM WELL. YOU SEEM WELL RESTED.
Your hair is artfully messy. You are calm, deliberate. Reserved.

You say I look thin. There is no tenderness in your voice.

I say, Not really *that* thin.

Are you okay, you say flatly.

Yes, I say, and feel a sudden jolt of joy. I want to grab your
hand, put it against my chest, see if you can feel ... *it* — it
pulsates and smiles inside me, the creation — not creature —
that's hatched and that's still too fragile, resting at this time but
sometimes expanding so hard and far I am no longer me but
*it*. Its beauty overwhelms me; I am giddy with its arrival, giddy
with the secrecy of it all too.

What is it?

No, nothing, I say. It's good to see you. I make a fist, keep
my hand to myself.

Is it.

Ouch, I say and laugh. An idiot's laughter. The *it* inside me stirs, one opaline eye looks up, then rolls in its orbit.

You don't tell me the latest story about your sexual conquest, you don't make jokes about dumb pursuits of others. You talk about politics — and real estate, of all things. It's time for me to get serious about investing, you say, your voice still flat.

I want to make an unfunny comment about the latest shipping-container trend, how tiny they are, how you could maybe buy one of those and move your torso in there, but I don't know — maybe you're buying a shipping container, maybe you're a more serious person now. You tell me that you've been getting your shit together, you've been exercising, you have memberships, and get hot shaves — imagine that — and once you say all that, you look at me a moment too long. Like I was the catalyst for your downfall and like you got better; you healed from me and here's proof.

What's on your mind? you say.

I say, Humidity index, because it really is quite wet. I watch as a bird swoops down and lands right on your head, but you don't notice, you don't know it's there. I blink and the bird is gone.

I giggle and stop giggling, then I giggle at stopping giggling, then I feel like crying. We walk past other couples. We are not other couples. I force a smile back at one, a girlfriend, or maybe she's a wife, hoping she will understand but she doesn't. She smiles even wider as if she and I *could* possibly be the same.

You look at me the way you used to but you don't do anything else, you don't stop to take my face in your hands, and so we walk, first to the water, then back, after sharing a cigarette, and I watch you watching an exhausted woman with two toddlers, trying to stuff them both into a baby carriage. You're strangely focused on them and I ask if you know who she is.

Who?

The mom.

Of course not, you say.

We walk again. I motion for us to sit down and we do, on a little hill overlooking the lake.

I blurt out, I don't know what was wrong with me. Perhaps it was the lockdown. Everyone went a little crazy. Forgive me.

You sigh and give a little cough. There's nothing to forgive.

No, but I'm really sorry, I say. (A *sorry* is so deficient it's almost offensive — why aren't there bigger words for causing pain? *Sorry* is too simple, sorry, sorry, sorry.)

Don't be, you say and then we don't talk for a long time, just sit untouching, like on a first date, all awkward and waiting for it to end.

I'm so tired, tired in my bones, in my core, the very bottom of my longing.

I prop myself on my elbows. My nipples are hard, braless. See? But you're looking ahead at the lake. I close my eyes and chant in my head, *Look at me, look at me, look at me.*

And then, suddenly, you turn and gently grab the back of my neck and you pull me toward you, and you pry my mouth open with yours, and you start to kiss me in that way I remember, the hungry, obsessed way, like a boy who just discovered a tongue.

And I grab back at you, grab the back of your head, dive my tongue right inside you, clean out your insides, your darkness, your sadness, the diamond that's turned back into coal, your pineal gland, your soul.

A praying mantis bites the head off the male and he still copulates with her, headless. Once he's done, she eats him. I am that, an insect eating you from the inside, a predator, a parasite, all those things you called me jokingly and not. At one point, you slow down, you want to stop, take a breath, but I don't let you. I have lungs bigger than my body. You know I'm not like other girls, I rarely gag — have you not thought this kiss through? Have you had no idea that I would try to kill you? By whatever means necessary, like this too.

You finally push me away and your eyes are wild, searching my face, What the fuck was that about?

I touch my lips.

A jogger runs past us and she does a double take. I want to shout after her, explain that this is not what it seems — but what is this exactly?

I gotta go, you say and get up abruptly and walk away so fast I don't have the time to lunge after you and grab your leg the way I want to.

## 2.

SEX IS A LIFE FORCE, A PHYSICAL ACT THAT IS SPIRITUAL with its power of creation and destruction.

Consider the Japanese geisha Sada Abe who killed her lover, Kichizō Ishida, by strangling him with her obi. Before that they'd spent a sweaty weekend barely separating for food or sleep, their genitals almost permanently attached. They were just like you and I used to be. There was some indication that Ishida was a willing victim. They had been playing increasingly dangerous games as his pregnant wife's cronies closed in on them.

When you open the door bleary from lack of sleep or something else, I feel it instantly, a draw, a pull that I didn't feel in the park. Different from how you were in the park, now you appear vulnerable, even physically smaller as if you were reversing back into a boy I used to see glimpses of. I like this.

*Hey baby*, I think and I smile at you, and you close your eyes and take a deep breath and open the door wider to let me in. It's like you don't have a choice. I sympathize but I also don't have a choice. Do you think I want to be here like a crazy person first thing in the morning? Yes, I do. Where else do you think I should be?

I'm not claiming to understand anything beyond rudimentary physics, but the definition of *force of attraction* is any type of force that brings objects together even if those objects are not near each other. The first force is the gravitational one. "What goes up must come down." The second is an electric force and this is the one I believe is at work with us, where one of us has lost too many electrons (you, losing me) and become positively charged and the other has gained too many electrons (me, my hunger) and become negatively charged. The attraction is instant when two objects of opposite charge are in close proximity, and the electrical force causes these objects to attract. The third force that may cause attraction is the magnetic force — when a north magnetic pole is brought into close proximity to a south magnetic force, we stick.

What? you say as I blather on about physics, and you sit down on the only unlittered surface, an office chair pushed against the wall.

I look around. What happened to your place? You're usually quite clean. There's a rust-stained blanket half thrown up on the loveseat littered with fast-food wrappers. The big chair has a mass of cables wedged in its crevices. There's a pile of clothes on the ground — laundry, clean or dirty, who knows? The glass coffee table gives the rest of the important detail to the story with its unclean surfaces and white dusty traces of whatever has been going up your nose. I count three empty baggies, but there's a little shiny white rock in a glass ashtray and there's a tiny folded square that looks untouched yet. There's glasses with various brown liquids, and one wineglass stained purple with residue on the bottom. Empty cigarette packs and another glass ashtray full. Two empty plastic pop cups. And then there's Sophie. A squishy teething toy known to every parent in countries that can afford to feed their infants expensive non-toxic rubber.

I pick up the box with the toy inside and wave it.

You look away briefly and run your hand through your hair. Then you look at me. We stare at each other for a while without talking. I watch you open the little folded square, tap some of the powder onto the glass surface of the coffee table. You've found the one clean spot. You take out a credit card, break the powder in uninspired taps, make two thin lines. You take a straw and put it against your nostril.

So is this like a nervous breakdown?

You look up, sniffing loudly. No. I don't know.

Are you okay?

I'm not. I'm fine.

I'm sorry.

You bend over the glass coffee table and chop the lines one more time, make them into two more even rows.

This is not for little girls, it's bad stuff, you gesture at the powder with the straw, press your finger against your nostril as you inhale.

What is it?

Daddy's medicine, you say, and inhale the second line. You murmur, *Daddy*, and shake your head.

We've never talked about *that*. And we won't start now.

I have no idea what to do. I don't have a plan but I especially don't have a plan for this turn of events. I walk up to you and then kneel down and lie my head on your knees, the way I used to in those star-eyed days we spent together. You would scratch my scalp, run your fingers through my hair. And you do it now but your hand shakes. It's a performance you're putting on for me. I'm uncomfortable on the floor but I don't move. I said I don't have a plan.

I do have a plan, actually, the only plan I know how to carry out.

I get off my knees, rise, and my hunger rises with me. I've been starving it, I wanted to see what will happen, and now, finally, I see, feel something shedding from within, a witch, a dragon, an egg, a phoenix, or none of these but yet some alien creature that's never been seen before, wet, silver-lavender. I am all light and titanium. And an afterbirth of scales and sinew. And thighs bathed in blood and juice, hair in the trees and howling wind and early morning mountain fog. And the ocean and all the fish. I am delirious, so many smells, flowers in the middle of a June or July kind of night, jasmine, every hair on my body electrified, I am sense itself. Your lips on mine feel charged and yet soft, a current being passed back and forth as your tongue explores the inside of my mouth, our mouths together again, sucking into each other. The kiss in the park was angry, confused, done for a show, or proof that we still want each other; this here is proof we *need* each other.

You get up and I press myself against you and I wrap my arms around your shoulders and carry us all the way to the ceiling, or at least it feels that way when, instead, you pick me up and I coil around your waist, still kissing you, drinking you, and letting you drink me back. I'm not a praying mantis now, momentarily, I am a life-giver, I am giving you my life. You are giving me yours, I feel it pulsing in your tongue, sneaking down my throat, my empty stomach, filling up my stretched-out veins.

You carry me to your bedroom and you lay me on the bed and you undress me. You are shaking all over. I don't know how long you've been up and I cannot see the ash in your skin in the darkness, but I can feel the fragile junky energy emanating from you. I caress your arms as you remove my dress, I massage your head as you pull my panties down, I keep touching you, never stopping, never not connecting with you, my hunger full-blown, my insides pulsating and waiting for everything you're about to give me.

There's a soft, large, yellow envelope on the bedside table and as you lower your head to shakily lick me between my legs, I reach for it and reach inside it and pull out the soft leather belt I knew would be there. After all, I mailed it to you earlier this week.

I am not nervous.

I feel you suck on my clit, little powerful pulls, the pressure is almost too much, almost too distracting, but I've been pre-paring for this without knowing for so long and now that I am here, it seems as if I'm just following steps I'd learned long ago, the steps I've been reciting in my sleep and while awake, un-aware of having been reciting them, but now that we're in this moment, I follow step *one, two, three,* the belt is around your neck. You look up briefly and in the semi-darkness our eyes meet. Then you dive back into my sea and you keep on sucking and I slowly move my hands away from each other. I unbend my elbows — you lose your rhythm, your tongue, your mouth trying to find the source again — and I stretch my arms wider and wider. I open my legs wider too, pull on the ends of the belt to mash your face into me; your fuel is whatever powder is helping to make this happen, baby. I love you, and you agree that I love you and you love me too, you show me, you elevate me, I rise higher and higher, my mons pubis, my mountain, and this is the only way we can be together, this is the only way I can satiate my hunger; the three of us — me, you, and my hunger — are one, no more misunderstandings, life taking the wrong turn, me filling my holes with wrong dicks, you plugging your holes with drugs. As I pull and pull — and you let me, you are complicit, you understand; none of this would be possible without you letting me — you start to cough and shake and twitch, you move your mouth away just in time for me to finally fall over the edge, explode all into myself, it's a flutter and violent bucking and my thighs clamp around your head as I orgasm right into you — your final breath.

### 3.

MAYBE THIS HAPPENED LESS POETICALLY BUT THAT'S HOW I write it out later on my phone, the white screen the only light in your apartment. It was a lot more grotesque. It takes almost five minutes for an adult to choke to death — but I don't want to think of what happened to us in those terms. What did you imagine before step one, when the soft leather touched the tired skin of your neck? I will never know.

    Once my breath steadies, I get up to look for the rubber giraffe. Maybe I will mail it to your son or daughter one day, along with a cryptic and psychotic note. *I knew your father.* I stuff the giraffe in the yellow envelope.

Briefly I try to think of ways to dispose of you. I fantasize about dropping you off on the bluffs somewhere, leaving you to get eaten by animals. But I'm exhausted; whatever strength I've had was spent on getting us to your final destination.

I fall asleep next to you and I drape your heavy arm around my concave belly. I dream of nothing. When I wake up, the day is fighting its way into the bedroom from behind the blackout blinds; it is high summer again. It is always high summer with you, and it is always hard to fight the sun.

I feel full. I love you. I love you and it doesn't matter if you love me back now, because there is no you now — this fullness, this contentment is enough. I never understood what people meant when they said it was all that we needed. What was I not getting, why couldn't I get it, why was I tired, I was tired of hearing *love, love, love.*

I've been in pain over loving you, I've debased myself, destroyed my days and my solar system, removed my sleep, focused solely on getting you back, on trying to stir something, and I made myself tragically unhappy.

But now that we're here, and now that I'm thinking about it, I know that my mistake was thinking that it was transactional, that it needed to be returned. It doesn't.

I don't need anything from you anymore. I don't need you to show up, I don't need to convince you. The gift is in me loving you, in being capable of loving this deeply and tragically, yes, but ultimately, this gift is freedom — no one can forbid me loving you, not even you. This is the power of love — it can exist independently of the parties involved. For the first time in my life, my contentment is not conditional and I am no longer hungry.

After the murder, Saba Abe told police, "Once I had killed Ishida I felt totally at ease, as though a heavy burden had been lifted from my shoulders, and I felt a sense of clarity."

# Cloudburst

AIMEE REMINGTON STOOD AT THE WINDOW OF ROOM 7 IN THE
Shamrock Motel, looking at the pool, where a woman with
long white legs slept in a lounger. She looked free. It was six
in the morning. Aimee wondered if she'd been there all night.
Had she passed out after a night of drunken revelry? Or did
she just have a boyfriend with apnea? The sky was clear but
dark clouds approached. Aimee looked over her shoulder at
her husband, sleeping on his back in the middle of the bed,
his arms and legs sprawling like suburbia. When Aimee looked
back out the window she discovered two things: the woman
was gone, and fully formed, fully erect dicks were falling from
the sky.

There were no men falling from the sky — only dicks, fully
formed and erect. Aimee thought she might still be dreaming.
Only after several failed attempts to wake herself up did she
accept that she wasn't. She stepped closer to the window to get
a better look.

The dicks were gorgeous. They were long without being too long, and had substantial girth. This was Aimee's favourite type of dick. It was as if these dicks were custom-made for her. After watching them fall for several minutes Aimee did something she'd never normally do — she opened the door of room 7 and stepped outside.

At first it was amazing. The perfectly formed cocks fell from the sky all around her. If she held out her hands she could catch as many of them as she wanted. Aimee stepped farther away from the motel and as she did something changed — the cocks became aware of her. The dicks falling from the sky started falling toward her. The cocks on the ground started moving toward her. There were so many cocks and they were everywhere and they were all focused on her. Aimee became, if not frightened, at least overwhelmed. She started running away and as she did the cocks began chasing her.

Aimee ran from the fully formed, fully erect cocks. She jumped over the cocks on the ground. She ducked and dodged the cocks falling from the sky. For several minutes she ran from the cocks, climbing a fence and running into a meadow. Then she was out of breath and a question formed in her mind — why was she running? She was aroused. What she really wanted wasn't to run from the dicks but to embrace them.

So Aimee stopped running. The cocks encircled her. They waited patiently as she took off her shoes and her dress and her underwear. She lay down on wildflowers. She spread her legs and opened her mouth and turned a bit on her side, offering her ass.

The cocks formed a line. Aimee smiled at the three cocks at the front of the line and gave a small affirmative nod. The cocks sprang into action. They were on her, hard. And after they'd had their way with her, the next three cocks got busy. All day long Aimee got fucked in her mouth and her cunt and her ass. The dicks kept falling from the sky, lining up behind her, waiting patiently for their turn and then having at her.

Hours later the last three cocks came and — just as all the others had — disappeared. Aimee lay in the grass looking up at the sky. The sun was setting. The world was full of pink. Eventually, she put her clothes back on. With the soreness provoking joy, she went back inside her motel room. Her husband continued sleeping.

Aimee silently closed the door and stepped noiselessly across the thin grey carpet. She showered. She changed her clothes. She packed and found the car keys in the right front pocket of her husband's pants. She did these things silently. Then she slipped off her wedding ring and set it on the dresser, in front of the remote, where she knew he would find it. She closed the door as quietly as she could and drove away.

# After Nicolette

IT'S ALMOST SUNSET ON A BLEAK WINTER DAY WHEN YOU
sink a knife into a gorgeous sourdough loaf. You cut a thick
slice and slide it into a pan of simmering butter; this is how
you learned to make toast without a toaster. A method that
produces a whole other exquisite something else that is less
"toast" and more lusciously chewy bread fried in nutty brown
butter. You bite into it, and a sigh escapes you. It's the caramel-
ized crunch, distinctive tang; it's soft yet springy, with a crust
so crisp it crackles and gives way to the warm salty richness of
melted fat.

Before this piece of hot bread, you harboured an increasingly intense frustration with your appetite. For example,
you hadn't eaten all day because even though you were probably hungry, you just couldn't be bothered. Nothing had been
compelling enough to drag you out of the too-soft bed in your
quaint hotel suite with its full kitchen and nostalgic nautical

decor. Essentially you were feeling sad, which, in all fairness, was an improvement from feeling nothing at all. An almost two-year-long span of feeling scarcely more than a stretched-out yawn of blankness had given way to a riotous medley of misery, fury, desperation, and some other vile emotions for which you're sure they've yet to invent names.

Your senses had been dulled since before the divorce; in fact, it seemed that your body began to curl in on itself as an act of self-preservation the moment Nicolette, your ex, asked for a separation.

Nicolette had, very calmly — with the kind of emotional detachment you now imagine a fucking asshole lacking empathy might display — explained that it had nothing to do with you. She had fallen in love with someone else and wanted to "see where that took her."

That's how she'd phrased it, like she was only asking to trade in an old ticket and hop aboard a different bus, train, or whatever.

Numb with shock, you'd listened, nodded, then left the apartment you'd shared for the previous four and a half years for a walk. Walking is how you make sense of things that don't necessarily want to make sense. It's how you attempted to process what Nicolette told you that evening. It wasn't until over an hour into your walk that your mind thawed, and many questions began to rush in, the loudest question being What the fuck?!

You'd jogged back to your place, raced up the three flights to your front door, frantically unlocked it, and barged in, shouting, "What the fuck, Nicolette?!"

But she'd already packed a bag and left.

•

YOUR HUNGER, IT USED TO BE LEGENDARY. YOU WERE proud of your voracity because it was directly proportional to your profound love for life. Your friends joked that you must have been monastic in a previous life; only someone with a lifetime of abstinence had any right to throw themself so thoroughly at every pleasure. They joked that you must be making up for lost opportunities this time around.

But Nicolette, her revelation levelled you.

Her falling in love with someone else was the only explanation she would give you. She moved out shortly after, cleaned the apartment of her and many of your shared belongings while you were on an unplanned trip to Lagos for the funeral of an old family friend. Your failing appetite was apparent, even then, to your mother, who had never spared a comment about your weight.

"Ahn ahn! This girl," she'd said a few days before your flight back to Montreal. "You haven't been eating o; what's wrong?"

You didn't tell her what was wrong because she'd never liked Nicolette, and you'd hoped that Nicolette would choose you again in the end. So you didn't want to give your mother any more reasons to dislike her. Now you wish you'd been honest; perhaps your mother could've cussed the bitch out, maybe even thrown a curse or two her way — oh yes, rage eventually ripped out from beneath your stupor.

By the time you signed the divorce papers, the robustness of your appetite felt like a distant memory. Fully functional in your despair, you threw yourself into work, previously nothing more than a means to an end, the end being money to use as you like. You became obsessive, meticulous, and speedy with your coding. You asked Femi, the chief technology officer at the start-up, for more responsibilities. But knowing you'd just had a divorce, he only scoffed and suggested you work remotely for the next few weeks.

"Your energy is a bit … manic these days; sorry if that's blunt," he'd said, wincing. You could see he was trying to be gentle. "It's just that some team members have mentioned they feel rushed, even though we're miraculously on schedule, so, yeah, take some time …"

This is what has brought you — a two-hour flight and an hour-and-sixteen-minute drive later — to Lunenburg, a tiny port town on the South Shore of Nova Scotia. You've never been before; you and Nicolette had considered it for your honeymoon but ended up going with a charming houseboat in Albufeira, Portugal, a gift from her parents.

You're in Lunenburg now, where the warm sweet aroma from a particular bakery by the boardwalk eventually drew you out of your hotel room late on your first afternoon in town. You bundled up and followed the scent. You gritted your chattering teeth against the sharp winds that cut through your layers until you found the source, a powder-blue building with massive windows and the word *Sourdough* displayed in bold white lettering on a bright red awning.

A bell above the door dinged when you opened it to enter; the heat of the bakery was already so delicious you didn't mind that there was no one at the counter.

"Be right with you," someone called out from behind the display case of bread and pastries.

"No worries," you said, your mouth watering slightly at the sight of flaky croissants, muffins chock full of nuts and chocolates, pillowy loaves of milk bread, and elaborately scored sourdoughs.

"What would you like today?" The person to which the voice belonged emerged at the counter, an umber-skinned stocky somebody with thick ropes of long dark locks and round, dimpled cheeks.

"I'm hungry," was all you could think to say.

"Well, you've come to the right place; these are all freshly baked."

"You're the baker?" You winced at your ineptitude, uncertain why you suddenly felt so awkward. You're not nearly as cool as you would like to appear, but you typically knew how to carry basic small talk.

"I am." The baker chuckled, the corners of their eyes wrinkling in amusement.

"Okay." You tried to compose yourself. "Cool, cool, cool."

"So you're hungry?" the baker coaxed.

"Yes," you nodded. "The thing is, I haven't felt this hungry in a while ...".

"I see. What are you hungry for?"

"... what would you recommend?"

"Mm." The baker feigned deliberation, stroking their chin with chipped yellow-painted fingers. "Well, the sourdough is award-winning."

"For real?"

"For real."

"Congratulations."

"Thank you!"

"I'll take a loaf."

"Which one?"

"You pick."

YOU STOPPED AT THE SMALL GROCERY STORE 'ROUND THE corner from the hotel to pick up some butter, fruit, jam, maple syrup, a bottle of sriracha, cream, overpriced avocados, and eggs. Then walked back clutching the large loaf of warm bread against your chest and wondering if you'd been flirting with the baker. If what you'd just done could be considered "flirting," if you'd even meant to flirt, or knew how to do it anymore. Though voracious, you'd never been the most forward; it was Nicolette who came on to you at that rooftop party all those years ago. You were far too high to be in public. Definitely too high to be on such a crowded patio. Your hands firmly clasping the railing as you looked up at the fat, bright moon, which seemed far too big and far too close to be real when this gazelle of a woman tapped you on the shoulder and asked if you had a light.

You didn't have a light, but she stayed anyway, asked you who you knew at the party and stared brazenly at your face as you explained that the hosts were friends of friends of friends and you were new in town.

"Where from?" she'd asked.

"Brooklyn, by way of Lagos."

"I like Nigerians." She smiled.

"That's good." You smiled back.

It was she who initiated the first time you'd fucked, in a bathroom at the cinema two days after the party.

This is what you remember now as warm butter slides down your chin, the taste of Nicolette's mouth — difficult to pinpoint precisely, but a certain zesty sweetness comes to mind. Something to do with the fruity gum she always seemed to be chewing. She had a particular way of kissing, a subtle thing she did with her tongue, like gently licking the insides of your lips or something, you're not sure exactly, but it always left you mildly desperate to be consumed. And there was how she moaned your name whenever she quivered at the brink of cumming. A familiar rush of desire tugs at a delicious swell in your abdomen, but you cannot bear any more memories of you and Nicolette because, the thing is, sex was never a problem between you two. You were always down to fuck, and she was always down to fuck, even during conflict when you could barely stand the sight of each other. Even in the back seat of your busted hatchback moments after leaving her Uncle Augustus's wake, where her aunt wept silently and stood unmoving as well-wishers offered their condolences. Augustus was her favourite uncle, and though devastated, she didn't cry over his sudden death — a fatal stroke that seized him while bent over in his garden, harvesting lemon balm, mint, and basil for tea — until after she came in the car that day. Her moans stuttered to ragged sobs after climax. "I can't believe he's gone," she'd cried repeatedly. "I can't believe he's gone."

So, no, you don't want to think of Nicolette in the summer, the season you loved her best. In the sunshine, her dark skin singed darker, her soft body barer, her smile just for you. You don't want to remember the way her eyes simmered to slits when she wanted to top, command your obedience, and ride your face before fucking you senseless. No, you really, really don't.

So another slice of bread it is then! Fried in butter again, but this one drizzled with maple syrup and a sprinkle of salt. The next piece of bread is thicker. Though you toast it without butter, you smear onto it most of an overripe avocado and a generous helping of sriracha before sinking your teeth in. Many sloppy mouthfuls later, you dust crumbs off your sweater's front. You wash your hands, and because you don't know what to do with yourself, you run a hot bath. The tub is too small to fully submerge your body, but it will do. You should put some time into work but don't want to. You want to think of the baker.

The baker with the nice shoulders and shiny eyes, nice lips too, if you remember accurately. You could imagine sliding the tip of your tongue into one of those cute little dimples. But the thing is, other than that drunken threesome that one time in Berlin, you haven't been with anyone other than Nicolette in six, close to seven years. And to be quite honest, it was incredibly hot, but it was Nicolette you had eyes on the entire time. The other woman was lovely, a full-figured American girl named Anna or Annie, something like that. She talked non-stop about her year surfing in Bali. Yes, she was gorgeous and slutty like overripe stone fruit in the height of summer, but it was Nicolette you wanted to fuck; it was her fingers you wanted in your mouth, in your cunt. But she mostly wanted to watch and touch herself from her perch at the top corner of the king bed. Then just as you were about to cum from Anna/Annie's mouth on you, Nicolette wrapped her long fingers around your neck and said, "Open your eyes, babe, look at me. Say my name as you cum."

And you did.

YOU FALL ASLEEP IN THE TUB AND DREAM OF NICOLETTE and the baker fucking against the glass doors leading to the balcony in your hotel room. Nicolette is wearing the supple leather strap you used to share and an oversized black T-shirt;

the baker is naked, and the sound escaping their throat is something between a moan and a grunt as Nicolette pounds hard into them. The baker clutches Nicolette's hips, her waist, and the back of her head, hands frantically moving to grasp something as their body rocks in ecstasy. You wake up in tepid water. It's dark outside. You are thoroughly aroused and utterly lonely, so you leave the bath and let the water drain in loud gurgles. You rub oil into your skin slowly before crawling into bed with your laptop in search of any decent porn. You are on a free porn site, the kind that usually sends a spike of anxiety through you because it doesn't align with your ethics. Still, the guilt makes the viewing all the more delicious. You don't allow your mind to wonder if the performers are adequately paid for their work, if they've consented to these particular videos being made available on this specific site; you simply sink into the hunger. You've brought no toys or lube on this trip because you had no reason to; now you berate yourself. You suck on your fingers as one of the actors, a tall busty femme with long red acrylic talons, sucks on the bared nipples of another tall busty femme, bound and suspended into submission with elaborate shibari ties. Red talon femme kisses, sucks, and teases bound femme until she begs to be fucked. All the while, you touch but never let yourself cum. You fall asleep with the light of the computer screen glaring in your face.

TOO EMBARRASSED TO RETURN TO THE BAKERY, YOU GET coffee from Number 9 Coffee Bar, a sleek café across the street from your hotel. The barista is cheerful and friendly, a curly haired cutie with a gold septum ring and a deep-cut V-neck showing off her freckled tits. The word *vixen* comes to mind the moment your eyes fall on her face, but you feel like shit and are very much not in the mood to subtly investigate the sexual orientation of every vaguely attractive person you meet in this postcard of a town.

You get your order — an oat milk flat white and large scone chock full of candied pieces of maple bacon and generous chunks of smoked cheddar — to go and wander down to the waterfront. The dock is slippery with tricky patches of black ice; you sort of slide and sidestep your way toward a cold bench at the edge closest to the rippling water.

Another frosty day, but the skies are clear and sunny. The water's surface glitters in brilliant bursts of light, and though you would like to rot in your funk, you find the weight in your chest lightening a bit.

The coffee is tepid when you get to it, but its flavour is robust and comforting even then. You scarf down the scone, a perfect blend of sweet, salty, and creamy. Damn, you enjoy it!

You might as well put some time into work, so decide to head back to your computer at the hotel. You walk past a bookstore with a sign reading *Lunenburg Bound*, past the vintage record store. You consider going to the bakery for another loaf or some other kind of treat and maybe to see if the hot baker is there. But you lose confidence a few steps away from the entrance. Ugh, you don't want to be a creep, and anyway, maybe the conversation from the day before only seemed flirtatious to you because you're incredibly sad and increasingly horny; you laugh at this thought, laugh at yourself, and decide not to go into the bakery after all. Best to hold fast and nurture whatever little scraps of dignity and self-respect you may still have.

However, you can't help yourself — you look through the bakery window as you walk past and see the baker at the counter. You smile sheepishly, raise and shake your hand slowly from side to side in a lazy wave. The baker's face lights up in recognition; they smile a big smile and wave you into the shop. You hesitate at the doorway momentarily before entering. Inside, a saxophone plays fluidly over a laid-back, groovy beat; instinctively, you bob your head to the music. The heady aroma of all those pastries — sweet, yeasty, malty, chocolatey, cinnamony, vanilla-y — it's nostalgic; it brings a warm, warm hug to mind and makes your mouth water. The baker's bashful smile leaves you feeling both shy and flattered.

"Hey," you say.

"Hey! Good to see you again! How did you like the sourdough?"

"It was great, yeah, I ate it all." You chuckle.

"Well done!" The baker laughs and nods. "You still hungry?"

"I could eat." You shrug.

"Why don't you try the focaccia today?"

"Yeah?"

"Yeah, it's a sourdough focaccia," the baker says, gesturing to the glass display case of loaves of bread. "With apples and cranberry and thyme."

"Sounds fucked up." You nod and smile, then add quickly, "Fucked up as in good, I'll try it."

"You won't be disappointed," the baker promises.

You point to a glistening pastry resembling a palm-sized parcel of many folded sheets. "What's this about?" you ask.

"Ah, that's a *kouign-amann*, one of my favourite things to make."

You raise one eyebrow in a question.

"You should try it," the baker suggests.

"Yes, please, I'll take two."

You pay and start to leave when the baker stops you. "I'm Silas, by the way!"

"Nice to meet you, Silas; I'm Khadijah."

"Nice to meet you too, Khadijah. That's a lovely name."

"Thank you."

You smile at each other for a moment, then Silas adds, "I don't know how long you're in town for, but we do this weekly-ish Beer and Bread thing."

"Beer and bread?"

"Yeah, folks from a few of the bakeries and breweries have a fire, some food, some —"

"Beer and bread?" you add, laughing.

"Yeah!" Silas joins your laughter. "Yeah, the next one is tomorrow if you're around and into it."

"I'd love to."

THAT NIGHT YOU EAT THE FOCACCIA WITH A SALAD OF CU-cumbers, red onions, soft-boiled eggs, parsley, and mint, dressed in olive oil, lemon, maple syrup, and salt. You revel at the softness of the bread, the tartness of the apples and cranberries cutting through the richness of the dough in all the right ways. The eggs in the salad are cooked precisely how you prefer them — yolk, a bright custard almost liquid in the middle. You scroll through your social media feed as you eat. Though you've blocked each other on most platforms, you see a picture of Nicolette and her new lover on a mutual friend's profile. Of course, a jolt of panic runs through you

— you hadn't expected to see pictures of her anywhere since you'd meticulously ensured this. And yet there she is in the embrace of a broad beauty with arms and neck covered in tattoos and a tumbling mane of dark curls. Many emotions rush to your surface, but you cannot help yourself; you click on her new lover's profile and see that her feed is filled with pictures of her and Nicolette. She and Nicolette in a tent, her and Nicolette on a hike in lush dark green woods, her and Nicolette on a beach in Barcelona, climbing in a bouldering gym in Montreal, kissing in the mist of a waterfall in wherever the fuck.

Without looking away from the screen, you fetch a mini kouign-amann from the paper bag by your bed and bite into it.

The thing is, you are certain Nicolette was cheating on you before she ever told you about being in love. You'd asked her when you signed the divorce papers; you'd looked her directly in the face and asked, voice cracking, "So all I get is that you're in love with someone else, huh? That's pretty psychotic, Nico, but I need to know if you cheated and for how long."

She never confirmed or denied it; she just shook her head and said coolly, "I'm really sorry that it's happened this way."

"You did it this way," you'd shouted. "You've done this! You're doing this!" Then you stormed out of the lawyer's office so they wouldn't see you break down in tears.

You scroll through her new lover's profile for a while and piece together that she's an EMT and very into weightlifting, being outside, and being with Nicolette. You wish you could warn her, say something cruel like, "Nico is going to ruin your life" or "She's going to chew you up and spit you out." But even in your vindictive fantasy, that's much too cliché, and the truth is that you don't know; maybe Nicolette will be good to the tattooed EMT, perhaps they'll be good to each other, and it will keep working out.

Your relationship and marriage to Nicolette were good as far as you can account for. You felt comfortably in love and thought your partnership was balanced and complementary. You don't know that there was anything "wrong" other than Nicolette falling in love with someone else and presumably falling out of love with you. You don't know because she never told you, and you're still working through how to move through this remarkably uneventful but wildly shocking wounding.

There's a picture of Nicolette's new lover in her navy blue uniform with her hair tied back, and her chin lifted so she is looking, unsmiling, down at the camera. You look at this photo, with her defined jawline and smouldering eyes, and think, *I get it.*

You imagine Nicolette grasping a fistful of her curls and commanding her mouth open before spitting into it. It's effortless to imagine this, effortless to see Nicolette commanding her lover to her knees before grinding her cunt on her face as if that is where it belongs. You put your phone away and wet your fingers with spit before touching yourself to memories of Nicolette's mouth, the taste of her cunt, and the way her fingers felt inside you. It feels good, and you so badly want to feel good. You want to disappear into bliss for a moment, but climax eludes you. You've rubbed yourself tender, and now all you can do is lie in your bed, in your sadness. Eventually, you just let yourself cry and fall into a fitful sleep.

THE NEXT DAY, THOUGH YOU'RE NERVOUS ABOUT ATtending Silas's Beer and Bread thing, you're also impatient for the evening to fall. You can't always tell the difference between nervousness and excitement in your body; they both incite a racing heart and queasiness in your gut. You work all morning through the afternoon, taking short breaks to eat what's left of yesterday's salad and the second kouign-amann. Earlier in the morning, you'd blocked Nicolette's new lover to create at least one additional barrier — even if only virtual and truly flimsy at best — between you and another evening of obsessing over your ex-wife.

With your work done, you shower, oil your body, and draw on some eyeliner before rolling a thick joint and heading down to the water. You smoke, watching the sun cast blood orange and purple light across the choppy water as it sinks slowly beneath the shimmering horizon. The wind whips your scarf and braids around your face, making you giggle. Seagulls squawk as they glide over the water, some finding perch on the posts along the dock.

You take out your phone and call your friend Celine; the phone rings for a long while, and you're just about to hang up when you hear her voice.

"Hey, girl," she pants. "How's life in the Maritimes?" You hear a tap running in the background.

"I'm looking at the water right now. How are you?"

"Good, washing baby shit off my favourite jeans."

"Yikes, how's Baby doing?"

"Other than having explosive diaper shituations? Great!" She laughs. "He's funny and keeps me on my toes."

"Toes are a good place to be."

"No other way to be for me."

You listen to each other's silence before Celine breaks it. "How's your heart, bud?"

"Beating," you reply. "Hey, a hot baker invited me to a thing this evening."

"You gonna go?"

"What do you think?"

"I think you should definitely go."

"Okay, I will. I want to."

"Let me know how it goes, babe."

You let Celine get back to swooning over her toddler, snuff your joint, and walk toward the bakery. It's dark when you get to it and find a piece of paper taped to the door. The message — "Beer and Bread in the bakery courtyard, go through the green gate on the left side" — scribbled on with black marker, as is an arrow pointing toward a wooden gate with bright green paint peeling off of it.

The smell of fire greets you, as does the din of a cheerful gathering. The courtyard, with a fire at its centre, is past the entrance and through a narrow alley. Wooden benches surround it, and folks roast sausages and marshmallows in the blazing coals. The yard is packed with more people than you've seen in your three days here; you assume they are locals, maybe a few sad strays like yourself. You spot Silas across the yard, squatting down and attempting to fit a bright pink toque over the large head of a squirming child. You wander over and wave hello.

"Hey! Khadijah, hi!" Silas says, standing up quickly. The child squeals and scurries away — their toque tumbles down their head and to the floor.

Laughing, you pick it up and hand it to Silas.

"That's my nephew, Benny," they say, exasperated. "I'm on last-minute sitting duty."

"I see."

"Anyway, hey! Thanks for coming."

"Thanks for inviting me. I was looking forward to this all day."

"Aw shucks." Silas motions for you to follow. "You should meet some pals."

You weave through the party with Silas, smiling, nodding, and shaking hands as they introduce you to friends, fellow bakers, brewers, small business owners, and neighbours. Then they bring you to a petit person with a shaved head and bleached brows assembling graham crackers, a piece of chocolate, and a burnt marshmallow to make a s'more.

"This is my partner, Saoirse."

"Oh hey." Saoirse gets up and offers a hug. "My hands are too sticky for a handshake!"

"I'm Khadijah," you say, accepting the hug and laughing at yourself; of course, the baker has a partner.

"So nice to meet you!" Saoirse says brightly. "Yeah, Silas hasn't stopped talking about you."

At this, Silas shrugs sheepishly and adds, "I've mentioned you, like, twice."

Saoirse only laughs. "Would you like something to drink?"

"Sure, yeah, what are my options?"

"Hot cider, mulled wine, and cold beer."

"I'll have a mulled wine."

With a hot cup of wine in hand, you perch on a bench by the fire with Silas, Saoirse, and a few other folks you won't remember.

"So, what's your story?" Saoirse asks. "Where are you visiting or moving from?"

"Visiting from Montreal, yeah, hiding out for a bit."

"Hiding out?" Silas asks.

"Yeah." You laugh. "That was a dramatic way of putting it."

"What are you hiding from?"

"Ah, just, uh, a bit of heartbreak." You wince at your words, then shrug.

"Oh, I know all about that." Saoirse sighs. "Is it fresh?"

"We officially divorced about a year ago, but she left me about a year before that."

"Damn," from Silas.

You laugh, light-headed and loose-lipped from the wine. "Damn, yeah, she 'fell in love with someone else.'"

"How long were you together?"

"About seven years."

"And that's it? She just fell in love with someone else?"

"That's all I got."

"Cold-blooded."

"Brutal."

"So you figured the South Shore was a good place to escape?"

"Yeah, as good a place as any. I'd never been here before, and I don't know anybody here, so nothing to remind me that I've deteriorated into a husk of my former self."

All three laugh loudly and for a long time at this.

"I'm sorry," Silas says eventually.

"Yeah, that really sucks," Saoirse adds. "But anyway, you know us now, and Silas has a bit of a crush on you."

"Jesus." Silas blushes and gently smacks Saoirse on the arm.

"Honestly, same," you reply, laughing. "How long have you two been together?"

"Mm, since college, so about thirteen years, maybe?" Silas looks to Saoirse to confirm.

"Thirteen-ish, about that, yeah."

"Wow, you're married?"

"In a way, yes, we're nesting partners."

"Poly?"

"Yeah, more or less ... We've definitely both 'fallen in love' with other people or whatever, but we also fall in love with each other all the time."

"You're going to have to tell me how that works." You mean to be lighthearted, but who knows how that landed.

Someone begins to drum on a bench, and another person joins in. Someone else calls for a speaker, and soon the smooth hypnotic rhythm of Gyptian's "Hold You" fills the courtyard. Not at all what you expected at this gathering, but you like it and start to sway a bit.

"Anyway, Silas, you're a baker," you say. "Saoirse, what do you do?"

"I'm a nurse practitioner!"

"That's so cool."

"Yeah, I think so too," Saoirse says and hands you a lit joint. "What are you doing tomorrow?"

"Ooh, thank you." You hold the smoke in your lungs before answering with a slight cough. "The same thing I do every day — mope around, work, eat."

Silas laughs at this. "It's supposed to be really nice tomorrow; we're going for a hike on the bluffs if you'd like to join?"

"Sure, I'd really like to." You pass the joint to Silas and drink the final dregs of your third cup of wine. "What time?"

"Around two?"

"Perfect." You get up to stretch. "Thank you for inviting me and for listening to my sad divorce story."

Silas and Saoirse laugh; you laugh, accept another cup of wine, and join a circle of dancers around the fire. Soon Silas also joins in the dancing, and Saoirse falls into another conversation. You dance until you're sweaty, until your body and Silas's body are only a breath away from touching. You hold each other's gaze for long moments, even after Saoirse joins in the dancing.

"I'm going to head back to my hotel," you say too loudly because you're a bit drunk.

"Would you like some company?" Saoirse asks, placing a gentle hand on your shoulder. "Or a nightcap?"

"Um, tonight I'm crashing hard and heavy." You chuckle. "But please, ask me again before I leave?"

"Will do." Silas smiles, eyes as glossy.

"When do you leave?" Saoirse asks.

"In a week or so."

"Well, I'll definitely be asking again."

You want to press your lips against Saoirse's shorn head and feel the prickly stubble of new growth. You want to run a shaky finger across her lips. You're curious about how they fuck, Saoirse and Silas; you suspect Silas enjoys being told what to do. You'd like to watch, slip yourself into whatever space there might be between them; you'd like to be their plaything for a night. But not tonight — you hug them, thank them for inviting you, and say you'll see them tomorrow.

You stumble home, tipsy enough to be unconcerned with the freezing winds whistling past you. It's been a minute since you felt so light. Who knows what great grief will descend upon you in the morning, but tonight? Tonight you're doing all right. You're basically skipping through the empty hotel lobby, cheerfully inebriated.

Back in your room, you take off your coat, peel off your dark jeans and white thong, and climb onto the king-sized bed whose sheets have been replaced with fresh, crisp white ones.

Straddling one of the oversized pillows, you reach one hand under your sweater to your nipples, the other between your sore thighs and touch yourself. For the first time in a long while, you don't think of Nicolette. You don't think of anything at all. You fall so slowly, so deliciously into the tension pulsing inside you. Cautiously, curiously, you ride the waves of pleasure gathering momentum in your abdomen as you grind against the pillow. A funny thing, you envision the moon; you've always done this whenever you play with yourself, no idea why. You imagine the moon growing full, full, fuller as you draw closer to climax. The moon is full when you peak, then it bursts, and it shatters into infinite glittering constellations that sear so bright on the inside of your eyelids. You soak the pillow in warmth, letting a loud high-pitched moan rip through you as you cum. You collapse into the bed, gasping, laughing in delight.

# Calliope

SHE WAS MIDDLING, IN A PHYSICAL SENSE, WAS MY COLD-hearted assessment, neither his most fetching nor his most revolting. But there was something about her that appealed to me. A joie de vivre, the sound of tinkling bells when she laughed. She lifted herself onto his dissection table, spread her legs.

"Like this?" she said.

A mound of ginger pubes pushing at her underpants.

She was twenty, she had told him — well past a marriageable age to be sure, even if she hadn't already defiled herself so completely. Her name, she said, was Calliope. The doctor had met her at Pitié Salpêtrière, on a visit to the morgue. She worked there, boiling gauze and cleaning sinks.

"Yes, just like that," the doctor said and, kneeling down, peeled off her panties and buried his face in her flea-ridden thicket.

Her eyes, so pale they appeared colourless, upturned to take in her surroundings — the doctor's flasks and forceps, splayed frog bodies, listing towers of books, cupboards crammed with tinctures, cabinet displays of shrunken heads and other curiosa, a cot, a piss-pot, bottles of rotgut, salted hocks hanging from a ceiling hook, a tangle of human spines piled in one corner, inkpots and pens, illustrated pornography of the most florid and transgressive nature, and an octopus, too large for its tank, floating listlessly in brackish water. Calliope was avoiding my gaze, steadfast in her refusal to acknowledge my presence there.

"Oh. Doctor," she said between gasps. "You. Are. An. Enthusiast."

At length, he disengaged from his inquiries and, wiping his mouth, said, "Please, dear, call me François. Are you close, or do you require some additional intervention?"

Her pallid face had turned rosy. "I am more concerned, François, with how I might satisfy you. What is your pleasure?"

*On your knees*, I commanded her.

"I find most pleasure, dear girl," he demurred, "in giving pleasure."

*On your scabby knees*, I commanded her.

"Well, what gives me pleasure," she said, "is this."

She tugged down her frock, unsheathed her bosoms. And then — just as I'd directed — fell to her knees, wrestled down his trousers, and unfurled his member.

"Shall I kiss it?" she said.

"If you'd like," François said.

And so she did.

And when François was done, some minutes later, Calliope made a show of swallowing his ejecta.

"May I ask you something?" she said then.

The doctor gripped the table to keep himself upright. "Whatever you'd like," he said.

"That thing," she said. "What is it?"

François glanced in my direction.

"What, you mean René?"

"It gives me the willies."

The doctor pulled Calliope to her feet. "Now, now," he said. "Don't be unkind." He nudged her forward, to the table on which I sat. "This is my best friend," he said.

The two of them gazed upon me, the doctor's kind regard, Calliope's astonished face.

I saw myself then as she saw me, reflected as I was in the humours of her eyes. How … ghastly. A brain, afloat in life-giving liquid, two eyeballs attached by the most frail of stalks, mutely watching.

"This is René," the doctor said. "René, I'd like you to meet my new friend, Calliope."

RENÉ, HE'D NAMED ME, AFTER DESCARTES, HIS IDOL FROM childhood.

More often, however, I felt like Renée, after de Créquy, the marquise.

It was a source of no small anxiety, this disparity between the doctor's understanding of me and my own. For who was I, after all? There had been a time before this one, this life in my home-jar. I had imperfect access to it now and again. Onrushing almost-memories, fractured glimpses, like shards of broken mirror: a smell — perfume; a half-remembered voice; the flaring of a gas lamp on a cobblestone road. A previous me. And who had that been? How I longed for a body to find out. To have appendages, like the doctor, like his friend, what bliss!

Was I one of these whiskered ones, like François, with a swinging thing between my legs, or one of the others, like his many visitors, their pleasure parts hidden like grottos?

IT HAD BEEN SOME YEARS SINCE MY FIRST BRIGHT SPARK of awareness. I recalled my awakening imperfectly. I had been deeply asleep and then — a jolt. François's face was the first thing I saw. Such a face it was. My love for him was instant.

And his, I dare say, was likewise. From that original moment, I was his confessor, his unspeaking oracle. He told me his secrets, his fears and desires, in the certainty, I suppose, that I would never tell — would never have a mouth with which to tell.

In the years that followed, I beheld his every mood. I watched him haggle with the landlord, with the bread man. I spent hours gazing at the crown of his head as he bent over volumes of obscure medieval texts. I witnessed his macabre experiments upon flesh both living and dead: human bodies, terrified octopi, beasts plucked lifeless from the cobblestones. I cast my eyes downward as he wept inconsolably, or desolately pleasured himself, or chortled maniacally at some insult he had devised for a member of the medical academy. I watched him, delirious with anger or frustration, grab beakers from the shelves and smash them into clouds of dust against the wall.

"Damn those pedants at the academy," he said to me, often. "Damn their tiny minds."

He was a pampered, handsome boy. I call him a boy, but he was well into his twenty-fifth year. He had lips like flower petals and soft blond hair, depthless eyes betraying thought and worry. He was the son — so he informed me in a fit of rum-sodden introspection — of an unhappy mother and an exacting father, both now dead. They had been wealthy — enough to put him through an education at l'Université de Poitiers — but these days, due to his extravagant appetite for science, laudanum, and prostitutes, François's inheritance, once an ebon mass, had been nibbled to a hillock. The current day had reduced him to a rented garret in the second arrondissement. His taste for women, undiminished in bankruptcy, had adjusted to account for his new circumstances. No longer scented and expensive, his visitors now were pustulous tavern slags in fetid frocks, or else washerwomen — young plump widows happy enough to bend over his table, lift up their skirts, and offer their dimpled rumps.

I watched his encounters with these women at close range, my eyes bobbing in my life-liquid with the rhythm of their passions, their thrusts and moans, their entreaties to please fuck them harder.

I didn't bother to remember their faces or names. The doctor never had return visitors.

Never, that is, until the day that Calliope returned.

THEY HAD COME INTO THE FLAT TOGETHER, SHE AND François, on this second date, in raucous mood, having — how coincidental — bumped into one another at his favourite café. She twirled her hair as they conversed, slapped at his arm, playful, when he made some ribald comment. Then they collapsed in sudden embrace onto the floor and performed in short order all of the Latin acts: fellatio, cunnilingus, *irrumātiō*, pedicatio.

When they were done, they engaged in post-coital chatter too tedious to relate, then Calliope rose, nude but for one errant stocking, rearranged her hair, approached my home-jar, spoke.

"René," she said.

Her ingratiating smile loomed, enlarged and distorted by my life-liquid. "It's lovely to meet you again, René. Aren't you a wonderful friend."

I did not care who François fornicated, or how often, or in what fashion. It was a biological imperative for the appendaged. But this awkward blandishment — it spoke of something more pitiful. She was smitten, the poor dear. I felt sorry for her in that moment. It was I who was his *complice*.

After that second encounter, her visits occurred with increasing frequency, much to my regret. Their intimacies moved from his dissection table to the beetle-eaten cot upon which he'd spent so many hours gratifying himself. From beneath his writhing blanket came their howls and exclamations, followed always by a period of light snoring. All of which served as prelude to a nauseating display in which she would fuss and dote like some hovering nanny: straightening his lancets, fetching him pastries from the *boulangerie*, scrubbing his intimates in the bucket she'd filched from the hospital, even administering an overdue haircut, flourishing her scissors as he sat upon a stool like a little boy, towel draped over shoulders.

"Aren't you the handsome one!" she had said when she had finished.

These furious ministrations persisted for some weeks. When Calliope was about, François ignored me; when she was not, he slumped in his armchair and pined.

•

"RENÉ," HE SAID ONE DAY. "DEAR FRIEND, LO ALL THESE years. Perhaps you've noticed something unusual. A strangeness in me. A change in patterns, an oddness in demeanour."

Well, but of course I had noticed this "change in patterns." Everything about our lives had changed since that woman's arrival. His working hours had become muddled with his Calliope hours. In evenings he disappeared, returning only at dawn's birdsong, filthy, exhausted. His important research interrupted now with yawns and armpit scratches, short naps with mouth agape, drooling upon the dissection table.

"Only, there's a good reason for it," he said. "You see, I have found the need to take on some extra work. Unsavoury work, I'm sorry to say ... bodysnatching, if you must know. For the medical school. The payment for which has allowed me to purchase this."

From the inner pocket of his jacket he pulled a crimson velvet bag, shook its contents onto the palm of his hand.

A thin brass loop.

A ring.

He stared at the thing with reverence, as though it were a sacred object.

"I am a stranger to myself, René. I have ... fallen in love. Such a circumstance, I admit, is improbable. But I've run the numbers and found it nevertheless to be the case. The young lady you have seen round here with some regularity. I intend to take her as my wife, should she agree."

*I hope she dies*, I thought, *wretched and alone.*

François secured the ring in the bag and stuffed the bag in the pocket above his heart. "I will ask her tomorrow," he said.

•

THE NEXT DAY, HOWEVER, SHE DID NOT COME.
Fifteen minutes after her usual arrival time, François consulted his timepiece. Fourteen minutes later he did it again. These half-hours accumulated, and as they did I watched him grow more agitated. He would pick up a book for distraction, only to set it down again immediately. He'd rush to the window and peer down at the alleyway below. After a prolonged episode of whimpering, he pulled on his overcoat and abandoned the flat.

The octopus undulated in its tank.

The sun went down, and stayed down, and rose again, pink streaks and dust motes through the mottled glass, before the door clattered, a key in the lock, and François, pale as a frog's spleen, eyes rheumatic, stumbled into the flat.

He carried with him a jar.

He placed this jar on the table beside me, then located a bottle of liquor and another of laudanum, and dropped to the floor, out of sight. For some hours he stayed there, recumbent, his laments like some tortured circus beast. I drifted my eyes over to the jar beside me, but already I knew what it contained: I could feel Calliope inside, pulsing weakly.

She had perished, so François later confided, when in a freak cloudburst, the spire of a Catholic church detached itself, tumbled to the street, and dashed her skull.


FRANÇOIS FELL INTO SOME WEEKS OF DESPAIR AFTER
this — weeks in which he kept to his noxious cot, weeks in

which his work went neglected, his experiments rotted in their jars. But the weeks that followed his return to health were no better, and in some ways worse, as old habits returned to him, albeit in more disturbing form.

The washerwomen, yes, and sluts from nearby cafés. Only this time, all of his guests bore a resemblance to his dead lover: fine-boned, pale, ginger.

His transactions with these impostor Calliopes were decidedly less lovely than with the original. He insisted, for instance, that they bind him with ropes and defile him in every manner: flogging him till his buttocks bled; brutalizing his manhood with candle flames; urinating into his forsaken face. Their reticence turning always, after a few lashes of the whip, into a mad enthusiasm.

All the while I felt Calliope beside me, her disordered alpha waves attempting to cohere. There was no rivalry between us, not anymore. I would have liked to connect with her, but in her weakened state it was to little purpose. I pitied her, she who had once been so gazelle-like. If it was painful for me to watch the dissolution of François, it must have been agonizing for her.

"YOU HAVE A PROBLEM," FRANÇOIS SAID TO HIMSELF ONE evening, after a particularly zealous session that required in its aftermath the attentions of a medical school acquaintance.

"Think it through," he said. He paced the floor, forefingers pressed into temples. "Think," he said. "Think."

Then snapping his fingers, stopped. As if in the throes of some whimsy, he bolted to the hat peg, grabbed his bowler, and rushed out the door.

He returned the next day in the company of an enormous cross-eyed fellow. Between them they carried a long, sagging canvas sack. They heaved it onto the dissection table. Thus relieved, François nodded at the behemoth and handed him some coins.

When the giant was gone, François located some shears and snipped the sack down the middle. The canvas fell away and there emerged from within the face of a young woman — small, pale, ginger.

Who was this unfortunate? Was she one of his flagellators, or some other who had found her way to the morgue? I could not say. With much flailing, François hoisted her from the table and deposited her in one of his fish tanks. Then browsing his shelves, plucked out an armful of books and, dropping them onto his desk, sat down to read.

There ensued a period of intense study. Days, weeks, the treetops turning from green to red, the ginger girl afloat in her tank, François flipping pages, jotting notes, taking no time to eat, drowsing at intervals in his chair.

At length, he said, as if to himself, "That's it." He straightened his papers. Rose. Yawned. Passed wind. Smiled. "That's it."

François announced his intention to visit a Turkish bath.

His return, hours later, found him much restored: bathed, shaved, colour in his cheeks. He came immediately to me. "My dearest René," he said. "With me all this time, never judging. My confidante, my boon companion." François gripped my home-jar, lifted it to his face. "I offer you now, dearest chum, an evolution of our friendship."

Could it be? Was he really saying what I thought he was saying?

I glanced at the girl in her bath of brine. Was this who I would become? Would I finally own a body and limbs with which to embrace him? I dare not even think it, lest the dream slip away like a mote in the eye.

The doctor plucked a vial from his tincture cabinet, returned to my home-jar. He filled a pipette, then lofted it above me. "I promise," he said, "this will not hurt."

The water in my home-jar turned an inky black, and I fell into the deepest of slumbers.

DREAMS OF FLIGHT. I WAS A STARLING. FLITTING FROM fountain to pine branch to park bench to statue. Alive! I cried. Alive!

When I surfaced from these dreams, and my confusion subsided, the first thing I saw was the doctor's face: his eyes, so kind. "René," he said.

I tried to speak, but produced no sound, so I blinked at him: once, twice.

"Good girl, good girl," he said. "Aren't you magnificent!"

How I longed to hold this man, to wrap myself around him. After waiting so long, I felt a sudden irritable impatience. I attempted movement but could not budge. I tried again: focused inward, searched my new form, mapped its many pitches and squeezes until, finally, with effort, indeed I moved.

But something was not right.

I tried once more — but my movements were not the same as those I had observed for so long in François and his women. I did not move as Calliope had moved, so nimble and lively.

I ... undulated.

Stricken now, I scrambled to confirm an intuition and found it in a corroded gilt mirror leaning against the wall opposite.

*Good God.*

"You are my proof of concept," François said. Tears of joy wobbled in his eyes. "I know now that my many labours were not in vain. The transplantation was a triumph."

Inside the mirror's gaudy frame was an octopus — that sad cephalopod I'd so pitied all of these years. A crudely cross-stitched incision bisected the cranium of this monster. Inside it was me. My eyes. My brain. The seat of all that I was. Me.

"With the knowledge I have gleaned from this procedure, dear René, I can finally restore Calliope to life," he said. "I assure you, your sacrifice will not go unrewarded." And with that, he reached into a bucket and threw a fistful of crabs into my tank. "Eat, my dear, eat," he said.

But I was not hungry, no, not for these crabs he was offering. Hungry only for his anguish.

With a sudden inner dynamism long forgotten in my home-jar but now vividly remembered, I sent brainwaves throughout my appendages — all eight of them. I felt them rising, tumescent. I slithered to the edge of the tank — and then, in one luminous burst of energy, flung myself onto him, wrapping his head in a dreadful embrace.

He stumbled backward — my body stifled his screams. With flailing arms, he knocked his implements and tinctures to the floor, he made mad grabs at my arms to pry them away. He implored me for mercy.

When he dropped to his knees on the floor of the garret, I peeled one tentacle from around his head and, sneaking it under my mantle, found his mouth and pushed it as deep as I could reach, past his epiglottis, down his esophagus, into his stomach, until he could no longer scream, no longer breathe — no longer cry out Calliope's name.

# An Archive

MY FRIEND FRANCES AND I WERE SITTING IN HER BACK-
yard, having cocktails in lawn chairs, our feet dangling six feet
away from each other. We were the kind of friends who would
have seen each other at social events all the time before the
pandemic. We used to go to bathhouses and sex parties in our
twenties, including the infamous one that got raided by the
cops, leading to the historic (victorious!) discrimination suit
that went all the way to the Supreme Court.

When I was hooking up at that bathhouse and heard the
banging of police billy clubs on the walls outside the tiny
white room, my first feeling wasn't fear or anger, it was *thank
God*. My hand was cramping up. Fuck the police, I'd said,
pulling a gauzy slip over my head and gathering my purse.
My lover was too taut, had too many muscles. I say "my lover"
because I can't remember their name. I'm the age now where
that is possible. Sex with perfect-looking people is boring.

You can't have an earth-shattering orgasm while thinking about your angles. I'd had to turn away to smile into the wall with the posters about where to get hepatitis vaccines. I don't like public sex unless there is an element of danger to it. When you have to sign a paper at the door agreeing to rules, I'd rather be at home watching *Law & Order*. The arrival of cops didn't make it dangerous in a hot way, as real cops are not sexy. They look like teenagers to me now, the kind of kids who won't ever stop being mad at their father. Perhaps one or two would make an adequate pounder in a pinch, but that's all.

I'd explained my ambivalent feelings about the bathhouse to Frances as *lesbians make everything like summer camp.* I remembered that at the beginning of the evening we'd lingered by the pool, still wearing hoodies over outfits we'd spent hours putting together so that they looked like we'd just thrown them on. We'd watched a lacklustre blow job given by a woman in both a fedora and a boa. It was some sort of organized blow job–giving game. A small crowd watched from the pool. The poor host was trying hard to make us cheer and clap when encouragement was called for.

Frances had nostalgia about the bathhouse days, thought I was being boring. Sex negative. Cynical. *So tell me about your best sex.* She twisted a lime slice dry and threw it into the garden. When Frances's boyfriend transitioned I promised her she could touch my tits any time she wanted, but we're otherwise platonic friends. *I want to hear about every time you were absolutely ruined.* I told her no way, but that got me thinking. So here are some lies, but most are true.

1.

I briefly dated a skateboarder I met on Hinge while travelling the west coast after my divorce. We were stuck in traffic on Route 35 between Santa Cruz and San Francisco. Usually we talked all through sex, trading off sentences of whatever narrative fantasy suited the mood. But the freeway was loud. Tyler reached over and slid a hand under my skirt. The song playing on the radio was on so many stations that we eventually gave in and decided to like it. It was about jealousy, sung by one of the guys from a boy band of brothers who'd just gone solo. I came after we drove by a semi-truck and Tyler said, *He can see you right now.*

A few miles later I saw a sign for Google headquarters that made me think of *The Simpsons* and also a fun, weird place to get Tyler off. I said, Turn off here. My hand was in their lap now and they were swerving slightly. We drove around what felt like a simulacrum of any American town, with security cameras and businesses that appeared as though they were on the moon. We pulled over in a parking lot. Tyler tipped the seat back. I scanned the horizon for people who may look in the windows of our rental car, not something either of us would truly get off on. But I liked the possibility of danger. When Tyler came I gripped their back and tried to memorize the sound of their groan. That groan is my favourite sound. I can still hear it, though we no longer speak.

Some little pompous asshole on TikTok, one of those pseudo-therapists that show up on your feed when you're depressed, like it *knows* you, talks into the camera and says, *The people you have the best sex of your life with are often the most toxic. It feels like the best sex of your life because it's the only time you truly connect.*

## 2.

The thing about Tyler is sometimes they want to have sex constantly. Sometimes not at all. I basically respond to their whims. Sometimes that's hot. It feels like the ultimate submissive fantasy. I am always available. They ask me to say, "I am yours," before they come. It ends up being my kink too. After a while I try to imagine the kind of sex life that I had some control over. But there's something so enthralling about giving that up. I would have given anything up for Tyler. I understand there is no glory, no personal triumph in that sentence. It's romantic at twenty and a thing you discuss in therapy at middle age.

We only dated for three months but it took me three years of therapy to get over it.

## 3.

I'm over Tyler! I write this in my journal. I don't know why I'm lying to myself in print in a journal. The pandemic is slowly making me dumber. I speak to my therapist on Zoom. She suggests I do small things to feel a part of the world again. So I go to an outdoor spa with a few friends, the also-singles. There are two of us who text each other every morning to report we have not died in our sleep. We send each other screenshots of dates we might have from Tinder, Her, and Lex. I've been flirting with a femme, and we have a date planned, one I'm very nervous about. I find my bathing suit in the bottom of my laundry bin.

There is still a layer of snow on the ground, and you can go between saunas and the hot salt pools and into resting cabins. While waiting outside the locker rooms for my friends, I watch a woman with long hair in a red robe stop to fill her water bottle at the spout and take a long drink. I don't normally look at straight women. She has a tattoo of flowers on her forearm, an undercut. Possibly not straight.

My friends book hour-long massages. I prefer to linger in the salt pools and dip in and out of the saunas. The heat of a sauna often makes me dizzy, so I go in and sit near the door on my towel, so that I can make a quick escape. Every time I pay money to relax I feel like an idiot later because I am not built for it.

It's empty except for the woman with the long hair, who is lying flat on her back, her eyes closed. Her silver water bottle is on the ground beside her. I watch her breathing slow and steady, envious that she is one of those people who can be in a hot cave and not feel anxious about suffocating. It takes me a moment to realize, as my eyes adjust to the dim lighting, that she is completely naked, her red wraparound underneath her like a towel. Most people wear bathing suits. I am. Because her eyes are closed I stare brazenly, preparing to avert my eyes and dash out if she were to catch on. Her breasts are full; she has one arm underneath them, propping them up. The other arm hangs down at her side. She stretches and arches her back, eyes still closed, but in a way that seems languid and dance-like, as though she knows she is being watched. And then she puts her one arm above her head and one rests on her lap, a thumb resting between her thigh and pussy in a way that might be a mistake. I want her to move her thumb so badly that if she does I'm worried I might come just from the sight of it.

I'm not normally attracted to femmes. So when it happens it's a remarkable thing, like when you live in a city and you never see an alpaca or a field of ponies and you never think about them, but the next time you're on a country drive and see them you're like, let's take a photo. This is worth remembering.

She is completely shaved. I think that anyone who came of age in the late 1980s or 1990s, as I did, will find a bare cunt hot because it likely resembles the first pornographic images we were able to scrounge up. I squeeze my legs together, imagining where I'd put my tongue when I swear to God she opens her legs slowly, eventually one foot resting on the floor, toes pointed. Her eyelids flutter. Is she deeply asleep? I scan the sauna for a camera. I keep staring, my mouth slightly open. I look away, trying not to be a perv.

Eventually I cannot control my body. I stand up slowly, even though my brain is telling me to sit down. I crouch down on the wood floor. Can I pretend I've dropped something? I'm close enough to see that her pussy is wet. Maybe she's having a hot dream. Maybe it's just the sauna's heat. The air is so hot and dry and rich with the smell of cedar. I stare at her long enough that my brain comes back online. I'm about to leave when she reaches one hand up and squeezes a nipple. She's in on it! I lean close enough that she must be able to feel my breath on her thigh. She spreads her legs even farther, moving down toward me. When I finally put my tongue on her clit, slow and softly, she whispers, Good girl. Good baby.

Do you like it hard or soft, I ask, like a fucking Girl Guide, but all she says is *Don't stop*.

The heat is easier to take lower on the ground, and once I start giving head I like to focus on doing my best work, listening carefully for every shift and sound. She starts to sound like she might be getting ready to come. When she does it isn't theatrical, but I can tell by how she grips my hair and shudders into my mouth.

Later at the hotel I look her up on Facebook. She posts about the Kardashians and works for a shady MLM, and eventually a few months later I have to block her because I don't want to buy her candles.

**4.**

My friend Rachel had an orgy for her thirtieth birthday party. She chose ten friends to come over and have cocktails and then take turns fucking her on the living room floor. I was young enough then, maybe twenty-three, to think thirty was quite old. I told a younger femme this story the other day and she gasped, what a great idea for a birthday! It wasn't that rare a thing, I said, back then. I sounded a hundred years old. My young friend's social circle is too busy arguing about how to honour asexuals during the pride parade to get group fisted as a way to celebrate life's big turning points. I include the story of watching Rachel get fucked, even the feeling of nervousness and imposter syndrome as I took my turn, bottom fucking someone in such a public way. I include it on the list because it's a good visual, a good story, more than anything. And sometimes that makes it notable.

**5.**

But the sexiest moment of my life wasn't even sex. I was nineteen and in a movie theatre in Ottawa on a date with the first person I was maniacally in love with, in a way that was reciprocated and deeply exhilarating. I think we were watching *The Birdcage*. It was just a moment that lasted maybe five seconds, when JT leaned over and touched the side of my breasts under my tank top. I remember very little from that far back, but the moment was so significant that I can recall the detail of the thread on the red cotton tank top. Later that night JT kissed me goodbye in the parking lot in the ByWard Market, and the kiss was unlike any kiss I'd had before or since. I got into one of those sketchy commuter vans that you could take between cities, that were cheaper than a Greyhound bus. I thought about how I'd done all sorts of crazy things by the age of nineteen, filmed art school porn movies and had sex in all sorts of places. But as we drove through a whiteout and I thought we were going to die in an accident, my only thought was, well at least I experienced that kiss, because it felt like the most exhilaration one could ever possibly feel, and that was enough.

# My Skin Isn't What
# It Used to Be

THE SKIN ON MY FOREARMS IS CRISS-CROSSED WITH TINY diamonds like a tangerine, and when I bend over, a small roll of flab hangs off my stomach. That's why I started with the tattoos. I had the first on my left shoulder, a Thai dragon in emerald and crimson, not especially original, even a cliché on a man like myself. A friend of mine, Damian, says we wear tattoos and rings to extend our skins out to the world. So we aren't cut off and left dangling in our cage of bones.

I'd quit the Thomas Fisher Rare Book Library, where I used to work on medieval manuscripts, and gone on to the job of teaching assistant at a large university in the suburbs of Toronto. It was the nineties, and I was writing my second novel, so part-time work suited me fine although the course was considered pretty lame. It was a humanities elective and it used Canadian novels from the nineteenth and twentieth centuries to explain "the Canadian Experience," as the course was called in the syllabus. The term was ironic since my course director began by telling our students there was no such thing. What he meant was that we should substitute the article *a* for *the* because the whole point of his course, he claimed, was that there were many Canadian experiences, not just one.

He shouldn't have said that on the first day. It wasn't what the students needed to hear: They were more knowledgeable about American culture than our own. So his ambiguous definition had lost them before we even started. Most of them didn't know the difference between a novel and a book of nonfiction, and they complained about reading anything over one hundred pages. The course director, Dr. Jonas Weinberger, said not to worry. It was typical of their generation. I don't think Dr. Weinberger knew I was only a few years older than they were, so he was implicating me in his assessment of cultural impoverishment. In any case, Dr. Weinberger was about to take early retirement and left me to my own devices. No directives on how I should run my tutorials, my few course meetings. All I had to do was keep my students interested. By that, I took him to mean I should keep myself interested. As it turned out, I did, but not in the way I expected.

I wasn't prepared for the sight of her in my tutorial on the first Monday, her yellow hair cropped in a buzz cut. She sat smirking at me with a punky arrogance that I admit draws me to women who aren't going to be very nice to me. She was older than the other students, about twenty-six — not so young, I found out later, that she could be bullied by my age and experience. Still, I was marking her essays and tests, and she had to more or less write what I wanted if she was going to get a decent grade.

As I said, my skin is not what it used to be. And when I had the second tattoo etched on my right elbow — a Japanese cross, in emerald and crimson (in keeping with the Thai dragon), and then a matching cross on my left — she was the only one who noticed and spoke to me about it. Damian had warned me about doing my elbows, had, in fact, tried to talk me out of doing it because he said the skin there was so close to the bone. And I'd ignored Damian just as I had the first time, when I went to him for the Thai dragon and he smiled at me in front of his shelves of inks, arranged in squeeze containers like ketchup bottles, and asked if I was up for a little pain. He compared the prick of his needle to a dentist drill and when I shrugged, he ushered me into a little room that actually looked like a dentist office, set me down in a tilt-back chair, and began. The radio was on one of those golden oldies stations you don't hear anymore, and Damian was humming along. I don't understand how people can listen to that junk, but I just nodded and closed my eyes. I've never minded going to the dentist. It's the kind of specific attention few of us get.

Each time the drill penetrated my skin I felt a sharp flare of pain followed by a tiny, surprising ecstatic thrill. I enjoyed the sensations, which were so interwoven, I couldn't tell where pain ended and pleasure began. The sensations soon became overwhelming, and halfway through our session I made Damian take a break on the pretext that I needed to visit the washroom. Alone in the toilet stall, I quickly squeezed one off before hurrying back to Damian, who said he was glad to see the grin on my face.

He pointed out that I might feel good now, but he warned there would be intense pain from the tattoos later and he was right. The next day my arms puffed up and two gigantic blisters hung off both my elbows. The little sacs of water swished when

I moved, and the pain, if I brushed one of my elbows against something, made me feel like I was going to pass out. I cringed whenever I had to dress them.

The day I'm talking about, the day she noticed the tattoos, I was coming out of the afternoon lecture where Dr. Weinberger had been showing the students a movie of Brian Moore's novel *Black Robe*. Other novels have been written about the encounter between Europeans and Indigenous Peoples, but Dr. Weinberger considered Moore's novel the definitive book on that cultural moment, and he liked the students to watch the film. He said the film helped them with their reading although I think he meant that for once, thank God, he didn't need to coax them into reading a text because they had seen it on the screen.

After the film, she was waiting for me by the door to the lecture hall, slumped against a wall. She beckoned and I went over. One of her friends was Anishinaabe, and he'd told her the Indigenous dialogue the girls spoke in the movie was just gibberish, an imitation of their language, the way, say, we might sound if we imitated Japanese.

"Don't you think it's an insult, Welsh?" (I always get students to call me by my first name.)

I couldn't speak; my elbows were killing me.

"I mean it wouldn't be so bad if it was the other way around. If you and I went to a Japanese movie, for instance, and the English character was speaking a gibberish English!" She waggled her tongue at me, and I noticed she'd had it spiked with a metal stud, dead centre. "At least, English is the dominant global language."

"You're right there." I began to look around for a place to sit down.

"Yeah — hey. You okay?" She grabbed my arm — my elbow.

I almost puked on her shoes. We were in a shopping mall on campus, the one with a computer shop, bookstore, and cheap takeout restaurants. A group of students from my course were looking our way and giggling.

"What is it?" she asked huskily. "Drugs?"

The pain was ebbing a little.

"Tattoos on the elbows," I said.

I heard a little laugh. She was rolling up the sleeve of her blouse. Along her arm, waves of black scalloped tongues licked the contours of her scrawny biceps.

"I have more," she said.

"Where?" I was interested.

She smiled. "I'll never tell."

"By the way," she said, "you shouldn't wear long sleeves over new tattoos. Not right after the bandages come off. It will slow down the healing. Didn't anyone warn you about that?"

Damian had mentioned something along those lines, but I didn't want anyone, especially my students, to see what a mess I'd made of myself.

She touched my hand and pointed to a nearby noodle shop. We went over and sat down.

"You're a writer, aren't you?" she asked after we'd ordered.

"No." I didn't like students to know about my writing.

"Don't lie to me," she said. "I saw your novel in the campus bookstore. Our prof made a big deal of it last year." She paused. "I haven't read you."

"So what." I grimaced a little and sat holding my elbows out from my sides, like an insect drying its wings. I didn't feel like talking and she seemed to understand. She ordered the day's special, a platter of rice and ribs, then wolfed it down while I sat watching.

We started sleeping together a few days later. Her name was Jen, and I'll never forget the first sight of her naked: she looked like a tribal warrior, a regular Xena. Her broad shoulders were covered by a Spider-Man web, and the backs of her calves and thighs were enveloped in the same intricate scallops as her arms. Jen was tall and sturdily built and I was relieved to see she didn't go in for Brazilian waxes. I prefer women who look like women, not prepubescent girls. As soon as we were in my apartment, she pulled off my jeans and began giving me head. When it was her turn, she told me she liked her lovers to talk dirty. For a moment, my mind went blank. Then I remembered "Roger the Lodger":

> There was a young girl from Cape Cod
> Who thought all babies came from God,
> but 'twas not the Almighty who lifted her nightie
> but Roger the Lodger, the sod.

"You think that's talking dirty, Welsh?" She laughed and recited some doggerel that's too lewd to repeat here. To my surprise, Jen had a butterfly tattooed on her genitals, a mourning cloak, she pointed out, not the same old monarch you see on a lot of girls, next to a daisy or their astrological sign. It was her favourite butterfly, with its jagged yellow-banded wings and blue spots; she'd had it done in an art deco style.

Quoting lewd verse soon became part of our lovemaking, which usually happened the night after my course. We kept our affair secret at the university and never talked to each other in class. Our situation was delicate even though she was the one who initiated sex. Student liaisons were forbidden even then, and I knew, if she fell out with me, I could be in trouble. Jen could decide to charge me with assault and sexual harassment and the responsibility for the affair would fall on me. Still, she was twenty-six, about to turn twenty-seven, a grown-up, so I didn't feel I was taking a risk. I enjoyed the thrill of knowing I'd see her later, especially after I had to make period relics like *Roughing It in the Bush*, by Susanna Moodie, sound relevant. Unfortunately, the students also found reading the poems in *The Journals of Susanna Moodie*, by Margaret Atwood, beyond their abilities. Both books were on the course, and it was my job to make sure they grasped how the two narratives refracted one another.

To please Jen, I asked Damian to give me an art deco arrow on my dick. He convinced me it would hurt less if I tattooed her name, Jen, and then he went to work. I will never forget that session. When I was a boy, my mother accidentally spilled hot tea on my crotch. She felt terrible because I was in agony. Although the pain took away my breath, every nerve ending in my groin was vibrating, and I experienced the most intense sexual pleasure of my life.

The same thing happened with Damian. I became aroused as soon as I walked into his studio, anticipating the pleasure ahead. I never mentioned my reaction to him. Maybe he noticed the bulge in my pants although he didn't comment. Maybe he didn't care if his male clients got erections. He was there to do a job, and that was that.

My new tattoo was only visible when I was erect so Jen was surprised the first time she saw it, just as I planned. Did I mention that Jen also felt upset? She said I didn't have to go to such lengths to make her happy and, besides, she liked me unadorned. I took this as a compliment but it was too late to fix the tattoo.

It hurt every time I penetrated her. I didn't tell her because I didn't want her to feel bad. However, the sensitivity there never quite went away and that was fine by me.

By this time Jen and I had begun to enjoy ourselves. At first, she tried to please me by giving me porn magazines. Her last boyfriend had left piles of them under their bed, everything from *Taste of Latex* to glossy French photo magazines specializing in women wearing catsuits. She said her ex loved that mag.

I explained that images don't stir me as much as words. I know guys like me are pretty driven, visually speaking, and I count myself in on that department, but words affect me the most profoundly, if you really want to know. So if a writer is going to describe a sexual experience, the writer should know a thing or two about the English language. For instance, D.H. Lawrence pulled off writing about sex in his novel *Sons and Lovers*. As a teenager, I stole that novel out of my father's office drawer and read it under my bedcovers. (My father is a Vancouver poet who publishes in small literary journals. The point is Dad had a fairly complete library, and one way or another, all of us made use of it.)

I read some D.H. Lawrence to Jen, who laughed her head off over "his purple prose." (Jen's phrase not mine.) Next I introduced her to Chaucer, and this line from "The Miller's Tale" cracked her up: "And Absalom had kissed her nether eye and Nicholas is branded on the bum and God bring us all to Kingdom come —."

She kept laughing so I treated her to a quote from *Fanny Hill*: "I had now totally taken in love's true arrow from the point up to the feather ..."

Jen said I was old-fashioned, and then she read me some Henry Miller along with some passages from the early fiction of Erica Jong. She liked Miller; I didn't — I grew up with a feminist mother who taught me to admire the way Kate Millett dumped on Miller in *Sexual Politics*. When I told Jen that Miller says *whore* and *cunt* a little too often for my taste, Jen laughed and told me I wasn't being honest.

It turns out Jen and I were both suckers for good prose. As a precocious kid, Jen impressed boys at her high school by quoting lines from dead American women poets like Sylvia Plath and Anne Sexton. It was the sort of thing men are expected to do, so Jen was a hit using poetry as her MO. After we'd been together for a month, she whispered a few lines from "The Ballad of the Lonely Masturbator": "*My little plum* is what you said. / At night, alone, I marry the bed."

The reference to "my little plum" seemed a bit cute for my taste, but now I carry around a memory of Jen with that passage the way Molly Bloom's soliloquy in Joyce's *Ulysses*, for instance, conjures up Jill, the woman I went backpacking with in New Zealand. But when I recited it to Jen, "... yes so we are flowers all a womans body yes that was one true thing he said ... And yes I said yes I will Yes," Jen just shook her head and said Joyce didn't know anything about a woman's orgasm.

Jen could experience twenty or thirty orgasms when I gave her head and often she was so out of breath she couldn't say when she wanted me to stop. I have to admit her capacity for pleasure was far greater than mine, even with my sensitive cock. "Of ten parts a man enjoys only one," according to Tiresias, the blind Greek prophet, and he would know because he changed genders.

In the meantime, I got another tattoo, Jen's signature, on my left thigh. It took Damian only half an hour to copy her big, widely looped letters. It felt wild to be sitting there as if nothing was going on when I was lost to sexual rapture.

Damian did the letters in Headhunter font, size 24, but the tattoo was still hard to see unless I was erect and sitting with my legs apart, a position that Jen and I used to find sexy. Meanwhile, the Canadian experience course ticked along, riding the usual highs and lows of the university year — a dip at the end of February when the students were drained from writing their essays and, finally, the accelerated end-of-year rush to the exams. Only this year, the last part of term was particularly turbulent. Just before the end of March, a film based on a short story by me unexpectedly won a prize for best foreign film at the Oscars. I hadn't thought much about the story because the filmmakers had ignored the clause in my contract promising to put my name in the credits. To make up for their slip, one of the American producers thanked me onstage at Oscar night, and the next day I was taking calls from all over. My father wouldn't speak to me after an article in *Time* magazine described him as "a regional poetaster." My photo appeared in the *New York Times* and some of the articles claimed that my single and largely forgotten novel was part of a Canadian literary flowering that included the short stories of Alice Munro in the *New Yorker*. These articles also cited a film based on the novel *The English Patient*.

My students, who used to look bored or confused any time I made a literary reference — these same students — began to bring my novel to the tutorials and ask me to sign it. Jen herself became a fan and started to pester me about the parts she guessed were based on my life. I explained that no writer wants to have his work examined for what is factually true and what is invented. I told her fiction is a composite of autobiographical truth and the writer's imagination and the two threads were usually so enmeshed you couldn't untangle them.

We began making love a lot less, although at first I didn't notice. I stopped reading something I'd written to Jen and ignored her when she wanted to talk about writing. One night, while I was kissing a scallop tattoo on one of her forearms, she ordered me to stop and began pacing angrily around the bedroom.

"You're a published author and you don't even know the right words to get me off!" she yelled.

I was dumbfounded.

"You think 'Roger the Lodger' is erotic! How dumb can you be, Welsh?"

"Maybe you expect too much, Jen."

"Whatever!" She threw on her clothes and stormed out the door. A few days later, during the last week of classes, our university went on strike. Everything, including my tutorials, was cancelled. Jen treated the strike like a holiday. She began to hang out in my apartment while I went on the picket lines. When I came home, I'd often find her in front of my computer.

If I asked her what she was up to, she'd stand so I couldn't see the screen. "Just hacking around," she'd tell me.

One day, I found my dog-eared copy of John Gardner's *On Becoming a Novelist* beside the bed. I knew then that Jen was trying to write fiction, and she didn't want to tell me until she had something to show.

I became irritable; the strike was taking up my free time. I'd been talked into bringing coffee to the full-time professors on picket duty, so I had to be at the university's front gates all day every day. There was little time to write although publishers and magazines had begun to press me for new work. So as you can imagine, the sight of Jen typing away in a trance was making me crazy.

Jen had written fifty pages inspired by an assignment in my seminar. It was a narrative in the voice of Annuka, the

Indigenous girl in Moore's novel *Black Robe*. I thought the writing was brilliant and I gave Jen an A-plus.

When she asked me if my agent would look at her book, I made encouraging noises, although I secretly thought publishers wouldn't be interested in her fiction. So I was surprised when Jen was paid a six-figure foreign advance for the novel. One of the American editors who bid on Jen's book called it "a lyrical debut reminiscent of Louise Erdrich." Her shy, bedazzled English publisher (who didn't realize Jen was white) said Jen's prose showed "the promise of youthful American genius." Jen claimed she owed this good fortune to me. If she hadn't used my name, no agent would have looked at her book. Meanwhile, the strike was still on, and although everyone was waiting to see what I'd write next and although I didn't breathe a word of it to Jen, I couldn't get past the first page. *Welsh, get a grip*, I told myself, *you have to produce.*

We began to argue. Jen told me that it's not unusual for couples to go through rough patches and her surprising sanity took me aback. I started kissing her passionately, and she drew me down on the bed, throwing her long muscular legs around my neck when I entered her. Her thighs squeezed my neck until the pain was so uncomfortable I felt as if my cock was made of high-tensile steel. That night, I clocked in at three orgasms but as always Jen had me beat. She came twenty-seven times, her orgasms cresting in ever-diminishing waves of ecstasy.

I decided to celebrate with another tattoo. I had Jen's mourning cloak butterfly tattooed on my groin. Damian teased me about it and said I'd become addicted. It happens to everyone, Damian told me. He cited the case of a customer who gets portraits of her cats tattooed on her thighs whenever one of her pets dies. Cats can live up to eighteen years so Damian figures it will be a while before this customer's skin is used up. Faith, another regular, paid Damian to tattoo her baby pictures down her back in full colour.

"Faith's a walking album," Damian said. Talking about this now, so many years later, I can see that's where I got my big idea, the idea that would transform me, because it was shortly after Damian's remark that I went back for the full treatment.

Right from the start Damian loved my idea (it meant hundreds of hours of paid work for him) but I didn't tell my sweetheart.

The selection from Chaucer was in a font called Alte Schwabacher, which looks like Old English. The typeface was Damian's choice but it was my idea to copy the rubrication technique the monks had used on their handwritten manuscripts. By rubrication, I mean the crimson red letters that start the first sentence of a chapter in one of these ancient documents. So Damian tattooed in blood red ink the first line from "The Miller's Tale" — "And Absalom ..."

Just under my chest, the Old English script fades into Fette Gotisch for the English poet Andrew Marvell. Damian let a verse from Verlaine run to my belly button and below, where the skin is especially tender, he tattooed in Plath's last stanza from "Daddy." It was touch and go cramming these five lines onto my belly, but my old buddy pulled it off.

On my back he used Flintstone and a bit of Headhunter for some romantic nonsense from Robbie Burns:

> O my Luve's like a red, red rose,
> That's newly sprung in June.

On my stomach, he added Jen's two favourite sentences from Erica Jong's *Fear of Flying*, "The zipless fuck was more than a fuck. It was a platonic ideal." And lastly, as our inside joke, I made Damian run Molly Bloom's soliloquy, from one buttock to the other, in standard Bodoni:

> ... first I put my arms around him yes and
> drew him down to me so he could feel my
> breasts all perfume yes and his heart was go-
> ing like mad and yes I said yes I will Yes.

I didn't consider de Sade even though Jen likes him. I'm against cruelty, and I wanted the tattoos to evoke my feelings for her. But she argued on de Sade's behalf and I told her I might add him later. Hell, I was a work-in-progress.

The tattooing lasted six months. I went three afternoons a week for a couple of hours. It was like having sex every day. That way, each tattoo healed without getting the older tattoos sore or infected. On average, skin with a new tattoo will look healed in two or three weeks, but it can take as long as three months to really recover. In the interim, I told Jen I didn't want to see her because I needed time off to start my new book. She seemed surprised and said that she would use our time apart to work on her novel.

Six weeks after Damian finished his work, most of the scabs fell off. That night I asked her to drop by, and she near-ly fell over when I took off my clothes. There's nothing like standing buck-naked in front of your special reader, wait-ing for the moment when the two of you start fucking your brains out.

I've just finished reading what I've written here and I have to kick myself for not anticipating Jen's reaction. Granted, I'm a lot older now, and I know better. But my exhaustion with the strike had something to do with my obtuseness. It had been going for four months and all of us were a little stupid by then.

"Welsh, put your clothes back on," Jen said when I showed her my tattoos. "You're creeping me out."

"You don't like it?" I asked.

"You look just like the guy I went out with before you, but even he didn't go this far. And he didn't copy my tattoos either."

"What do you mean?"

"Don't look so dumb — you had my mourning cloak tattooed on your groin! That symbol is personal. Like hello. It's part of my identity."

"But I did this for you!"

"No, you did this for yourself — to show me you are the big shot writer and I'm your cheesy little reader."

Feeling glum, I covered myself up with a towel and sat down on the floor.

She sat down beside me and tenderly kissed my shoulder. "Welsh, you have writer's block. Is it because I'm writing too?"

"Maybe. There you are typing away and I can't produce a fucking word."

"Darling, don't worry about it," she said. "I'll get an office outside the apartment and you can type away in peace."

ALL THIS HAPPENED YEARS AGO. JEN'S NOVEL WAS A critical success but it sold twelve hundred copies. My novel, *The Last Days of Somebody's Life*, sold poorly too, although it was nominated for a prize that another writer won. Then nothing. Neither Jen nor I were able to sell our next books because the bottom had dropped out of book publishing. My agent says the situation is not our fault; we live in the digital age, with its endless distractions, and nobody is pulling down advances the way they did. The year following my novel's publication, Jen went back to school and became a social worker. The same year my teaching position at the large suburban university was lost in a budget cut so we moved out of the city. I work at a community college where the students are more interested in their screens than in reading print books. Instead of creative writing seminars or an academic course like the one on the Canadian experience, I co-teach a MOOC, short for massive open online course. My section of the course focuses on business writing, and it stresses some of the same guidelines that John Gardner once recommended in his books about writing fiction.

I still emphasize the need to write specifically and concretely. Business types, like novice novelists, think that vague, general language gives the reader more freedom to interpret, and it's my job (just as it was in my creative writing seminars) to disabuse the students of this notion. I take comfort in knowing that I'm wringing truth out of language.

In fact, I'm more comfortable about a lot of things, including the unforeseen accommodations that used to drive me nuts when I was young, and I look back at the days when my fiction was reviewed in publications like the *New York Times* the way you might look back at your years in high school. Success in the world of literature isn't the ongoing condition I imagined.

Now that we're past the physical labour of raising our twins, Michelle and Erin, Jen and I are having sex again. Of course, I'm still prone to fits of optimism, so last year I published my first ebook. I spent half a year promoting it on social media to no discernible effect. To cheer me up, Jen rented a cabin on a

Quebec lake and we left the kids with Jen's mother. The writing has been going slowly, and I find myself spending a lot of time on YouTube. Yesterday, I came across a photograph of the late Michael Jackson. His skin had turned the colour of chalk. I showed it to Jen and she gave me a hard look. "Are you thinking what I think you're thinking?" she asked.

"I'm thinking Damian could do some laser work on me — salt scrubs don't go deep enough." I shrugged. "I know it's time consuming. They have to burn the same spot over and over to erase one tattoo. But a little pain has never stopped me before."

Jen shook her head, smiling. "Welsh," she replied, "you slay me."

# Party, Party,
# (Sex) Party

IT HAD BEEN THREE WEEKS SINCE I HAD FELT DESIRABLE; NOW I was lost somewhere on the streets of Outremont, my vision blurred. The pulsing between my ears was like a rabid bass line, as if I were still perched under the speakers from one of the night's parties. I couldn't say which one for sure. Wherever I was had a balcony. Those speakers were bigger and louder than they had any right to be. The wind was the same. None. I missed home. That brisk island breeze that used to rub my bones numb. It was a two-hour walk down Avenue du Parc to my apartment under the staircase in the north end of the city. A year's rent left enough money in my grad school stipend for what was really important for my survival. And that was barely enough. The approaching lights of a bus were a lifeboat I couldn't refuse.

In the twenty minutes I was on the bus I collected enough warmth and odd looks from the other late-night passengers.

Their gaze affixed on my ensemble. Wrinkled, raised eyebrows deemed me too fabulous for public transportation. My nods echoed a sincere, wholehearted agreement; my gold platform shoes and holographic glitter leotard made me feel like a super-model, even as it wedged itself between my balls. Thankfully, my shorts hid the severe camel toe caused by the leotard. I belonged on a runway or in a limo. Not on this bus. I got off at the next stop. It may have been a new year, but that was about all that was new.

It was, unquestionably, A Friday Night. I think there was a gay dance party. There was an after-party, and I was defin-itely turned all the way up. Whenever energies dipped, there was also an empty bathroom to do a bump or four. Then back to dancing or whatever else my state of being would allow. Customary behaviours when one is kicking a wretched year to the curb. My body screamed from dancing too hard. The after-party was at my old roommate's sister's friend's house. They, my old roommate's sister and her friend, did Live Sculpture 438 together last semester.

I had quenched a bit of my thirst with some regulation hottie at the gay dance party beforehand, but those details are fuzzy, so did it count? My roommate's sister found a bag of M on the floor at the after-party. We sprinkled it into our shots and danced around in a haze of doobs until I knew I needed to leave. It was so random, not my exit, but this leap from sobri-ety. Fun was had but was it so much fun because my reality was so altered? Or because everyone was just as fucked, fucked up, as I was. Every scene, every party I found myself at, was basic-ally the same. On the mainland there was always an after-party. They felt like an institution in the culture — these post-party spaces existed where you could let things simmer and wear off or you could amp the fuck up to go another round. This city was crazy like that. I tried not to get sucked in, still desperate for that big gay romance.

A rich orange sun splashed ripples across the sky, grand brick silhouettes carved into the distance. The bus had meandered through a web of side streets that brought me no closer to home. Miss Tiny, as my asshole was affectionately called by those who have used her, wanted a reasonable exercise. I needed some amount of dick in one or both of my holes. My fleeting data be dammed; I didn't care if I went over my phone plan limit for the month. I loaded the DMs with unbridled desire. An early morning fuck always helped me sleep away decisions from the night before.

The battery alert sounded as soon as I opened Facebook. Five percent remained. I dared not open anything else on my phone. The green dot told me there was a message from someone online. Jacques. We had gone on two dates. Both times I presented myself as more wholesome than someone who would appear at your door with exposed ass cheeks at three in the morning. I clenched my fingers anticipating their soothing crack. It didn't disappoint. The heat was a rush. I put my phone away.

Rue Durocher. Diego lived farther down this street. God bless queer safe spaces in the big city. Everyone in his building was gay and I had only fucked half of them, not Diego, not for lack of trying. And not the guy in the basement, John, who had let me into the highlighter-blue building many times. His buzz cut still fresh, the mohawk and pompadour from before distant memories. The mullet that accentuated his waist-length, wild, puke-green curls, an obvious result of a dye job gone awry, was my favourite look.

John's apartment wasn't exactly in the basement; it was on the first floor. He had the only apartment on that floor. No one hung out there. John grew the dankest weed but had managed to find an even more pungent-scented spray to conceal the ripening cannabis smell. No one was fooled. More were repulsed. John saw every visitor, even though his guest log lacked entries. He had told me twice my ass looked good in my black cut-offs. John was always up.

My body reverberated with the familiar pains of difficult digestion. That half-off grocery store sushi was eager to make an exit. A complication for what I craved. My body begged to go home or to do something I preferred to only do at home. I had no way of getting into Diego's for a quick shit, my phone, cold and lifeless. The cold couldn't be the only one sucking the life out of things. I had come to the city to go to school. Not be this mess. I pulled the tiny bag of powder out of my fanny pack and loaded a key. It was humid and clumped so I rubbed some on my gums. This was the closest I would ever be to peace. Could I live with that?

THAT LAST WEEK, I HAD FINISHED A CHAPTER IN THE *Oxford Handbook of Political Science* on Interest Groups. It was an okay read; I only fell asleep once. I woke up immediately. Somewhere between dream and dread, I came up with a final topic for my Canadian politics seminar. The decline of political parties and their actors to make way for the rise of grassroots interest groups. It was a total long shot and sounded like a lot of work. The hardest part would be convincing my professor it was a valid argument. This man was the Google image search result for *curmudgeonous*. A bitter-looking, old white man. He enjoyed being a contrarian as much as he considered it appropriate to wear a dashiki when lecturing on South African race relations.

I needed to be a bit of a mess to deal with being in school. The mental and physical toll it took to maintain somewhat decent grades and an active social life was downright harmful to one's well-being. How was I supposed to squeeze a job into my life? I had spent the Christmas break collecting data for my thesis, but I also spent it sober. It always felt like a different world when that farce faded.

Any exposed part of my body was coated in glitter, my belly trapped by my sailor-blue vest with the gold epaulettes atop the leotard. The freezing air brushed against my exposed midriff. My stomach stirred some more. This part of Rue Durocher was lined with two-story single-family homes. Pristine paint jobs left their exteriors shining whether night or day. All detached, fenced properties. Cold hardy evergreens upped the curb appeal, adding winter interest to sidewalk gardens and audacious life to winter drab. Diego's building was too many blocks away. Smack in the middle of the part of Durocher where the buildings were only being held up by hopes and prayers. No one had gardens, front lawns. A back alleyway exit was cause for celebration and a chance for an escape from the crippling August heat that locked itself into the building during the peak of summer. Another wrenching pain forced me to assess my options. The manifestation of a rendezvous the main priority.

When shit came to crown, I was face to boxwood before a pink mansion. It had a pair of aged red brick steeples, surrounded by ten-foot-high cedars. The perfumed air transported you outside the city walls. There was an open yellow gate between the massive evergreens. I was propelled through them onto the brick pathway by my fight-or-flight response. The air was even better inside the cedar hedge. I imagined the red brick–outlined gardens that lined the outskirts of the pink mansion in the summer, and how they must have flourished. The boxwoods planted for winter interest were stiff from cold but less prickly than the remnants of the mature, thorny rose stalks left unpruned. I tucked myself into the front corner of their garden, facing their mostly stained-glass door in case I needed to make a fast escape through the cedars.

This shit was ready. It would be quick. I squatted with fingers crossed and snapped open the pins of my leotard. My shorts and briefs dropped to my ankles. Just the tip of my top knot visible.

Party. I hovered over the invisible toilet. Relaxing my ass muscles after each thud. This all seemed rational considering my irrational need for cock and the cocaine coursing through my veins. The cedar in the air calmed me. I loaded another key into my sinus cavity before pulling up my pants. Heaven. Streets were clear; I knew I couldn't just stand by my shit in shock.

The walk afterward felt anything but rational. Five minutes ago, wiping was the least of my concerns. I had spread my cheeks as wide as they allowed, but this was an unfortunate situation. With every step I felt the effortless slide of each cheek. I questioned my resolve; I could do everything but get fucked. My track record dictated at some point I would ask, "Do you wanna put it in me?" How was I going to get fucked now?

Another covert mission was the only option. I knew cleanliness was next to Godliness.

I rang Diego's doorbell to test my luck. Miss Tiny felt ashamed being covered in shit in public. I tried to console both

Miss Tiny and myself of the rarity of such an occurrence. We were proud "clean bottoms," according to the doctor at the McGill student clinic.

"He's asleep." It was John. An orange bathrobe strung over his shoulders. His hairy belly looked sweaty. He looked warm. I wanted that.

"Oh. Hey." I stepped back before he had a chance to open the door, clenched my butt cheeks in hopes of masking any smells. My ass and penis barely covered. I put a hand by my tuchus and waved it quickly, then stopped in case I was only fanning the shit toward him.

"Wanna come in?"

"Sure."

He pulled the robe over both his legs. He held it in place and fumbled his hands through the armholes.

I needed to sneak into his bathroom. His fumbling made it easier. The dankness that emanated from his pores gave me hope.

"Really?" John looked around when his body was properly placed in his garment.

I was already past him, nearing his door; I had never returned his advances with much more than a smile. Tonight felt like the stars had aligned for me and John, a perfect storm.

I had been in enough of the apartments in this building to know the layouts were all basically the same. I pushed open his front door and beelined it to his bathroom.

None of the tissue paper stuck to my crack. I wiped inside my asshole with some wet towel to freshen her up.

By now I admit my meter of rationality may have been skewed. I took my time in the bathroom, my face arguably cute if I smiled but more worn than how I left the house. I heard a loud gurgle. My stomach wanted a round two. I winced at the thought and clenched my belly. It was calm underneath my grip. I turned the tap on when another, louder gurgle erupted; I pushed the faucet and water gushed onto the orange tiled backsplash. A large, discoloured water bubble rose and fell in the toilet bowl — it beat out of synch with the covering flow from the tap. Above the toilet, a sign. *Three Sheets Per Flush.* That was a foolish place for an important sign. The bubble rose slowly. Too empty to throw up, it was all I wanted to do. I looked over as the bubble neared the rim of the bowl and prayed. Pleaded with HaShem that if this water vanished, I would observe Shabbat more appropriately the next week. The water rose higher still.

"Are you okay in there?" John's perfectly pitched baritone susurrated through the cracks. He had not grown up in Montreal. His drawl gave him away within seconds.

"Really needed to wash my face. Be right out." I spoke toward the space under the door as I was already near the toilet. This time it was my stomach. A stream of water rolled down the side of the toilet, and the pipes gurgled. My stomach gurgled. Please, HaShem. Please. I looked down and it seemed my prayer worked. The water level receded, the rising bubble gone. I scanned the bathroom floor and wiped whatever splashes I saw. The puddles by the base of the toilet, drawer handles, and the garbage bin. Great care taken to wrap the used tissue into a tight ball and throw it into the trash. My leotard sank deeper into my skin; I couldn't breathe. It had run its course on my body. I stuffed the flimsy bit of fabric into my pockets and put back on the rest of my clothes. I breathed.

I faced myself again. I looked into myself and at HaShem. He knew me better than to take my last promise seriously. The mirror revealed all. My face told the story of the night.

Smudged lips and faded blush. I was a far cry from the meticulous portrait I had created in my room. My mother always said, even on my worst day, I was still a ten. It wasn't my worst day. I pulled out the baggie and my house key. Deep inhales. Rational actions for rational actors. I took solace in that and left his bathroom.

John had an executive one-bedroom version of Diego's two-bedroom apartment. It was twice the size. There were three other men in the room, not including John. Unbeknownst to me, I was joining a party that was already roaring.

John jumped onto his bed. His back pressed to the blue paisley sheets. The robe slid open as his dangling legs carved letters in the air.

A couple of men, one with a Swiss flag tattoo spanning his left pectoral, the other a brunette, were fucking on the right side of John while a tall redhead masturbated his curved penis above them. The brunette getting railed by the above-average-diameter dick sucked on the redhead's balls like a baby desperate for a nipple. John played with his hole as he watched the unfolding coitus. The redhead spat in his palm and rubbed his dick around in his saliva. He walked over to John's puckered asshole and slid his entire shaft deep inside him. John reached back and twirled his fingers through the ball hairs making direct contact with his taint. The redhead looked me deep in the eyes as he moaned as if to say, this is how it's done. He showed his pride with a bitten bottom lip and a quick wink. John screamed and stuffed handfuls of his bedsheets into his mouth. The redhead tossed his head back. Eyes closed, the redhead clenched his hands tighter around John's pelvic bone. I felt the rush of blood to my penis; it was ready to join the festivities.

John grabbed the guy with the Swiss flag tattoo fucking the brunette. Swiss flag tattoo guy then leaned down to lick John's armpits, his partner pressed into the bed beneath him. My shorts rode up as my boner twitched more; my dick was on the verge of crowning. I wondered where I belonged. This wasn't why Mummy shipped me to foreign from Jamaica with her whole pension.

I knew I should try to do things differently, stop having so much casual sex. If the sex were sober, it wouldn't be so bad that it was all casual. It was a new year, make Mummy proud. It all felt incredibly futile. I knew from previous failed attempts that true and honest change was hard. Maybe impossible. I would be a fool to try; I needed these habits. Would my life have been complete without seeing that Swiss flag flying and flexing as this stranger fucked? If I were able to make peace with myself, my nature, these desires — that alone would be such a marvellous accomplishment for the new year. Instead of the vitriol I spewed at myself when I failed. That last week I'd finished *Queer as Folk* again; that show was a total mindfuck to me when I was eleven years old. Now the characters' antics all seemed run-of-the-mill. Who were these men really? John, if that was his real name. Swiss flag tattoo guy? Redhead guy? Was I where I belonged? I guess it felt right.

"Coming in?" John stuck his tongue out at me, his right index finger accompanied the dick inside his hole. The redhead pulled out of John's asshole and slipped his dick into the next available orifice.

I reconjured my position when releasing the shit earlier. John pushed my shorts up to access my privates. My dickhead brushed John's tongue. He put his cold hands on my exposed midriff. Sucked me. Swallowed my freckled dick to the base.

When my dickhead was slick with his saliva, I turned John around and shoved my cock into the depth of his asshole. My first time topping. His right thumb found my own asshole. That made me so hard it hurt. I fucked John harder, his fingers dug into my ass cheeks holding me close. My vest barely clung to my body. I wanted to free myself of these clothes.

The TVs, there were two of them, flashed pornographic images and videos. Half-smoked joints littered the bedside table. Stifling aromas from the lube and latex suffocated me, much different from the potent cedar from earlier.

"Take a shot." The Swiss flag tattoo guy had every muscle I knew of and ones I didn't. I could tell he used every machine at the gym. The redhead didn't miss a stroke. His penis looked long. I watched him pull out many times, the head of his cock never visible. Where did it end? I wanted it inside me; I pulled out of John.

After my first shot, I was fully naked. In the bed after my second. Eyes fixed on the black-painted stucco ceiling. A little tired from fucking John when he placed his asshole over my nose. I breathed deep before putting the tip of my tongue into him.

"Fuck me again." John pushed a finger inside himself. Lube and cum coated his asshole. My dick throbbed harder than it ever had.

"Yeah?" I whispered rolling on top of him. "You want this?" That felt appropriate. I slid into him again, channeling the redhead. His eyes pinched shut. Inside him felt more welcoming this time. His lips disappeared between his teeth. I looked at the porn, his body below mine. I held his ankles in place and pushed his knees into his body. He didn't want to move; he couldn't. The tip of me pushed his soul open. My mouth drowned his moans, the pressure he put on my tongue between his teeth his recompense. I slid in and out.

This felt better than my usual fruitless pining. The boys in grad school were only attracted to my brain. No moves made to tap the booty. I wasn't meant to find love in the corridors of conservative academia like my hetero friends. Wrong major, maybe? It wasn't like I was looking for love in this basement either. Maybe another paper topic that my politics professors would never approve. Another line would have made it ecstasy.

I still needed to finalize the syllabus for my Media and Feminist Thought reading course. There had been no feminist theory in my honours degree; adding this element to my master's thesis brought a new dimension to the literature review and the overall paper. Would I ever de-stress from cramming my entire program into one year? This course needed to be tough enough for my supervisor to approve it for full credits. Planning an entire master's level class was not in my skillset. I couldn't afford to do a second year, my lucrative funding package not guaranteed beyond three semesters — a condition I had agreed to before accepting their offer of acceptance to the program. What I really wanted was a doobie when I got home. I flicked my eyes to the back of my head in hopes of remembering if I had taken the PBR tallboy out of the freezer before leaving the house.

"More lube." John jammed his tongue toward my eardrum. He guided my hand to my dick. We both rubbed on the red head of it when it popped out of his hole. John spat in his free hand and smeared the saliva all over my dickhead. I spat on his hole. My dick slid in without much effort. The Sea of Reeds parted. I pushed into him as far as my body would allow. We composed an intoxicating melody in tandem with all the other orchestral sections. The redhead put his dick next to my cock and kissed John. He tried to push his dick into John while I was still inside him. I grabbed John's waist and pulled him close enough for our tongues to connect. The redhead pried my mouth open and traced my teeth with his tongue. I licked the chipped filling in the back of his mouth. John's hole stretched to accommodate us, his pupils all but vanished. I wanted to feel what John was feeling but what if my hole never bounced back? Could I call her Miss Tiny if she wasn't as snatched anymore? We fucked John for seven more minutes; my dickhead caressed the inside of his stomach. He was still tight and warm. It felt as good as a thick long line. The redhead fucked me for the next five minutes. The three of us, a luscious sandwich. As we switched positions, I noticed the redhead's asshole was covered in curly red hairs that crept over half of his butt cheeks. His carpet matched the drapes, it was a refreshing honesty. Our bushes became friends instantly. Was any of my behaviour a rational reaction to not getting a kiss at the stroke of twelve on New Year's Eve? I couldn't wait to step foot inside my quiet, comfortable abode.

The sun had finally clocked in for work and the streets were amuck with people preoccupied by their days by the time I emerged from John's pleasure palace. If I had stayed sober the entire break, I would have been one of these people. It is unclear how much fun me or Miss Tiny would have had if that were the case. With no more change for the bus, and not enough money for a taxi, there was a two-hour walk home ahead of me. I didn't have enough data left to call Mummy on WhatsApp while I walked home either. But that was probably for the best. She had a way of detecting regret in my voice. I don't know how much of it I would take back if given the choice though. That was a safe space to top for the first time. I rubbed the last bit of powder from the little baggie on my gums.

The spot where I had shat looked undisturbed to the naked eye. I prayed nature would take its course with haste. John needed to keep last night between us. Speaking it out loud would only make this all even more real. It had been another great party, and I was beyond glad I went. Just uncertain it was something I needed to do again. There was no way that kind of behaviour would make Mummy proud. It might have been time to start doing the hard work in trying to change some things about me. The last bit of semen that refused to be swallowed found itself spat out of my mouth and lost somewhere on the streets of Outremont.

# Maria

IN A TRANCE OF HITTING THE X SOMETHING ABOUT HER froze his thumb. She looked absolutely nothing like his ex-girlfriend for one. She was white and dirty blond and had green-brown eyes with sleek wings of mascara and lips of kissable pink. The profile said she was twenty-four and from Chicago where she was in school, just visiting Toronto for a couple of nights. He scrolled down. Everything about the profile indicated a thrilling straightforwardness. One pic had her in front of a mirror, her torso twisted so she could capture her plumlike ass in grey yoga pants. Where the prompt said, I'm looking for ..., she'd written, Nothing serious. He liked one of the pics, not the ass one, and tossed the phone to the other side of the couch and turned on the TV. In just a few short minutes he got a notification. You have matched with Maria.

He waited as long as he could before starting the chat. Hi Maria, he wrote. How do you like Toronto?

He watched the circles bounce as she formulated a reply.

hey

it's pretty good

a little boring maybe

A glimmer of light wedged open in his mind. With a frankness that amazed him he thumbed in the words, I wonder if I can find some way to amuse you?

He'd been single for six months but didn't identify as single. He identified as alone. His girlfriend had dumped him. They'd lasted five years, living together for three, and though he knew her better than anyone in the world, his soulmate basically, he'd been totally unaware of his impending doom. She executed the break with immaculate stealth. On a day like any other she simply announced that she was leaving. She already had a place lined up. That was astonishing, the new place, that she'd gone through the unspeakable difficulties of finding an apartment, charming the landlord, passing the credit check, providing first and last months' rent. Within hours of the announcement she was established in an altogether different life and he was alone.

The whole thing filled him with unbearable shame. There was no longer any bedrock to his world. If he could be so deceived by his soulmate then what was solid, what would still be there tomorrow? He'd been terribly fooled and he moved through life with a sense that everybody could see his foolishness. The faces on the street, they saw it. If they were looking at their phones they were reading about it. And when he turned on the TV the people on TV saw it too.

Anything like lust would be ridiculous for a man in his condition. It was like his dick had died between his legs and he let his pubes overgrow it like an unimportant ruin. Only once before had he experienced an aversion to desire like this, when his now-ex gave him chlamydia. This was right when they were getting together, years ago. The first time they fucked no condom she gave it to him. She was asymptomatic but he was not so fortunate. It manifested first as a disconcerting burn, then in the morning he woke up with a boner on fire and squeezed it and a runny yellow snot gasped out. For the next few days until the antibiotics did their thing it was like someone had cracked an egg in his underwear. His dick was just a useless appendage, tacked on like the tail in pin the tail on the donkey. It was horrible, really the worst, but what he wouldn't give to get chlamydia from her now.

The final insult of the breakup was to be spat into a dating world so alien to the one he'd known before. In the five years of their relationship the apps had become the all-pervasive mode of meeting people. Before, he met women in what he considered the traditional way, sitting in the same coffee shop day after day, month after month, hoping that an attractive woman would sit within a reasonable distance to strike up conversation. That's how he had met his ex, God or science or whatever conspiring to bring them together. But now it all happened on the apps. The few times a friend coaxed him to a club or bar he sensed in the armoured postures of the women that introducing himself would be weird. Meeting people was not something that occurred in public, it occurred while you were on the toilet swiping through an app.

Whenever he'd dared imagine what it would be like if his relationship ended it seemed impossible that he could ever build another like it. Now it felt like a hurricane had levelled his metropolis and he had to rally the strength to lay the first of a billion bricks. But he couldn't be alone forever, he was only thirty-two, there was still time to get it all back.

He downloaded the app and built his profile. He had a few decent photos of himself, all taken by his ex who had an eye for that sort of thing. He uploaded them, then he took a selfie for something up-to-date. He'd never been good at that, never knew how to grip the phone, never understood what angle was most flattering, and do you look at yourself on the screen or stare into the lens? After a dozen takes he thought he'd got something decent but when he reviewed it the image was reversed like in a mirror and looked totally different. His ugliness embarrassed him. He couldn't meet his own desperate eyes on the screen. He uploaded it anyway.

Then he spent a while swiping through the app. Every so often he found someone attractive and hit the like button. He imagined this little Cupid's arrow pinging off a 5G tower and soaring toward her heart. At first nothing happened, then one morning he awakened to discover he'd matched with somebody. She was pretty, he was excited, he told a friend about it. The friend asked to see a pic. He screencapped the profile and sent it over, only to be met with silence. After a little while he asked, Something wrong?

i gotta be honest with you man, came the reply.

she looks exactly like your ex

That was a real eye-opener and for a few days he didn't trust himself to like anybody. It would be the most pathetic thing in history to try to physically replace his ex. He'd seen *Vertigo* and wasn't going out like that. He consciously worked to expand the horizon of his desire and soon started matching with women that didn't inspire concern.

One of these chats evolved into a date. It was enticing at first, just the idea of maybe kissing someone new, but his anticipation collapsed in the moment before leaving and he felt like lying under every blanket that he owned. He looked hard in the mirror and told himself it had to happen, he had to go out, it was time to be a man about his life.

It was one of the first nights of winter so he had to wear one of his thicker, uglier coats. They met at a bar. She had short bleached hair and a furry upper lip and a lot of colourful tattoos. They ordered cocktails. It would be an understatement to say that his date had more energy than him. She rushed him through the conversation, most of which consisted of her taking out her phone and showing him things on social media that made no sense to him. He tried not to drink too much, both because that would be a red flag and because the price of cocktails had skyrocketed in the years of his relationship. It all seemed like a waste, he was unbelievably tired after like an hour, but she wanted to go to another bar so he followed. This place was more of a dive. They drank beer. She wanted to play a game of darts. She said she liked games and was extremely competitive. He couldn't care less about the outcome of a darts game but played anyway and got unsurprisingly destroyed. When she hit the last bull's eye she yelped and raised her hand for a high-five. He reciprocated weakly, feeling like the most un-fun person in the world.

By the end of the night they'd been hanging out for hours and he knew almost nothing about her. Then again he never planned to see her again so what did anything matter. He figured it was time to walk home in the cold wind of this empty universe but to his amazement she asked if he wanted to come back to hers, she lived right around the corner, they could have another drink. He said yes, thinking he should take this chance, what kind of man says no? He found himself in a studio apartment. There was a futon, some yellowing houseplants, and an old electric organ that was unplugged and being used as a kind of table. They made out on the futon, which was in couch formation. One time he asked his ex frankly if she had any criticisms of how he kissed, hoping she'd say nothing at all, he was perfect, and after thinking for a moment she said he generated a lot of saliva. As he kissed this strange woman he was partly kissing her and partly working to restrain the activity of his glands.

They had sex or made the attempt. The thing is that it had been five years since he'd used a condom. His ex always went down on him right away, then he'd get on his knees and jerk off while licking her up, her cool hands pressing his face into the wet, altogether making him so maximally hard that he didn't have to think about it. Now he had to think about it. This woman did not go down on him, the foreplay was perfunctory, she just wanted to get fucked. He didn't know how to ask for what he needed and anyway he should not be fucking the way he fucked his ex, it should be new. She lay back on the futon. She was objectively hot and deserved whatever she wanted but when he rolled the condom onto his cock it was like he was erasing his boner. For the first time in his life he went soft and couldn't get it back, a complete terror. He ate her out for a while and she worked herself to an O but when he left her place he was a hundred years old.

Since then he'd kept his distance from what could be called the dating scene. Every once in a while he chatted with a woman on the app but it never quite arrived at a solid plan to meet. The idea of sitting across a table from a stranger filled him with shame, as if his face were private parts. He tried telling himself it was noble to be alone. With these long quiet nights he would read a lot of books and maybe get a dog and find that the dog was his best friend. But after a month, less actually, his depression had become indistinguishable from an almost agonizing horniness, an inner weeping for touch, and he felt like he was living in a crater on the moon.

Then he matched with Maria. There was just something different. She was really cute and only here a couple of nights. Who wouldn't like to kiss a stranger in Canada? It was possible anyway.

I wonder if I can find some way to amuse you?

He stared at his own words, all the courage of his heart dangling out in digital space. He turned his phone off, unable to wait, then turned it on again and waited. He didn't know what he expected, for her to rush into his arms or something, but her reply set him back.

hmm, she wrote.

maybe

tell me more about yourself

In a hurry not to seem like it was all about sex, though it was all about sex, he said sure and gave her some humanizing details like his last name and a bit about his job.

What about you? he said. How's university?

dont remind me, she said.

He lol'd and she lol'd. They had a nice little rapport going on.

ugh, she said, i hate this app. so glitchy.

Really?

for me anyway. do u have snap?

He did not have Snapchat and said as much.

oh

i think im gonna delete this app

Already he was downloading Snapchat and hastily setting up an account.

If you do, he wrote, add me.

He gave her his username. Nothing happened. The minutes passed. He was sitting by the window. It was night and he watched the snow swirling in the orange streetlight. He was also just a particle falling through time. He couldn't go on like this. He went to the kitchen and placed his phone on the counter and started making dinner. As he chopped the vegetables and tossed them in the wok he held the black shape of the phone in his peripheral vision. Then it lit up, a notification. Maria had added him on Snapchat.

so much better, she said.

what r u doing tonight?

He served his food and sat at the little kitchen table.

I think I'll just stay cozy, he said, maybe drink some wine at home.

Then it arrived, a photo. He opened it at once. It was her, it was Maria. She was standing before mirrored closet doors that reflected a small bedroom. It was a chaste photo, very sweet really, just a slight inquiring expression on her heart-shaped face. The black strip across the middle of the image had a caption, can i have a glass of wine?

The thrill overcame him so forcefully he lost his appetite.

Is pinot noir okay? he wrote and wondered why he wrote that.

yeah?

Then yes.

take a selfie 4 me? she asked.

He paused. He'd just forced some food into his mouth.

Um, he wrote, I'm actually eating right now. But here's an older one?

He swiped through his photos searching for something sufficiently cute. All he had were rejected selfies. He chose a borderline one and put it in the chat. There was something powerful about sharing it, the glory of the risk, the final exposure, and when her reply came it rushed through him like blood.

so handsome :)

This was the moment, a hinge in time. He tried a few variations and then sent, I have a glass waiting for you.

But again his momentum was checked.

hmm, she said.

maybe we share some photos first?

I'm still eating.

ill wait

It made sense that she wanted to see more. His dating app profile didn't suggest much by way of body type. He could be absolutely monstrous for all she knew. He put the dishes in the sink and went to his bedroom.

He didn't know exactly what to do in there. He sat on the edge of his bed and faced the full-length mirror, then took out his phone and framed his reflection. The lamplight softened all the edges and made things almost pretty. It was a kind of confidence. He took his shirt off and studied himself in the mirror in the phone. He remembered how Maria posed in her pics. If he twisted a little like her it tightened his torso like a screw. He rapidly snapped some photos. One of them was fine, possibly good, and without letting thought intervene he sent it.

She replied with emojis with hearts for eyes. She was so good to him.

maybe i should take off my shirt too, she said.

He lay down on the bed and waited for the photo. It came, a topless selfie, her perfect breasts, smallish with small pink nipples. All he wanted to do with his life was have them in his mouth. His pants filled, a blessing. He wanted her to touch him now before anything changed.

I'll send a cab for you? he said.

The reply was long in coming. His cock slumped to one side and started caving. He tried looking at the photo of her tits again but it had expired.

i cant tonight, she wrote.

my friend wants to go out later

She sent that eye-rolling emoji.

tomorrow? she said.

No problem, he said. Tomorrow works.

He was about to turn off the phone and go watch TV or something when another photo arrived. Now she was wearing just a black thong and she'd turned her ass to the mirror and he wanted to die by suffocation in its curve.

The caption said, but im so horny rn, with some wailing emojis.

The pic sent him past articulation and all he could do was send drooling emojis.

show me something? she said.

He needed commands. Like what? he said.

your cock baby

He fully undressed and knelt on the bed. His cock was hard, drifting slightly left. Some pre-cum had leaked and with his thumb he painted the head and it glistened in the light. With the phone he framed his reflection in the mirror, everything below the neck. His belly was a little distended after dinner but his dick looked thick. He could see someone wanting this dick. He massaged it slowly.

god i wanna ride u, she wrote, and sent one of herself sitting on the floor, her long legs spread. Her pussy was a beautiful shadow.

tell me how bad u want this

He was still on his knees, jerking off insanely. Behind his eyes he lapped up the pink between her legs.

I need to know what that feels like, he wrote, slathering his frothed pre-cum on the screen.

A video came. Maria was on all fours, her ass to the camera, a sharp pink nail visible as she pressed between the lips of her cunt.

hold me down and fuck me

Yes baby

tell me im a good girl

You're a good girl

He filmed himself jerking his cock as pictures of it disappearing inside her flashed upon his brain.

These balls are so heavy for you

i wanna drink every drop

I'll give it to you

show me ur face when u fuck me

He angled the camera so he was fully visible in the mirror. He felt hard and glorious and like their souls were flying away holding hands.

omfg im gonna cum so hard, she said.

You want me to cum?

ya baby

fill me

fill this pussy

He lay back and filmed his cock. He coated the whole shaft in pre-cum and stroked it as she glanced over her shoulder, her mouth open wide, her eyes disbelieving this thickness and this depth. He buried himself in her pussy and she took it and the first cum spurted, his eyes crushed closed, hot white spilling through his fingers. He felt huge and there was love in the world. Then he gasped and his eyes shot open and he was dizzy and happy in his sudden emptiness.

With a playful flop he got on his stomach and reversed the camera direction, the cum webbed between his fingers. His face filled the screen. He smiled and took a photo, just one, and when he looked at it he was touched. The face was so sweet, so serene. He sent it off and wrote, Thank you. Come get the real thing tomorrow.

As soon as he hit send he received a reply, several long messages with images attached. He looked at the images. They were screenshots of his friends' Facebook and Instagram accounts and the website of his company.

Hey, the message said. I've been screen-recording everything. I have your photos and videos and I'm gonna send them to all your friends and family and post it on all social medias. I don't care if you block me or do any kind of shit I'll make sure I get your nudes posted. Now don't panic, you can make this go away. You transfer me 3000$ (US dollars) in BTC to this address 13rZuNK8rbWkReQNxghvc64CPS8T9jZUy4 and I will erase all your pics from my machines and never contact you again. I will count to 10 and if you don't respond I will click to send your video. Will you be able to gaze into anyone's eyes after that?

More messages started arriving.

10

9

8

He closed the app and deleted it. A notification came in from Instagram, a new follower and a message.

If you think this is a prank check Facebook

With unsteady hands he blocked and reported the user and made his account totally private. Then he went to his Facebook. He hadn't used it in a while, only old people were on there, but someone with a name not Maria had just posted a photo on his wall. It was the first pic he'd sent, the shirtless one, and the user wrote, If you want to see what's below then I have lots message me

He deleted it and blocked and reported and turned all the security settings to maximum.

An email arrived. The subject line was, You think you're so smart blocking me but just watch

Then another. I will do everything I can to destroy your life

He reported that as spam and then everything fell silent. He was still naked, his hand still sticky with cum. He felt the weight of the snow on the roof over his head. He curled into a ball against the headboard and googled around about what to do in situations like this. The advice was all the same, just ignore it, if the scammer can't reach you then they'll go away. They might send some pics to one or two friends but there was nothing you could do about it now. The advice always came with a censure. Why would you think a woman wants a picture of your dick after a few minutes of chatting online?

He turned off the phone and plugged it in and placed it on the bedside table. Then he lay down flat and stared into the stucco up above. It's true, he was a fool, that was obvious. But his calm surprised him. How could he be so unbothered by some psycho in Côte d'Ivoire or whatever blackmailing him? Why did it not seem to matter if his boss or grandmother woke up to a video of his dick exploding? The cold finally got to him and he slipped under the covers and cuddled into himself. Then he realized it's because he looked good. So he's alive in the world, there's nothing shameful in that. Let everybody see. He switched off the lamp and as he waited for sleep he thought about his smile in the last photo and felt nothing but grateful for Maria.

# Labefactions of a Thwarted Patootie

I AM THE LABEFACTIONS OF A THWARTED PATOOTIE.

I am her downfall, her *untergang*, her demise itself; I am inevitable putrefaction and entropy.

Little is known of the life of said Patootie, save that she was "thwarted" in ways that are said to irretrievably compromise an individual. She was put to rout in the same way that a military battalion suffers defeat at the hands of a conquering barbarian horde — she was brutalized, with no consideration given beyond her total ruination.

I am also the Ministrations of the Dread Penalty and the Recrudescence of Venereal Indiscretion. The Abrogations of a Noble Spirit and (no relation) the Calumnious Defiling of Sinless Innocence I consider close friends.

I am the Patootie grinding her shapely hindquarters into the denticulated bridgework of travelling salesmen, bathroom

attendants, mail carriers, telegram boys, office managers, psych-
ometrists, custodians, supply teachers, civil servants, dentists,
hair stylists, servers, soda jerks, typing pool marauders, grocers,
overlooked authors, and one circus performer (sword swallower)
as she hand-spunked variously apportioned cocks to comple-
tion, before inserting a fabled finger into their squalid, sweaty
netherdoms.

They called this sexual service the Devil's Jump while she
went by the *nom de guerre* of Smut-Matron (bless her undigni-
fied heart).

Her admirers brought her asafoetida, desiccated chicory,
bulking agents, and glucomannan derived from the konjac
plant, none of which she obliged. She had presence of mind to
know that browning someone off took on an altered meaning
on this side of the Atlantic.

She retained an unfaltering sense of decorum about the
service she provided, so much so that she never veered from its
stable ingredients and proportions, that it might approximate
the allure of a widely enjoyed cocktail or an elite club that could
claim some unifying social feature among its members (having
all slept with some local celebrity, having all been chewed out by
some local celebrity, having all been autodidactically enamoured
with the unpronounceable surname of some local celebrity).

Said Thwarted Patootie, the engineer of many sexual mir-
acles, eventually left such diversions behind her and settled
down with a charmless Californian investment banker who
knew nothing of his dearly beloved's former life.

One day while in queue at the butcher's shop, a voice whispered into her ear, "Patootie, is that you I behold?"

It need not matter what name this Gentleman Caller answered to, nor what circumstances had fortuitously arranged

for him to meet his long lost inamorata. The Gentleman entreated Patootie to make off with him in his Arctic (Wimbledon) white Lincoln Continental, but nothing — not shelling out for the cost of her poundage of mesquite-tinged brisket, not the Porcaloca-sized billfold he produced from his inside pocket — could shake her indefatigable powers of indifference.

She took no notice of the Gentleman driving alongside her and jabbering through the passenger window until he mentioned a "corset-wearing factotum employed in his office" who had performed the same Devil-Jumping courtesy for him one night in a granary of his farmstead estate.

Without turning to face him, Patootie stopped in her tracks and asked, "What did your boy call it?"

"He called it the 'Nonesuch Handbrake' or something like it. The secret's out and you along with it. But I know better. Accept no substitutes. I'm sad to say that the last paying customers you entertained were too addle-brained to remember its mechanics properly. No one drinks the Martinez anymore, correct? And soon the Nonesuch will be all that remains."

"Unacceptable," Patootie muttered under her breath.

"What was that, poppet?"

"Drive us up to Mount Whitney," she said, "and I'll take you someplace humankind has seldom been."

"That's over a hundred miles from here."

"Have Ardour, will travel. Only my husband has experienced it."

"What will it cost me?"

"You, Marcus Winstone, accounts manager at Taggart and Young, who engaged my services on five occasions, all at the Hotel del Coronado from 1972 to 1973?"

"I knew you were something special. I say it again, ungrudgingly. What will it cost me?"

"How about some executive visibility?"

"Well, I do like the sound of that."

I am the Labefactions of a Thwarted Patootie, soon to become the Sanctification of a Transfigured Patootie, who so placed her hands on the Gentleman's treacly member as one would start a friction fire, manoeuvring her palms like oily paddles of seed-spilling misadventure. Gentleman felt the unendurable pressure build, felt his head swim from the rapid change in air pressure lying down on a scarped edge near the base of Mount Whitney.

His bottom lip began to quiver, signalling to Patootie that the agony-muck still flowed copiously through him despite his enfeebled appearance. With her thumb pressed down like it was fastening a thumbtack through a stubborn piece of cork, Patootie pushed on the tip of Gentleman's cut cock and improbably wrapped the surrounding folds of flesh over it. She held this makeshift foreskin together between her shapely index and middle fingers the same way a stylist is accustomed to handle hair that is about to be sheared.

The Gentleman yowled from the pain sullying his pleasure-seeking. It was only when Patootie released her fingers that Gentleman's rapturous mewling echoed down the Whitney Portal and the Mount Whitney Trailhead.

The Gentleman began to swoon and pressed his hands against his temples in an effort to control the massive headache-induced megrim that was sure to follow.

"What do you call that?" he asked as his chism dripped along the ridges of his scrotum like moraine from a glacier.

"Egads, woman. I can't even stand properly."

I am the Labefactions of a Thwarted Patootie.

Little is known of the life of said Patootie, save that she was responsible for the creation of the Devil's Jump and the Vamp Stamp you enjoy with shameless regularity, which you request at houses of ill repute and temples of carnal worship and in bedrooms with familiars all across the land, with the sang-froid of having your pants pressed.

There was dignity to these youthful labours. As she lingers over the threshold of death, her body racked with pain and suffering, take heed to never speak of her "gracious withdrawal from perfection, keeping a hint of former majesty withal."

# Patience

I KNOW WHEN SHE ASKS ME TO FIX THE EARRING HOOK CAUGHT in her hair. My hands don't shake even after all the times I've jerked off thinking about how soft her hair would be in my fist. We've been learning about where each other comes from, and why we're here, for months now. Why are we getting bored at a juice stand in the mall? She is observant and coy, and I feel my stomach clench like the fist I imagine working into her every time her ass in those jeans goes up in the air when she bends to unpack the oranges. She wears the same jeans all the time and I bet they're a little bit dirty. I've thought about it, what that seam smells like.

At the earring moment I know she's thought about what I smell like too. At least my neck. At least my armpit. It's good, for the record. A girl I'd seen recently described it like this: grassy and warm. So I asked her for a drink.

Girls like me. Girls at specific bars, at specific hours of the night, who don't know anything about my family and would never see me anxious and tired in the daylight, jonesing for a smoke break. This girl I see almost every day. I haven't spent so much time with a girl since high school, when I would turn constantly, pretending to check the time in class to catch a glimpse of this other, this long-necked ponytail girl. Great posture that showed off her neck and breasts and her lips always parted. The space between her lips alone would make my mouth water.

After her, her kisses and tantrums, after high school, I learned some things: dropping my jaw like a flower opening, vapidly checking girls out to find them grinding in my arms on the dance floors, exuding tequila, hair on my pillow, again like a flower. So sweet to see her in my unmade bed with her eyes shut, grinding and yearning and wetting my hand, my thigh. Another her. Another her. Different bodies that made my eyes widen like new clothes. They had new clothes that they took off half-ashamed or laughing while I kept my pants on, loose around my hips. My eyes appraised and desired and that's most of it. Their wetness made me focused and calm. I floated above them like a dream, dreamt myself in the pleasure of night girls and their pussy lips like deerskin, arched backs and stiff nipples. I noticed details like a silver ring on every finger or a soft blond patch of hair on the tailbone. Details about concealing and revealing, hard and soft, fast and slow, what made them nice and juicy. I dress kind of country but I'm not. But I started thinking about fishing. Still patience. My eyes the pond, my hands the line.

And I let them out in the morning, both of us soft-eyed and embarrassed, disappearing from each other's lives again and again. I'd go back to my life of smoking weed and reading poems in my boxer briefs. I ate tuna fish and rice. On and off welfare, in and out of the evening, in and out of wondering if I'd be better off dead.

SNOW, TEARS, RATS. THEIR PLEASURE SAVED ME.

My juice-stand girl makes me react like the ponytail teen dream. My chest gets red under my pearl-snap shirt. I speak softly, getting her to lean in close enough to smell me at this straight bar after work. Her eyes dilate. She's wearing this incredible top I've never seen before, with a round hole for the dark line where her breasts meet, and I keep imagining working up that other dark line of hers, the one I haven't seen yet. I'm not saying much, saying much less than our gossip. We're enjoying the turn things have taken quietly. I'm warm from my drink and waiting. She's making fun of me.

"I see you looking."

"Looking where?"

She runs her finger up and down the line. Heavy, beautiful tits without a bra.

"You're beautiful." I'm honest.

"Thank you, you're beautiful too!" she says cutely, and then recognizes she's said the wrong thing when I lean back and hide my hands. Really, I want to put her over my knee. I imagine making a hole in the jeans, where I've checked her round ass so many times, bigger, making that ass wobble in my two hands, smacking it and rendering her speechless. I imagine her biting the mattress while I make her red, then dipping my fingers inside while I lift her by the hair with my other hand to make her taste her wetness. I imagine us sharing the pleasure of her wet, happy cunt.

"So I think I really am going back to school this winter," she's saying. She's looking into her drink and can't see my thoughts in my gaze.

"I'll miss you at work."

"You're staying? I thought you were there for me," she jokes. I notice her seem to think about who will be my next companion, crushing ice. "How long are you really going to stay?" Her eyes are wide, caring dark holes. I shrug and stretch.

"To be honest I'd rather be in the moment. Do you want to get out of here?" When I help her with her coat, I cup her ass gently for the first time and she arches back into my hand easily. She's wonderfully ready.

We tiptoe past my roommates and I turn on a lamp that doesn't illuminate the mess, just the big rumpled bed. Spotlight on the edge where I sit her down and bring my face close to her beautiful face like I'm about to kiss her tipsy, happy mouth, but I don't. I fall to my knees and look up in a devotion that feels like fun theatre. My hands run up and down her sheer stockings as if smoothing her legs. Her breathing is changing, her hands in my buzz cut. Her lips are swollen like we've been kissing but we haven't. Just talking together, drinking together, teasing each other. I run up a little farther — I'm dying to really feel the weight of her perfect ass — and my hands are on her thighs under her tight black skirt. I pull the thighs open and she lets me release them, then I look at this blank white space covering what I'm here to please. I slip into the sides of her thong and peel it down. After months, I'm looking straight at her pussy. Her pussy is closest to me, the shape of her pussy, this dark little walnut made to suck. It's shy, furred. The darker colour of it spreads across her thighs. The smell of her is something impossibly deep and warm. All the smells I like are descendants of this one.

But it's closed still, and her thighs fall together slightly. I want to lick the inside of her thigh and stroke it with the back of my hand, but she's pulling me up by the shoulders, pushing my shoulders back against the headboard. I think she wants that kiss, but she pulls back and is smoothing her hands across my chest, reaching for my shirt snaps. I try to be playful, try to catch her wrists to stop her, but she grabs mine and places them at my side.

Her knees are on either side of my face. Her skin is as soft as water, and her pussy, hovering above me, surrounded by the ring of its skirt, is getting wet. I smile and open wide, stick my tongue out, and exhale down it like a dog or laughing god, knowing the warmth of my breath will reach her. Her face is floating far away, lips and eyes half parted, the space between all those soft lips making me crazy to fill. I would even lick her eyeball. I would stretch her mouth with my hand, but she wants to play with her own control. It's important for her to feel powerful, although most of my dates don't get there this way.

She hovers lower, low enough that when I stretch, the tip of my tongue brushes the edges of her sweet cunt lips, then moves upward with control. I'm getting antsy and my jeaned hips buck up past where she hovers. She reaches back and grabs my crotch full in her hand. I'm stunned and inch away, so she moves to the thigh. Her touch is not what I'm used to, though. She holds my thigh like it can take abuse and like I'm holding her up at the same time. Her hips push forward and she's starting to smear on my face. I lap at her, animally eager. She rubs her pussy down on my mouth a bit, our eyes still locked, until hers start to look bored and she falls back.

I'm wondering what I don't know when she pulls her shirt off and her tits bounce into view with the drop of their significant weight from above. I try to lift my hands to seize them and she locks me easily with her knees. I want to love them with my tongue, make them shine above me. She's holding her body not like it's mine to admire. Not like a toy, but an instrument. Her nipples are hard, her eyes are sharp. She pushes her hips back down to my knees and rubs herself on the denim with the same look on her face as when it was my mouth. Leans forward and offers me a tit to suck. I'm willingly not moving my hands now, accepting them at my sides like a soldier and my hips are starting to rise again. She unsnaps the jeans like she did the shirt, her eyes on me, and moves her face down to my boxer briefs.

"I don't usually go there," I croak, and she nods, eyes on me with a question in them now, cheek pressed fiercely against my mons. I lift a hand to hold her there and press her cheekbone to my bone there. Consent. I'm beginning to accept. She nuzzles the top, the bone. Her hand goes over my underwear to the crack of my ass through my underwear, presses the dampness up into it, pressing my hole through the cotton. I am surprised to wriggle back against the side of her hand. She is pulling down the underwear now but ignores what's there and climbs back up above my face so air is hitting my bare crotch, where I find myself sensitive. It's a shock. Usually, what I have down there is as internal as my heart.

Now she hovers again and I see her cunt is open, I see the shining pink inside, available, her orange juice honey sticky. So she wants to stay up above me. I'm beginning to feel like I'm sinking through water. Her pussy starts to fold over me and I'm licking, sucking, trying to feel the current of her with my tongue. I'm feeling it, I'm there. She's there. She is throbbing in my mouth like a live mussel. She is briny and hot and sweet and deep too. I am myself with my slack jaw from the club, doing what makes me happy, but somehow my jeans and underwear are pulled down to my knees, the full weight of the woman on my face, air stinging me below like a blow. Her breathing gets more laboured. I can dimly see her own hand over her mouth muffling her moans, which is hot. She's coming. She comes, her full weight down on my face. I didn't know that was my favourite.

She is lifting off me, sliding down, keeping her heavy gaze on mine, running her hands over me in circles, moving my stiff energy. She drops down to me and presses her hand, knuckles up, against the bottom of me, against what I just sucked on her. I'm stunned to feel myself lubed. She is rubbing me, looking at me. Hard, even strokes like a punch. She's running her other hand all over me, letting my energy go in circles. The softness on my body melts away under her fingers. She massages a hand and I realize I can move my arms. There's a new strength in them as I reach up to hold her like someone powerful I want to protect.

She flips so her ass is in my face but sensitive and tired, still out of reach. She's touching me and how I move through the world is altered. I'm on my back and she is sucking what I have so much, more than enough to be a cock. Her hand is up my centre. She is holding me down above my heart. What made me put my arms up in the air, twist my fingers around each other? The way she pulses my heart down it's like I'm all muscle. When I come, my throat reveals itself the way she revealed the cock I know I have. It's like I'm coming through what I swagger around imagining, but it reaches out the top of my head, long beyond the ends of my toes.

In silence, she covers me with herself, all woman. She made me a man. My pleasure saved me, and she floated above me like a dream.

# Gold Star

I SHIFT DOWN INTO FIRST, AWARE OF GUY'S EYES ON MY hand, the soft frost making symmetrical puzzles on the windshield glass, and there at the top of the hill is Massey Drive pond, dark and clear like a promise. I can feel him grin at the stick shift, my mom's old rusted Tracker bringing us back twenty years to the last time we were up here together. Back then we looked similar, both of us foxlike and angular, with blue eyes and black hair, and the memory of our likeness shoots through me; he still looks like an icon, clean and sharp, where I am something else now, weak-chinned and soft, my lower back hot with strain, a testament to slow and constant downward movement.

If I told you that I'm not what I was when it happened between us, I know that some long-quieted part of me would be lying. The first time it was dark as pitch, just our bodies, wet and hot. He synched up the rabbit rhythm of our hearts somehow, one steady quick beat between us, pressed his long fingers down my slicked abdomen and reached them inside of me, lighting up a whole world I hadn't really known about. The animal noise that came out of me, dark and masculine, surprised us both, and we laughed like there was nothing to hide. I moved my way around him like I knew what I was doing because I didn't have to think about it, slipped him into me, and pressed my hips against him with an urgency as desperate and intuitive as prayer. The pain was good, and once he was inside I wanted him deeper, all of him, wanted him up through my chest and throat as he held me down firm like a threat, his hands pressed hard against my shoulders, fucked me until I couldn't tell the difference between inside and outside, both of them spinning into a flurry of heat and light, and I came in such a rush it left me flayed, stupid, and loving. We were just kids and we didn't know anything, but then and after, we knew that.

At the funeral, I told Guy how shocked I'd been about Teddy, grasping, I realized too late, the buttoned sleeve of his black linen coat, wrinkling it in my clutch. We stood close as if for warmth through the eulogy, Guy's arm playfully a-sway, gently grazing my bare skin, his hand sometimes reaching down to squeeze mine. He whispered to me mid-speech that it hadn't surprised him, said that he'd always wondered about Teddy's ability to keep going, how he wasn't really set up properly for all of that living, is what he said. Guy's always been that type of person who will say what other people don't even want to admit they're thinking.

In high school the three of us had been best friends, but I had since mostly lost touch with Teddy, whereas he and Guy stayed close, moved to Montreal together and then Toronto nearly the same time too. I went to music school, for piano, in

Antigonish instead and now teach it. The truth is, I probably wouldn't be at the funeral if I wasn't living at home again, the acrimonious split with Josh sending me and my girl, Maddy, back to where rent was cheap and schools were easier to enroll her in, plus the family support we both needed. Guy flew in from the mainland, hadn't been home in years. We chatted a lot online the last few, but I had forgotten the effect of him, that voice, low and veering in a flash between sardonic and kind, the slight lisp, the smirk hiding in every word. Teddy had been so in love with him and I think it was mutual, at least in a way. We used to sneak out, the three of us with our parents' liquor in our backpacks, run laughing up the steep length of Massey Drive, and once at the pond play Never Have I Ever. The usual rules of the game go like this: each person gets a turn saying the words "never have I ever" and then finishing the sentence with something they have never done. If a member of the group *has* done the stated claim, then that person takes a drink. The purpose of the game, more than anything, was to learn secrets about one another, ones that might not come up in conversation. We did this, but with the added removal of one article of clothing for each drink, so it was also a stripping game, the first person naked forced to jump into the inky cold water.

On the dock, the silence between us is known and thick. I break it.

Remember how Teddy used to lie, I say. So that he could follow you into the water?

Teddy had been pudgy and acne-scarred around the jaw, colicky as a baby, and something of that carrying into teenage-hood, his teeth yellow for no discernible reason, maybe just a lack of enamel. He was a gamer, never got enough sunlight, his parents alcoholics and slot addicts who never made dinner and were worse when around than an empty house. Like Guy said, Teddy wasn't set up right. But something about him drew you in, some dark secret his vibe tempted, though most people seemed repelled, not wanting to be a part of that ominous club. If you opted to be a member, then Teddy was sexy in his way. His confidence in lying about something so obvious, for example. And Guy needed his absurdity, the bravery of it.

Guy fans his hand out and looks at his nails, bites the middle one for a moment.

I remember that, he says. I remember he took off his socks when you said that thing about cigars. What was it? Never have I ever stolen Cuban cigars from my father and resold them? You said it because you wanted to call me out on it, wanted to see Teddy's expression when he saw me drink. And he and I both took a drink. Ha!

At first I used to wonder if you guys were maybe soulmates, all that random stuff in common, I responded. There was just all of this, like, *energy* that came through the two of you in the water, fanning waves around, fighting and going under for longer and longer every time.

It was the only place he'd be like that, Guy says, looking me in the eye for longer than a beat.

I think about the last time I had sex. Josh and I had divorced two years earlier. He never got it back after Maddy was born, used to hold my breasts up to his face contemplatively and say things like "you're a restaurant now." At first it was funny and the damage from the birth was too much to even consider being touched, but when eventually my body healed and the jokes kept coming, curdling us both in repetition, I saw what I was to him, and I couldn't be that type of woman they talk about, the one who skulks around in a short skirt at home, bending over to show the fabric of a trashy pink thong, the kind of woman who begs for it. I *wanted* to beg for it, but not to him and not like that. And after Josh there had only been a couple of one-night stands with strangers, the sex athletic and drunken under too-bright lights. The bleak memory breaks as I notice Guy taking off his shoes and then socks, like how Teddy used to, but I don't say anything. You can't really say anything to Guy like that; to question a decision he's already made always feels confusingly embarrassing. No one else I'd ever met was like him.

After that first time, we kept it going in secret, Guy and I. What do I remember? The sound of construction in the distance, the rough bark bloodying our knees as we hid up against a tree behind his parents' house at dusk, his hand somehow under my braid and through it, pressing the crown of my head forward, the pressure, the mess. The sky highlighter blue, its diffuse light dancing over our faces, the dirty maple leaves that he used to wipe me down with after, how later I'd find bits of leaves stuck to the insides of my thighs like secret messages. Or other times on school nights when he would sneak in through my bedroom window, knocking over picture frames, sliding into my twin bed, taking me there like that in resolute near-stillness so that my parents couldn't hear and all I could feel was him hard inside of me, the slightest shift electric like I could track his moving blood. And what else? Unopened Gatorade on the floor, matching socks confusing to reclaim, how if in the hour after I had to speak to my parents or anyone, every word came out of me a second too late, so that I was overlapping my words with theirs, stunned and pretending to be the same person but blunted in the aftermath and caught. Or that time on the ferry for a band trip, the loud drip of the faucet in the janitor's closet, my head dodging the tendrils of a leaning mop as I felt myself unfurl from the inside, climaxing through my arms and legs and stomach as he held his hand firmly over my mouth. But what was it like between us otherwise and through that? It was unspoken; Teddy couldn't know, and beyond that I can't really remember. Just that I thought life would continue that way, that I would keep feeling it like that with him, or not, and it didn't, and I didn't, and I was the last and only girl he was ever with, and he didn't set me up well for living either, not that he had to, not at all.

Guy and I dangle our feet over the dock and he lights a smoke, his hand shaking more than the cold would cause, and I consider his sharp jawline, his tired eyes, how maybe he hasn't managed to rein in the party. He pulls a sixty of tequila out of his tote bag and takes a long swig before handing it to me. A single star beams in the sky over us, stark and too big for the night, and I wonder if it's Teddy.

You lied at least once too while we were playing Never Have I Ever, I mention, hoping the threat of it will get his socks back on. Instead, he takes off his jacket, his shirt underneath a thin summer linen. Clears his throat.

You still smell the same, he tells me. A drop of patchouli, soap, girl hair.

I think it's just, like, seeped into my skin by now, I admit. I hadn't put it on in years.

I take the bottle out of his hand, drink way more in a swig than I think I'm capable of, and swallow, his eyes on me energizing, making the challenge feel easy, and I remember how in love I had been with him, despite myself.

He and Teddy had something that I envied so much. How they wanted each other but with this poetic, active restraint that was only curtailed for moments like this one, late at night in the water.

Can I ask you something, I say.

Go on, he responds, which everywhere else in the world means continue but in Newfoundland also means stop.

Did you ever carry it over into real life? Like, did you guys ever date, or try to?

Guy contemplates the bottle in his hand, the glint off the moon and single star lighting up tiny edges of it in brief flashes.

Not really, he says. We tried some stuff in Montreal, when we were older. But it always felt risky, like if I did, if I leaned into it, I would have to give it everything. Like, forever. Like, it would be too much to stop, he says, his lisp thickening in the cold.

But then you *did* stop, if it *was* something at one point.

We did, he says, and the weight of it hits me newly, and I see what he's carrying.

Before we started having sex in high school, Guy came over one night before the semi-formal, disappeared into the bathroom down the hall, and came out wearing a cling-tight lilac dress from my closet, a hot pink wig, emerald stilettos that made him look a hundred feet tall. I just looked at him, thought about how much better he pulled off the dress than I ever could. I did his makeup on his command, softly brushed a sparkling blush over the edges of his cheeks, revelling in the intimacy of how he let me touch him like that. That night, at the dance, I kissed a boy from school while slow dancing to "Purple Rain," and after, the boy asked me who my friend was, interested. The question was gutting. You wouldn't know her, I told him.

219

Guy ditched the dance early, his beauty too gossip-provoking to allow him a low profile, and told me he was going to Broadview West, the seedier bar-heavy area of town where they don't card anyone, to get fucked. He had started doing that the fall before, using sleepovers at my house as an alibi and staying out. That night I worried about him like a mother would, how vulnerable he might be to some lonely old man in the pay-per-hour hotel down by the mill, comforted only by his self-assurance, his coy, distanced demeanour that held him at bay from other people, making him powerful and invulnerable, the right kind of woman.

We sit quiet for a long time and I think about the lie he told, wonder whether I should bring it to him. At first I think not, but when he starts to unbutton his pants, the cold of the night chattering his jaw, I consider it, hoping to slow him down.

If I ask you to tell me the lie, you might say a different one, and then that's double bad for you, I say to him.

Double trouble, he responds laughing, and I'm quiet.

I lied to you less than to other people, he says after a bit, pulling his black pants down his thighs, revealing a tattoo of a cross I had forgotten about.

The one I remember hurt me, I say, and we both know.

I never wanted to hurt you, Jessa, he says to me, a warble in his voice. I just figured you could handle it better than Teddy could.

I challenge him with a look and bite my tongue.

That night fell at the very end of the summer we had spent sleeping together, something that I could tell no one about. Maybe if I had girlfriends I would have told them, but I didn't, just Guy and Teddy. It was almost the start of our final year of high school, Labour Day weekend, already a chill in the air. I got drunk on the walk because I wanted the courage of it. Guy went to pee in a bush by a pink house, and I asked Teddy to dare Guy to kiss me once we reached the dock. It was a cruel ask because of how it might make Teddy feel, but I needed it. The rest of the walk, Teddy kept his distance from me, Guy filling the space between us, singing "The Leanover," by Life Without Buildings, in a chaotic, feral way.

I pushed for Truth or Dare once on the dock, the heavy air threatening rain, and as soon as Teddy gave the dare, Guy knew I had been in on it. He could just tell. He looked at me violently, put his finger on my lip the way he did other times when it was just us, and leaned toward me, his arms akimbo, just his lips on me and nothing else. It was like all those secret moments between us but uncanny for the distance of his body, no pulling me in but the pressure of his tongue on mine, the performed hunger of it, where usually it had been real. He was relaying something between us and I thought of him in those hotel rooms, seducing strangers. He pulled back and clicked his tongue, unable to look Teddy in the eye.

Enough of this, he said. Let's go back to Never Have I Ever, it's more fun.

Never have I ever had sex with a woman, said Teddy, looking at Guy closely. We all held our breath for a moment that seemed then and ever to stand outside of time. Guy cleared his throat, lifted the bottle in front of him without taking a sip, and then put it back down with deliberate slowness, and Teddy started to breathe again as a sharp pain cut through me, as real and emptying as a birth.

In our twenties, I followed Guy on Instagram, and he got a big following for posting humorous and performative details of his sex life, his Instagram handle @goldstar1987. A gold star is a gay man who has never slept with a woman in his life, a standard that few people met, it seemed. It was a joke and a revered symbol, as singular and shining as the star above us that night, the one that could've been Teddy, or maybe a satellite, or maybe just a real star exploded, gone now but still visible to the naked eye, tricking us all.

Guy and I huddle on the dock, remembering, and I feel the liquor rushing through me, the grief of the week having suppressed my appetite. The booze hits me harder than it normally would, and I lean into Guy, feel myself grip his bare leg. Then I feel his hand on my back, the pressure of it rising up under my shirt to my exposed neck, the heat in him warming me as I realize that the babysitter is probably waiting and I'll be up so early, that Guy will head back to Toronto soon and his hand will break contact with me, and once again I won't be equipped for the day, not a shape-shifter able to dream through it, not set up right. The thought hits me like a shock as he kisses me hard on the mouth, quick and real, reminding me of everything undeniable that still doesn't make sense. I feel myself come to life again there for the first time in years as he breaks contact, jumps up, and strips bare before me, his body taut and timeless. He kicks his clothes into a pile on the damp wood where I sit and dives without a splash into the impossible cold of the water, breaking the mirror of it and sending ripples extending outwards like the years in a tree, all of those years collecting. I try and find a ring close to him so that I can latch my gaze onto it and follow it to the shore, but too quickly it grows away from me under the glint of the moon and I lose it to the night.

# Content Farm Confidential

YOU HAVE FINISHED YOUR FIRST BOOK, AND NOW YOU must apply to the only jobs available to twenty-six-year-old freelance writers with zero life skills: writing copy for content farms. All these farms want the same thing: staggeringly long articles thousands of words long, stuffed with keywords to trick Google into vaulting their website to the very top of organic searches. A race to the top via the very bottom. A flattening, a meaninglessness made of a trade that was nearly redundant before you finished university.

You need to temper your feelings about content farms and other digital sweatshops by saying it's better than a lot of other gigs. You know, of course, that this is the era of Big Content, and it's a massive scam — the battle was lost as soon as everyone all agreed, for some reason, to call what you do content, as opposed to, you know, articles, photography, programming, music, interviews, documentaries, prose, reportage, criticism. Calling it content made it all nothing but a commodity. It's like exceptional barley, run-of-the-mill barley, and lousy barley all end up mixed up together in the same grain elevator.

You get through three interviews with [Content Farm] and write them a six thousand–word pillar page titled "Top 25 Tips to Raise the Value of Your Business Property — #12 Will Surprise You!" It's an "audition" piece, the chipper hiring manager reassures you. You smile painfully and blush through the "culture fit" interview — yes, you love Ping-Pong; no, you hate leaving the office before a task is finished. A 60 K salary had been advertised, but you're gently informed in a call with the hiring manager — the pops of a Ping-Pong game in the background — that the posting wasn't necessarily reflective of the nature of the actual position, and you'd be looking at about half that. You express dismay before you can stop yourself — a very human moment, the first one you've shared in your hours together on the phone — and you don't hear from them again for five days. You assume they've passed on you, and it's their loss, you tell yourself, deeply crushed. You eat ice cream with your roommates and liken big data to toxic waste and call Silicon Valley the gestapo in hoodies. And then your phone rings again.

"I'm the CEO of [Content Farm]," a man says.

"Oh, wow, hi." You are peeing; you only answered because you didn't recognize the number, which looks incredibly exotic — it could be Los Angeles, it could be Sierra Leone.

"You'd be such a strong addition to our team. You've never seen a team like this, I promise. You'll get the most amazing mentorship, and you'll become a rock star mentor."

"It's the money," you say frankly. Your pussy stings from stopping the stream so quickly, and you realize with horror that you're aroused. You pull on your underwear, bunched around your ankles; the elastic has gone loose. You notice your toothbrush is in the garbage again, wedged in with bloody Kleenexes — one of your roommates, perhaps making a symbolic gesture, keeps throwing it out.

"How about twenty-nine thousand," he says, "and we offer you [a series of bullshit benefits you don't understand]. How do you like that?"

Good Lord. He doesn't even *sound* good. A horrible memory sprouts up unbidden, a pale mushroom from rot: phone sex with your high school boyfriend — *What are you wearing? Do you like my big dick? Am I your daddy? Do you like that?*

"I'll have to think about it," you say, dismayed: How much functional underwear do you have left? People wear underwear in offices, don't they? Will you get a bladder infection?

"Well, I heard something in your voice just now," he says, lowering his own. "It sounds like you want it. And when I want something, I just go for it. Trust your instincts."

Were these your instincts?

You take the job.

Everyone is unimaginably young, and everyone is an expert, and everyone sits at one long table. It's January; the sun has barely risen, the clouds are thick and bruised, and the rows of fluorescent light glare back at you from the glass.

Management tracks the copywriters' progress using an incomprehensible supervision program, and on Friday, the twenty-one-year-old office manager turns on the giant screen by the exit, brings out trays of wet sandwiches so the copywriting team might have some choking hazards to grasp as she calls up a series of charts. You are the only girl copywriter. None of the guys look at you as you all roll your wheely chairs up to the screen. Each copywriter is assigned a percentage grade based on their productivity during the week. Every minute is accounted for. Your first week, you receive the worst grade: 68 percent, the office manager observes in a sombre, worried tone.

"I work slow, but I'm meticulous," you say, which is true; your brain is like a water mill, turning over and over. But this week, nonetheless, you produced the fewest articles on the Top 5 Security Cameras to Protect Your Legal Marijuana Business, the fewest articles on The Top 10 Most Romantic Places to Vacation in Ontario This Year, the fewest pillar pages on the Top 3 Ways to Structure a Pillar Page, and so on, and the office manager is disappointed in you.

You realize quickly that the CEO has promoted certain particularly soulless young workers very quickly to "management" roles, and they get off on micromanaging the copywriters. It's so strange to have your piece torn apart with mystifying edits — like, truly mystifying, and you do appreciate a good edit — when the piece is itself just a long, cynical strand of garbage about The Best Security Cameras on the Market Right Now, and then Five Tips to Make Sure You Get the Best Security Cameras on the Market Right Now, all to trick the Google Algorithm — possibly. Playing tricks on the Google Algorithm seems to you total folly, unadvisable and puny, like trying to fool God. You say, "FUCK," when your keyboard freezes, and your phone's digital assistant wakes up and chirps beside you — "Hello [Name], I'm afraid I can't help you with that."

So your coworkers, these kids (and they are all kids), stay late and work for free all weekend and say really interesting things like "[Content Farm] company managers have no life but we're always hustling." What product they are hustling, to where, or to whom is unclear. What is clear is they are under-slept, resentful, unsexed, and incredibly young. They don't have time to sit down for a meal, to look out the window, or even to fuck; fucking isn't really hustling, so what's the point? One of them proudly tells you that he's a dirty, dirty capitalist. Not the good kind of dirty, you figure — he seems unwashed, covered in coal dust, his childhood birthdays passing in a Victorian garment factory. You ask the Dirty, Dirty Capitalist why he doesn't request overtime pay, or an appropriate salary, and he ignores you for a week.

Wednesdays are compulsory chair yoga during lunchtime. Every other Thursday, the office manager marches the team to the Philthy McNasty's around the corner, and you drink enor-mous margaritas and chew on your tongue. You know that the workplace culture is uniquely toxic but only later realize how unviable it was. It's like a shitty gold rush with no gold and none of the prospectors bothered to wear un-smelly sneakers to work. But you find pleasure where you can: sometimes you ask the Dirty, Dirty Capitalist if humans really landed on the moon, or whether 9/11 was an inside job; his answers rarely disappoint. One copywriter, a chubby man who churns out copy at a cold-blooded, alarming rate, deigns to talk to you sometimes, and it's always to present a fact. "When you fly United Air Emirates, they cover the windows so that you don't see whether or not the Earth is flat," he says one morning, as you're peeling a banana.

Never underestimate the allure of the only man who gets the office in a content farm. Not even [CFO Name] gets an office. He sits at the long table beside the Content Managers and hears them talk about Jell-O shots and worries about his stepdaughter — she's just discovered weed too young. [CEO Name] is the only man with an office in [Content Farm], and it's a big one with a cheap, massive desk. He'll take calls on speakerphone and spin his chair around to his floor-to-ceiling window to take in the expansive view of the parking lot, the Vietnamese nail salon, and the gigantic, down-at-the-heels Western buffet.

One morning, he invites you in for a belated entrance interview and asks about your writing; you say a stupid, grad student word he doesn't recognize, and he frowns slightly, then smiles, and writes the word on a Post-it, confirming the spelling with you — the first handwriting you've seen in an office full of writers. He's an idiot, you tell yourself. But you're touched, and you don't know why. And when something shifts between you, and you know it's time to go and close the office door behind you, you find that you don't want to.

Relations with your roommates have grown tense. They make their beds and sweep their floors every morning and leave their doors wide open, and the sun seems to shine through their pristine windows right out into the hallway. Your door is always shut, emanating a dark sense of fullness, like a deep, rotting hedge in summer. You know that you can't keep doing drugs that are probably made in vacuum cleaners; you know you can't keep living on spaghetti and sriracha; you know you can't keep being about to become. You want to find a sense of empathy and kindness and beauty everywhere, and you look everywhere for it, too. And if you can't find it, you construct it — in just about anyone who holds still long enough. So you begin to see tenderness in [CEO Name]: one day, he brings his mother to the office. She is wearing heels and stumbles a bit on a fold in the carpet — he reaches out, a practiced, gentle gesture, and takes her hand.

Proximity to power, even in a flimsy, transparent environment, is seductive. [CEO Name] is very rich and won't let anyone forget it; he bought his house — which, he assures the girls
in the office, is enormous — with cash. You wonder if he knows
there is something off-putting about him; that his sole capital
is his literal capital. Isn't that lonely?

Somehow you understand that it is only within the context
of this little digital fiefdom that you'll find this man attractive, and you want to savour the thrill it gives you. Bad drugs
have blown out your serotonin; you rely on masturbation at
night, imagining him fumbling with his fly, yanking down
your loose-elastic panties, kissing you deeply. The helpless in-
evitability of it pulls you in further.

Maybe your roommate is right about manifestation, because late the next afternoon, [CEO Name] calls you into his
office. The only other copywriter who talks to you gives you a
sympathetic little smirk — just last Friday, you scored 71 percent (he is always in the nineties).

"If you could get the door ..."

You are halfway through closing it already. Something in
the air shifts and changes, and something animal about you
smells it. Your scalp prickles.

And it happens.

He pulls the blinds against the bright white of the office,
the rows of eyes, the long, open, purple-carpeted expanse. You
imagine him telling you he loves you, leaning back away from
you to take your face in both of his hands and gaze at you, as
you guide him inside of you, so slick his cock comes out covered in long hot strands of you. Yes — that works. You want
to talk to him, to make it good for him. To pierce and deepen
whatever this is. "I'm so fond of you," you whisper into his

ear, your legs wrapped around his bare ass. He sighs into your mouth; his breath has grown hot. He closes his eyes and rests his head on your shoulder. You wonder — suddenly — if he'll cry, and it turns you on all the more.

Afterward, he helps you into your clothes, holding your hand like he holds his mother's, steadying you as you pull up your skirt. He sighs.

"Do *you* think this is working out, [Your Name]?" he says, with a practised gentleness that is as closed and rhetorical as a triple-locked door.

"This job?" You do not hesitate. His hand smells of you. "No."

"The numbers don't lie, [Your Name]," he says, adopting a concerned tone that the twenty-one-year-old office manager, you realize, has picked up from him. Clever. "You're barely clearing the seventies, you know? And I think we've been very patient in terms of scope adjustment." He collapses back in his swivel chair, his bedside manner impeccable. "You're just not cut out to be a content producer. Don't feel bad: it's not as easy as it seems."

"I see."

He pushes an envelope forward. "I'm providing four weeks' severance. For five weeks of work with [Content Farm], I'm sure you'll agree that's more than generous."

It is.

"May I share something, in the spirit of full transparency?" he says, and as always, it's not a question. Though you're wet all over, he's barely broken a sweat. He clasps his hands, and you realize, with a jolt, that his earpiece has been in the whole time.

"I know I'm in good shape, and I work hard on that," he says. "I run every morning and every night; I meditate, and aside from that glass of wine I shared with you, I only drink herbal tea. But I'm forty-four years old, [Your Name], and juggling two careers, especially with such unique demands of music and business, well. It leaves no time to grow a family. And that's incredibly important to me. And you know what? I'm fond of you."

You are astonished. Not by the implicit proposition, but by his awareness of biological reality. Since he shared powerful reverence for a future merging with tech to erase mortality, you had him pinned as a transcendental humanist.

Right down by the sparkling lakeside, in an opulent suburb from which even the trees whisper wealth, you walk through his house. It is indeed beautiful and smells terrible: he keeps it like a thirteen-year-old boy whose parents leave for months at a time. A display case for a cake, full of ancient crumbs, sits next to a wooden bowl containing his vape, the keys to the pool shed, and six shrivelled lemons.

"A woman makes a place a home," he says. It's not an observation, but rather a directive. Were you to move in, you would naturally arrange for another woman to scrub the floors with chemicals and a man to suck the brown swollen leaves and cicadas from the pool; you'd coordinate gardeners, cook dinners, and fold laundry. You'd find contractors to address the horrific smell in the master bathroom and to fix the fourth spare bedroom door that just wouldn't close, which in a moment — you assume — of rare rage, [CEO Name] has torn off its hinges. Bright white, the door now rests across the bed in the spare bedroom, like an enormous, unsent letter.

[CEO Name] makes you watch *The Red Pill* and talks to you earnestly about negging and other well-worn pickup-artist tactics during a weekend at a fabulous spa — he details the pickup artist oeuvre with a kind of earnestness that leaves you baffled. "I could have waited a few days to connect with you after our first date so you'd feel insecure, but I liked you," he says beatifically. You look at him. He looks at you. He's sprawled out, his long body draped over a woven chair. He crosses his coltish legs; you watch him pick at a bread roll, pull the middle out, and then put it back on the plate.

He stands up. He cups your face in his hand and kisses you. You leave your eyes open, a little game of resistance you've played since your sixth-grade English teacher kissed you in an empty classroom: What if he opens his eyes and sees the terrified whites of yours? Isn't that some kind of betrayal? [CEO Name] whispers your name and lifts you from your chair — he does this a lot, to your dismay — then lowers you on the scratchy rug. You whisper his name back, and he exhales, roughly, into your hair, sweat-caked from the sun, and there it is — the thread that turns you on — he is lonely, so lonely, and you are his, and he is becoming yours the way only a lonely person can — and oh, he *wants* that. And one day he might love you the way you know love. You close your eyes and kiss him back, deeply, and his response shocks you: a kind of stillness akin to surprise. Shifting beneath him and then swinging up around, you straddle him — his hip bones so sharp from this angle, you want to kiss the thin skin stretched between them — and his hands are gripping yours, guiding yours — you've both closed your eyes, yet you're guiding each other along. Something deeply painful flits across your mind. You remember that a certain gold-throated songbird is the world's cruellest delicacy. ([CEO Name] moans, and you moan back into his mouth.) The little bird is overfed brandy-soaked cakes with a cloth over its cage, disoriented in the dark. Its bones soften, sweeten; it takes weeks. (He kisses your stomach, your rib cage, one of your breasts.) The man who eats its flesh must drape his own head in cloth, to keep in the smell, and to hide himself from God.

You cry out together.

After he finds out about the weekend at the spa, your brother stops lending you money. Your best friend won't be your best friend anymore if she keeps buying you groceries. You had the four-thousand-dollar severance from [Content Farm], but you blow money; it's almost gone. You inherited this from your father: a grand stag of a man, he'd show up on your birthday with a paycheque so hot it burnt his fingers, presenting childhood-you with incredible gifts — a fluffy pink telephone for your bedroom! — and order massive spreads of sushi, then disappear again. Two winters ago he took you out for beers, his mind heavy with all the root canals his girlfriend required, and warned you about your family history of alcoholism. You remember scanning your father's face urgently, knowing not to beg him to stay. [CEO Name] knows this without knowing: it's all over you. People are what he reads, and he's incredible at it. He closes deals over sake minutes after disembarking from eighteen-hour flights to Japan.

After about a week at [CEO Name]'s house, your roommate texts you and you reply, tepidly reassuring her you're alive. You're dicing cabbage, green onions, and carrots to make slaw; it's 3:32 p.m. and you're halfway through a glass of cider. She texts that she's worried, and you assume it's about rent, but you know you're being unkind — though it's brittle and finite, she cares about you. You're used to assessing the limitations and conditionality of caring. [CEO Name] is working in the spare bedroom, a makeshift office into which he's recently hauled three of his computer monitors: you feel his roving, pointed energy. You put down the knife. Through the kitchen window, you see a starling land on the edge of the ruined fountain, then flutter down to the tiles lining the pool. It cocks its head at the bright blue expanse of the pool. Nobody else will ever see this moment just the way you do, no one will care so deeply for this bird like you do in this moment — it'll fly away, flit to another backyard, and you'll forget about it in time. You must care about yourself.

# Mirror, Mirror

7:13. LIKE CLOCKWORK EVERY WEDNESDAY AND FRIDAY night, he enters his apartment, throws his computer case on the sofa, and takes off his overcoat. This he hangs carefully on a hook, beside a black umbrella that never seems to move from its place. Then he disappears. Perhaps for a glass of water in his kitchen. Perhaps to relieve himself in the washroom. His leaving is never more than five or six minutes. Today is no different. When he returns, his top button is undone, his tie loosened. He goes to his closet and closes the door he's left open all day. He stands, dressed, before a full-length mirror.

I see him from behind but can just make out his reflection so that his actions are clear while his expression is not. Is he bored with the ritual or does he discover something new every time?

One shoe slips off, then the other. I have never seen his shoes but I imagine they are loafers, burgundy leather with tassels perhaps. How easily they slip off. How easily they are discarded. But for all the grace of the shoes, the removal of the socks cannot help but be a tad awkward. Thankfully he does this quickly. I know, now, to glance away. By the time I look back he is removing the tie. He undoes it; he does not simply loosen it and pull it over his head the way my last boyfriend had. Later, he will hang it up. On a tie rack on the inside door of his closet.

He unbuttons from the bottom of his shirt first. Pulling it free from his trousers. Today it's a pale pastel linen. Ecru, I think it's called. This he does not hang up. Instead, he folds it in half and lays it, gently, onto the sofa, slipping his hand out from underneath its folds. This too he will hang up later. Later, when it is all over and my apartment lights are turned back on.

Daylight saving time is my best friend. Before the time change, I had to duck down, out of sight, catching only stolen glimpses, imagining the rest. Now in the early darkness of autumn, I can watch without interruption, lights turned off, and him completely unaware of me. Of my gaze. I have become so bold that I've even placed my armchair in the middle of my living room, facing my window, directly across from his window. Would I have done anything like this before? No. Isolation has changed us all.

Although he cannot see me, I remain fully clothed. I never touch myself. Not even when I feel myself dampening with physical wanting. Not even as I imagine his hands on me, undressing me as he kisses my neck, my collarbones, my nipples. Not even as I imagine the texture of his tongue as it maps a path from my breasts, down my belly, over my hip bones. When I close my eyes, I can almost feel the heat of his breath as he burrows his face into my panties. God, this year of isolation has made me desperate for human touch of any kind, if only my own. It would be so easy to slip my fingers between the fabric of my panties and my wet cunt. Who would it hurt? He wouldn't know. As he peels away the layers of his clothing, I could just pull the fabric to one side, spread my legs wide, with one knee on each arm of the chair. Lean back into the recline of the cushions, hips lifted off the seat. He would never see me in the darkness of my apartment. Would never know that I was pleasing myself while he did the same. But no, I will not distract myself from watching him by pleasuring myself. Instead, I will remember every move, every detail, and then, later, when I lie in my bed I will attempt to remember the ritual exactly. How he took off his clothes. How he pinched his nipples between his forefingers and thumbs. How he took his cock into his hand and how his slow rhythm increased as he stroked himself, never once taking his eyes from the mirror. Then, and only then, will I take out my sketchbook and put him to paper.

I have never really been aroused in my art classes. Never desired a model. I have watched as poses have changed and clothes have been removed and put back on. I have seen it all. Robust women with low-slung breasts and dimpled thighs. Skeletal ones, with bones protruding like weapons. Men both hairy and hairless, some with six packs and some with the first swell of a middle-aged pot-belly. Bottoms high and round like a dancer's, or thin and flat like a day-old crepe. Tight bodies. Loose bodies. Fleshy and sinewed. And with every change of pose there is another, more intimate, view. This one has more pubic hair, this one has a large cock even while flaccid, this one has flesh that is yellowing with age. Every model's body exists only for my purposes. Every model is aware of my pencil, my easel, and my unflinching gaze. But my man across the courtyard is different. He is real. There is no artifice in his posing.

No premeditation in his movement. This is not a body offered but a body stolen.

It is a lovely body, though a little on the thin side. His legs are long, defined but not very muscular. His ass is round and lifted, though small. He is an upside-down triangle, with a chest that is wider than anything below it. When his back is toward the window, I can see the tautness of his muscles below his skin. I could point at each muscle, label it with the right name. There is the trapezius, the latissimus dorsi, the rhomboid major, the rhomboid minor, and levator scapulae. A good artist knows the muscles of the body. Knows how they look. How they would feel. I know every muscle in his back. I sense how they would feel, but still want to know them by touch. The hand longs to go where the eye has already been.

I have never seen him orgasm. I don't really know what his cock looks like, his body obscures its full reflection in the mirror. Sometimes though, I can just make out the purplish hue at the tip. And that he is circumcised. I imagine it is a grow-er, not a show-er. Maybe a slight curve upwards when hard. I like that. A curved penis touches places that the straight penis cannot. But I cannot imagine that now. That is not part of the exercise.

His stroking intensifies, gains vigour. It must feel hard in his hand, though the skin would be smooth, soft. Yes, soft skin that moves as his hand moves over the firm shaft of his cock. His eyes are likely closed now and I wonder whom he imagines. A past lover. Someone he's recently met. A co-worker. When I think of who's in his mind I cannot help but feel a little jealous, but he doesn't know I exist, doesn't know I watch him, and so how can he possibly think of me? I am a shadow, a whisper, an echo only. I lean slightly forward in my seat, still safe in a cloak of darkness around me. Maybe this time it will be different.

Maybe this time he will see it through to its proper conclusion. Just once I would like to see him finish. Watch his back move with the irregular breath of excitement and then a sudden convulsion or shudder before his body is spent, slackened. I want to witness him after, in repose on his sofa, splayed out like the Barberini Faun. His penis softening to something more fragile and benign. A trail of stickiness on his belly. The warmth of his cum turning cold, before he wipes it from his flesh.

Instead of cumming, he goes into the shower. I know this because he always reappears with a white towel around his hips and another around his neck, which he uses to dry his hair and ears. What I don't know is whether or not he finishes himself off in the shower or if he takes a cold shower.

I pick up when my phone rings, turn away from the window.

"Hey, what're you doing?" It's my ex, checking in on me. He no longer wants me but needs to know I am fine. That I am weathering the isolation.

"Nothing much. Just watching *Rear Window*," I lie, sort of.

"What, again?"

"It's a great film."

"All those films creep me out."

"What films?" I ask him, not really caring.

"You know, films about stalker chicks who solve some murder or crime."

"What's wrong with that?" I glance at the window. He's still not back.

"Well, we forget that they were being creepy and obsessive in the first place. If it were a man instead of a woman in *The Girl on the Train*, it would be different."

"I guess." I want him off the phone. God, he judges me even when he doesn't know he's judging me!

"I picked up some extra groceries. Want me to drop some by. I worry you aren't eating."

"I am."

"How? You never go out. You don't shop ..."

"I'm eating!" I yell at him.

Food triggers me. My ex was a chef. Properly trained, at the Savoy Hotel. He showed his love with food, never with touch. He was so orally obsessed that I sometimes wondered if a thing existed to him if he couldn't put it into his mouth. Needless to say, he was stellar at eating me out. But the fucking was a little lacklustre. Once he got me off with his tongue, it was all about him. I always came on his tongue, but I never came on his cock. I wonder if it is the same with my replacement. If she is content with the long sessions of his mouth and the quickness of his cock.

"How's Kelly?" I ask him.

"Come on. We promised. Boundaries, remember?"

I glance back at the window. Across the courtyard the lights are now off. I missed the white towel part. Now he's disappeared. He might be in another room. Perhaps he has gone out for the evening. Although it is November, there are still heated patios at some of the restaurants that have managed to survive.

"Look, I have to go," I say into the phone.

"Go where?"

"I just have to go. I'm working."

"Working? You drawing? Painting?" His voice is quick. He doesn't want me to hang up. He must have had a falling out with Kelly.

"A few groceries would be nice," I concede. "I don't like going out."

I put down my cellphone and turn on my light. I look across and can see little when I glance at his window. If he is there, though, he could see me. Imagine being seen? Not being invisible. To be witnessed. To exist.

I can justify my watching. I'm an artist. I study the body, I put it to paper or canvas. I am in isolation. There is no one stripping off for me now, allowing me to objectify them. But perhaps my ex is right. Perhaps this is creepy.

I face the window, face the darkness of his apartment. I stand under my ceiling light. I pull my worn cashmere sweater over my head. There is no bra to remove, we've all stopped wearing them. My nipples harden as I brush my hand over them. Then I pop the top button on my jeans. I stare ahead as I wiggle the denim over my hips, then step out of them. I pause before touching the waistband of my panties. I use both my hands, moving my fingers along the top before slowly easing them down. I wait. Nothing. So I reach for the oversized white T-shirt I sleep in and let the soft cotton fall over me.

It has to stop. My sketchbook is filled with him. I close the cover, vowing that I will not watch him on Friday. I curl in my bed, a row of pillows along one side to help me forget my loneliness as I sleep.

I don't know if it is because of the phone call or the fact that I didn't masturbate before I fell asleep, but I dream of my ex. He's pumping away on top of me, eyes are closed because there is someone new in his head, and I am only the receptacle of his desire and not the object. I turn my head and there he is, the man across the courtyard. He sits, fully clothed, on a wooden chair beside my bed, one long leg casually thrown over the other. He watches intently. I stare at him, confused that he is in my room. I watch him as my ex fucks me, unaware that there is now another man present for me. The inside of my pussy is tightening around my ex's cock. I have never enjoyed my ex's cock as much. The other man smiles at me. Nods as I near orgasm. I awaken, my stomach tensing in uncontrollable spasms.

I get up and move the armchair away from the window. I put my easel in its place. Then I pull the drapes and shut out the world.

In the morning there are three bags of groceries left outside my door. I venture down, not bothering to dress. When I open the outside door, the cool morning air wraps around me. My legs are too bare. My T-shirt is too thin. My nipples are too hard. But the street is quiet, there is no one there to see me.

Except him.

He's leaning against the brick of his building. Smoking a cigarette. Funny, I never pictured him as a smoker. He's watching me. It would be so easy to wave, to acknowledge him in a casual, neighbourly way, but I can't. I am frozen with embarrassment. He throws down the last of his cigarette and grinds it under his foot. I pick up my groceries and retreat back inside.

I cannot help myself. After I drop my groceries I go to my living room window to draw open the curtains. I tell myself that it is only to let in the morning light. But there he is. Shirt already off, his smooth chest pressing against the glass. He nods, consenting. I reach for the hem of my T-shirt and pull it over my head. As his hands reach for his trousers, I watch, and he unbuttons his fly. He looks at me and waits, not lowering his trousers until I make a move for my panties. He smiles, gestures for me to peel myself free from that bit of silk I have left on my body. I slowly lower them and he slips free of his pants. He is wearing no underwear; his cock is suddenly there in front of me, free and alert. I am taken with its beauty, its simple perfection. He runs his hands over his chest down his belly, and because he is watching me with such intent, such demanding eyes, I imitate him, drawing my hands over my breasts and down my belly. He puts his fingers into his mouth, I do the same. When his moistened fingers wrap around his cock, I bring mine down and separate my lips, run my fingers the length of my cunt. I watch him, keeping pace with his rhythm. His cock is now almost touching the window. I open up to him, so he can see me slip two fingers inside. I rest my head on the cool of the glass, steady myself as I stare at him, following his lead, until we surrender with violent spasms.

Today I am no longer his watcher. I am his mirror.

# Portrait of a Lady

THE LARGE RED AND BLACK TILES ON THE BODEGA FLOOR were bloated from water damage. Some of the tiles were missing. In their place were layers of newspapers used to soak up all the excess water. It didn't matter what the story was, it still got covered in snowy footprints. All those politicians and stars and criminals. All the murders lately! Bodies that had been found in rivers. Bodies that had been shot in the head. Bodies that had been found in the trunk of a car with their throats slit. It had been a violent year. I couldn't help but be proud to see all my bodies on the front pages.

I stopped to look at myself in the security camera's TV screen. I looked just barely legal enough to buy cigarettes and get into clubs. My blond hair was hanging in pretty strands across my freckled cheeks. You could see my blue eyes piercing through behind the strands, like prowling wildcats in the Sahara fields.

I suppose I am bragging. But it's one trait all vampires share. Vanity is definitely among all of our various vices.

THERE WERE TIMES IN MY LIFE WHEN I KEPT MYSELF AWAY from everyone. I avoided all manner of contact. There was a time when I stayed in a basement for three years. I didn't speak to anyone at all. I only read books. It is a strange gift to not be able to sleep.

But I had been concerned with the amount of time I had begun to spend in close quarters. There were vampires who became more and more stationary. I knew one who had locked himself in a trunk and had it tossed overboard. There were vampires who had themselves buried alive in coffins. They wanted to be alone to contemplate their thoughts. They became so introspective, they tired of having a body at all. They were just ideas underneath the earth.

Whenever I found a place to be quiet and disconnected from the world around me, I thought I could stay there for-ever. I would stay there for years. Something would cause me to come out. I was living in an abandoned mansion for eighteen months when a crew arrived to tear it down.

I was only out in the world several hours when I went back to my stalker ways. It was a young blond boy. I could not resist. He pulled over next to me, unrolled his window, and asked whether I might enjoy taking a ride in his car. I did very much want to.

I liked the way he looked at me. I liked the feeling of his gaze. It was like silk. It was as though my body was covered in whipped cream. He would lick it off and we would both taste it. I was transfixed. It was as though he had put me on a stage under a spotlight. So everyone could pay attention to me.

I mistook the feeling for happiness. There is really no such thing as happiness. It is only the beginning of an addiction. If you asked a donkey that was following a carrot tied in front of it whether or not it was hungry, it would certainly say yes.

I was sitting on top of him, riding him, when the wings came out of my back for the first time in so long; it felt as though a corset had been untied from my back as I lifted my face up to the roof of the car in order to fill my lungs up with air.

AND ONCE I STARTED, I COULD NOT STOP FEASTING. I OFTEN gave myself the name of a character in a novel I had been reading. Why not? I had no relatives to be named after. I was a fictional character for them also. That was why they never caught me. They refused to see me as a person. They didn't want to give me the satisfaction of acknowledging I was visible.

I danced naked on the coffee table of a man who called me Alice. A large man with hair all over his back and belly tit-fucked me and called me Emily. A man who blindfolded me while he buried his nose in my ass as though he were a marvellous pig rooting for truffles called me Cleo.

There was a man who called me Violet. I liked that. He asked me what I liked to drink. He said, "What do you want to drink, Violet." My heart kicked against my chest. As though it were a neighbour signalling that I was making too much noise.

I liked when a businessman who had a very large penis called me Clementine. It made me feel as though I were actually a girl who had parents who had named me Clementine. And I had had a group of school friends who had called me Clementine, too. The next day I went to the grocery store. I held a clementine up to my nose and inhaled. It was then I noticed there was still blood underneath my finger. I put it in my mouth and sucked on it.

I LIKED WHEN MEN LOOKED AT ME WITH DESIRE AND DISgust. One man tied me to a chair. He kept slapping my face. He told me I was a skanky little bitch. He turned a video camera toward me. He left it there and he went to work. When he came back, he leaned over me to check that my arms were either properly tightened, or that my fingers had not turned blue. The thought that he was now going to enact his final violence on me turned me on. So much that I couldn't hold my wings in anymore. I sank my teeth into his neck.

The blood comes so quickly. You have to drink and drink. You have to drink as much as you can before their heart stops beating.

All his hopes and dreams. All his violence. I saw his life flash before my eyes. There was a moment where he was receiving a puppy for his birthday. It was sweet enough. There was nothing particularly unusual about his childhood. Nothing that would turn him into a murderer of women. My wings pushed out so hard, they broke the straps and the back of the chair.

I took a shower in his bathtub. The soap dish was shaped like a large peach-coloured seashell. He had a fluffy orangish-yellow toilet lid cover. There were pill jars in the bathroom cabinet with an old lady's name on them. He must have inherited all his toiletries from a grandmother. Men went through life having the objects in their life derived somehow from women.

HUMANS ARE ALWAYS ASSOCIATING SEX WITH LOVE. A vampire always conflates sex with death. Who knows how long I have been a vampire, or if I was ever anything other than a vampire, in the same way that humans can't remember being born and what they might have been before.

I have memories of this country when it was all forest and there were no buildings at all. It was all chaos and murder, really. There was always mud on my boots. They believed in me then. When my bodies would turn up, they would cry out it was the work of the devil, that there were evil forces afoot in the new land. Which amused me since I had come over on the same ship they had.

I once saw another vampire captured back then. She had a woman's body, like me. They thought she was a witch, whatever that was. They believed women were conduits for everything evil. Someone had noticed that she slept all day and that was enough to have her sentenced to death. I adored a witch craze. Even though it put the likes of me at risk.

There was quite a lot of work trying to kill her. They tried hanging her. Everyone gathered to see. I have often been at a ballet and found myself wanting to whisper to the person next to me, This is all right. But what you really need to watch is a public hanging. Watching her body drop felt almost like sex and it made my wings twitch and move as though they were about to burst out.

Anyway, she survived. I watched her be tied by a steel shackle around her ankle to an anchor and be tossed into the water at the harbour. I'm sure she is at the bottom of the harbour still, standing there like a woman at a rural bus stop, with the wind blowing her hair all over the place.

To be honest, I was happy to see her go. She had come over on the boat with me from Europe. I had been hoping there were no other vampires on the boat, but I suppose we are more or less like rats.

One of the reasons I left Europe was because of the other vampires. I can't even recall what I did that so incensed them all. But they said I was rash, going on killing sprees in cities for too long, and it put them all in danger. They picked on me because I have the form of such a young, beautiful girl. And it allows me to get away with all sorts of things. And they hated that my wings are the colour of glass, and I can be naked and my victims can't even see them.

I am who I am. Every being has the right to pursue their own particular path toward happiness.

I had been in this city for far too long. It was dangerous because it allowed other vampires to find me. But knowing this, I still decided to stay. Perhaps I was staying with the express purpose of other vampires finding me. Perhaps I wanted to be dragged or forced out of this city.

I WENT TO THE NIGHTCLUB THAT HAD BEEN ESTABLISHED in an abandoned post office. I was wearing a sleek black coat I had taken off a dead man. I thought I looked great. Everyone else seemed to think so too as I could feel eyes turning to look at me as I passed. Tonight would be easy. I could tell from the way people were looking at me that I was already in the process of transforming. They were enchanted. They would believe anything I told them about myself.

Underneath my coat I was wearing a peach-coloured baby-doll dress. I had on a pair of black tights. If I were to untie my boots, you would see that there were holes in my stockings and that my toes stuck out of them. I wondered who in the club would be foolish enough to untie my shoes.

I wasn't afraid of anyone because I was the predator. If you want to know what it feels like to be a predator, I will tell you. It feels like you are superior. It made me feel as though I were the same colour as the night. It made me feel like a jaguar, if a jaguar were granted human form for the night, so that it might do something like ride the subway without drawing attention to itself. And so I was given the body of a skinny girl. If you looked at me, you were probably in trouble.

The cold made the eyes of the patrons at the club tear. Everyone looked as though they were crying. They did not look as though they were weeping. They looked as though they were trying to hold back the tears. And the second they spoke a word, they would burst into tears. They looked as though they were pained by melancholia. They looked as though someone had whispered something unkind to them. Something that had unwittingly hurt their feelings profoundly.

I WENT TO THE COUNTER. I FELT A PARTICULARLY MOROSE gaze directed toward me. I turned to see it was coming from a woman at the end of the bar. It was a plump, short woman with a black bob and bangs hanging almost to her eyes. Her face was pale. Her black hair made her face seem more pale. She was wearing a long black wool coat that seemed three sizes too big. All black coats had originally belonged to men. And when they got tired of them and shrugged them off, women crept inside them, like mollusks into abandoned shells. Then they were able to move around more carefully in the night. I had one on myself.

She seemed more vulnerable than anybody else in the whole place. She was setting herself up to be a victim. Surely some man was going to mistreat her. It excited me.

I noticed she had a novel on the bar. It was a copy of *The Portrait of a Lady*. I had read that book maybe forty years before. I had wanted to talk to someone about that book for decades. Some books were so relatable and resonated so deeply with me that I was quite convinced they might have been written by a vampire.

"I've read that book," I said.

She looked over at the book with curiosity, as though she was seeing it for the first time.

"What did you think of it?" she asked.

For some reason I could hear every word she was saying over the music. I really wanted to tell her that I thought Isabel Archer was a vampire. She had had the same brilliant naïveté as a vampire. She had that same desire to see everything there was to see in the world. Instead, I answered, "Oh, I just adore Isabel Archer."

"I don't," she said, looking at me with a gaze of almost despair. "I feel so sad for her. She's so weak and dumb. She's doomed from the beginning, isn't she? From the first second you meet Isabel, you think, oh, she is doomed. Don't you? She is happy and free, so she is doomed. She has all this money, so she is doomed to have someone steal it."

"Well what could she have done not to be doomed?"

"She should have stayed in a small house somewhere reading books and never met anybody at all. To do anything else would be idiotic."

This was a peculiar reading. At no point did I think Isabel was an idiot. I found it upsetting. I was leaning away from the bar, about to move along, when she said, "Do you want to do cocaine with me?"

I fell back against the bar. I loved doing cocaine. It was the closest I got to feeling as though I had killed someone without going through the trouble of actually killing someone. It made my blood buzz as though I had killed someone. Although it was more or less foreplay, as it made me want to kill so badly; it made me feel as though I could kill an entire legion of men.

"Do you have some?" I asked.

"No," she answered. "But I know a guy. We could go to your place and call him."

Then she looked into my eyes. I thought I should like to see her humiliated by a man. I should like to kneel next to her, as a man we despised slapped his dick against our cheeks and then came over both our faces.

She seemed as though it would not be her thing at all. And that was what was so thrilling. On some level I could never believe in my complete degradation, because I knew that I liked it. It was what I had sought out. It made every molecule in my body start to buzz and feel alive. But she would actually feel degraded. She might start to cry afterward. Maybe she would feel suicidal. I needed to live vicariously through her suffering. I put my arm in hers. It was so unlike me because I really lacked a certain empathy for human beings.

"Will you call me Isabel," I asked as we walked down the street.

"Yes," she answered. "If you will call me Madame Merle."

I laughed. She was capable of wickedness then, or at least she thought she was, since Madame Merle was Isabel's undoing in the novel.

WE WENT BACK TO THE HOTEL ROOM I HAD RENTED. IT was tiny. But the windows were large and beautiful. You could open them up like doors, sit on the wooden plank on the radiator, and call mean things out to passersby. The stars looked as though they might be painted on the windowpane and the night sky was black outside.

There was wallpaper on the walls. And there was a framed drawing of a woman, with a fur shawl around her neck, laughing. I would never be able to part with her. I would probably steal her when I left. She had been waiting for me. No one else had noticed her.

If Madame Merle wanted cocaine, then she should call and get us cocaine. She was acting odd about everything. She went to the telephone by the bed. I sat down next to her.

"Tell him that we don't have any money. Tell him that we will have sex with him for cocaine."

"Why?"

"Or I will do it. Tell him you want cocaine and that I will have sex with him for it."

"I have money for it."

"It's not about the money! It's not even about the cocaine. It's about degrading ourselves. Don't you want to degrade yourself with me? I want to make love to you very much. But I also want someone to watch. I want us to be pornographic together."

"No," she said. She dialed the number.

I wanted to slap her in the face. Nobody loves us. Nobody wants us. Nobody decent wants us. It is only possible to be desired by the most grotesque of men.

A MAN CAME TO THE DOOR NOT TEN MINUTES LATER. HE WAS odd looking. He was tall and more or less well dressed. He was wearing a cheap navy-blue suit with pens in the blazer pocket and a black coat that went down to his ankles. He had a briefcase that he carried his drugs in. He came in the room and looked around. He sat on the armchair next to the television and put his briefcase on his lap and tapped on it. The girl motioned for him to follow her. They went to talk in the bathroom.

They left the bathroom and he stood there. I wasn't at all worried. I wanted him to be insane and violent with us. But I would probably not have any such luck. How boring, I thought. At this point I wanted him to leave. I felt we might as well do the drugs together. And see where that led. I don't know why I had brought her along for my adventure.

After he left, she poured some of the baggie of cocaine onto the nightstand. We both inhaled it. I lifted my head back and the last year flashed before my eyes.

When I lowered my head again, Madame Merle sat cross-legged on the bed. The mattress sagged underneath her. There was a nimbus of light around her. Her skin began to twinkle. As if none of the snowflakes from outside had melted on her skin but sat there sparkling. She looked at me as though I had been making her cry for a hundred years.

She took off her large black sweater and dropped it on the floor next to the bed. Underneath it, she was wearing another sweater. It was black again, but had flecks of yellow in the yarn. And in the middle was a pattern of a yellow horse. It was still loose. She pulled that sweater off. She had another sweater on! She was like a nesting doll of sweaters.

When you dressed in the winter, you ended up often accumulating layers of clothing without even knowing it. You could keep peeling off different layers. Like in the way there would be different layers of wallpaper on an apartment wall. Each representing the taste of a different person.

This sweater she had on now was tighter. It was red and had blue fighter jets on it. You could see the outline of her frame in this one. She had very large breasts and her belly sat on her legs. Her head was now separated from the rest of her body by a neck.

She pulled off the final sweater. It made a crackling noise from the static electricity in her hair. Strands of her bangs stood up, revealing her pale face and large sad eyes. She had just a bra on. It went underneath her breasts. Covering the bottoms of them in black lace. They were paler than her face. She made me feel as though I were in a black-and-white movie. Or at least she was from a black-and-white movie.

She twisted her torso so I could see. I thought at first that I was looking at a large tattoo of some sort of Giger-like drawing. Folded up against her back were wings. They were so carefully concealed I could not see them at all from the front. I did not know she was hiding anything at all behind her back.

As soon as I realized what I was seeing, I felt my wings begin to react. I felt a terrible dread in my body when they moved. It was as though I could open a drawer in my chest and take out a dove that was trembling and set it free. It made me feel tiny in the universe. It humbled me. It made me want to cry. It made me suddenly want to be home, even though I had no idea where home was. It made me long for a childhood I didn't have.

The wings lifted off my back. It was so good to just allow them to come off. I never realized the extent to which they were heavy and restricting until they were loose. I felt so much lighter. I was so alive. I turned away from the window. The colours of the neon lights were always too bright when my wings were out. The flowers on the wallpaper began to twitch and move around.

"Well, Isabel," she said. "Your body count has been extraordinary. You've been too naughty and free for us to let you carry on. It's a shame, isn't it? You are so lovely, after all."

AND ALL I KNEW WAS THAT MY WINGS WERE OUT WHEN she bit into me. And I never felt such deep satisfaction as when I was dying. It was different than drugs. It was like sex, but different.

The softness of the dawn light was the last thing I saw. It reminded me of hard-boiled eggs. If I took a spoon and tapped it on the light, it would crack. It reminded me of girls' underwear hanging from a laundry line. Heaven for me would be walking through a field of laundry lines that only had girls' underclothes hanging from them. I will run my fingers through the tights. The underwear will brush up against my face.

# Contributors

**ANGIE ABDOU**'s first novel, *The Bone Cage*, was a Canada Reads finalist, and her two memoirs have hit the Canadian bestseller list. Her most recent book is *This One Wild Life*. Abdou is a professor of creative writing at Athabasca University.

**JEAN MARC AH-SEN** is the author of *Grand Menteur* and *In the Beggarly Style of Imitation* and the forthcoming *Kilworthy Tanner*. The *National Post* has hailed his writing as an "inventive escape from the conventional."

**TAMARA FAITH BERGER** writes fiction, non-fiction, and screenplays. Her work has been nominated for the Trillium Book Award and her third novel, *Maidenhead*, won the Believer Book Award. Her latest novel is *Yara*.

**JOWITA BYDLOWSKA** was born in Warsaw, Poland, and lives in Toronto. Her most recent book is the novel *Possessed*.

**XAIVER MICHAEL CAMPBELL**, born and raised in Jamaica, has considered Newfoundland and Labrador home for over a decade. His fiction has been published in *The Malahat Review*, *Riddle Fence*, and the anthologies *Us, Now* and *Hard Ticket*, by Breakwater Books, and in *Release Any Words Stuck Inside You, III*, by Applebeard Editions.

**K.S. COVERT**, a devoted observer of human nature, enjoys putting her characters in morally dubious situations and seeing how — or whether — they might transform themselves to suit. Her first novel, *The Petting Zoos*, was described as a dystopian sex adventure. She lives in Ottawa.

**francesca ekwuyasi** is from Lagos, Nigeria. Her debut novel, *Butter Honey Pig Bread*, was awarded the 2022 Dayne Ogilvie Prize for LGBTQ2S+ Emerging Writers. It was longlisted and shortlisted for numerous other awards, including the 2020 Giller Prize, the 2020 Governor General's Literary Award for Fiction, and the 2022 Dublin Literary Award.

**ANNA FITZPATRICK** is the author of the novel *Good Girl* and the children's book *Margot and the Moon Landing* (published as A.C. Fitzpatrick, because some things are best kept separate).

**DREW HAYDEN TAYLOR** is an award-winning playwright, novelist, journalist, and filmmaker. Born and currently living on the Curve Lake First Nation, he has done everything from stand-up comedy at the Kennedy Center in Washington, D.C., to being artistic director of Canada's premiere Indigenous theatre company, Native Earth Performing Arts.

**VICTORIA HETHERINGTON** is the author of *Mooncalves* (2019) and *Autonomy* (2022). She lives in Toronto.

**MARNI JACKSON** is an award-winning journalist and the author of two works of fiction (*Don't I Know You?* and a forthcoming novel, *You Again*). Recent collaborative writing projects include two stage shows — *The Secret Chord: A Leonard Cohen Experience* and *The Shape of Home: Songs in Search of Al Purdy.*

**ANDREW KAUFMAN** has published seven novels, including *All My Friends Are Superheroes, Born Weird,* and *The Ticking Heart.* His non-fiction has appeared in the *Guardian* and the *Globe and Mail.* His novels have been translated into eleven languages and published in eighteen countries.

**MICHAEL LAPOINTE** is the author of *The Creep* (2021). He has written for the *New Yorker* and the *Atlantic,* and he was a columnist for the *Paris Review.*

**PASHA MALLA** is the author of, most recently, *Kill the Mall,* a novel. He lives in Hamilton, Ontario, and teaches at York University.

**SOPHIE MCCREESH**'s first novel, *Once More, With Feeling,* was published in 2021. She lives in Toronto.

**LISA MOORE** is the author of four novels, *Alligator, February, Caught,* and *This Is How We Love.* She wrote the story collections *Degrees of Nakedness, Open,* and *Something for Everyone.* Lisa is the co-librettist, along with Laura Kaminsky, of the opera *February,* adapted from the novel by the same name.

**HEATHER O'NEILL** is the author of seven books, including *Lullabies for Little Criminals* and *The Lonely Hearts Hotel*. Her essays have been published widely. Her most recent novel was *When We Lost Our Heads*. She lives in Montreal.

**LEE SUKSI**'s debut, *The Nerves* (Metatron), won the 2021 Lambda Literary Award for Best LGBTQ Erotica. They have recent work in the *Brooklyn Review*, *Peach Mag*, and *BESIDE* magazine. They are an artist's model and astrologer in Toronto, where they write horoscopes for the *Grind*.

**SUSAN SWAN**'s fiction has been published in twenty countries. She is best known for her novel *The Wives of Bath*, a gothic tale about a girls' boarding school. Swan is working on a new *Stupid Boys Are Good to Relax With* story collection and a memoir, *Too Big*, about how her size shaped her destiny.

**HEIDI VON PALLESKE** likes to switch between acting and writing. Although most memorable for her role in *Dead Ringers*, Heidi has since starred in many films, most recently *My Animal*. Her novel *Two White Queens and the One-Eyed Jack* was a Loan Star's pick and was shortlisted for best literary novel for the Foreword INDIES Awards.

**ALEY WATERMAN** is a writer of fiction, poetry, and music, from and living in Newfoundland. Her first novel, *Mudflowers*, was published by Rare Machines in 2023. She has had work appear in the *Brooklyn Review*, *Bad Nudes* magazine, *Riddle Fence*, the *Trampoline Hall* podcast, and elsewhere.

**ZOE WHITTALL** is a bestselling author of five novels, most recently *The Fake*. She also works as a TV writer. Her debut short story collection, *Wild Failure*, is forthcoming in 2024.

**DAVID WHITTON** is the author of *Seven Down*, a finalist for the 2022 Crime Writers of Canada Awards of Excellence for Best Crime First Novel. His short fiction has appeared in a number of journals and anthologies. David lives in Toronto.

**MICHAEL WINTER** has been writing down overheard erotic confessions for over thirty years. Some of these monologues have appeared in his two collections of short fiction and four novels. He lives in Toronto, where he likes to germinate delphiniums, raise a kid, and follow a dog through parks and laneways.